Praise for the novels of
New York Times bestselling author
Suzanne Brockmann

"Zingy dialogue, a great sense of drama and a pair of lovers who generate enough steam heat to power a whole city."
—*RT Book Reviews* on *Hero Under Cover*

"Brockmann deftly delivers another testosterone-drenched, adrenaline-fueled tale of danger and desire that brilliantly combines superbly crafted, realistically complex characters with white-knuckle plotting."
—*Booklist* on *Force of Nature*

"Readers will be on the edge of their seats."
—*Library Journal* on *Breaking Point*

"Another excellently paced, action-filled read. Brockmann delivers yet again!"
—*RT Book Reviews* on *Into the Storm*

"Funny, sexy, suspenseful and superb."
—*Booklist* on *Hot Target*

"Sizzling with military intrigue and sexual tension, with characters so vivid they leap right off the page, *Gone Too Far* is a bold, brassy read with a momentum that just doesn't quit."
—*New York Times* bestselling author Tess Gerritsen

"An unusual and compelling romance."
—*Affaire de Coeur* on *No Ordinary Man*

"Sensational sizzle, powerful emotion and sheer fun."
—*RT Book Reviews* on *Body Language*

SUZANNE BROCKMANN

Nowhere to Run

Recycling programs
for this product may
not exist in your area.

ISBN-13: 978-0-373-60608-5

NOWHERE TO RUN

Copyright © 2014 by Harlequin Books S.A.

The publisher acknowledges the copyright holder of the individual works as follows:

NOT WITHOUT RISK
Copyright © 1995 by Suzanne Brockmann

A MAN TO DIE FOR
Copyright © 1995 by Suzanne Brockmann

HARLEQUIN®
™ www.Harlequin.com

Printed in U.S.A.

CONTENTS

NOT WITHOUT RISK 7

A MAN TO DIE FOR 279

NOT WITHOUT RISK

CHAPTER ONE

EMILY MARSHALL was in the bathroom. No, not the bathroom, the head. On a boat the tiny bathroom was called the head.

And as long as you're correcting yourself, Emily thought as she leaned closer to the mirror to reapply her lipstick, *this floating castle with sails can't really be called a boat.*

Boats were unassuming, functional little things you sat in and used oars to row. Or they were things with sails attached that gave you calluses on your hands, sunburn on your face and a healthy lungful of fresh ocean air. Sometimes they took you from point A to point B, but mostly from point A to nowhere, and back again.

Despite the fact that there was, indeed, no destination for this evening's sail, there was nothing unassuming about the sailing vessel Emily was standing on. True, the *Home Free* wasn't large enough to be called a ship, but somehow the word *boat* didn't fit, either.

Yacht, thought Emily as she adjusted the straps of her new black party dress. Alexander Delmore's boat really had to be called a yacht.

She looked at herself critically in the mirror. She'd picked up this dress in a fancy department store's bargain basement. Even marked down the way it had been, it had put her out nearly half of one of her weekly paychecks.

Spending that much money was a big deal to her. It meant she'd have to watch her grocery money for the next few weeks, and really try to keep her expenses down. But to real estate tycoon Alexander Delmore, the amount she'd spent on the dress would have been laughably small. When Alex took her out to dinner, he spent that much on one bottle of wine.

Of course, he made significantly more money wheeling and dealing in real estate than she made as a high school English teacher. That was just one of the simple facts of life. And it was typical of Emily to have fallen in love with a job in a city school system that couldn't afford to pay a decent salary. Sure, she could have applied for a job in a more affluent district. Or she could have stuck to her original college major and gone into business or gotten a job working with computers. It was her own fault that she never seemed to have enough money.

Emily made a face at herself in the mirror. But even with her tongue sticking out, she still looked sophisticated, thanks to the elegant lines of the dress.

Earlier this evening, Alex had asked her out again, for next Tuesday night. He wanted to take her to a party at a local country club. If she spent the other half of her paycheck on yet another expensive dress, she'd be eating pasta or tomato soup until the end of the month.

Emily didn't like eating pasta day in and day out. She liked lobster. And veal. And expensive cuts of filet mignon. She liked asparagus, regardless of the season. She liked watermelon in the winter, and imported chocolate.

She liked houses like Alex's, houses that overlooked the clear blue water of the Gulf of Mexico. She liked houses like Alex's, with six bedrooms and four and a half baths. She liked fluffy new towels that weren't fraying around the edges. She liked cleaning ladies and dinners out. She liked big floating weekend parties on Alex's yacht—parties like this one that started early in the afternoon on Saturday and didn't end until late Sunday night. She liked big-screen stereo TVs and state-of-the-art compact disc players.

She liked the thought of having enough money that she'd never have to worry about the phone bill or the electric payment. She liked the idea of vacations and cruises and trips to Europe.

She also liked Alexander Delmore.

But she didn't love him.

It was clear that he was interested in her. He had as much as told her that he was looking to settle down, to start a family. He was one of Florida's most eligible bachelors, and Emily was flattered that he found her attractive.

But…she didn't love him.

Her neighbor, Carly Wilson, said so what if you don't love him? Love was overrated. A good strong case of like could outlast the most passionate love affair, particularly if it was combined with an enormous bank account. How often does real love come along, anyway? Carly had asked. According to Emily's neighbor, the answer was usually never.

Emily stared at herself in the mirror, searching the familiar blue of her own eyes. She was amazed that she could be wearing this gorgeous, expensive dress that made her look like a million dollars, and be standing here, in the bathroom—head—of millionaire Alexander Delmore's luxurious yacht, thinking about…James Keegan.

After seven years, you'd think she'd be over the man. And she *was* over him, Emily told herself firmly. Her affair with black-hearted Jim Keegan was dead and buried, deep in the past. Jeez, it had been over almost before it even began.

So what the heck was she doing thinking about him?

Because of love. She was thinking about Jim because she had honestly loved him. As rotten and cruel as he had been, as badly as he had hurt her, the fact remained that Emily had loved James Keegan with all of her heart and soul. And deep inside she knew that never, not in a billion years, would she ever love Alex Delmore even half that much.

Still— Carly's voice seemed to echo in her head, as if she were a little devil perched on Emily's shoulder —*who says you have to love Alex to marry him?*

"I do," Emily said out loud to her reflection, then winced at her poor choice of words.

She gave the short skirt of her new dress one more yank southward and quickly ran her fingers through the short, blunt-cut of her chestnut hair. She took a deep breath to further exorcise James Keegan's too-handsome ghost, then turned to open the door that led out into Alexander's tiny shipboard office.

She heard the angry voices as soon as her hand was on the doorknob, but it was too late to pull back. The door swung open, and the arguing men immediately fell silent. Alex and another man—Vincent something—looked up at her, and she could see surprise and annoyance in both pairs of eyes.

"I'm sorry," she said. "I didn't mean to interrupt...."

Alexander Delmore shook his head. "No problem," he said, crossing the tiny cabin with a smile on his tanned, handsome face. "I didn't realize you were using the head." He glanced back at the other man as he took Emily's hand. "If I'd known, we would have gone somewhere else to have our...chat."

Emily couldn't remember the other man's last name. They had been introduced earlier that evening, when all the party guests first boarded Alex's yacht. Vincent what? she thought. Martino? Or was it Medino?

Whoever he was, he was a heavyset man. His dark complexion and body-builder's physique offset Alex's golden slenderness. And, unlike Alex, Vincent still looked annoyed at the interruption.

"If you don't mind..." Vincent said pointedly.

Emily slipped her hand free from Alex's. "I'll get out of your way," she said.

"It'll only be a second," Alex promised. "I'll meet you up on deck."

The office door closed tightly behind her.

Emily was halfway down the hall when she realized that she'd left her purse in the head. She turned back, but when she got to the door to the office she could hear that the two men were arguing again. They were keeping their voices low, but there was no mistaking the underlying current of tension.

She had just lifted her hand to knock when Vincent's voice rose slightly.

"If you don't like *that* deal," she heard him say quite clearly, "how about *this* one—I waste you and take *all* of your profits."

Waste? Had he said *waste?* As in...*kill?*

Alex's voice rose enough for Emily to hear him, too.

"I had a deal with your uncle that worked out fine for years," he said, his voice shaking with emotion.

"My uncle's dead," Vincent said. "And *I'm* in charge now. You want to deal, first you gotta deal with me."

"Fine," Emily heard Alex say. "In that case, you can deal me out."

Vincent laughed, but there was no humor in it. "You don't expect me to believe that you'll get out of the business just like that, do you?"

Emily could almost see Alex's shrug. "Believe what you want, Marino."

There was a loud thump from inside the office, as if someone's head had hit the bulkhead, hard. Emily's heart was pounding, but she couldn't move, couldn't run away.

"I *believe*," Vincent's voice growled, "that I just might break your face. I *know* that there was a snowstorm somewhere off the Gulf Coast last night, and I *know* that this pretty little boat of yours was there to intercept. You cut me my share, or you're dead. That's your deal. Take it or leave it."

A snowstorm? In July? In *Florida?*

With sudden clarity, Emily remembered waking up in the early hours of the morning to the sound of a small outboard motor. The yacht's motorized dinghy had quietly pulled up alongside the bigger boat, and even as she watched out her cabin's tiny porthole, the gentle throbbing of its engine had been cut.

Someone had been out on the deck. Emily hadn't been able to see who it was, but she had heard the sounds of movement. The little boat had been secured to the side of the yacht with a rope, and a ladder had been thrown down. The person in the boat had turned, and in the early dawn Emily had had a clear view of his face.

It had been Alex.

When she asked him about it at breakfast that

morning, he'd apologized for disturbing her, and told her that he'd been out fishing.

Fishing? Fishing for what? Something Vincent Marino would threaten to *kill* Alex for?

Snowstorm. Snow. *Snow* was slang for cocaine, wasn't it?

God in heaven, was it possible that Alex was dealing *cocaine?*

Emily turned and ran.

CHAPTER TWO

EMILY SAT at the interrogation room table in the St. Simone police precinct, her hands clasped tightly in front of her.

The police officer who had first taken her statement had called this the interview room, but Emily knew better. It was an interrogation room. A mirror lined one wall. It was clear that it was really a window, and that people could stand on the other side and observe and hear the conversation without being seen.

The clock on the wall was covered with a protective grid, like the clocks in the gym at the high school where she taught English. The walls were a drab cross between beige and green, and the tile on the floor was gray. It was pitted and cracked from age.

Yes, this was an interrogation room. And after three hours, with seven different police officers asking her the same questions, she could safely assume that she was being interrogated.

The room smelled like stale cigarette smoke—until the police detective she'd been talking to came back into the room, carrying two ceramic mugs of steaming coffee.

"We have those foam hot cups," he said, in his gentle Hispanic accent, "but I don't like to use them—not now that I know what they do to the environment. But these mugs are okay—I washed them myself, and I am very careful to get them clean."

Emily could believe it. The detective—Felipe Salazar, he'd said his name was—was neatly dressed and meticulously well-groomed. He was a young man, probably even younger than her own twenty-five years, with short dark hair and a face with high, exotic cheekbones that might have looked dangerous if not for his open, friendly smile. He reminded her of a puppy—a Doberman puppy who had potential, but hadn't yet learned to be dangerous. With the exception of the few minutes he'd spent getting coffee, he had remained with her for the duration of her questioning.

Six other police officers had come into the room, and she'd told her story over and over and *over* again. She realized they didn't believe her when she told them that Alexander Delmore—one of the pillars of St. Simone society—was running drugs. She knew that was why she had to tell what she had heard and seen again and again— the police were waiting for her to slip up, to make a mistake, to mess up on the details, to change her story in some way.

All the other police officers and detectives had expressed their doubts about what she was telling them. Some had said she must have misheard the conversation between Delmore and the man she'd ID'd as Vincent Marino. Some had said she must have mistaken someone else for Marino, allegedly the new kingpin of a statewide crime syndicate. Others had implied that her story was a load of baloney. They had implied that she had some dirty, rotten motive for wanting to smear Delmore's good name.

Emily had been asked countless personal questions

about the nature of her relationship with Alex. Had they recently had an argument, a falling-out? How long had she been seeing him? How long had she been *sleeping* with him?

Emily couldn't see how those questions had anything to do with Alex's involvement in drug running. But she'd answered them truthfully. And the truth was, she wasn't intimately involved with Alex. When they went for weekend sails on his boat, his crew had always been on board with them, and she had always had her own cabin. She had *not* slept with him.

But she could tell that none of the other police officers believed her about *that,* either.

But young Detective Salazar had been nothing but kind. He'd said he *did* believe her. He'd asked her to be patient and put up with the skeptics. He said that if Delmore was guilty of distributing cocaine, then Delmore should go to jail—regardless of the amount of money the man had donated to the widows-and-orphans fund over the past few years.

As Emily took another sip of black coffee, Salazar shuffled the pages of notes he had been taking throughout the three hours of questioning.

"Do they believe me yet?" she asked him bluntly.

He smiled at her apologetically. "My boss, Lieutenant Bell, will be coming in to talk to you," he said. "And my partner is around here somewhere. He'll be in soon, too."

The door opened, and Emily looked up to see a woman come into the room. She, like most of the others, wasn't wearing a police uniform. She was wearing a dark blue jacket and skirt and a utilitarian white shirt. She was short and wire thin, and she could have been anywhere from forty to sixty years old. Her brown hair was streaked with gray, and she wore a pair of half glasses on her thin nose.

She peered over the tops of them at Emily. "Emily Marshall?" she said. "I'm Lieutenant Katherine Bell."

The older woman didn't hold out her hand to shake, so Emily stayed in her seat and didn't uncross her arms. Bell sat down next to Salazar and appropriated his notes. "I understand you believe Alexander Delmore is involved in some sort of illegal activity," she said, looking down through her glasses to read Salazar's perfect handwriting.

Emily didn't say anything. She waited for Bell to finish reading through the notes.

"You claim that your relationship with Delmore is casual," Bell commented. She glanced up at Emily, with one eyebrow elevated in an expression of disbelief.

"It's more than a claim," Emily said, keeping her voice at its usual controlled calmness. But her blood pressure was rising, and she was long past the point of merely being annoyed. "It's a fact. And I fail to see exactly how that question pertains to my suspicions that Alex is bringing cocaine into the country."

Bell sat back in her seat. She tapped her fingers on the table as she studied Emily carefully. "We're asking these questions because we're trying to figure out what you're doing here," the police lieutenant finally said. "These are serious accusations you're making. We need to be sure you're not a jilted lover, or someone out for revenge. For all we know, you're psychotic. For all we know, you've never even *met* the man, and—"

"Do I look crazy?" Emily asked.

Bell shrugged. "Believe me, honey, it takes all kinds."

Emily leaned forward. "I'm here, Lieutenant, because I teach high school in the seventh district."

Bell actually looked surprised.

"I assume you're familiar with that part of the city," Emily said.

The seventh district was in the part of St. Simone located on the wrong side of the proverbial tracks. There were guns and crime and drugs in the poverty-stricken seventh district, and those guns and crime and drugs didn't stay politely outside the high school doors. Emily had seen students arrested at gunpoint in the corridors of her school. She'd seen students sick and shaking from withdrawal, desperate to get their hands on more of the drugs that would temporarily ease their pain. She'd had students, mere children themselves, bring their babies into class with them, unable to afford day-care. She'd seen empty seats, desks made suddenly vacant because some kid had overdosed on crack and died the night before.

"I know what crack does to people—especially to children," she told Lieutenant Bell. "If Alex is selling drugs, he needs to be stopped. I refuse to just sit by and do nothing."

"And you think he *is* selling drugs," Bell said.

"How else can you explain what I overheard?" Emily asked.

"She correctly identified Vincent Marino from a photo lineup," Salazar murmured to Bell.

"Marino doesn't exactly keep a low profile," Bell replied, with a shrug of her narrow shoulders. "Any number of people could ID him."

"Still, it's worth checking out," the detective said. "I have to wonder what Vincent Marino—a man nicknamed 'the Shark'—is doing on Mr. Delmore's guest list. *Someone* is bringing drugs into town. We have been trying to trace the source for years. Maybe it's Alexander Delmore. Maybe not. But we won't know if we don't at least investigate."

Bell was shaking her head. "It would take months to set up that kind of investigation," she said. "Months, and more money than it would be worth spending on a wild-goose chase. No, I don't think so."

Bell pushed back her chair, about to stand up and leave.

But Salazar caught her arm. "Wait, Lieutenant. I have an idea," he said. "Look at Ms. Marshall's eyes. They are the same shade of blue as Diego's."

Bell looked pointedly at her watch. "Is there a reason you're telling me this, Detective?"

"I say we get Diego to go undercover as Ms. Marshall's…I don't know…brother, I guess. With those eyes, they look like they could maybe be related," he said. "And if Ms. Marshall keeps on seeing Delmore, she can get him to take her on another one of those floating parties, and Diego, playing the part of her big brother, can tag along. Then he can check this guy out." He glanced at Emily. "Diego is my partner," he said. "He's the best in St. Simone. And probably all of Florida, too."

Bell was silent.

Salazar continued. "Provided Ms. Marshall is willing to cooperate—and I think, from what she has told me, she is—we have got a quick and easy way to pull off this investigation. If Delmore is smuggling drugs, wham—we nail him. If he's not, we pull out, and no one ever needs to know we suspected him in the first place."

Bell's flinty gray eyes flicked over to Emily. "*Are* you

willing to cooperate?" she asked. "Are you willing to put up with one of my detectives moving into your apartment for a week or two, posing as your brother?"

The thought was not at all appealing. Emily's apartment was tiny, with only one bedroom. But if she needed to do this to help catch Alex... She lifted her chin. "As long as your detective is willing to sleep on my couch and share the bathroom," she said.

"And what about the risk?" Bell asked. "If Alexander Delmore *is* responsible for bringing shipments of cocaine into the country, he could be an extremely dangerous man."

"I think it's worth the risk," Emily said.

The door opened, and Salazar broke into a wide grin. "Hey!" he said. "Diego! Just the guy we were talking about...."

Emily turned to get a look at the man Salazar thought so highly of, and froze.

His name wasn't Diego. It was James. James Keegan.

For the first time in over seven years, Emily Marshall was face-to-face with Police Detective James Keegan.

"Ms. Marshall, meet Detective Keegan," Salazar said.

But of course. Diego was Spanish for James.

"Emily?" Jim said, his voice hardly more than a whisper.

Emily tried valiantly to regain her composure. But it was hard. It was terribly hard. He was standing there, staring at her as if he couldn't believe his own eyes.

His brown hair was shaggy and long—longer than it had been seven years ago, when he was a newly recruited detective on the Tampa police force. His hair was long enough to pull back into a ponytail at the nape of his neck, but he wore it down around his shoulders. It gleamed, thick and wavy, in the overhead light. And soft. Emily couldn't help but remember how incredibly soft his hair was to touch.

His face was instantly familiar, yet there were visible changes. His nose was still crooked, his lips still full, his mouth still generous. But his cheekbones were a little more pronounced, adding a ruggedness and maturity to his face that hadn't been there before. The crow's-feet and laughter lines around his eyes and mouth had gotten deeper.

His deep blue eyes, though, were exactly the same. They still seemed to sparkle and burn with life and heat. And they still were shadowed by some inner darkness his quick, easy grin couldn't hide.

She'd forgotten how big he was. At six foot four, he seemed to fill the room. His shoulders were broad underneath the thin cotton of his T-shirt, and the muscles in his arms stretched the sleeves. His faded blue jeans were the new, loose-fitting kind, and they somehow seemed to emphasize his lean, muscular physique. Emily wondered if he still ran five miles every day, rain or shine.

She exhaled noisily, realizing she'd been holding her breath. "What are you doing here?" she asked.

"I transferred down from Tampa, about three years ago," Jim said. His deep voice was still husky. And he still hadn't lost that slight trace of a New York accent. "What are *you* doing here?"

Jim Keegan had been living in St. Simone for three years. Emily had trouble catching her breath again. Only chance had kept her from running into him before this. St. Simone wasn't *that* big....

She was silent as Salazar quickly sketched out his plan, realizing with a sudden icy shaft of fear that James

Keegan was the man they'd all been talking about. James Keegan was the man who would be posing as her brother. He was the man who would come and live in her apartment for a week or two.

No way. There was no way on earth she'd ever agree to *that*. She couldn't even handle seeing him for a minute or two. No way could she put up with him for two whole weeks.

"No way," Jim Keegan was saying, shaking his head. "It wouldn't work."

"Are you kidding, man?" Salazar said. "It's a great way to gain Delmore's confidence."

"And it would provide Ms. Marshall with round-the-clock protection," Lieutenant Bell pointed out.

"May I speak to you, Lieutenant?" Jim asked. He opened the door. "Out in the hall?"

He glanced briefly at Emily as Lieutenant Bell pushed back her chair and stood up, and Emily knew that Jim Keegan didn't want to spend the next two weeks with her any more than she wanted to spend the next two weeks with him.

Jim politely held the door open for his boss, not daring to look back at Emily again. Damn it to hell, what was she doing here in St. Simone? He'd been so sure that she'd returned to her parents' home in Connecticut after she finished her four years at the University of Tampa. Whenever he thought about her—and, damn it, he tried hard not to make a habit of it—he imagined her happily married to some well-mannered business suit, living somewhere in New England.

So what was she doing here in Florida? And what the hell was she doing dating a well-known playboy like Alexander Delmore?

And—God!—how had she managed to become even *more* beautiful in the past seven years?

She'd been eighteen when they first met—and eighteen when they'd said good-bye.

She'd been a college student. A freshman, a lousy *freshman,* at the University of Tampa, with waves of long reddish-brown hair that fell down past her shoulders and blue eyes he was convinced were the color of heaven. Her heart-shaped face had been soft-looking, and she'd had full, beautiful lips that were usually curved upward into a smile. She'd looked exactly like what she was—a nice young girl. Too nice. And way too young. And, God, how he'd loved her....

Lieutenant Bell's raspy voice interrupted Keegan's thoughts. "Was there something you wanted to discuss, Detective?"

"Yeah," he said. "You've got to find someone else to take this case. I can't do it."

"Can't?" Bell said.

"I was once involved with Emily Marshall," he said bluntly. No use beating around the bush. "I'm sorry, Lieutenant, but there's no way I can play house with this woman."

"Involved," Lieutenant Bell repeated. "Intimately, I assume, or this wouldn't be an issue."

The muscles in his jaw tightened. "It was a long time ago," he said.

"Who dumped whom?"

"I was the one who broke it off," Jim said. "She was just a kid, and—"

"Spare me the sordid details," Lieutenant Bell said, "and just tell me if you think she's here right now because of you."

It took Jim a solid ten seconds to understand what she was suggesting. "You mean, do I think she's concocted this story about Delmore because…"

"She wants to get your attention?" Bell finished for him. She watched him, waiting for an answer.

He shook his head. "No. You saw the look on her face when she recognized me," he said. "She was surprised as hell."

She'd been so surprised, she forgot to hide the hurt that still glimmered in her eyes—hurt from the way he'd treated her all those years ago. God, he could still close his eyes and see her standing outside that University Boulevard bar, shock and pain and disbelief on her sweet face.

"Besides," he said, shaking his head slightly to banish the image from his mind, "what happened between us—it was over seven years ago."

"Good," said the lieutenant. "Then you shouldn't have any problem working with her on this case, right, Keegan?"

She started back toward the interview room.

"Lieutenant," Jim said, "give me a break here. Please."

Lieutenant Bell turned back to face him, crossing her arms. "You and your partner are the only detectives available right now, and I suspect that Alexander Delmore won't buy into believing that Felipe Salazar is Ms. Marshall's brother," she said. "If you tell me you're still emotionally involved with this woman, I will have you removed from this investigation. But that will mean waiting a number of weeks before another detective is available. And *that* means there will be a number of weeks that Ms. Marshall is out there, by herself, with a man she suspects is running drugs." She pinned Jim with her stern gaze. "I am not keen on the idea of Emily

Marshall being a part of this investigation in the first place, but Detective Salazar is right. If we start immediately, we can get this done quickly and easily. And then Ms. Marshall will be out of your hair, Detective."

She was watching him closely, and Jim knew that she was unerringly reading the tension in his shoulders, neck and jaw. The idea of Emily being in danger was making him crazy. God, it was even worse than the picture that kept flashing in his head of Emily together with her new boyfriend, Alexander Delmore....

"Now," Lieutenant Bell said. "Are you telling me that you are still emotionally involved?"

Emotionally involved? No way. Impossible. Not after seven years. Yeah, sure, he'd thought about Emily Marshall now and then, but that didn't mean he was emotionally involved. And yeah, sure, seeing her again was a real surprise, so it was only natural that he should feel so off balance. And add to that the amazing fact that she was still so damned pretty. He'd always thought that imagination and memory tended to exaggerate things, that he'd somehow built up his memory of her until he remembered her as some staggeringly gorgeous woman. But she was even more beautiful than he'd remembered.

But so what? He still found her attractive. Big deal. That didn't mean he was emotionally involved.

Besides, what good would being emotionally involved do you, a little voice inside of him asked, with more than a slight trace of sarcasm. You dumped her, pal. It's not likely she'll come back for more.

"Are you, Keegan? Are you emotionally involved?"

"No," Jim said, but his voice sounded unnaturally hoarse, unusually raspy.

He hoped to God he wasn't lying.

CHAPTER THREE

JAMES KEEGAN.

Didn't it figure that it had to be James Keegan?

Ever since Emily had overheard Alex's argument with Vincent Marino, ever since she'd first come to realize that the wealthy society man that she was starting to think of as her boyfriend might be a drug runner, she'd felt as if she were living in some kind of dream world.

Last night on Alex's sailboat, she'd numbly pretended that nothing was the slightest bit wrong. She'd smiled at Alex as he came up beside her on the main deck and draped his arm casually around her shoulders. She'd kept up a steady stream of conversation as he drove her home in his BMW after the sailboat returned to its yacht-club mooring. She'd even let him kiss her good-night the way he always did.

It had been late—long after two in the morning— when she unlocked the door to her tiny apartment.

She would have gone to the St. Simone police right away, but she'd suddenly gotten scared. What if Alex suspected that she'd overheard his conversation with Marino? What if he was watching her apartment that very moment? If he saw her leave in the middle of the night, and if he followed her to the police station, then he would know for sure that *she* knew he was involved in something rotten.

So she had waited for morning, then showered and changed into her favorite pair of khaki shorts and the T-shirt that was on top in her T-shirt drawer.

Morning had taken forever to come. The hours between three and five-thirty had seemed centuries long. But then, finally, it had been six and then seven o'clock. Cars had started moving on the street. People in her building had woken up. Emily had managed to wait until eight-thirty before she left her apartment.

Talking to the police detectives had been just another unreal part of that horrible, weird dream.

And then James Keegan had shown up.

That had been the final bizarre touch to an already surreal experience. Boy, how many times had James Keegan appeared out of the blue in her dreams at night? Too many to count.

She would be having some nice, friendly, soothing dream. She'd dream she was out shopping with Carly, or having dinner with some of the other teachers from the high school. But then everything would shift, and Jim Keegan would suddenly be there. Sometimes he would just look at her, with that familiar hunger in his eyes. Sometimes he would touch her, the way he'd touched her that one weekend they'd shared, the weekend he'd made love to her. But sometimes she'd see him, not in his own bed, but in that horrible hospital bed, after he'd been shot, with all those awful tubes and wires connecting him to all kinds of monitors and respirators. She would beg him not to leave her, not to die, but he would never even open his eyes.

Never, not even in Emily's wildest dreams, had James ever gotten assigned by his boss to move into her apartment and pretend that he was her brother.

And that made *this* funky real-life dream a true nightmare.

She was trapped. Sure, she could say no, she didn't want Jim to move in, she didn't want him to invade her life again. Of course, that would leave Alexander Delmore free to bring as many kilos of cocaine as he wanted into the city.

Emily stumbled on the rough blacktop of the parking lot outside of the police station. Brother, she was exhausted. And this nightmare was only beginning.

The hot July sun beat down on her mercilessly as she fished in the pocket of her shorts for the keys to her car. She dropped the key ring twice before she realized there was a reason her hands were shaking and her vision was blurred.

She was crying.

She'd held up so well while the police asked all their questions. She hadn't lost her temper even once—she had remained calm and cool, even when she felt insulted and embarrassed. And, most importantly, she hadn't screamed hysterically when Jim Keegan walked into the room. She hadn't burst into tears. She hadn't even looked more than surprised.

This must be a delayed reaction, she thought dazedly. She'd felt like crying ever since she'd found out that she had misjudged Alex so completely.

Emily futilely wiped her eyes with the back of her hand and tried one more time to get the car key into the door's lock. The lock popped up, and she opened the door. The inside of her car was hotter than Hades, but she got in anyway and started the engine. She opened all four of the power windows and cranked the air-conditioning.

Why James Keegan? Why *now?* What had she done to deserve this?

Emily gave in to the flood of tears. She rested her arms against the hot plastic of the steering wheel, put down her head and let herself cry.

JIM KEEGAN broke into a run as he headed down the corridor, Emily's purse in his hand. He pushed open the door that led out into the municipal parking lot and braced himself for the almost solid impact of the humid outside air.

Damn, Emily was nowhere in sight. He hadn't been *that* far behind her, had he?

As he scanned the rows of cars parked in the lot, he was well aware that he didn't have a clue what kind of car she drove. Something expensive, no doubt, he thought sourly, a gift from her millionaire boyfriend.

But then he saw her. She was sitting in the front seat of an unassuming little Honda, slumped forward, her arms and head resting on the steering wheel.

As Jim walked toward her, he realized almost immediately that she was crying, and his heart lurched. Calm, collected Emily, who never lost her temper, who never was rattled, who never allowed any of her anxieties to show, was crying as if the world were coming to an end.

He'd only seen her cry one other time before. It had been in the hospital, about a week after he was shot. She'd stayed with him for days, first waiting outside ICU while he was in critical condition, then sitting beside his bed after he was out of immediate danger.

He'd been unconscious most of the time, but the few times he came to, she'd been there, smiling at him. He'd felt reassured by her serenity. He hadn't noticed the lines of strain and worry on her beautiful face. He hadn't noticed—until the night he woke up to find her crying inconsolably.

She'd thought he was asleep, and she was weeping as if her heart were breaking.

That had been the beginning of the end. Jim had known that he was the cause of Emily's unhappiness. Of course, he'd already known that he was poison, that he didn't deserve her. Seeing her cry like that had just hammered it home.

Yet here it was, seven years later, and he'd made her cry again. He had to assume he had something to do with her tears. Damn, seeing her again made *him* feel like crying.

She didn't hear him as he walked up to the open window of her car. She didn't hear him when he stopped, either. So he crouched down, making his face level with the window, and cleared his throat.

"Emily?"

Emily jumped. She lifted her head and found herself staring directly into Jim Keegan's dark blue eyes.

"You okay?" he asked.

Emily tried to dry her face, but she was perspiring from the heat inside the car, and she succeeded only in smearing her wet face with her damp arm. Thankfully, the air coming from the air-conditioning vents began blowing cold.

"I'll live," she said shortly.

His mouth twisted in what might well have been an apologetic smile. "You left your purse in the interview room," he said in his rich, husky voice as he handed it to her through the window. "Some things never change, huh? You should get one of those belt packs, and just never take it off. That way, you can't leave without taking your purse with you, you know?"

"These days I don't usually leave my purse behind," Emily said stiffly. Then she remembered that forgetting to take her purse out of the bathroom on the *Home Free* was what had made her overhear Alex's conversation with Marino. "At least not all the time."

She glanced over to find Jim studying her. He was close enough that she could see the soft, dark fans of his thick eyelashes, and the specks of green and gold mixed in with the blue of his eyes. He was close enough for her to see the roughness of his two-day-old five-o'clock shadow, and the supple smoothness of his full lips. He looked tired. The lines of laughter that creased his face and wrinkled the edges of his eyes seemed more like worry lines in the harsh afternoon light. She could read his tension clearly by the way he clenched and unclenched his teeth, making the muscles move in his jaw.

"You look good, Em," he said softly.

Oh, sure. If he was standing close enough for her to count the stubble of his five-o'clock shadow, then he couldn't help but see that her eyes were red and swollen from tears, and that her face was puffy and pale from crying and lack of sleep. Frankly, she looked like hell. And she knew it.

"Don't cry anymore, okay?" he said. "I know that working with me isn't going to be a lot of fun for you—it's not going to be easy for me, either—but we'll do this quickly and get Delmore in jail, where he belongs. Then everything will be back to normal."

Emily actually laughed. "Normal?" she said. "I'm going to help send my boyfriend away for twenty years to life. Do you think he's still going to want to go steady with me after that?"

Jim was silent. God, what an egotistical bastard he was. Here he'd gone and assumed that she was crying because she was upset about seeing *him* again. But she wasn't. She was crying over *Delmore.*

"I'm such an amazingly lousy judge of character," Emily continued. And it wasn't as if this were the first time she'd misjudged a man. Seven years ago, she'd totally misjudged Jim Keegan, too. "I thought Alex was nice—I thought he was basically a good man. A little stuffy, maybe. A little pompous. But basically good."

God, maybe she'd loved Delmore, Jim thought, feeling an odd twist in his gut. Maybe she *still* was in love with him. Yet she believed so strongly in right and wrong that she felt compelled to turn him in. That couldn't be easy. In fact, it had to be torture.

"I'm sorry, Em," he said.

"Don't call me *Em,* Detective," she said sharply, putting her car into gear. "You don't know me well enough anymore."

She pulled out of the parking lot and was gone.

THERE WAS A MESSAGE from Alex on the answering machine when Emily got home that afternoon.

"My twelve-o'clock appointment cancelled," he said without ceremony, and without introduction. It was clear he expected Emily to recognize his voice. Of course, she did. "If you get back from wherever you are before noon, give my secretary a call. She'll page me, and we can meet up for lunch. If not, I'll see you on Tuesday."

See you on Tuesday.

Emily didn't want to see Alex on Tuesday—or any other day, for that matter. She didn't want to see him ever again.

She didn't want to see Jim Keegan ever again, either,

but he was going to show up at her apartment in a few hours and she was going to have to spend the next week or two seeing him every single day. He was going to be the first person she saw every morning, and the last person she saw every night.

Emily opened the sliding glass door that led out to a tiny deck overlooking the courtyard of her apartment complex. The courtyard held a modest-size swimming pool filled with sparkling-clean blue water, but it was the lush plants and trees that grew on the tiny grounds that Emily loved.

She sat down on one of the two lounge chairs that just barely fit on the minuscule deck. Emily put her head back, listening to the relentless buzzing and sawing of disgruntled insects protesting the day's heat. It had to be a hundred degrees in the shade, with humidity that hung almost visibly in the air, creating a haze that seemed to magnify the power of the sun.

It was summer in Florida, and Emily loved it. The droves of winter residents had migrated north, and the streets seemed empty, the pace so much slower. Of course, as a teacher, she had most of her summers free, which added to the sense of laziness. She had the time to kick back, to walk instead of run, even to stroll instead of walk.

Emily had loved Florida from the start—from the first time her parents took her family here on vacation. When Emily was twelve, Dr. and Mrs. Marshall had bought a beach house on Sanibel Island. From then on, school vacations and a hefty part of the summer had been spent on Florida's Gulf Coast. It had seemed only natural that Emily would attend college at the University of Tampa.

The university. She had only been there about a month

when it became clear that a serial rapist was stalking the campus. Emily had joined a student organization formed to promote student safety. She'd helped get the word out that there was a serious danger to young women walking alone on campus—at any time of the day, and particularly at night. She'd helped set up an escort service so that no one would have to walk anywhere alone. And she'd worked closely with the Tampa police force as they'd tried to catch the rapist.

Many of the kids on the committee had been in awe of the police detectives. Although they were barely in their mid-twenties, the detectives were so obviously men compared to the college boys. And Detective Keegan— he looked like a cross between Mel Gibson and Kevin Costner, with his charmingly crooked grin and smoldering blue eyes—was the number one topic of conversation on the girls' floor of the dorm. Emily had been determined not to be one of the many who developed a schoolgirl crush on the man.

Still, she often looked up during meetings to find him watching her. He'd smile at her, then look away, but moments later, he would be watching her again. Staunchly she tried to ignore him. She always left the meetings quickly, careful not to dawdle, wary of the strange attraction that seemed to spark between them— afraid it was all due to wishful thinking on her part.

Wishful thinking, because Detective Keegan was more than just an incredibly handsome man. He was sharp and funny and smart and so electrifyingly *alive.* But deep in his eyes, and hidden behind his boyish grin, Emily could see real sadness and pain. No one else seemed to notice it, but she knew it was there. She imagined he'd seen awful things on the street, even in the few short years that he'd been a police detective. Rumor had it that he'd recently moved to Florida from New York City. No one seemed to know why.

Despite her resolve to steer clear of James Keegan, the truth was, Emily *would* have given just about anything to spend more time with him.

She could still remember the first real conversation she'd had with Jim. The rapist had been evading the police for weeks, managing to attack four more women, despite the added security measures. Emily had been sitting in on a task force meeting between the police and campus security, and it had suddenly occurred to her that the rapist could very well know their every plan and every move if—and this was an awful thought—he was one of the campus security guards.

After the meeting was over, Keegan's partner left before Emily could approach him. That meant she'd have to share her theory with Jim Keegan.

He was surrounded, as usual, by a crowd of adoring coeds. Emily waited in the doorway, leaning against the frame. He glanced up at her, and somehow he knew that she wanted to talk to him.

"What's on your mind, Emily?" he called across the room.

Emily was surprised. She hadn't realized he even knew her name.

"I was hoping to have a word with you," she said.

He glanced at his watch. "I'm late for a meeting downtown," he said. "Can you walk me to my car while we talk?"

Emily nodded. "Sure."

"Excuse us, ladies," Detective Keegan said, smiling at the other girls.

The girls disappeared down the hall, with more than one catty look thrown in Emily's direction. Jim noticed, and grinned.

"It's nice to be so popular," he said.

"Watch out," Emily said dryly. "You just might find yourself voted this year's homecoming king."

Keegan laughed, coming to stand next to Emily. He was outrageously tall—at least eight inches taller than she was. She had to tip her head back to look up at him. And he had a nice laugh, rich and full and husky. It was sexy, just like his speaking voice. Emily felt her pulse kick into a higher gear, and she chastised herself, determined not to let him know how much he rattled her.

He opened the door that led to the outside and stood back to let Emily go through first.

"So, what's up?" he asked.

Praying that her voice wouldn't give away her nervousness, Emily explained her theory about the possibility of one of the security guards being the rapist as she walked Jim Keegan down to the back campus parking lot.

He was silent for a few minutes after she finished talking. They arrived at his car—a battered silver Chevy—and he leaned against the door and just looked down at her from his intimidating height. Somehow, she managed to hold her own, calmly meeting his eyes. Somehow, she managed not to blush under his scrutiny.

"I'm going to let you in on a little secret," he finally said. "Meyers and I came up with that same idea just yesterday." His blue eyes became even more serious. "You can't talk about this with *anyone,* okay?"

She nodded, her own eyes wide.

"That meeting we just held?" the detective continued. "It was a setup. We're not going to have our patrols and our stakeout teams in the places we planned to have 'em. Instead, we're going to send out decoys in the areas we told campus security that we *weren't* going to be tonight. If this son of a bitch *is* working for the campus security, and if he decides to have some of his twisted idea of fun tonight, we have a good chance of nailing the bastard."

"That's an awful lot of ifs," Emily said.

"Yeah, I know." Keegan reached up to rub the back of his neck, as if it ached.

"Is there anything I can do to help?"

"Yeah," he said, pushing himself up and off his car and aiming the full intensity of his neon blue gaze at her. "Stay in your room and lock your doors and windows. Until we catch this bozo, you—and every other woman on campus—are not safe. Don't forget that, Emily."

He reached forward to push a stray lock of her long brown hair off her face. Emily stepped backward, startled by the heat of his touch, and then embarrassed that she had reacted so obviously. But Jim looked away, as if he were embarrassed, too, and murmured an apology. He stared down at his boots, scuffing them slightly in the dust of the parking lot.

"Remember what we know about this guy," he said, glancing back at her. "He's partial to brunettes. And we think he stalks his victims. We think he picks them out in advance, then follows them around to get their schedule, to find a time they're regularly alone and vulnerable. If you get the sensation that someone's tailing you, don't ignore it, okay?"

Emily nodded, unable to keep from smiling slightly. "That's *my* speech, remember?" she said. "I've just spent the past two weeks visiting all the floors of all the dorms, saying those exact words."

Keegan smiled, too, a quick flash of white teeth. "Yeah, I know." His smile faded. "It's just…if this guy *is* somebody we've all been working with, he might get a real perverse kick out of hurting somebody like you— you know, one of the women on the student committee. And I'm afraid, 'cause you…I don't know…you really stand out in the crowd, you know?"

Emily had to laugh. "Me?" she said in disbelief. "I don't think so. Kirsty Conlon or Megan West, maybe. They're always the center of attention. Not me. I don't get noticed, not the way they do."

"What, you think bouncing around the room and monopolizing the conversation is the only way to get noticed?" Jim asked, almost fiercely. "You're wrong. Because I noticed you. I noticed you the first time you walked into that meeting room."

Emily felt her pulse skip a beat. He'd noticed her. This grown man, this real-life hero, this undercover cop, with a body to die for and the face of a movie star, had noticed *her*. But she was quick to scoff at her reaction to his flattering words. Because they were surely just that— flattery. He'd probably said similar things to Kirsty and Megan and all the other girls who followed him around, fluttering their eyelashes at him.

But his next words surprised her.

"I can't believe you're only a freshman," he said, looking down at his boots again, talking almost as if to himself. "You seem so much older than the other girls." He glanced up at Emily, his eyes frank and honest. "You know, if you were a senior, I would've asked you out. Hell, if you were a *sophomore,* I would've…. But a *freshman*…" He shook his head in disgust, as if being a freshman were her fault.

"What makes you think I'd go out with you?" Emily asked.

"When I first noticed you," he said frankly, "I also noticed that you noticed me, too."

"You're outrageously self-confident, Detective," she said, crossing her arms, determined not to let him see how his words were making her heart pound.

"You're outrageously pretty," he countered.

Her heart leapt higher, but then reality intervened. Inwardly Emily rolled her eyes. More blatant flattery. She knew darn well what she looked like. Sure, she had pretty eyes. And her hair was an exceptional shade of brown. But there was nothing special about her face, nothing that made her qualify as outrageously anything.

Keegan leaned back against his car again, looking for all the world as if he were preparing to stay right there, flirting with her, all afternoon long.

The man's smile was way too charming, and his eyes seemed to hold a warmth and an intimacy that implied that she was the only woman in the world worthy of his attention. Emily knew that couldn't possibly be true. Still, the heat in his eyes was intoxicating. She could get addicted very easily—she was already wondering when the next task force meeting would be, when she'd next see James Keegan. That, combined with the fact that she had discovered she truly liked the detective's open honesty, not to mention that mysterious sadness in his eyes, could be very dangerous. If she stayed here, talking to him much longer, she would develop a full-fledged crush on the man. Assuming, of course, that she hadn't developed one already.

"Didn't you say you were already late?" she asked him. "You better get going."

"Yeah, I should," Jim said. He unlocked his car door. "Hop in."

Her surprise must have shown on her face, because he laughed.

"Don't worry, I'm not trying to kidnap you," he said. "I'm just not about to leave you all alone out here in this parking lot."

Emily looked around. It was broad daylight. Of course, three of the seventeen rapes had occurred during the day—one of them in the back seat of the victim's car, in the north campus parking lot. She shivered. And climbed into Jim Keegan's sedan.

"Thanks," she said.

"My pleasure," he said, with his quick grin.

He drove her the quarter mile back to the main campus building and pulled over to the sidewalk. She started to open the door, but he reached out and held her arm.

"You know, I was serious about what I said before," he told her. "About wanting to ask you out."

Emily didn't know how to answer, so she said nothing.

"I was wondering—" Jim stopped, then shook his head and laughed. "This is going to sound really stupid, but…can I call you? In about a year or two?"

He was still holding her arm, and Emily gently pulled herself free. "You're right," she said, getting out of the car. "That *does* sound really stupid."

But in the end, Emily thought, closing her eyes as she lay on the lounge chair on her tiny deck, *she* had been the stupid one. Seven years of hindsight made that more than clear.

From inside the apartment, she heard the faint sound of the doorbell ringing, but she didn't open her eyes. She wasn't expecting Jim for another few hours, and she didn't feel like talking to anyone right now, not even Carly. Maybe especially not Carly.

But the bell rang again, and then again, and Emily pushed herself to her feet and went inside. Carly had probably seen her car in the parking lot. She knew Emily was home, and she wasn't going to give up until they talked.

With a sigh, Emily opened the front door.

"I *thought* you were home," Alex said, with his smooth, charming smile. He leaned against the door-frame. "I didn't wake you, did I?"

What was he doing here? Emily's heart was in her throat as she stared at him, and she swallowed, trying to push it back down where it belonged. Just because Alex was here, that didn't mean that he knew she'd gone to the police. Just because he was here, that didn't mean that he suspected her of anything. As long as she kept her cool and acted normally…

"No, not really," Emily said, trying to keep her voice even. "I was sitting out on the deck, thinking about dozing off."

"Mind if I come in for a minute?"

Yes. "No, of course not," she said, stepping back to let him into her apartment. "Can I get you something to drink? A glass of iced tea? Some wine? A beer?" Good grief, she sounded like a waitress. If she didn't relax, he *was* going to get suspicious.

"Actually," Alex said, "I can't stay long."

Thank God.

"I just came by to give you this," he continued, taking a slim black jeweler's box from the inside pocket of his suit jacket. He held it out to her with a smile. "I saw it when I was out at lunch, and it made me think of you, so

I gave in to the urge to be self-indulgent." He wiggled the box. "Open it."

Emily slowly took the box from him. It was heavy, and it felt cool in her hands. Why was he doing this? He'd never bought her anything before. Was he using this expensive gift as an excuse to drop by, to see how much of his conversation with Vincent "the Shark" Marino she'd overheard?

But he was smiling at her, and his smile seemed genuine enough.

Of course, this was a man who was a suspected drug smuggler. Was *anything* he did or said genuine?

"Go on. Open it," Alex said again.

Emily slowly opened the box.

It was a necklace. It had a simple yet substantial gold chain with a single enormous sapphire pendant in an equally simple setting. It was elegant, and it had surely cost Alex a small fortune.

But what had it cost the people he made his money off of? What had it cost the addicts and the kids looking for a kick, for a high, or for a quick fix for their poverty and depression? How many people had had their lives ruined, how many people had overdosed and died, in order for Alex to be rich enough to buy her this necklace?

"I can't...I can't accept this," Emily said. No way was she going to wear this necklace. No way could she put this piece of gold, bought with Alex's tainted money, next to her skin.

"Sure you can," Alex said. "It's nothing, really."

Emily closed the box with a snap and held it out to him. "I'm sorry," she said. "I'm just...I'm not comfortable accepting this. It's not appropriate."

Alex laughed. "Oh, come on."

"I'm serious, Alex," she said. "I'm not dating you so that you'll buy me expensive jewelry." *I'm dating you so that I can help the police get the evidence they need to put you in jail, where you belong.*

"Think of this necklace as an apology," Alex said. "I thought maybe my conversation with Vincent Marino upset you, and I wanted to say I was sorry about that."

Panic. For one mind-numbing instant, Emily was frozen with fear. He knew. Alex knew she'd been out in the corridor, eavesdropping. But he was still smiling at her. He wouldn't look so calm, so confident, if he thought she knew about his illegal activities, would he?

"Vincent *who?*" she asked, playing dumb, praying he would buy it. "Alex, I'm not sure what you're talking about. I wasn't upset at all last night."

His smile broadened. "Well, good. My mistake. Keep the necklace anyway."

She wanted him to leave, but she wanted him to take the damned necklace with him. If he left it, he'd wonder why she didn't wear it tomorrow night at the country club. And she wouldn't wear it. She *couldn't.*

"I can't accept this," she said, forcing it into his hand. "People will get the wrong idea."

He laughed again, but this time with good-natured resignation. "Can't it be an early birthday present?"

"My birthday's not till October," Emily said. "Even then, it's too expensive a gift. It's just not appropriate."

Alex slipped the box back into his jacket pocket. "Well, then, I'll hold on to it until it *is* appropriate," he said. "Is that okay?"

He'd be holding on to the necklace until hell froze over. And that was just fine with her. Emily nodded.

"I've got a dinner meeting I need to get to," Alex said. "I'll see you tomorrow night."

Emily nodded again.

He stepped toward her, and she turned away, afraid he was going to kiss her goodbye. But then she was even more afraid that he would wonder why she didn't kiss him. She leaned forward and lightly brushed her lips against his, praying that her revulsion wouldn't show.

"See you tomorrow," she said lightly, opening the door.

And then he was gone, leaving behind only a trace of his expensive cologne.

Emily locked the door behind him. She turned the dead bolt and fastened the safety chain.

She went into the kitchen and dug through the cabinet underneath the sink until she found a spray can of disinfectant. Then she sprayed the living room until the last of Alex's scent was wiped clean from the air.

CHAPTER FOUR

JIM KEEGAN sat and stared at the computer screen on his desk. In real life, Emily Marshall's brother, Daniel, was an astronomy professor. She couldn't remember what she'd told Alexander Delmore about her brother, so Jim was taking this crash course on the computer in basic astronomy. He was learning the lingo so that he wouldn't look stupid—or suspiciously unscientific—when someone mentioned pulsars or red dwarf stars or God only knows what else.

He glanced at his watch. He was supposed to show up at Emily's in less than three hours. Three hours to learn ten years' worth of facts and theories. Jim was known as something of a quick study, but he wasn't *that* quick.

No, he was just going to have to pray that Alexander Delmore knew even less about the universe than he did.

Still, he dragged the cursor back up to the explanation of a black hole, and tried to concentrate. A black hole was a collapsed star with such an intense gravitational field that everything around it was irresistibly sucked toward it. Even light couldn't escape its pull.

Jim shook his head. He knew all about irresistible pulls. He'd experienced one himself, seven years ago.

He had been well aware that he should stay away from Emily Marshall. He had been well aware that she was too young, too sweet, too damn *nice,* for a man like him. And after they caught and locked up that bastard who had raped all those college girls, Jim *had* stayed away from Emily—for all of two weeks.

But, just like a stray beam of light bouncing around the universe, he'd found himself constantly pulled in the direction of the irresistible black hole that was the university—and Emily.

One evening, he found himself standing outside her dorm. When he realized where he was, he tried to tell himself that he had no idea what he was doing there, that it surely was a coincidence that he'd ended up on that particular street in this particular part of town.

But the more pragmatic side of him knew that his excuses were a load of bull. He'd come to the university campus for one reason and one reason only—to see Emily.

He could have flashed his police badge to get past the guard at the high-rise dorm's security checkpoint. But he wasn't here on official police business, so he used one of the telephones in the lobby and dialed Emily's room. As the phone rang, he half prayed that she was in, half prayed that she wasn't.

"Hello?"

She was in.

Jim cleared his throat. "Uh, yeah, Emily?" he said. "This is Jim Keegan. How ya doin'?"

There was a brief pause, the tiniest of hesitations. Then: "Fine." Emily's voice was musical, even over the telephone wires. "What can I do for you, Detective?"

"You can start by calling me Jim," he said.

"Jim," Emily repeated. "Thanks for calling that night—my roommate gave me the message that you called to say you caught the rapist. I was glad to hear that he was off the streets."

"You never called me back," Jim said.

There was another pause. "I was going to," Emily said. "In about a year or two."

Jim laughed. "Touché," he said. "Look, I'm in the lobby of your dorm. You want to come down? We could go get something to eat."

"I already had dinner," she said.

"We could get dessert then," he said. "Or, I don't know—a cup of coffee?" All of a sudden, he was positive that she was going to turn him down. "You're still on the student safety committee, aren't you?"

"Yes, but—"

"There are some things I'd like to talk about, if you've got the time," Jim said. It wasn't the truth, but he would have said damn near anything to get a chance to see her again.

There was another brief pause.

"All right," Emily finally said. "I'll be down in a few minutes."

He leaned on the edge of the security desk for nearly twenty minutes before he saw Emily come out of one of the elevators. She smiled as she walked toward him, and his heart started beating so damn hard he was sure the security guard could hear it.

She looked fabulous. She was wearing a pair of faded jeans and a turquoise T-shirt that hugged her slender curves. Her long chestnut hair was shiny and loose around her shoulders, and she wore very little makeup— just a touch of lipstick and some blush on her cheeks. Her eyes were the color of the ocean.

She walked with the poise of a much older woman.

But she was only eighteen. He'd have to remember that. She was just a kid.

"How're your classes going?" he asked as they went out the doors into the early evening. In Florida, November nights were still soft and warm. The sidewalks were alive with people out for fresh air.

"Great," she said, smiling up at him as they began to walk.

Her skin was soft and smooth looking, and her features were delicate, almost fragile. Her freckle-covered nose tipped up a tiny bit at the end, and her chin was a touch too pointy, making her look slightly elfin. She was gorgeous—an incredible mix of woman and girl, of sophistication and innocence. The woman in her was emphasized by the peaceful calm of her lovely blue eyes.

Jim took her arm and pulled her out of the stream of pedestrian traffic.

"I lied," he said bluntly. "I didn't come here to talk about the student safety committee. I came because I wanted…"

He couldn't find the right words. Why *had* he come? Because he wanted to see her again? But he didn't just want to see her. He didn't just want to talk to her. He wanted…

"What?" she breathed, looking up into his eyes.

Jim realized he was still holding her arm. He realized he was standing close enough to breathe in her sweet, fresh scent, close enough to feel the heat from her body, close enough to kiss her….

He bent his head, drawn irresistibly toward the tantalizing sweetness of her lips. But he made himself stop, a whisper away from a kiss, giving her a chance to pull away, to pull back. But she didn't move. She didn't use the opportunity to escape. She simply looked up at him, her lips parted breathlessly, a spark of anticipation, of excitement, in her eyes.

So he kissed her. Right there, on the sidewalk in front of the university dorm.

He didn't intend for it to be anything but a sweet kiss, a gentle kiss—a single kiss. But one kiss wasn't enough, and he kissed her again. And again. He pulled her against him, and the softness of her body made him crazy, and he forgot all about gentle and sweet. He ran his tongue along her lips and, God help him, she opened her mouth to him, granting him access, inviting him in.

It wasn't an invitation he needed to be given more than once.

Jim felt her fingers in his hair as he drank her in. He kissed her again and again, long, hard, deep kisses that made the world spin dizzily around him and made the air suddenly thin and hard to breathe.

He might have gone on kissing her for hours, days— hell, even *weeks*—but she pulled back. She was breathing as hard as he was, and her beautiful eyes were nearly molten with desire as she gazed up at him.

Her voice shook slightly as she spoke. "Does this mean you don't want to wait a year or two before you ask me out?"

Jim had had to laugh. With hindsight, he knew that was the exact moment he'd fallen in love with Emily. But at the time, he hadn't recognized the sensation. All he'd known was that she made him smile, that she took the edge off all the pain he carried around with him day in and day out.

Jim stared blindly at the definition of a nebula that was displayed on his computer screen.

He'd never told Emily that he loved her. Not even that one wonderful, exhilarating, *terrifying* weekend they'd spent together, that weekend he'd lost all control and made love to her. He'd never told her, never said the words.

He couldn't. Because if she'd known, she wouldn't have let him walk away from her without a fight. She would've known that the cruel things he'd said to her were said out of fear and pain.

Jim shut the power on his computer down, then went to pack up the things he would need over the course of the next two weeks.

Two weeks that would be spent with a woman who had every reason to hate him.

What had Lieutenant Bell called this investigation? Quick and easy? Yeah, right. This was going to be as quick and easy as a canoe trip around the world...without a paddle.

EMILY WOKE UP drenched with sweat, with the setting sun glaring in her face. She pushed herself up from the deck chair, slid open the glass door and went inside. The living room was cool and dark, and as she closed the sliding door behind her she shut out the noise of the traffic and the raucous cries of the seabirds that wheeled overhead. The steady hum of the air conditioner joined with the gentle throbbing of her refrigerator, making her apartment seem like some kind of environmentally controlled spaceship, detached and separate, independent and remote from the rest of the planet.

Emily went around the corner into the small galley kitchen and opened the refrigerator. She poured herself a large glass of seltzer, and drank it thirstily as she glanced at the clock on the wall.

It was 5:38.

Jim Keegan would be arriving in less than an hour.

She pushed her sweat-soaked hair back from her face and searched her cabinets for an aspirin. She didn't have a headache yet, but she could feel a real doozy coming on.

Of course, it wasn't too late to call off her participation in the investigation.

Emily poured herself another glass of seltzer and drank this one more slowly, swallowing the extra-strength aspirin tablets with the first sip.

What if she had guessed wrong about Alex Delmore? What if she had misunderstood his conversation with Vincent Marino? What if Alex really had been out fishing in the dinghy that morning? What if he was innocent? He had acted innocent enough an hour ago, when he dropped by.

But if he *was* innocent, what was he doing socializing with one of Florida's most powerful mob bosses? And Emily *hadn't* misunderstood that conversation. She knew exactly what she'd overheard. And, come to think of it, why would Alex have bothered to take the dinghy if he wanted to fish? Why wouldn't he simply have done his fishing from the deck of the *Home Free?*

No. Something odd was going on, and her every instinct screamed that Alex was involved.

If she backed out of this investigation now, she'd always wonder how much crack Alex had brought into Florida during the time wasted because she refused to cooperate with the authorities. She'd wonder how many people—how many *kids*—died from drug overdoses, from heart attacks, from knife fights over possession of those drugs.

How many kids would die because *she* was too chicken to spend a little time with Jim Keegan?

This was good, Emily realized, grabbing this course of reasoning as if it were a lifeline. Thinking this way would help her stop focusing on the awfulness of her situation.

True, working with Jim Keegan would be terrible, because she'd be forced to face the embarrassment of knowing that he'd once played her for a fool. She would have to face the fact that she had misjudged him so absolutely, that seven years ago she hadn't really known him at all. True, she'd have to face the constant reminder of the pain he had caused her. And, true, she'd be forced to confront her own stupidity every time she looked into Jim's blue eyes and felt her heart *still* leap and her pulse *still* kick into double time.

But maybe, Emily thought, just *maybe,* it was also true that spending the next two weeks with Jim Keegan would be a good thing. Aside from the fact that helping with the investigation could save lives, maybe two weeks of close, day-to-day contact with this man would be helpful to her. Maybe it would help her see the real Jim Keegan—the same Jim Keegan who had lashed out at her so cruelly all those years ago….

Emily closed her eyes, remembering with stark accuracy the night she and Jim had broken up. It had been April, early spring, only about three weeks after he was released from the hospital. It had been only three *days* after she went to his apartment, looking for him—and ended up staying overnight. They'd made love for the first time that weekend….

Emily shook her head, unwilling to let herself remember the way he'd touched her, kissed her, *loved* her—and left her. *That* was what she had to remember. Not quite three days after they made love, he had left her for good.

It had been a Wednesday night, and Emily had been standing outside her dorm. She'd been ready for their date a little early, so she'd gone down to the front of the building so that Jim wouldn't have to come inside to get her.

But he was late. Fifteen minutes. Then thirty. She went inside to use the pay phone, but there was no answer at his apartment. He hadn't even left his answering machine on. She called her own machine, checking to see if he'd called to tell her that he'd be late. But there was nothing. No message.

After another fifteen minutes, Emily was well past worried. It wasn't unusual for him to be late, but he'd always left messages before—either on her machine or wherever they were planning to meet. Refusing to think about hospitals or gunshot wounds or the growing number of city police officers who had been shot dead on the streets over the past few years, she walked briskly to the sports bar on the corner, where they had been planning to go that evening. Maybe he'd left a message for her there. Maybe he wasn't lying in some pool of blood somewhere. Maybe—

Jim was there.

He was there, sitting at the bar.

With his arm around a pretty dark-haired woman who had to be wearing the shortest skirt Emily had ever seen in her life. Disbelief flooded through her.

She must have made some sort of sound, because Jim turned toward her. He looked surprised to see her at first. But then he laughed.

He actually *laughed*.

She knew she should turn and walk away. But she was a fool. She just stood there and stared at him, thinking that there must be some mistake….

"What are *you* doing here?" he asked. The woman he had his arm around peered curiously over his shoulder at her.

Emily couldn't speak. She just looked at him, unable to move.

He sighed heavily and turned back to the dark-haired woman. "Don't go anywhere, babe," he said, and kissed her. On the lips. Then he slid off the bar stool and walked toward Emily.

Jim staggered once before he reached her. He laughed again, as if his inability to walk a straight line was something he found funny. He stank of whiskey as he walked past Emily, motioning for her to follow him.

She walked woodenly behind him, out the main entrance and onto the sidewalk in front of the bar.

"What'd I do? Mess up the dates again?" Jim asked, turning to face her. "I thought we were on for tomorrow night."

Emily shook her head no. And suddenly, through all the disbelief, through the hurt and pain of having seen him with that other woman, came waves of relief. At least he wasn't dead. At least he wasn't lying in some ambulance, racing to the hospital while the paramedics tried to keep his heart from pumping his blood out of a bullet hole in his chest….

Thank God.

"What did you say?" Jim asked, his eyes narrowing slightly.

Emily realized she must have spoken out loud.

Her eyes filled with tears as she looked up at him. "I

thought you'd been shot again," she said, her voice shaking. "I thought you were dead."

"Oh, God," he said, recoiling as if she had hit him, turning away, covering his face with his hands. But he turned back almost instantly, his eyes flashing with anger, his face nearly contorted with rage.

"I'm *worse* than dead, damn it!" he shouted. "So stay the *hell* away from me!"

He moved toward her. His anger and his sheer size were menacing, frightening, but Emily stood her ground. If there was one thing, and only one thing, that she could hold on to as a truth in all this insanity, it was that, drunk or sober, Jim Keegan would *never* hit her.

"I don't understand," she said. "What are you doing? I love you. And I thought—"

"You were wrong," he said, backing away when he realized that she wasn't going to be the one to move. "Whatever you thought, you were *wrong,* damn it!" He lowered his voice. "Yeah, it's been fun, and last weekend was a blast, but— You don't *really* think that I've slept alone every night since we started dating in November, do you? Get real, kid…."

The shock of his words overcame her relief, and Emily turned and ran.

Last weekend was a blast.

Emily had let him touch her in ways that she'd never let a man touch her before. She'd given herself to him, heart, body and soul. But to Jim, it had merely been "a blast."

She had heard the expression "Love is blind" a hundred times in the past, but before that night she'd never experienced the phenomenon firsthand.

Love was, indeed, blind. She had seen Jim Keegan as

some kind of superhero, some kind of perfect man. She'd seen someone tender, someone kind and sensitive, someone she thought loved her as much as she loved him.

Wrong.

Seven years ago, her imagination had obviously clouded her vision.

But now there was nothing to keep her from seeing James Keegan clearly. Over the next few weeks, she would have an opportunity that most women never had…she would be able to see, *really* see, this man that she had once loved so desperately. She'd get a chance to see, firsthand, that he wasn't the perfect man she'd once thought he was. She'd have a chance to dissolve the superhero myth that still surrounded him in her dreams, despite the way he had treated her that awful night. She'd be face-to-face with the real man—the insensitive, selfish, impolite *bastard* that he truly was. And maybe then she'd stop longing for the sound of his laughter and the warmth of his touch. Maybe then, finally, she'd be free.

THE DOORBELL RANG as Emily was stepping out of the shower. She quickly dried herself and slipped into a terry-cloth bathrobe. On the way to the door, she glanced at the clock. It was only quarter of. It figured that Jim Keegan would be early. It figured that he'd catch her wearing only her bathrobe—

She stopped short, halfway across the living room.

Oh, brother, if she answered the door in her bathrobe, what was he going to think? Stupid question. She knew exactly what he was going to think, and it wouldn't be good.

"Hey, Emily, open up! I know you're home—I saw

your car in the lot!" a voice called from the other side of the door.

But the voice didn't belong to Jim Keegan. It was Carly's voice.

Emily opened the door to her neighbor's familiar face and shining...*blond* curls?

"What d'ya think?" Carly asked, needing no invitation to come inside. She turned, posing like a model on a fashion runway, showing off her new hair color in the middle of Emily's living room.

Carly Wilson, thrice divorced before the tender age of twenty-nine, rarely stood still. And when she *was* standing still, it was usually because she was laughing too hard to move.

Carly had moved into the apartment down the hall from Emily not quite a year ago—after her most recent divorce. At the time, the diminutive woman had had thick, straight, nearly jet-black hair. Since then, she'd gone through a wide variety of perms and cuts and hair colors, the most recent being a not-quite-believable shade of red.

Carly was, of all things, a librarian. With her flamboyant wardrobe and her ever-changing hair color, she was far from the stereotype. But she *did* love books. In fact, she claimed to love books even more than she loved men. And that was saying something.

"Blond, huh? It looks good," Emily said, closing the door. "What's the occasion?"

Carly laughed and plopped herself down on the couch. "No occasion," she said, in her low, scratchy voice, which was incongruous with her petite size and cheerleader-cute face. "Just time for a change. Speaking of changing, I caught you fresh out of the shower, didn't I? Don't let me stop you. Go on, get dressed."

"I'll just be a minute," Emily said.

Carly turned, raising her voice so that Emily could hear her even in the bedroom. "You know what triggered this new color?"

"Nope," Emily called back, pulling on fresh underwear. "What?"

"I was out with Mac again on Saturday night," Carly said from the living room. "We went to the Crazy Horse Saloon, 'cause his band was playing there, and during one of their breaks I found out that that man can really dance. And I mean *really*. So he's leading me around the line of dance like some kind of cowboy Fred Astaire, and I suddenly realize that I'm daydreaming about dancing with him at our wedding reception!"

"Uh-oh," Emily said. She brushed out her still-damp hair as she came back into the living room, wearing a clean pair of shorts and T-shirt.

"Uh-oh's right," Carly said, her brown eyes merry with suppressed laughter. "Now, Mac is undeniably good-looking, and I confess he's got the ability to make my poor heart beat twice as hard as it should, but *marriage?* Good Lord, it wouldn't last a month. Three months, tops. And, quite frankly, I can't afford another divorce. So I figured if I wanted a change in my life that badly, I'd skip the wedding and just color my hair and rearrange my living room furniture instead. Besides, in a few more weeks, after old Alex pops the question, I can help you plan *your* wedding, right? I'll get plenty of vicarious thrills that way—no need to suffer through the experience again myself."

Emily stared out the sliding glass door, her good humor suddenly gone. But Carly didn't notice. She chattered on about the new curtains she was thinking about buying for her kitchen windows until the doorbell rang.

Emily turned then, her hairbrush still in her hand. Oh, shoot. This time it had to be James Keegan.

"Are you expecting someone?" Carly asked curiously.

The smaller woman beat Emily to the door and threw it open wide. Even though she couldn't see who was at the door, Emily knew it was Jim simply by the sudden change in the way Carly was standing.

"Well, hel-lo," Carly said. "*Who* are *you?*"

"I'm looking for Emily Marshall," Jim's husky voice replied. "I thought she was in 6B. Am I wrong?"

Emily stepped behind Carly, and Jim's face relaxed into a smile. "Well, hey, Em, how ya doing?" he said. "The directions you gave me from the airport were great."

It was odd—his words and expression were relaxed and friendly, but the message Emily was getting from Jim's eyes was anything but. Who the hell is this, he was silently asking about Carly, and what the hell is she doing here?

"You gonna invite me in?" he asked.

"Please…come in," Emily said, pulling Carly back with her, out of Jim's way.

Jim lugged a duffel bag over the threshold and closed the door behind him. His long hair was pulled back with a rubber band at the nape of his neck, and he was dressed in a pair of khaki pants and a white polo shirt.

Emily realized that she'd rarely seen Jim wear anything besides jeans and a T-shirt, or the sloppy, army-issue shorts he sometimes wore when it got too hot for long pants. Every now and then he'd worn a suit because he had to. Of course, it occurred to her that Jim was undercover right now. He was wearing what he figured her visiting brother might wear—and he was pretty darn accurate. Except Danny never looked so good in *his* Dockers.

Jim slid a gym bag off his shoulder and onto the floor next to the duffel bag and turned toward Emily. Before she realized what he was doing, he'd put his arms around her.

"It's been a long time," he said, pulling her in close to him.

Damn, she smelled great. She still used the same sweet-smelling soap when she washed her face. She still used the same brand of shampoo. She still didn't bother to wear perfume. She still smelled young and fresh and achingly lovely. Jim let go of her, fast.

Trying to hide how off balance he felt, he turned to the blond woman and made himself smile. "Hi," he said. "I'm Dan Marshall. I'm Emily's brother."

The blonde held out her hand. "I'm Carly Wilson, Emily's neighbor."

"I'll get some iced tea," Emily said as Carly dragged Jim into the living room.

Jim sat down on a couch with pale floral-patterned up-holstery. Emily's apartment was small, smaller than he'd expected—proof that Alexander Delmore wasn't subsi-dizing her living expenses. He was relieved about that, more relieved than he should have been. What was wrong with him? He didn't have any reason to feel jealous of Delmore, and certainly didn't have any reason to feel pos-sessive toward Emily. Seven years was a long time.

As Carly gave him a detailed narrative of exactly when and where she'd met Emily, Jim looked around the place that he was going to be calling home for the next few weeks.

Several framed pictures hung on the white walls. They were photographs—two of the ocean, one of an older man and woman on the front porch of a house, and one of the earth taken from the moon.

There was an entertainment center directly across from the couch, with a small, inexpensive TV and stereo inside a cabinet. A wicker-and-glass coffee table sat in front of the couch. Rows of bookshelves lined one of the other walls. A single rocking chair was the only comfortable place to sit besides the sofa. A small, round dining table and two hardbacked chairs were at the end of the room, in front of a sliding glass door and adjacent to what Jim figured must be the kitchen. He could hear Emily moving around back there, could hear the clink of ice cubes in glasses, the sound of the refrigerator door opening and shutting.

Jim looked up at Carly, suddenly aware that she'd asked him a question. "I'm sorry—?" he said.

"Jet lag, huh?" she said sympathetically. "Where'd you fly in from?"

"Colorado," he lied. "Denver."

"You know, I can really see the family resemblance," Carly said. "It's in your eyes. You're definitely Emily's brother."

Jim looked up as Emily came into the room, carrying three tall glasses. She set them down on the coffee table, then handed one to him. His fingers brushed hers accidentally, but she didn't seem to notice. Hell, he nearly stopped breathing at the slight contact, but she didn't even blink.

Emily offered Carly one of the glasses, but the blond woman shook her head and stood up.

"I'm outa here," Carly said. "You guys have some catching up to do."

"Oh," Emily protested. "You don't have to go…."

"No, no," Carly said. "You don't need me butting in."

She smiled at Jim. "Besides, your brother's tired. I'll come back tomorrow, after he's had his rest."

Jim fought the urge to join in with Emily's protests. Having the neighbor there was something of a relief. Having her around meant that he and Emily weren't alone, together, in this tiny apartment. It meant that they wouldn't have to look at each other or talk.

But he knew that Carly's presence would simply put off the inevitable. He and Emily *had* to talk. He had to find out more about her childhood and her parents. He had to find out if Emily remembered what she'd told Alex about her brother.

And, sooner or later, they had to talk about their history. There was no way he could stay here for any length of time without at least *mentioning* their past relationship. It would be too weird.

So he stayed on the couch while Emily walked her friend to the door. He heard them say goodbye. He heard the door close. And then he heard...silence.

Keegan looked up to see Emily pick up her glass of iced tea and sit down across from him in the rocking chair. She met his gaze calmly, and again he felt a stab of frustration. How could she act so cool when just the idea of them alone together was making him sweat bullets?

He covered his discomfort with a smile. "So," he said, "here we are."

She didn't comment. She didn't say anything equally stupid simply to break up this damned silence. She didn't do anything except sip her iced tea. And watch him.

God, she was beautiful. And so damned unaffected by his presence. Jim clenched his teeth.

Emily was holding her glass of iced tea so tightly that her fingers were starting to cramp. She forced herself to loosen her hold and take a sip. She could see the tension in the way Jim was sitting. He was nervous. Well, rightly so. He *should* be nervous. Seven years ago he'd taken advantage of a young girl's trust and love. Quite frankly, he'd used her in the most blatant and obvious way. He'd treated her abysmally.

It was clear that he had never imagined he'd see her again, let alone be forced to occupy the same space for anything longer than a few brief, embarrassment-tinged moments.

She gazed at him, not having to bother to ask herself the timeworn question *What had she seen in him?* She knew exactly what she'd seen in him—she was looking straight at it. Thick honey-brown hair that waved around a lean, handsome face that could have made a fortune on a movie screen. Dark blue eyes surrounded by thick black lashes, a slightly bent, very masculine nose, and a million-dollar smile—although he wasn't smiling now, was he? Still, smiling or frowning, James Keegan was outrageously attractive.

And that was just his face. His body was more of the same story. He looked like he might have put on a few pounds over the past seven years, but they were all pounds put on in the right places. His stomach was still flat, and his hips were still slim and his legs... Yeah. He was in even better shape than he'd been in at age twenty-five.

He cleared his throat, clearly ill at ease. "We've got a lot of ground to cover here," he said, reaching into his back pocket for a small notepad. "Where do you want to start?"

Emily leaned forward slightly to put her glass down on the coffee table. "Where do you want me to start? With Danny? My parents? Our house in Connecticut?"

"How about we start with Delmore?" Jim suggested, flipping to a blank page in his pad.

Her eyes met his suddenly, a startling flash of blue in the grayness of the rapidly dimming room.

"Alex," she said.

"Yeah," Jim said. "Your boyfriend."

Emily crossed her legs with a sudden quick movement. That, and a slight flaring of her nostrils, were the only signs that he had touched a nerve. And he wanted to touch a nerve, he realized suddenly. He wanted her to be as rattled as he was. He wanted to see some kind of evidence that she had missed him these past seven years as goddamned badly as he had missed her. Had she cried the way he had? Had she ached just from wanting to see him, the way he had for her?

He'd imagined her so many times, walking on the beach, staring out at the ocean, feeling so utterly alone and lost—the way he'd felt without her. But he'd also imagined her finding some nice safe guy and settling down. *Settling,* that was the key word. He'd imagined Emily settling for someone else, but still wanting *him.*

"Alex is a little old to call a *boyfriend,* don't you think?" Emily said.

"Maybe we should call him…your lover." Jim added just the slightest tinge of nastiness to his voice. He was needling her on purpose. There was no way she could have missed it.

But she didn't react. No intake of breath, no flicker of her eyes, no tension in her shoulders. She just looked at him. And then she smiled.

"Alex Delmore and I dated," she said quietly. "That's all you need to know, Detective. Anything else isn't your business."

What the hell did that smile mean? It was as if she were keeping score, and she'd just won a point.

Jim reached forward and took a healthy slug of his iced tea, trying hard to keep his cosmic balance. He put the glass back on the tabletop with just a little too much force, and it made a loud noise in the room's silence.

"Mind if we turn on a light in here?" he asked.

Emily shook her head, standing up in one graceful motion and crossing to a halogen lamp.

"Also, you better get used to calling me Dan," Jim added, squinting slightly as the bright light seemed to fill the room. "Or Danny, or whatever you call your brother."

"Danny," Emily said, moving back to the rocking chair and sitting down again. "But he calls himself Dan now."

"I need you to try to remember what you might have told Delmore about your brother," he said. "Any little mention, anything he might remember."

Emily chewed thoughtfully on her lower lip. "You know, I don't know if I've ever even mentioned my brother to Alex," she said. "I guess I must've. We've talked about Guilford, where my parents still live—you know, in Connecticut—so I must've mentioned Danny. But only vaguely. Like, 'I have only one brother, no sisters. My brother lives in New Mexico. He's an astronomy professor.'"

Keegan's eyebrows slid upward. "That's it?" he asked, in obvious disbelief.

Emily shrugged. "Alex and I really haven't talked that much," she said.

"I'll bet," Jim muttered under his breath. If she heard him, she gave no sign, except for another of those damned smiles.

They worked for close to two hours, going through

Dan Marshall's background, and the details of Emily's childhood home in Connecticut. A little after nine o'clock, Jim rubbed his hands across his face and stretched.

"I gotta stop," he said. "I'm losing my concentration. I'm sorry, but I pulled a double shift last night—I haven't slept more than two hours in the past forty-eight. Mind if we finish this up tomorrow?"

Emily shook her head. "The couch pulls out into a bed," she said. "There are sheets and a pillow in the linen closet. A blanket, too, but it's pretty hot—you probably won't need one. Feel free to use the shower."

"Thanks," he said.

He looked down at all the notes he'd taken, and cleared his throat. "I know…" he said hesitantly, his voice huskier than usual. He stopped, then started again. "This has got to be difficult for you. Working with me, I mean." He looked up and forced himself to meet her steady gaze. "Especially with me living here like this."

Emily was silent for a moment. Then she shook her head. "No," she said with a small smile, "actually it's not that bad."

Jim couldn't hide his disbelief. He stared at her, and exhaled shortly—a quick burst of doubt that under other circumstances might have been called a laugh. "You're kidding," he said flatly.

Again she shook her head. "No."

"You don't hate me?"

If she was at all surprised by the directness of his words, she didn't show it. She *did* consider his question carefully, though.

"No," she said finally, as if the answer were as surprising to her as it was to him. "I don't. It's true that I dislike you, but dislike is different from hate. Hate's much too strong a word." She stood up. "If we're done for tonight, I'm going to run out to the grocery store. I have a couple things I need to get. Want anything?"

Keegan shook his head. He felt oddly dizzy. Emily didn't hate him. She only *disliked* him. Somehow that was worse. "No," he said, realizing suddenly that she was waiting for an answer to her question. "No thanks."

Emily picked up her keys and went out the door, closing it firmly behind her. It wasn't until she was down in the parking lot and sitting in her car that her knees began to shake.

God help her, she was such a liar. She didn't know *what* she felt for Jim Keegan, but it sure wasn't the cool indifference she'd pretended to feel. She wanted to feel indifferent, though. She wanted to be able to look at Jim and feel only mild distaste, not this…jumble of emotions, this mishmash of intense feelings.

She took a deep breath, and then another, and another. She'd seen glimpses of what she assumed must be the real James Keegan tonight. Rude, arrogant, selfish, impatient, conniving…the list went on and on. She was noticing all the imperfections and flaws that she hadn't been able to see when she was dazzled by his rugged good looks and the kind gentleness that she knew had to have been an act.

After two weeks of eye-opening reality, she *would* feel nothing but cool indifference toward him.

Wouldn't she?

CHAPTER FIVE

EMILY WOKE UP at eight-thirty, and got dressed before she left her bedroom.

But when she opened her door, the rest of her apartment was quiet. Too quiet. She ventured down the hallway and peeked into the living room.

The pullout mattress was back inside the couch, and the sheets that Jim had used were folded in a neat pile on the coffee table. His bags were out of the way, in the corner of the room, and he was nowhere in sight.

The kitchen was just as empty, but there was a note for her out on the counter.

"Emily," Jim had printed in his big, bold handwriting, "I went out for a run. I'll be back before nine." He'd started to sign the note "Jim," but had crossed out the *J* and signed it "Dan" instead, underlining the name twice for emphasis.

His handwriting was so familiar. It brought back a barrage of memories so intense that Emily had to sit down.

Over the course of the five months they had dated, Jim must've left her a hundred little notes like this one. Sometimes the notes had been tacked to the corkboard on her dorm room door. And sometimes he'd sent them through the mail, on silly postcards or even just scraps of paper stuffed into a business envelope. Often she'd opened her mailbox to find more than one envelope with her name and address printed on the front in Jim's neat block letters. She'd opened them to find clippings from newspapers or magazine articles he thought she might be interested in, along with a quick note. Sometimes he'd only send a note, and sometimes it would be only one line. But no matter what he said or what he sent, the message had been clear—Jim Keegan had been thinking about her.

So how did his thoughtfulness fit into the picture now?

Instead of being part of the softer side of a tough man, all those notes had probably just been another way Jim manipulated her into trusting him. And, boy, it had worked, hadn't it?

The fact was, he'd dumped her only days after he got her into bed with him. It seemed safe to assume that, therefore, his sole goal in courting her had been to have sex with her.

When you looked at it *that* way, then yes, all those wonderful little notes did seem nasty and manipulative.

Emily stared down at the paper she was holding in her hand. But what about *this* note? There was nothing manipulative about this one. He had nothing to gain by telling her where he'd gone and when he'd be back. It was simple consideration.

She crumpled it up and threw it in the trash. So what? Even an ax murderer could be considerate now and then, she thought sourly.

The front door opened slowly, and Emily looked up.

Jim poked his head around the edge of the door, saw her, then stepped into the room.

"You're up," he said.

He was wearing a pair of running shorts and a muscle

shirt that had more armhole to it than shirt. His skin—and there was so much of it showing—glistened with sweat, and his hair clung damply to his neck and the sides of his face.

He was carrying a white paper bag, and he brought it into the kitchen and put it on the counter. "Breakfast," he explained, with an uncertain smile. "I picked up some bagels at that place down on the corner. You ever go there? It's called Stein's. I walked in and, you know, I thought I was back in New York City."

As he talked, he poured water into Emily's coffee-maker and searched the cabinets for filters. He found them on his second try, then opened the refrigerator and grabbed the can of coffee.

"You want more than one cup?" he turned to Emily to ask.

She was watching him, eyebrows slightly raised, and he stopped. "Um…" he said, "you mind if I…you know, make some coffee?"

Emily shook her head. "No," she said. "As long as you don't mind chipping in to help pay for the beans. Or whatever else you use."

"Of course," he said.

"Then, by all means," she said, "make yourself at home."

He smiled sheepishly. "I already was," he admitted.

"I noticed," Emily said. But then she smiled. At him.

But it was just a little smile, and it was over nearly as soon as it started. Still, Jim stared at her, momentarily lost in the blueness of her eyes.

He forced himself to turn away, pretending to concentrate on measuring out the scoops of coffee as he regained his equilibrium.

Sure, it was just a little smile, but it *was* a smile. A real smile, not one of those odd smiles she'd given him last night—one of the ones that suggested that she knew some kind of joke and she wasn't going to share the punch line with him.

He pushed the filter into the coffee machine and put the can back in the fridge. As he glanced up, he saw that Emily was still watching him.

"Well," he said, uncomfortable under her steady gaze, "if it's okay with you, I'll take a quick shower while the coffee's brewing, and then we can get back to work."

She nodded. "That's fine."

"Help yourself to the bagels," he said.

Emily watched him walk down the hall to the bathroom. Jeez, he was *still* a hunk and a half. She pulled her eyes away before he could turn around and see her checking out his long, strong legs and his incredibly perfect rear end.

Many men hit their thirties and started losing their hair and developing beer bellies. But not Jim Keegan. No. He had to be one of those men who became more perfect with age. It wasn't fair.

"I'M DAN MARSHALL," Jim said, looking over his notes. "I'm thirty years old, a professor of astronomy at the College of Santa Fe in New Mexico. I went to Yale for two years, then transferred to the University of New Mexico in Albuquerque, where I got my bachelor's degree. I went to Denver, Colorado, to get my master's, then back to UNM for my doctorate—"

"Have you ever even *been* to Colorado or New Mexico?" Emily asked.

He shook his head no. "I stayed on at UNM for two

years, teaching, until I got the offer to head the department in Santa Fe—"

"How can you pretend that you've lived in the Southwest for ten years, when you've never been there even once?"

Jim looked up from his notes and smiled. "I've seen a lot of Westerns," he said.

"I'm serious," Emily said. "Alex's mother lives in Phoenix. And I know that he's been skiing in Colorado, but I don't know exactly where. What if it was near Denver? What if he asks you a question that you can't answer? It won't take much for him to realize you've never been out West."

Jim shrugged. "I'll get by."

Emily was leaning forward slightly, watching him, sitting in the same rocking chair she'd sat in last night. She wasn't wearing much makeup, but her face had that glow that a person could only get from good health and the persistent Florida sunshine. Jim's eyes traveled almost involuntarily down the long, slender lengths of her bare arms and legs. She had one hell of a perfect tan, not too dark, but a delicate golden brown. She sure didn't get that tan from sitting inside, in her living room, all day. She had to be as antsy as he was, as eager to get outside and stretch her legs, work off some of this nervous energy.

Talk about nervous energy. Jim hadn't felt this restless in a long time. Of course, the fact that he'd spent last night only one room away from a woman he'd once felt a powerful and irresistible sexual attraction toward had a lot to do with it. His eyes moved back up Emily's long legs. God, she was gorgeous. She was a knockout, with those killer legs and that body—

Damn, who was he kidding? The attraction he felt wasn't a thing of the past. It was extremely present-tense. It was here and now, and he couldn't deny it. Seven years later, and he *still* lusted after this woman.

But if the attraction was mutual, she sure as hell wasn't showing it.

"You hungry?" he asked her. "I know this great lunch place down by the beach. What do ya say we go get something to eat? My treat." He stood up and put his file of notes into his gym bag. "Come on. It's nearly one-thirty, and I'm starving. This place has the best jerk chicken in the universe." He forced a grin. "And I oughta know. I'm an astronomer, right?"

Emily glanced at her watch. Was it really one-thirty? She hadn't even had breakfast—only a cup of Jim's ridiculously strong coffee. She wasn't hungry, but she stood up anyway. Getting out of the confines of this apartment was a decidedly good idea. "Just let me get my sun hat," she said.

Jim was waiting by the door when she came out of the bedroom. "You wanna take your purse?" he asked.

Emily pretended that she had forgotten her little canvas bag on purpose. "I thought this was going to be your treat," she said.

He smiled. "I thought maybe you'd want your sunglasses."

She knew she hadn't fooled him, and she sighed. "I'm twenty-five years old," she said. "I'm an organized person. I'm relatively neat, and always punctual. Why do I forget my purse all the time?"

"Get a purse that's really heavy," Jim said as they walked down the stairs to the apartment complex's parking lot. "Then you'll notice when it's not hanging on your shoulder. Like, you know, right now I'm really aware that I'm outside without my shoulder holster on. It doesn't feel right. Something's missing, and I know it."

Emily glanced at him. He'd changed out of his shorts when she went to find her hat, she realized. He was wearing long pants and a pair of cowboy boots now, despite the hot weather.

"Are you—"

He finished the question for her. "Carrying? Yeah. I've got a gun in my boot. It's not as easy to get to, but I didn't think it would be believable for your brother to wear a jacket in this weather. And a shoulder holster would look a little funny without a jacket to cover it up." He paused as they left the building's protective awning and walked into the uncovered parking lot. The heat was intense, reflecting off the blacktop and making the air feel thick and suffocating.

"But I've been carrying a weapon for so long, it feels unnatural for me to be without *something*—even a gun in my boot," Jim said, watching as Emily unlocked the door to her little car. "That's how you've got to get with your purse. You've got to feel like it's an essential part of you—that something's missing when you don't feel it there, next to you. You know what I mean?"

"But I hate carrying a purse," Emily said. "I don't *want* it to be an essential part of me."

"Then maybe you *should* get a belt pack," Jim said as he squeezed himself into Emily's subcompact car. He had to recline the seat slightly, and still his knees nearly touched the dashboard. "By the way, *that's* how I do it."

"Do what?" Emily looked away from the rearview mirror to glance at him as she put her car into reverse and backed out of her parking space.

"How I handle questions that I can't answer when I'm undercover," Jim said. "I get around the questions. I answer vaguely, and then I change the subject, like I did with your question. Remember, you asked me what I'd do if Delmore asked me something about Colorado that I couldn't answer, right? I turned around and asked you to lunch."

"Yeah, but what if Alex asks something specific, like have you been to his favorite restaurant in Denver?" Emily said. "Won't he be suspicious if you don't even know what part of town it's in?"

Jim rested his elbow out the open car window as she pulled on to the main road. "I'll say something like 'I didn't get out much when I was living in Denver—not on a teaching assistant's salary.'"

She shot him a skeptical look, and he said, "I'll also do some research. I'll look at city maps, memorize street names, learn the addresses of major attractions…and restaurants."

Emily glanced at him again.

"I've gone undercover before," he said, "with much less preparation. I guess I'm just a good liar."

She didn't say a word.

"Take a left up here on Ocean Ave.," Jim said. "You know, I was surprised you live so far from the beach. I thought for sure you'd be within a block or two of the water."

"The only way I could afford to live near the beach was with a roommate," Emily said. "And after all those years of college roommates, I really wanted to live alone."

"I remember you wanted to live in a house *on* the beach," Jim said. "You wanted to be able to roll out of bed, open the blinds and have the ocean be right there, in your face."

Emily laughed, despite her growing discomfort at the easy familiarity of Jim's words. "Yeah, right. Last hurricane season, there was a time or two when the people who owned beachfront property actually *had* the ocean in their faces. Literally."

He was watching her, a smile playing at the corners of his mouth. "You don't really expect me to believe *you'd* be scared away from the beach by a little bad weather."

"No," she admitted. "It was purely a financial decision. If I could afford to live by myself in a place that's on the beach, I would. But, unfortunately, I can't handle a higher rent with my current salary."

"When did you decide to become a teacher?" Jim asked. "You took all those computer courses your freshman year. Weren't you majoring in computer science and business?"

She glanced at him. "Is this more research?"

He was silent for a moment, looking out the window at the rows of fancy condominiums that lined Ocean Avenue. "Yes, I need to know more about you," he finally said, "but no, that wasn't why I asked." He pointed to the public beach's parking lot. "Park here. We can walk to the lunch place."

Emily put on her right blinker and moved carefully into the right lane. Just as carefully, she said, "I'd prefer to continue the type of interview we've been using to give you the information you need to know about my personal life. I'm not comfortable pretending we're old friends chatting and catching up on the past seven years."

She pulled into the parking lot and drove down a long row of cars, looking for an empty space.

"So, what you're saying is, after I get the information I need from you in order to pull off masquerading as your brother, you don't want us to have any other conversations," Jim said. "Is that it?"

Emily glanced at him. His mouth was tight, and he used his left hand to rake his hair back from his face. He wasn't pouting, but maybe if she pushed him, he would start. And she found grown men who pouted extremely unattractive...

"Yes," she replied. "That's what I'm saying."

Ahead of her, a car pulled out of a spot, and she quickly zipped into it. She switched off the motor, took the key from the ignition and turned to look at Jim.

To her surprise, he *wasn't* pouting. Instead, there was very genuine regret in his eyes, and a resigned sadness on his face.

"I'm sorry, Emily," he said quietly. "I'll do my best to respect your wishes."

He smiled at her then—a small, bittersweet smile. Emily could have sworn she saw a sudden glimmer of moisture in his eyes, but he turned away before she got a closer look. He opened the door and hauled his large frame out of the tiny car.

Emily followed him to the lunch stand, where they waited for their sandwich order in subdued silence.

Why couldn't he have pouted? Why couldn't he have been a baby, or acted rudely, or... She would have preferred *anything* to the honest, humble regret she'd seen in his eyes.

"Let's find a picnic table in the shade," Jim said, leading her toward the beach.

Heat waves shimmered over the wide expanse of fine white sand and even over the deep blue-green of the Gulf waters. Emily sat down across from Jim on the bench of a wooden picnic table aged silver-gray by the sun, the wind and the salt air.

She still wasn't hungry, but she unwrapped the chicken sandwich Jim had bought her and took a bite.

"Great stuff, isn't it?" he asked.

Emily nodded. Surprisingly, it was.

"Ready for more questions?" he asked, getting out his little notebook, making their conversation official.

He'd put sunglasses on, and she couldn't see his eyes. She nodded again. "Fire away."

"I pretty much know all the basics," Jim said. "You know, like the year you were born, your middle name, your birthday—"

"You remember my birthday?" Emily was surprised. "And my middle name?"

"October seventeenth, and Sara." Jim smiled. "God, you know, I even remember the name of your favorite elementary school teacher. Mrs. Reiner, fourth grade, right? You used to talk about her all the time."

Emily was staring at him, her sandwich temporarily forgotten. She was frowning, her delicate eyebrows wrinkled in disbelief, her usually clear gaze cloudy with uncertainty.

It was the first real, heartfelt look she'd given him. It was the first glimpse he'd had past her cool, controlled front. And it *was* a front, he realized suddenly. It had to be a front, or he wouldn't be able to see past it, right?

"How can you remember that?" she asked, her tone incredulous. "After all this time?"

"Because I was crazy about you," Jim said. He knew as soon as the words were out of his mouth that it was something he shouldn't have said. His habit of saying what was on his mind, of laying his thoughts and feelings out on the table, had gotten him into trouble before, and he knew right away that this wasn't going to be an exception.

His uncensored comments often got uncensored reactions, but Emily just stared silently at him.

He knew he was in trouble, though. He knew that his words were worthless in her eyes. And there was no way on earth he could back what he'd just said with any proof or evidence. In fact, the very way he'd broken up with Emily seemed proof that he hadn't cared about her in the least.

Jim looked down at his sandwich, sitting on top of its white paper wrapper. Suddenly he wasn't feeling very hungry.

But when he glanced up at Emily again, she was smiling. It was one of those private smiles, though, one where the joke was on him. The uncertainty in her eyes was gone, replaced by confidence and determination.

Her smile disappeared, and her gaze became positively steely as she looked him straight in the eye and said, "You are so full of crap. Don't you dare try to whitewash the past. I know exactly how you felt about me." Her voice was quiet, but her even tone left no doubt that she meant business. "If you insist on continuing to insult my intelligence with further ridiculous interpretations of our…sordid little affair, I'll be forced to go over your head, Detective. I won't hesitate to issue a complaint to Lieutenant Bell."

Sordid little affair. Jim's relationship with Emily had been the greatest, most treasured love affair of his life. Hearing her refer to that time as nothing but a sordid little affair was a slap in the face.

But what could he say? If he stood up and shouted at her the way he wanted to, shouted that he had *loved* her, damn it, where would that get him? She wouldn't believe him, and he'd be off the case—as fast as Lieutenant Bell could say the words "Keegan, get your butt into my office."

Without his participation, the investigation would be postponed and Delmore would be free to continue shipping kilos of cocaine into Florida. Then Emily would have even more reason to dislike him.

And Jim knew with a sudden, startling clarity that he didn't want Emily to dislike him. He didn't know what the hell he *did* want, but he knew for damn sure that he didn't want *that*.

So he didn't shout. He didn't tell her she was wrong. He didn't say anything at all. He simply took off his sunglasses, rested his elbows on the picnic table and tried to relieve the ache that was starting to build up inside his head by pressing his forehead against the heels of his hands. He could hear the seconds ticking by on his watch as they sat in silence, neither of them moving.

After many, many of those seconds had gone by, Jim looked up, running his hands down his face. He rested his chin on his thumbs and his lips against his fingers as he looked across the table at Emily.

She was staring out at the ocean, her eyes soft and unfocused. He nervously cleared his throat, and her gaze flickered toward him before returning to the distant horizon.

"Emily," he said. He cleared his throat again, but it didn't make his voice any less husky. "I'm sorry. Can we…maybe…start over, here?"

She looked at him dead-on. Her expression was so chilly, he could've gotten frostbite.

"Start over?" she said. "I intend to start over. After Alex is in jail and you're out of my apartment, after I don't have to see *either* of you *ever* again, I'm going to start over. Definitely in a different city, maybe even in a different state."

"That's not what I meant—"

"I know what you meant. And the answer is no. Next question, Detective."

Jim stared at her, shocked by the hard edge to her words and the equally hard set to her usually soft mouth. This was a side of Emily he'd never seen before. It was a side he suspected hadn't existed back when she was only eighteen years old, back before her contact with men like Alexander Delmore had jaded her. Men like Delmore, and—yeah, who was he kidding?—men like him.

He'd left her because he thought the short-term hurt would be better than the pain he would cause her in the long run. He'd felt he didn't deserve the happiness he found with her, *and* he'd thought he would poison her if they stayed together. Instead, he'd managed to poison her by leaving.

But then he saw her lower lip tremble. Her eyes filled suddenly with tears that she couldn't control. She said one choice word, one he'd never heard her say before, as she turned her head away, trying to hide her tears from him. But it was too late. He'd already seen.

Jim reached for her, across the table. But she jumped back, away from him.

She tripped over the piece of wood that connected the bench to the table and went sprawling in the soft sand. Jim was up in a flash, but she was faster. She scrambled to her feet and started running down the deserted beach.

"Emily, wait!" Jim said, but she didn't stop.

Damn, she'd left her purse on the table. Jim dashed back for it, tucked it securely under his arm and went after her.

She had one hell of a head start, but his legs were longer, and he was used to running distances. Still, he had to work hard to catch her.

"Emily, stop!" he said, but she didn't, so he grabbed her arm.

"Leave me *alone!*" She struggled to get away, but he tightened his grip.

She swung angrily at him, but her aim was off and her fist bounced ineffectually off his shoulder. Jim knew the blow had hurt her hand more than it had hurt him.

She was crying—thick, hot, angry tears. She wiped at them as if she were trying to make them go away, but they wouldn't stop. She struck out at him again, and he pulled her in tightly to his chest.

"Emily, come on. *Please...*"

Emily felt the fight draining from her as soon as his arms went around her. She couldn't stop crying. Sobs racked her body, and she wanted nothing more than to lean against Jim's warm solidness.

If she closed her eyes, she could pretend she'd somehow gone back in time to when she was eighteen. She could pretend that he really *had* loved her, and—

His fingers trailed lightly through her hair, and she felt the familiar surge of sexual heat she had always felt when he touched her that way. It was his gentleness, his tenderness, that had turned her on—that obviously *still* turned her on.

Brother, what was *wrong* with her? How could she think of Jim Keegan this way? How could she allow herself to be attracted to him now, when she knew the kind of man he really was?

With her last bit of strength and her last scrap of fight, Emily pushed herself away from him.

But she couldn't break free. His arms just tightened around her. Angrily she lifted her tear-streaked face toward his. His face, his mouth, were mere inches from hers. And as she looked up into his eyes, she saw the deep blue of his irises nearly swallowed by the widening expanse of his pupils as he looked into her eyes. She knew without a doubt that he was going to kiss her. Her anger was transformed instantly into fear. Fear, and something else. Something far more disturbing.

"Emily," he whispered, leaning down toward her.

"Don't," she whispered, and he froze, leaving less than an inch between his lips and hers. "Please, if you have even a shred of decency left…"

Jim released her immediately. God, what was he doing? What had he been thinking? Apparently holding her in his arms that way had knocked all sense clear out of him.

She stared at him, her eyes big and accusing. She had stopped crying, but her face was still wet, and one last tear hung on her lower lashes. Though he knew damn well that he shouldn't, Jim couldn't resist reaching out and, with one knuckle, gently brushing that tear away.

Emily flinched as if his touch had burned her.

"I'm sorry," he said.

"Don't touch me," she said. "Don't *ever* touch me."

Jim looked down at the sand, out at the ocean, up at the sky, and finally at Emily. "Emily," he said huskily, "I've got to confess—it's hard not to. I can't seem to stay away from you."

"You had no problem seven years ago," she said, and walked away.

What could he say to that? Silently he followed her back to the car.

CHAPTER SIX

JIM WAS PACING. He moved from the front door to the sliding glass door that led to Emily's tiny deck. He moved back to the small dining table, lingered there for a moment, then went back to the front door. Then he went to the sliding glass door....

Emily brought her eyes and her attention back to the slim Hispanic man sitting across from her on the couch.

"I will be in the room," Detective Salazar was saying in his soft, charming accent, "or at least somewhere in the country club, the entire time you and Mr. Delmore are there."

Emily nodded.

"If you have a problem, Emily..." Jim said, speaking for the first time in nearly twenty minutes. Both Emily and Salazar looked up at him. "Any problem at all, find Phil. He'll get you out of there."

"What kind of problem could I possibly have?" Emily asked, crossing her legs as she coolly gazed up at Jim. "It's a society dinner. I seriously doubt Alex intends to perform any illegal acts in front of the gossip columnists from the local newspapers."

Jim pushed his hands into the front pockets of his pants and leaned his back against the wall, finally standing still. "You're right. He probably won't," he agreed. "But this is a man you suspect is a felon. You're going to spend hours with him, pretending that you don't know how he really makes his money. That's not always easy. If you find that you can't do it, if you get overwhelmed, if you get scared—"

"I'm not scared," Emily said, raising her chin in defiance. But what was she defying? His words, or their underlying kindness? Or maybe it was the quiet gentleness of his voice...

"Well, that's good," Salazar said, smiling at her. "Now, your goal tonight is not to get any information from Mr. Delmore. You're gonna leave the information gathering to my buddy Diego, all right?"

Diego. James. Emily's gaze flicked over to where Jim was still leaning against the wall. He was watching her, and she quickly looked back at Detective Salazar. "All right," she said.

"Your goal is for you and your 'brother'—" Salazar gestured toward Jim with his head "—to get invited along on one of Mr. Delmore's floating weekend parties. That shouldn't be too hard. It also couldn't hurt for the two of you to get an invitation to Mr. Delmore's home. The investigating we've done shows that Alexander Delmore does most of his business either at home or on board his yacht—" His eyebrows drew together, and a look of concern crossed his face. "Is there some kind of problem? You don't look happy."

Emily *wasn't* happy. "My relationship with Alex is kind of...odd," she said. "He's told me on more than one occasion that one of the reasons he likes dating me is that I never pressure him for anything. I've never asked him when I'll see him again, I've never asked him for *anything.* He's told me that in that respect I'm different from the other women he's gone out with."

Jim stared down at his cowboy boots, listening to Emily talk about her relationship with Delmore. She might as well have been describing *their* relationship, seven years ago. Because she hadn't pressured him for anything, either, not even his attention. That was what had drawn him to her when they first met—after the initial shock of physical attraction, anyway. She'd been so low-key, so laid-back, so cool and collected. If she had dangled her body at him like bait, if she'd sent him long, meaningful looks and body-language telegrams the way most of the other college girls had, he would never have given her a second glance. Well, he might have given her a second glance, but he wouldn't have become so intrigued by her.

Even after they'd been dating for months, Emily had never assumed anything. She'd never demanded anything from him. Or had she? He could still picture her, that Saturday morning she'd come by bus all the way out to his apartment because he hadn't returned any of her phone calls. He'd been home from the hospital for only a few weeks, and she'd been worried about him. Still, even then, she hadn't demanded anything from him— except maybe the peace of mind of knowing he was all right.

"Do the best you can," Salazar said to Emily, interrupting Jim's thoughts. "Don't say or do anything different from what you would normally say or do. It won't help to get him suspicious."

"*I'll* ask Delmore to take us for a sail," Jim said. "I'll do it when he comes to pick you up tonight, after you introduce him to me, okay?"

Emily nodded, her blue eyes flashing in his direction.

God, he could see wariness in her eyes every time she so much as glanced his way. It had been stupid of him to hold her in his arms like that, down at the beach. What was he, some kind of idiot? Had he really thought that Emily would want comfort from *him?* Yeah, she'd want that about as much as she'd want a pink slip along with her next paycheck.

The truth was, *he'd* wanted an excuse to touch her. He'd wanted to run his fingers through her hair…wanted to feel her body pressed against his. He'd wanted to kiss her. God, he still wanted to kiss her. And she knew it now, too.

Perfect, Keegan, he thought. Just perfect. She was under a ton of stress, and here he was, making it worse for her.

The doorbell rang. Jim glanced at his watch. It was only quarter to four. They had nearly three hours before Delmore was due to arrive.

"Who is it?" he asked.

"I don't know." Emily stood up, uncertainly eyeing the door. "It could be Alex. He dropped by yesterday without calling first."

Salazar got to his feet, too, as the bell chimed again.

"Phil, get out of sight," Jim told the other detective. "Go down the hall, into Emily's bedroom. If it *is* Delmore, we don't want him to see you."

Salazar nodded and vanished down the hall. The bell rang again, this time twice in rapid succession.

"You want me to get it?" Jim asked.

Emily shook her head and went toward the door. Her heart was pounding as she opened the door.

"Thank *God* you're home."

Jim looked over Emily's shoulder at the painfully skinny young woman standing in the doorway. She had long red hair and the kind of pale complexion that burned almost instantly in the hot Florida sunshine. She also had one hell of a black eye, and a grubby little boy, probably around three years old, with matching red hair and big, solemn eyes, clinging to her hand.

The woman looked up at Jim, and the relief faded from her face, replaced by shuttered reservation. She was clutching a brown paper shopping bag filled with clothing and baby toys. A dingy yellow Big Bird doll peeked out of the top.

"Sorry," she muttered. "You got company, don't you?"

"Jewel," Emily said. "What happened? Who hit you? Please, come in."

Jim stepped back as Emily took the younger woman by the elbow and pulled her gently into the apartment. The redheaded woman was younger than he'd first thought, no more than a girl, really. She was pretty in an old-fashioned, Victorian way—or at least she would be if she washed off the layer of dust and grime that covered her, and maybe smiled a little. She had aristo-cratic features—a long, elegant nose, delicate lips, a graceful, if dirty, neck. She was eyeing him with distrust, and he smiled at her. Her expression didn't change.

"Jewel, this is…my brother, Dan," Emily said, her eyes meeting Jim's briefly in acknowledgment of her lie. "Dan, this is Jewel Hays. She's a former student of mine." She ruffled the hair of the little boy who still clutched Jewel's hand. "And this is her son, Billy." She turned her full attention to the girl. "Are you all right?"

Jewel shook her head no. "I'm in big trouble," she

said, her gaze skittering toward Jim and then back to Emily. "Can we talk…in private?"

Emily nodded. "Why don't you come into the bathroom? We can get you cleaned up," she said. She looked at Jim. "Will you keep an eye on Billy?"

"He's hungry," Jewel said, looking down at the little boy. "He hasn't had nothing to eat since night before last."

"I'll get him some food," Jim said.

"Thanks," Emily said. "I'm not sure what I have that he'd like…"

"I'll improvise," Jim said. "We'll be fine."

As she led Jewel toward the bathroom, Emily glanced back to see the tiny little boy tipping his head to look way, way up at Jim.

EMILY CAME INTO the living room to find Billy, perched atop several telephone books, sitting at her dining table, finishing up a sandwich—peanut butter and jelly on pita bread, the only bread she'd had in the house. Jim was sitting across from him, and Felipe Salazar was in the kitchen, leaning against the counter.

"Hey, guys, how's it going in here?" Emily said, smiling brightly for Billy's benefit.

"He's eating his second sandwich," Jim said. He smiled, too, but his eyes were full of questions. What was going on? Why the hell hadn't this kid been fed before this?

"I need your help," Emily said, looking from Jim to Felipe and back again.

Jim stood up. "Why don't we go out onto the deck and talk?" he said. He looked at Salazar. "Stay with the kid, okay?"

"No!" Billy looked up at Jim, his eyes wide. "Don't go!"

To Emily's surprise, Jim crouched down next to Billy's chair, so that he was at eye level with the child. "Hey, Bill," he said, "I'm just gonna be out there on the deck. You'll be able to see me through the window, okay?"

The little boy was not convinced.

"And your mom's in the shower," Jim continued. "She'll be out soon, and then maybe you can take a bath. In the meantime, what do ya say you and my friend Felipe here go into the living room and see if you can find a good cartoon to watch on TV?"

Billy looked at Salazar. "He's your friend?" he asked.

"My *best* friend," Jim said. "So be nice to him, okay?"

Billy nodded.

"Great," Jim said. "I'll be right outside, Bill, if you need me."

He opened the sliding glass door, and Emily followed him out onto the deck. She'd thought Jim would be absolutely lost when it came to taking care of Billy. But he knew just the right way to talk to the little boy. He spoke to him as if he were an equal. He didn't talk down to the child at all.

"Do you deal with children very often?" she asked, closing the door behind her so that Billy couldn't hear their conversation.

Jim leaned his elbows against the wooden railing, looking out over the courtyard. "Not so much these days, no," he said.

"You were great with him," Emily said. "You know, I've never even heard Billy speak before. I didn't know he could."

"He told me someone named Uncle Hank hit his mother," Jim said, turning to look at her.

Emily swore softly.

"What's going on?" Jim asked.

"I don't know what to do," she admitted. "This is way out of my league."

"Tell me what's going on."

Emily took a deep breath. "Okay. When Jewel got pregnant, her parents sent her here, from their farm in Alabama. She was supposed to live with her aunt until she came to term, and then give the baby up for adoption. When the time came and the baby was born, she refused. Her parents wouldn't let her come home, so she and the baby—Billy—ended up staying on with the aunt, who isn't exactly a pillar of the community. Jewel picked up some nasty habits from the woman. She got addicted to crack, and started hooking to support her addiction. Apparently—and this is something I didn't know before today—her good old uncle Hank is quite the little pimp."

"Damn…" Jim breathed.

"Exactly," Emily said, anger making her eyes seem an even darker shade of blue. "Jewel's been in and out of rehab at least three times in the past two years. She just got out, again, a few days ago. Guess what Uncle Hank gave her as a homecoming present?"

"You mean, besides the black eye?"

"Yes," she said. "Besides the black eye."

She reached into the pocket of her shorts and took out three little glass vials. Crack. It was crack.

Jim swore. "That son of a bitch—"

"He wanted her to start walking the streets again," Emily said. "I guess he figured the easiest way to get her to do that was to make sure she stayed dependent on the drugs." Her fingers clenched tightly around the vials. "Do you know how hard it is for an addict to stay clean? Especially right out of rehab? Jewel couldn't bring herself to throw this stuff away, she just couldn't do it. She wanted it. But she was strong enough to come here and ask for help."

She sagged, sitting down on one of the deck chairs. "I've been trying to help this girl for years," she said. "I knew her home situation was bad, but this is…awful. She's got to get out of there. Permanently. But she says she's got nowhere else to go. She refuses to press charges—she thinks that she'll lose Billy if the police and the social services department get involved. I honestly don't know what to do." She stared down at the vials in her hand. "I don't even know how to dispose of this. Do I flush it down the toilet, or will it contaminate the water? What do I do?"

Jim held out his hand. "I'll take care of it," he said.

With relief, Emily gave him the drugs. "Thanks."

He sat down on the chair, next to her. "Em, you can't let her stay here. You can't take on that responsibility."

Her eyes flashed. "I certainly can't send her home."

"I'm not telling you to do that," Jim said quietly. "Maybe there's some kind of halfway house or shelter—"

"She's tried that," Emily said. "All the places she's contacted won't let her bring Billy along. She'd have to have him placed in foster care. And that's unacceptable to her."

Jim nodded, looking out at the crystal blueness of the apartment complex's swimming pool. "He's a sweet kid," he said.

"What am I going to do, Jim?"

Jim. She'd called him Jim. Not Detective. *Jim.* He took a deep breath, letting it slowly out. "Let me talk to Phil, okay?" he said. "Maybe he's got some ideas. He grew up in this city, he's got all kinds of connections. We'll try to find a place for her to go, Emily."

She was looking at him, looking searchingly into his eyes, with the oddest expression on her face.

"What?" he said.

She shook her head and stood up. "You're not supposed to be so nice," she said as she opened the sliding door and went back into the apartment.

Not supposed to—? What the hell did *that* mean?

WHEN EMILY WENT into the living room, Jewel and Felipe Salazar were sitting on the couch, with Billy between them.

Jewel's hair was still wet from her shower, and she was wearing Emily's spare bathrobe—a white terry-cloth robe that enveloped her slight frame and went all the way down to the floor.

Felipe was smiling, and Jewel's cheeks were slightly flushed as she smiled shyly back and answered the detective's gentle questions. It was heartrending to see that this girl, who was so experienced in many ways, was socially inexperienced, even shy.

"Phil, got a minute?" Jim called from the door to the deck.

With one last smile at Jewel and a murmured request to be excused, Felipe joined Jim outside.

Jewel looked up at Emily and smiled.

"Feeling better?" Emily asked, sitting down across from her in the rocking chair.

Jewel nodded. "Yeah. Thanks."

"Do you have any clean clothes?"

The girl's smile faded. "No. I only had time to grab some of Billy's things before we left."

"I'll lend you something of mine," Emily said. "And I think I've got some things that shrank in the dryer. A couple of T-shirts, some sweatpants, stuff like that. They're too small for me now. You can have them."

"Thanks." Jewel looked toward the big glass door that led onto the deck. The two men were standing out there, talking seriously. "Felipe says he's a friend of yours," she said.

Emily smiled, thinking *Your friend, the neighborhood police officer.* "Sure," she said. "I guess you could say he's a friend."

Jewel glanced back at the men on the deck. "He's cute," she said.

Emily looked out at Felipe Salazar. He *was* good-looking, with his easy smile, his exotic high cheekbones and his dark, chocolate-brown eyes. He was, as usual, impeccably dressed in a dark suit. His shirt and tie were the same color as his suit, and the effect was striking.

"He told me Billy was such a nice little boy, I must be a real good mother," Jewel said, and blushed.

Felipe had managed to totally captivate Jewel Hays, Emily realized with a smile. He *was* charismatic and handsome. And his kindness seemed genuine. Emily might have been attracted to him herself, if...

If what? If she didn't already have a boyfriend? She didn't have a boyfriend. She'd stopped thinking of Alex in those terms the night she overheard his conversation with Vincent Marino.

So how come she *didn't* find Felipe Salazar attractive? Her gaze moved almost involuntarily from Felipe to Jim.

She could still feel the way Jim's arms had felt around her when he held her on the beach. She could still see that look in his eyes as he'd bent his head to kiss her....

Jim looked up and through the glass of the door into the living room, directly at Emily. Their eyes met.

The connection was instantaneous, and so strong Emily almost gasped out loud.

Instead, she looked away.

But she'd answered her question. The reason she didn't find Felipe Salazar attractive—or any other man, for that matter—was that she was still tied to the past. To James Keegan, to be exact.

He was an insensitive, selfish, uncaring man...who had a special way with little kids. He was a heart-breaker...who sometimes seemed to have a heart of gold.

Emily had opened her house to Jim, thinking his presence would give her a clear view of the awful person he really was. And, sure, he'd given her instances of imperfect behavior to focus on. But he'd also shown her that he could be alarmingly kind, which left his bad-guy image extremely obscure and undefined.

The sliding glass door opened, and the two men came inside.

Jim sat down on the couch next to Jewel. "Emily told me about the trouble you're in," he said, coming straight to the point. "She says you need a place to stay."

Jewel nodded silently.

Felipe came farther into the room. "I know of a place in my neighborhood, a kind of a shelter, that might have room for you and Billy," he said. "I have time to take you over there now, if you would like."

The wariness was back in Jewel's eyes. "What if they don't?" she asked. "Have room for us, I mean."

Felipe smiled gently. "Then I will find you someplace else to stay," he said. He glanced at Jim. "I have a friend whose apartment is empty right now—but that would be a last resort, of course."

"Come on, Jewel," Emily said, heading toward the bedroom. "I'll find you something to wear."

But Jewel didn't move. "Why are you helping me?" she asked the two men. "What do you want in return? 'Cause I know nothin's free," she added flatly.

"Jewel—" Emily started to protest.

Jim stopped her. "No, she's right," he said. "Nothing comes for free." He turned to Jewel. "You've got to stay clean—no drugs, no alcohol. And *that's* the easy part. You live in the shelter, you don't just sit around, watching TV, sponging off the state. You either enter a program to get your GED, or you take vocational classes, learn a trade."

"What I *meant* was, what do you get?" Jewel said.

"Jewel, I am a police detective," Felipe said. "I will get the satisfaction of knowing that I will not have to bust you someday."

The girl's eyes were wide. "You're the *man?*"

Felipe nodded. "Yes."

"Come on, Jewel," Emily said gently. "Let's find you some clothes, and get Billy into the tub."

AT SIX O'CLOCK, Emily returned from Carly's apartment with the dress she had borrowed for tonight's date with Alex. The dress was blue, scattered with sequins, way too tight and much too short. But, it had the distinct advantage of not being the same dress she'd worn to the last country club function to which Alex had taken her. Holding it up on the hanger, it looked more like a blue tube of crinkly material with spaghetti straps than a dress.

"Do you and your friend borrow clothes from each other all the time?" Jim asked when she came back inside.

He was sitting on the sofa, reading the newspaper, with his feet up on the coffee table. He'd changed back into his shorts, and his feet were bare. He looked entirely too comfortable sitting there. He was far too at home.

"I only have two formal dresses," Emily said. "I wore them both last week, and I can't afford to buy another. My budget's strained as it is." She made a face as she looked at the dress she'd borrowed from Carly. "Unfortunately, Carly's tastes aren't very conservative. On top of that, she's shorter than me."

Jim pulled his feet off the table, folded the newspaper and put it down. "Won't Delmore buy you clothes? He's got more money than God."

Emily crossed her arms. "I'm not Alex's mistress, Detective."

Jim looked up at her. "I know," he said. "Actually, my sources tell me that you were on track to become Mrs. Delmore. The whole town is predicting a Christmas wedding."

Emily laughed. "Then they're going to be disappointed, aren't they?"

She turned to go down the hall toward her bedroom, but his words stopped her.

"You could've looked the other way, and half of everything Delmore has could've been yours," Jim said. "You never would've had to borrow someone else's dress, ever again."

He was serious. He was sitting there, looking up at her, his eyes intense and devoid of any humor or teasing.

Emily laughed again. It was a small, mirthless sound. "You never did get to know me very well, did you?"

It was meant to be a rhetorical question, but he answered it anyway. "I thought I did," he said. "But I guess I didn't really know how tough you could be."

Jim had always thought of her as someone fragile, someone to be protected from the harshness and unfairness of life. But here she was, taking a stand for something she believed in. For Emily, there was no gray to the black-and-white issue of drug trafficking. She believed that it was wrong, and that it had to be stopped. End of discussion. The fact that the leading suspect in the case was her almost-fiancé made no difference to the overall picture.

"I hate drugs," she said, her words somehow more emphatic for the lack of emotion in her voice. "I hate crack. It kills my kids. Or, worse, it turns them into animals."

"Your kids?" Jim said.

"My students," Emily said. "For every kid like Jewel who makes it into rehab, there are plenty of others who don't. They wind up on the street. They steal or turn tricks to support their habits. If they don't end up in jail, they usually end up dead." Her voice shook slightly, and she stopped and took a deep breath. When she spoke again, she was back in absolute control. "You're a cop. You know the story."

"Yeah," Jim said. "I do."

"If Alex Delmore *is* bringing drugs into the country," she said, "then he's made a fortune from other people's misery." She disappeared down the hall. "And I'm going to make *damn* sure he goes to jail."

CHAPTER SEVEN

"THEY ARE SITTING at a table with four other couples," Felipe Salazar's voice reported over the telephone. "Everything is—"

Jim interrupted him. "What about Emily?"

He was pacing the length of the living room, carrying the phone with him as he impatiently walked back and forth, back and forth.

"Emily looks enchanting," his partner told him from the telephone at the country club's bar. "She is wearing a very...beautiful dress..."

"I *know* how she looks," Jim said, fuming. God, he couldn't *believe* how Emily looked in that blue dress. He'd known that she had gorgeous legs, but in that short, sexy dress, with black high heels, her shapely legs looked five miles long. And the way that dress clung to her slender curves should be illegal. She was wearing her hair up, off her smooth, bare shoulders, in some kind of elegant twist thing that emphasized her long, graceful neck.

In that dress, with her sweet girl-next-door face, Emily was an incredible combination of fresh innocence and pure, unadulterated sex. It was mind-blowing. When she first walked out into the living room, Jim's blood had run hot—and then cold, as he remembered she was going out to spend the evening with Alex Delmore.

So far, nothing about this evening had gone right.

Delmore's limo had arrived nearly twenty minutes early—without Delmore. The millionaire had been tied up at the office, and would meet Emily at the country club, or so the limo driver had informed them. So much for their plan to introduce Delmore to Emily's brother Dan. And so much for Jim's chance to finagle an invitation onto Delmore's yacht.

But worst of all was the fact that, with Delmore's limo driver standing sentinel in the living room while Emily put the finishing touches on her makeup, Jim hadn't gotten a chance to talk to her, to make sure she was okay, to make sure that she hadn't suddenly gotten cold feet. He hadn't had the chance to give her any advice, any warnings—or any reassurances.

Then she had come walking out of the bathroom, wearing that amazing blue dress with her amazingly long legs, and Jim's heart had nearly stopped beating. But he'd barely had enough time to focus his eyes before she was gone.

After an hour and a half of pacing the floor, he'd given in, called the country club and paged Salazar.

"Emily is eating the veal Oscar," Salazar told him. "It's very tasty. I was eating it myself, before I was called away to the telephone—"

"Phil."

"Diego. She is fine. I am here—"

"And I'm not," Jim muttered.

"You care for this girl more than just a little, don't you, man?" his partner asked.

Jim evaded the question. "Nothing's gone right tonight, Felipe. Make sure Emily knows where you are at all times, in case she needs assistance. God knows what else will go wrong."

"She knows where I am," Salazar told him. "She is doing fine. She's quite good at pretending that she is enjoying herself."

"And Delmore?" Jim asked.

Salazar laughed. "Mr. Delmore does not have to pretend that he is enjoying himself. Ah, I see them now, out on the dance floor. You tell me—what man wouldn't be pleased to hold a woman as beautiful as Emily Marshall in his arms?"

Jim briefly closed his eyes, trying to banish the sudden, vivid picture of Emily dancing with Delmore's arms around her, swaying in time to some old romantic song. "Damn," he said.

"Excuse me?" Salazar said.

"Stay accessible," Jim ordered him. "And call me when they leave."

EMILY MADE HER WAY SLOWLY to the ladies' room, taking her time and stopping to chat with a group of Alex's friends who greeted her. In between the small talk, she glanced toward the bar, where she'd last spotted Detective Salazar, hoping that he was still there. She was in luck— he was. And he was watching her. She caught his eye, hoping he would be able to read her mind. She needed to talk to him. To her relief, he nodded, almost imperceptibly.

She went out into the lobby where the ladies' room was located, to find that it wasn't deserted as she had hoped. Instead, groups of men and women were standing and talking, away from the noise of the dance band. Emily hesitated, unsure of what to do. A soft touch on her arm made her spin around.

"I'm sorry," Felipe Salazar said. "I didn't mean to startle you."

Emily stared at him. Were they simply going to stand here, in full view of everyone, and carry on a conversation, as if nothing were wrong?

"Ms. Marshall, is it not?" the detective said, and suddenly she understood.

"Yes," she said. Of course they could stand here and talk. As long as they appeared to be making party chatter, talking here, out in the open, would look far less suspicious than whispering together in some dark, secluded corner.

"Felipe Salazar," he said, holding out his hand to her and smiling charmingly. "We have a mutual friend, remember? A Ms. Hays."

"Yes, of course," Emily said. "How is Jewel?"

"She is doing as well as can be expected," he replied, then lowered his voice. "There was space for her and Billy in one of the mothers-and-toddlers dorms. I had her put on a waiting list for a semiprivate room. She was very frightened when I left. I'll go back tomorrow to see how she's doing."

"Don't go out of your way," Emily said. "She's a tough kid. She'll be fine."

"It's not out of my way," he said.

"Be careful that she doesn't get too dependent on you," she warned him.

"Better to be dependent on *me* than on crack," he said with a shrug. He lowered his voice even further. "Was there something you wished to tell me? And don't look so serious. This is a party. You're supposed to be having fun."

Emily smiled at him brightly. "Right. Fun. Alex has to leave. He says it's business, but it seems odd to me. It's a little bit late at night for regular, legitimate business, don't you think?"

Felipe glanced at his watch. It was nearly ten-thirty.

"His driver is going to take me home," she said. "But I wanted to tell you, in case you wanted to follow Alex, see what he's up to."

He nodded. "Thanks."

"I'm sure I'll see you soon," Emily said, as if she were ending just another casual party conversation. "Take care."

"I will," Felipe said. "And say hello to your brother for me."

Her pretend brother. Jim. Who was waiting at home for her. Who had looked at her as if he wanted to devour her whole as she nearly ran out the door tonight...

Could this night get any worse?

EMILY HEARD CARLY'S familiar husky laughter as she opened her apartment door.

Jim was sitting in the rocking chair, his feet still bare and his shirttail untucked from his shorts. He looked up at Emily with real surprise in his eyes. "Hey!" he said. "What are you doing back so early?"

"Wow!" Carly said from where she was sitting cross-legged on the couch. "My dress looks *great* on you."

"Alex had to cut our date short," Emily said, closing the door behind her. As she crossed toward the kitchen and put her purse on the little dining table, she could feel Jim's eyes on her. "He had his driver bring me home. Apparently he had some unscheduled business to attend to."

She turned toward Jim, to emphasize her words with a silent message, but his eyes weren't on her face. They were traveling slowly up her legs, then up her body. Finally he met her eyes and smiled. Emily felt herself flush. The nerve of the man! He was practically propo-

sitioning her with his eyes, yet not even five minutes ago
he'd been getting cozy with Carly.

"Poor baby," Carly was saying. "So you didn't even
get properly kissed good-night."

Jim was still watching her, and Emily felt his gaze in-
tensify. She pointedly turned her back on him and looked
into the oval mirror that was on the wall beside the front
door. "I'll live," she said. She began unfastening the clips
that held her hair in place.

Actually, she'd been relieved when Alex didn't give
her more than a cursory peck on the cheek as he said
goodbye. She'd been dreading the moment all evening
long. It had been hard enough to dance with him, to have
him hold her as close as he had.

Emily tossed her hair clips on the table next to her
purse and ran her fingers through her hair.

"So," she said to Carly, "I go out for only a few hours,
and when I get back I find you hitting on my brother."
Her tone was light, teasing, but inside she was feeling
oddly off balance. The thought of Jim and Carly together
was disturbing. She glanced at Jim. "Or were *you* hitting
on Carly?"

"Oh, I wish," Carly said, with a flirtatious smile at Jim.
"No, I was working late, and got home about a half hour
ago. I saw the light on, so I came over. Dan was telling me
about how he used to chase you around the house, making
monster faces at you, when you were kids. You know, *I* had
an older sister, and I remember that she used to…"

Emily sank down next to Carly on the couch and put
her head back. Brother, she was exhausted. And…
relieved? Oh, shoot, was it possible that she was actually
relieved that Jim hadn't invited Carly over here, that he
hadn't been hanging out with her all evening long?

Jim met her eyes and smiled, and Emily realized that she'd been staring at him. She quickly looked away, hoping that he hadn't somehow managed to read her mind. Lord, if he got the idea that she still found him desirable, he would be all over her. Relentlessly. She closed her eyes, trying to banish the unbidden memory of Jim holding her on the beach.

"...she was *awful*," Carly was saying. "No redeeming qualities. Her one goal in life was to torture me. Was Dan like that, Em?"

Carly was talking to her. Emily opened her eyes. "Dan?" she said foggily. Dan who?

"I wasn't awful all the time." Jim jumped in and saved the day before she blew his cover. "I tried to take care of her—she was so little. Big brothers are supposed to do that, right? They protect you, keep you out of trouble, make sure you fly straight. They're always there for you, you know?"

Something about Jim's voice caught Emily's attention. He wasn't just making things up in order to keep Carly believing he was Emily's older brother. He was speaking from experience. But it sounded like it was the experience of a younger brother who had had an older brother to look up to and admire.

That was odd. Emily knew that Jim had several older sisters, but the only brother he'd ever mentioned was much younger than he was. She would've remembered him talking about a big brother, wouldn't she?

"Look, Carly," Jim said, standing up, "Emily looks beat, and—"

"We should let her go to sleep," Carly said, also getting to her feet. "So...do you want to come over to my place?"

Jim looked surprised, as if he hadn't expected Carly to issue such an invitation. And then he actually looked flustered. "Ah…" he said. "No. Thank you," he added quickly, "but…I don't think that would be a good idea. You see, I'm—"

"No need to explain," Carly said good-naturedly, handling the obvious rejection like a pro. "It was just a thought."

"I'm involved with someone," he said. "It's pretty serious."

"You are?" The words were out of Emily's mouth before she could stop them.

Carly laughed. "Uh-oh," she said, opening the door. "I think you just woke your sister up. Gee, maybe you two can have a double wedding, save your parents some bucks. See y'all tomorrow."

Emily could feel Jim watching her as he closed the door behind Carly.

"I'm sorry," she said, bending to pick her shoes up off the floor. "Whether or not you're involved with someone isn't my business."

"I'm involved with someone the same way you're involved with Delmore," Jim said quietly.

Emily looked up at him, not understanding.

He sat down next to her on the couch. "It's fictional, Em," he said. "See, I don't need Carly hanging around all the time, getting in the way of this investigation. So it's easier to tell her I'm involved. You hear what I'm saying?"

Emily nodded, looking down at the shoes she held on her lap.

She looked so tired, and so damned fragile. Jim wanted to touch her. He wanted to hold her close and—

"Tell me more about this unscheduled business of Delmore's," he said.

"He got a phone call," Emily said. "At about ten-fifteen. When he came back to the table, he apologized and said he had to leave, that some important business deal was finally going to go through." She glanced up at Jim. "I managed to tell Felipe, and he followed Alex."

"*That's* why Phil didn't call me when you left the country club," Jim said.

"Oh, *no!*" Emily said, sitting up straight.

"What?"

"I just realized…" She turned to Jim, her eyes wide with dismay. "Alex left so quickly, he didn't…we didn't make another date. As it stands now, I have no plans to see him again. What if he doesn't call me?"

Jim had to laugh.

"What's so funny?"

He was grinning with genuine amusement, his eyes sparkling and dancing with humor as he looked at her. "Trust me, Em," he said. "The guy is gonna call you."

"There's no way you can know that for sure," Emily argued.

Jim scratched his head, still smiling at her. "I'm as sure of this as I'm sure the sun's going to rise in the morning. Delmore will call."

"Suddenly you're a psychic?"

"No, just a man."

She still didn't understand.

"Come here," Jim said, standing up. She didn't move to follow him, so he reached down and took her hand and pulled her up off the couch.

"What are you doing?" Emily halfheartedly tried to pull her hand free, but he wouldn't let go.

"I want to show you something," he said, leading her down the hall.

Emily's bedroom was dimly lit by the streetlight that shone in through the open blinds. Jim tugged her gently into the room and pushed the door closed.

Her heart was pounding. What was he doing? What was he—?

He stood behind her, held her gently by the shoulders and pointed her toward the full-length mirror on the back of her bedroom door. "Look," he commanded.

He was standing so close behind her that she could feel his body heat. His grip on her shoulders tightened slightly as she met his eyes in the mirror.

"Look at *yourself*," he said.

Emily looked. She saw…herself. Sure, the dress was fancy, and its style flattered her trim body in a way that could be called sexy, but underneath it all she was still Emily. True, she rarely showed other people the side of her personality that liked wearing little blue sequined dresses, but it was part of her just the same.

Her legs were long and in good shape. In fact, her entire body was well toned. Her face— It was the same face she'd had all her life. It was pretty enough, she supposed. At least, taken all together, her features seemed to fit in the space provided for them. Separately, her nose was a little too big and slightly crooked, her mouth was a touch too wide, her chin a little too pointed.

She looked closer. She should have looked tired—jeez, she had been exhausted just a minute ago—but she couldn't see even a hint of fatigue in her eyes. No, they were bright with an odd mix of wariness, fear…and anticipation.

"Look at how beautiful you are," Jim murmured, and Emily looked up at him. "And that's just the wrapping on the package. There's no man on earth who wouldn't call you for another date."

He ran his rough fingers down the lengths of her arms, lightly caressing her bare skin, as Emily stared at him, frozen in place. In the mirror, his lean face looked mysterious, almost frighteningly intense. He'd long since stopped smiling, and his deep blue eyes glittered colorlessly in the darkness with unconcealed desire.

But then his eyes met hers.

Jim pulled his hands away and took a rapid step back, putting some space between them. She was still staring at him, and he knew from her expression that everything he'd been feeling and thinking had been clearly written on his face. "Sorry," he said. "I'm sorry."

He ran one shaking hand through his hair. Damn! What was he doing? Another minute and he might have started undressing her. God knows he wanted to. He couldn't remember when he'd last wanted a woman this badly—

Yes, he could. Seven years ago. Then, too, the woman he'd wanted so desperately had been Emily. He'd wanted her enough to throw away all his good intentions. He'd actually gone and made love to her, despite his resolve to stay away from her.

He still found her that irresistible. Only this time around, Emily wasn't going to come to him the way she had seven years ago. This time around, she knew better.

Jim took a deep breath. "You're tired," he said, forcing a smile. "I know. I know what it's like to be out there pretending to be someone you're not for hours. You can't relax, not even for a second, for fear you'll say something wrong or make a mistake."

"Excuse me," Emily said, and he realized that by standing there the way he was, he had penned her into the corner.

Jim moved aside, and she opened the bedroom door. He was in the middle of her bedroom now, not two feet away from the big double bed Emily would be sleeping in tonight. He could picture her lying there, and it didn't take much to go another step farther and picture himself there, too. And oh, baby, that was one dangerous thought. He yanked his eyes away from the miniature flowers on the print of her bedspread to find her watching him. Self-consciously he smiled and moved past her, out into the relative safety of the hall.

"I'm exhausted," Emily said, and her voice shook very slightly. "And you're right. It's not easy spending so much time with a man I despise."

That statement seemed to be loaded with hidden meanings, and Jim tried to look into Emily's eyes, to see exactly what she had meant. Was she talking about Delmore—or God, was she talking about *him?* But she didn't look up at him for longer than an instant as she murmured a good-night and closed the bedroom door.

Jim walked slowly back into the living room, forcing himself to face the facts. He was poised at the brink of an emotional avalanche. He wanted this woman physically, there was no denying that. But it also seemed that she'd awakened more in him than merely his libido. He felt all sorts of frightening sensations whenever she was around—hell, he felt them whenever he so much as thought about her. And he thought about her damn near one hundred percent of the time.

He felt protective. Possessive. He felt proud—God, she was undeniably her own person, standing up so firmly for the things she believed in. He respected her, he admired her, he liked her. Yeah, he definitely liked her.

But feeling those things didn't mean that he loved her, did it? No, even *he* wouldn't be stupid enough to fall back in love with a woman who disliked him—and probably even despised him.

CHAPTER EIGHT

EMILY'S DREAM started the way it always did. It started the way that awful evening had started—with deceptive calm and normality.

This time, she was having dinner with Carly. They were at that new place on Venice Road, the restaurant with all the big-screen TVs. Country Music Television was playing, showing a Dwight Yoakam video.

Carly was telling her about the latest stud she was dating, but right in the middle of a description of the guy's peculiar eating habits, Carly turned into Michele Harris, Emily's college roommate from her freshman year.

Michele was talking about something just as important and gripping as Carly's latest conquest, but although her mouth moved, Emily couldn't hear the words. Yet she knew that whatever her old roommate was saying didn't matter. She knew as soon as she saw Michele's face that the nightmare had begun.

Sure enough, the restaurant on Venice Road disappeared, replaced by Emily's freshman dorm dining room. She and Michele were sitting in the corner, at a round table near the television. They were sitting exactly where they'd been that awful night.

The television was set to a channel showing reruns of

*M*A*S*H*, exactly as it had been. And the show was interrupted by a late-breaking news story, exactly as it had been.

Emily had dreamed about it hundreds of times before. She'd even lived through it once. But the horror was no less intense as the television newsperson reported live from the scene of a recent downtown shoot-out between local police and an escaped convicted killer.

"The killer, Laurence Macy, has been declared dead at the scene," the reporter's dispassionate voice said as the camera panned across the area. "But he didn't go down without a fight."

Emily watched in disbelief as the news camera lingered on Jim Keegan's beat-up old car. A portable police light still flashed from the roof. The car had been riddled with bullets, its windshield shattered.

"Two police officers have been shot," the reporter continued as the camera cut back to him, "and one is in critical condition." He turned to look over his shoulder at an ambulance parked haphazardly in the middle of the street. A crew of paramedics came into sight, shouting as they ran toward the vehicle, pulling a stretcher with them.

"The unidentified policeman," the reporter said as the camera zoomed in tighter on the figure on the stretcher, "is being taken to University Hospital."

It was Jim. His eyes were closed, and his mouth and nose were covered by an oxygen mask, but Emily recognized him immediately. And—oh, God! His chest was covered with blood. The paramedics scrambled around him, pulling him up and into the ambulance and slamming the doors tightly shut.

"We'll report in later from the hospital when we have information on the police officer's identity and condition," the reporter said, but Emily was no longer watching. She was already halfway out of the dining room.

The taxi ride was interminable. The hospital was only a few blocks away, but it seemed to take forever to get there. Still, Emily managed to arrive before the ambulance.

The emergency room was bustling, preparing for the ambulance. Emily stood in the lobby and prayed. *Please, God, let Jim live. Please, God, don't let him die.*

The ambulance pulled up with a squeal of tires, its siren wailing. The doctors ran outside to meet it, opening the van's doors and taking over from the paramedics. And then Jim was inside. Emily followed as they wheeled him down the hall.

His eyes were open and glazed with shock and pain. He was laboring to breathe, every breath a rattling effort. Bright red blood was everywhere, seeping through the bandages and the blanket that covered him, even flecking his lips.

How could someone lose that much blood and still live?

"Jim, hang on!" Emily cried, but he didn't, couldn't, hear her.

"We're losing him," a nurse reported, her voice cutting through the noise.

The medical team moved faster, but not fast enough.

As Emily watched, her own heart hammering in her chest, the machine hooked up to monitor Jim's heart rate flatlined.

The doctors and nurses worked frantically to revive him. Emily stood there in the hallway, watching in horror.

She felt the last of her control slipping, sliding away,

as the doctors attempted to start Jim's heart with a jolt of electricity.

He was dying. He was going to die.

"No!" she cried. "No! It's not supposed to end this way! Jim! *Jim!* No—" She threw back her head and screamed, a piercing, primitive, throat-burning cry of grief and rage.

The door to her bedroom burst open, and light from the hallway flooded into her room and yanked Emily out of her dream.

She sat up with a start as Jim made a quick circuit of her room, checking the window locks and glancing into the closet. He was wearing only a pair of running shorts, and his hair was disheveled from sleep. He held a gun with an easy familiarity, as if it were an attachment to his arm.

"Are you all right?" he asked, putting the gun's safety on as he came to stand next to the bed.

Emily nodded.

He was still breathing hard, his broad chest rising and falling. She could see the faint scars where the bullets had struck him and where the surgeons had operated. He *wasn't* dead. He *hadn't* died. He was standing right here, in front of her, living, breathing proof that her dream had been only that—a dream.

Still, she couldn't seem to stop the tears that were streaming down her face.

"Nightmare?" Jim asked gently.

She nodded again, still silent, hugging her knees tight to her chest and closing her eyes. She heard the clunk as he put his gun on her bedside table, then felt the mattress sink as he sat down next to her on the bed.

"It must've been a bad one," he said. "You called out

for me, and then you screamed. You scared the hell out of me, Em."

Emily lifted her head, pushing her hair out of her face with a hand that was still shaking. "I'm sorry—"

"Hey, shh…no," Jim said. "That's not why I was— You don't need to apologize." He reached for her before he realized what he was doing. It wasn't until he had his arms around her, until he felt her body stiffen, that he remembered she didn't want him to touch her. But before he could pull away, she put her arms around his neck. She held him so tightly it nearly took his breath away.

This had nothing to do with him, Jim told himself. Right now Emily needed someone to hold her, someone to hold on to, and he happened to be here. That was all this was, nothing more.

Still, he closed his eyes, breathing in the sweet fragrance of her hair as he rocked her back and forth. He gently stroked her back, soothingly running his hand up and down the soft cotton of her T-shirt.

"It's all right," he murmured. "It was only a dream."

After a while, he could feel her start to relax. He felt her stop trembling and heard her ragged breathing return to normal.

"I won't let anything bad happen, Emily," Jim said. "I promise you. Whatever you were dreaming about, it's not gonna happen, I swear."

"But it already did happen," Emily said.

Jim pulled back to look searchingly into her eyes. "Has Delmore hurt you?" His jaw tightened. "Damn it, I'll kill him—"

"I wasn't dreaming about Alex. I was dreaming about you." Tiredly, she let go of him. She moved away from

him on the bed so that her back was against the head-
board—and so that she was out of his reach.

"Me?" he said.

She could see the surprise on his face. He was surprised that she'd been dreaming about him—and equally
surprised that she would admit it.

Emily pulled her knees up and rested her elbows on
them. She supported her forehead in the palm of one
hand. "I was dreaming about the night you were shot,"
she said. "I don't know, I guess seeing you again brought
back the old nightmares."

"Nightmares?" he asked. "Plural? You mean, you've
had this kind of dream before?"

She nodded. "I guess having my boyfriend shot made
kind of an impact on me."

"You never told me."

"I didn't have them until after you were out of the
hospital for a few months."

Until after they had split up. Until after he had staged
that ugly little scene in the University Boulevard bar.
Emily hadn't mentioned that night, but Jim knew that she
was thinking about it.

"In my nightmare," Emily said, pulling the sheet
higher up the bed, as if she were suddenly cold, "you
always die, right there in the hall near the emergency
room lobby." She looked up and briefly met his eyes. "It's
as if my mind is playing out the worst-case scenario. It's
as if I get to experience what I was most afraid of when
I saw them wheel you in." Emily shrugged, sweeping her
hair back from her face. "I don't know. I had a roommate
who was a psychology major, and she said—"

She looked up, startled, when Jim caught her wrist. He
was watching her intently, questioningly. "You saw them

wheel me in?" he asked. "You *were* there. I thought I'd only imagined hearing your voice."

She was staring down at the fingers encircling her wrist, but he didn't release her.

"I got to the hospital before you did," she said.

"But how?" he asked, realizing suddenly that he'd never asked her how she'd first heard that he'd been shot. They'd never talked about it. "Who called you?"

"No one," she said, looking up into the piercing blue of his eyes. "I saw you on the news, being put into the ambulance."

"Oh, God," Jim breathed. He could remember the sense of disbelief he'd felt when the bullets hit him. No way. No way could he have been shot. He was off duty, he wasn't wearing a vest, he wasn't ready for it. There must be some mistake. But the only mistake was his. There was so much blood. There was blood *everywhere*.

And Emily had seen him that way. On television. Without warning.

Emily's eyes filled with tears. "Then, when they brought you in, they wouldn't let me near you. They wouldn't even let me hold your hand."

"I thought I heard your voice," Jim said. "I tried to find you. I wanted to tell you…"

He'd been so sure he was going to die. In fact, he'd been damn near ready to give up the fight. He'd been so tired and… But he'd wanted to tell Emily that he loved her. He'd tried to tell the doctor to give Emily a message from him, but the man wouldn't listen. He'd kept telling Jim to save his strength.

And then Jim had heard Emily's voice again. He'd heard her tell him to hang on, to keep fighting.

So he had.

But he hadn't really believed that she was actually there, in the hospital. It was bad enough that she'd seen him in the hospital bed, with all those tubes and monitors hooked up to him, after he was moved out of ICU. But, God, down in the ER, when he'd first been brought in, he'd been a real mess. That was enough to give anyone nightmares for the rest of their life.

"Emily, I'm sorry," he whispered, blinking back the sudden sharp sting of tears in his own eyes.

She wiped at her eyes, at a tear that threatened to roll down her cheek. "I am, too," she said.

Jim wasn't holding her wrist anymore, she realized. He was holding her hand. And she was holding on to him just as tightly.

"Sorry," she said, releasing him. She managed a watery smile. "Usually when I have these dreams, I don't have access to such solid proof that you really *are* all right."

He was looking at her with such wistful sadness in his eyes that she didn't flinch or pull away when he reached out to push her hair back from her face.

"I really blew it, didn't I?" he asked quietly. "By getting shot that way. I knew it was rough on you, but I had no idea…"

"It wasn't as if you got shot on purpose," Emily said. "It wasn't much fun for you, either."

"I didn't want you to have to live through something like that ever again," Jim said, cupping her face with his hand. His fingers were so rough, but he touched her so gently. Emily felt her pulse kick crazily into double time. "I never thought you would have nightmares."

She was looking up at him, her eyes wide and her lips slightly parted. She was wearing a faded white oversize

T-shirt that didn't quite succeed in hiding her body from his view. The cotton was thin, and it clung to the soft fullness of her breasts. He forced his eyes back to her face. Her skin was so soft, and her beautiful hair was tousled from sleep. She looked sweet, so sweet and so innocent, as if somehow the past seven years had never touched her, as if she were somehow still eighteen years old, even after all this time.

He ran his thumb lightly across her lips. "God, Em, you're so beautiful—"

Desire. It was suddenly so palpable, it might have been a living thing, swirling around them, surrounding them, connecting them.

Emily knew that the desire she could see in Jim's eyes was mirrored in her own. Like him, she was helpless to hide it, powerless to conceal it. She could see it on his face, hear it in the way he breathed, feel it in his touch, in the heat of his skin.

She wanted him to touch her. She wanted to touch him. She wanted—

He kissed her.

Gently his mouth met hers in a kiss so sweet Emily nearly cried out. It had always amazed her—it *still* amazed her—that a man who was so much larger than life, a man who lived his life so passionately, so intensely, could be so breathtakingly tender.

Even as he deepened the kiss, as his tongue sought entry into her mouth, even then he was unquestionably gentle. Emily felt herself melt. She felt her bones turn to liquid, felt her body molding to fit against his as he took her into his arms and kissed her again and again.

His touch and taste were so familiar, it seemed as if they'd last made love just yesterday. Her memories were incredibly vivid. They'd tumbled together on his bed, a double bed just like this one, kissing and touching, exploring….

Emily felt Jim yank the sheet out from between them. She gasped as he rolled over, pulling her on top of him. Their legs intertwined, the roughness of his against the soft smoothness of hers. She could feel the hard bulge of his sex pressing against her as he kissed her again. He wanted her—it was undeniable.

She knew she could tell him that she wanted him, too, without saying a single word. All she'd have to do was to keep responding to his kisses. Or maybe, more obviously, she could pull her T-shirt up and over her head. No doubt he'd catch on pretty quick if she was lying naked in his arms.

Emily could remember the way he had caressed every inch of her body as he made love to her. He had made her feel as if she were the most beautiful, most desirable, woman in the world. She could remember how he had somehow seemed to know when to unleash his passion, when to leave his sweet tenderness behind. She could remember how he'd let himself lose control, giving himself over to her completely, crying out her name as waves of intense pleasure exploded around them both.

She could remember how totally, how absolutely, how with all her heart, she had loved him.

Her memory of that love was so strong, she could almost feel it. It was as if she'd been thrown backward in time, back seven years, back before Jim had hurt her so badly, back before she had known the kind of man he really was.

She could make love to him again, as if it were seven years ago. She could pretend that she was eighteen again and in love for the first time.

But tomorrow morning, when they woke up, it wouldn't be seven years ago. It would be now, and they would be here, and it would be awful.

She wiggled free, escaping his arms. He sat up, as if to follow her, but stopped suddenly. She turned to look at him, and saw the expression on his face as he realized what they'd been doing—what they'd been about to do.

"Oh, *damn,*" he said. "Emily, God, I don't know what happened. I didn't intend to—"

"I know," she said. "It's…all right. It wasn't your fault— I mean, it was my fault, too. I think talking about that night you were shot made it easy for us to…kind of…slip back into our old relationship. It was easy to pretend that we're still lovers." She looked down at her hands, clenched tightly in her lap. "But we're not."

"Em," Jim said.

She looked up at him. He was watching her intently. His lean face looked mysterious, and hauntingly handsome, in the shadows. He didn't smile as she met his eyes.

"We could be," he said softly, seriously.

Lovers. He was talking about them being lovers.

Emily swallowed, remembering his taste, his touch…

"No." She shook her head. "We couldn't." She turned away from him. "I need you to leave."

He left.

WEDNESDAY, the phone rang only once. It was Felipe Salazar, calling to say that Delmore's odd business meeting on Tuesday night had been exactly what it appeared to be—a late-night meeting with a client. Nothing illegal had transpired.

Thursday, the phone rang twice, but neither time was it Alexander Delmore.

By Friday, Jim had had enough. He wasn't sleeping worth a damn, not with Emily in the other room. She was well within reach—or she would have been, if his hands hadn't been tied behind his back. He wanted her so badly he could barely remember his name, but every time he so much as said two words to her, she jumped a mile high, then thought up some phony excuse to get away from him. Time to do the laundry. Time to get groceries. Time to wash the deck furniture. Wash the *deck* furniture, for crying out loud...

Something had to happen soon, or he'd lose his mind.

At ten o'clock, he went out onto the deck, where Emily was repotting several of her houseplants. She only glanced up at him, but it was long enough for him to feel the now-familiar jolt of awareness. Still, she seemed determined to ignore the powerful chemistry between them.

"Can you be ready to go out in about an hour?" he asked. She was wearing a faded old pair of cutoff jeans that had ripped several inches up the outside seam of her right leg. The effect was outrageously sexy—and all the more so because she seemed so oblivious to it.

"Where are we going?" she asked, moving some kind of plant with lots of long, green-leafed vines into a larger pot. She packed potting soil loosely on top of its roots.

Her hands were covered with dark brown dirt, and she used the back of her arm to push her hair out of her face as she looked up at him, waiting for him to answer.

"Your 'brother' is going to take you someplace nice for lunch," Jim said. He smiled. "And—what a coincidence—it'll just happen to be the same restaurant where Delmore's having lunch. You'll introduce him to me, I'll get us invited out on his boat."

Emily raised a skeptical eyebrow. "Alex never goes to the same place twice in a row," she said. "And sometimes he doesn't decide where he's going until he's halfway there. There are about seventeen restaurants that he really likes. So we've got a one-in-seventeen chance of guessing where he's going. And that's assuming he doesn't try someplace new."

Jim shook his head. "We aren't going to do any guessing," he said. "We're going to be dressed and ready and sitting in a car downtown near Delmore's boat slip. Phil Salazar is going to follow Delmore to wherever he's having lunch, then call and tell us where to go."

"Then we walk in, sit down and pretend we're surprised to see Alex, right?" Emily laughed, her eyes flashing with amusement. "Nothing like having the police force on your side when you want to get a date." She rinsed her hands in a bucket of water, then dried them on a rag. "I need to take a shower, but I can be ready to go in about a half hour."

She opened the sliding glass door, but paused on the threshold, turning back to look at him. "Some of the places Alex likes to go for lunch require a jacket and tie. Do you have something to wear?"

Jim smiled. "I've got that under control."

Emily nodded. Under control. At least *something* here was under control.

"I'M READY."

Emily came out into the living room wearing a white denim skirt and a pale blue T-shirt and carrying a white sweater over her arm. The skirt went down to midcalf, and she wore flat leather sandals on her feet.

Jim shook his head. "No, you're not," he said.

"Sure I am," Emily said. "I even have a sweater in case the air-conditioning is up too high."

Jim went down the hall toward Emily's bedroom. "You look like a high school English teacher."

"I *am* a high school English teacher," Emily said, bristling slightly, as she followed him into her room.

"Right," Jim said, opening her closet door. "But today you've got to remind Delmore that you're also an incredible-looking babe."

Emily rolled her eyes.

"You've got to wear something more along the lines of that blue dress." He looked quickly through the clothes hanging in her closet and pulled out a long, flowing skirt with a bold floral print. "This is good," he said, tossing it onto the bed.

Emily crossed her arms. "You don't *really* think I'm going to let you pick out my clothes," she said. She looked at him pointedly. "Wearing *that* tie with *that* jacket isn't exactly going to get you on St. Simone's list of the best-dressed men of the year."

"My tie doesn't match?" he said, looking at himself in the mirror on the back of the bedroom door. He was wearing dark blue pants with a light, grayish-blue tweed sport jacket. His tie was a dull mix of drab green and yellow. He shrugged and pulled three other ties from the pockets of his sport jacket. "I hate these things. *You* pick, okay?"

Emily glanced at them. "The blue is the least awful," she said.

Jim laughed. "The least awful wins." He put the other ties back in his pockets.

Emily watched him as he took off the green tie and put on the blue. She was wrong. Jim Keegan would make anyone's best-dressed list—provided "anyone" was a woman. Jim could wear damn near anything, and *still* be better-looking than most of the rest of the male population.

His pants fit him sinfully well, hugging his long legs and stacking neatly around his boots. His jacket might well have been tailor-made for his broad shoulders. And the way he wore his tie with the top button of his shirt unfastened was charming, rather than sloppy.

He looked into the mirror to adjust the tie and caught her watching him.

The last time he had been in her room, he'd kissed her. Jim knew she was thinking about it, too—how could she not be? She'd spent most of the past few days avoiding any possibility of a repeat encounter. Yet here he was. Back at the scene of the crime.

As Jim watched, she smiled briefly at him and looked away, moving toward the bed and the skirt he'd thrown there. Okay, so she was going to play it cool. They'd come pretty damn close to making love right here on her bed a few nights ago, but she wanted to pretend it had never happened. It was not to be mentioned, not to be discussed. But, damn it, he *wanted* to discuss it.

"Emily—"

She knew what he was going to say, and she didn't want to hear it. She picked up the skirt and held it up to her waist, gesturing to indicate the blue T-shirt she was wearing. "Do you want me to wear this shirt with this skirt?"

As she met his steady gaze, she clenched the skirt's hanger tighter.

"Emily, I really think we should talk—"

"What's to talk about?" she said swiftly. Jim could

hear a trace of desperation in her voice. "Either you want me to wear this shirt or you don't. A simple yes or no will do."

"That's not what I meant, and you know it."

As he watched, Emily took a deep breath, visibly calming herself. When she spoke, her voice was even. "Look, just tell me what to wear so that we can get this investigation over with."

"And me out of your house," Jim added flatly.

"Yes."

It couldn't get much clearer than that, could it? But what was he expecting? Did he really think that they could sit down, have a quick heart-to-heart, and become lovers again? Because that was what he wanted, wasn't it? He wanted back into her bed.

Except if it was just a physical thing, if it was mere lust, he'd be able to control it. The way he'd felt the other night had been beyond control—*way* beyond control.

"What do you want me to wear?" she asked again.

Jim made himself focus on the skirt.

The floral print was a mix of blue, black and off-white. Jim shook his head. "Don't wear a T-shirt," he said. "You got one of those— What are they called? You know, it ties at the back of your neck and behind your back, at your waist?"

"A halter top?" Emily said.

"Yeah." Jim nodded. "Something like that. Something you'd never wear to teach a class."

"I don't have anything like that."

"I'd bet Carly does," he said, glancing at his watch. "If we're lucky, she hasn't left for work yet."

"Oh, have you memorized Carly's work schedule?" Emily said, with a sudden flash of something that *couldn't* be jealousy. It didn't make sense for her to feel jealous.

She followed Jim out into the living room and watched him open the front door.

"She told me she works at the library afternoons and evenings," he said evenly. "Right now, it's still morning. Maybe she's home."

He was gone only a few minutes, and when he returned he was triumphantly waving something that looked an awful lot like a tiny black silk scarf.

"We're in luck," he said, handing it to Emily. "Carly had just what I was picturing."

"You want me to wear *this?*" Emily held the black silk up, and the sunlight streaming through the sliding glass doors made it seem almost translucent. "With *nothing* underneath?"

"Yeah. It'll look amazing with that skirt."

"Amazing," Emily echoed, nodding her head. "Right." She looked up at Jim. "Why bother wearing anything at all?" she said tartly. "Why don't I just go naked?"

He crossed his arms and leaned back against the wall, giving her a long, appraising look. "That would be okay with me, too."

She held the halter top out to him. "Thanks, but no thanks."

He didn't take it. "I thought you wanted to get this investigation over with." She didn't move. "At least try it on," he said, more gently.

Emily turned and went back into the bedroom to change.

CHAPTER NINE

AT ONE-FIFTEEN, Jim's cellular phone chirped, and he flipped it open.

"Yeah." He held Emily's gaze as he listened to Felipe Salazar report which restaurant Delmore had gone to for lunch. "The Stone Wharf." He gave Emily a questioning look.

"I know where that is," she said with a nod. "I've been there with Alex several times. It's near those new condos, about three miles from here. It's part of that new development of expensive stores called the Quay."

Jim nodded, taking his sunglasses from his pocket. "Thanks, Phil," he said into the phone. "We're on our way."

He clicked off the telephone and put Emily's car into gear. They'd been sitting in it, with the motor running and the air-conditioning on full, for ages.

"About time," he said. "I'm starving. I was beginning to think Delmore was never going to eat lunch."

Emily looked over at him, startled. "We're not really going to eat there, are we?"

"We can't go in, sit down and only order a glass of water while we wait for Delmore to notice us," Jim said. "That would look a little suspicious, you know?"

"The Stone Wharf is really expensive," Emily said,

gazing out the window at the posh hotels and high-class condos that lined the streets in this part of town. "Lunch for the two of us could easily cost eighty dollars. I can't afford that."

"It's covered by my expense account," Jim said. "You won't have to pay. You know, don't go crazy and order champagne or caviar or anything outrageous. But don't worry about getting stuck with the bill."

Emily nodded. "Thanks." She pointed out the window. "It's your next right. See the sign for the Quay?"

"I've driven past this place," Jim said, signaling to make a right turn into the upscale mall's driveway, "but I've never gone in. So far they've had no crimes committed on the premises, and as far as the restaurants go, an eighty-buck lunch date is a little out of my league."

Emily was silent as he found an empty space and parked the car. He turned off the motor and the air-conditioning, and the sudden lack of noise was deafening. But she didn't seem to notice. She stared out the front windshield, her eyes unfocused.

"Hey," Jim said, and she turned and looked at him. "You ready to go in?"

"Ready as I'll ever be," she said coolly, "considering that I feel half-naked wearing this ridiculous excuse for a top."

Jim's gaze dropped to the whisper-thin silk that covered Emily's full breasts. It was true—the halter top didn't leave a whole lot to the imagination. But it wasn't as blatantly revealing as she feared. The fabric was gathered, sort of like two large triangles of silk that were bunched together and attached to a wide band that went below her breasts and tied in the back. Sure, when she moved a certain way and the weight of her breasts strained against the silk, her nipples were clearly outlined. But that happened only infrequently—just enough for Jim to wish it would happen a little more often.

"You look great," he said. His voice was raspier than usual, so he cleared his throat. "You're really gonna turn heads when you walk into this place. You look sexy, but in a real classy way, you know?"

"And you're an expert on classy, right?" Emily said, suddenly wanting to lash out at him. His words, his voice, the soft look in his eyes, it suddenly all seemed too intimate, too personal. She didn't want him to look at her that way. She didn't want to care whether or not he thought she was sexy. She wanted to dislike him. Forget dislike— she wanted to *hate* him. At the very least, she wanted him to hate her. Either way, she wished he would stop being so damned *kind* all the time. "And how do you know whether or not I'm going to 'turn heads'? You've never been to this restaurant before. It's out of your league, right?"

Jim got quiet, very, very quiet, as he studied the front of the restaurant out the windshield of the car. But when he turned to look at Emily, she could see the flare of emotion in his eyes. She saw anger—and something else. She looked away quickly, praying that what she'd just seen in his eyes wasn't hurt.

"Just because I don't earn my money running illegal drugs," Jim said tightly, "just because I choose not to spend an amount that would feed an entire family of six for an entire week on one lousy meal, doesn't mean I don't know class when I see it. I don't pretend to have any class—I never have—but I'll tell you one thing I know for a fact, Emily. I've got a hell of a lot more of it than your boyfriend in there."

He got out of the car and slammed the door shut.

Emily couldn't breathe. She'd gotten him mad at her, all right, but she couldn't blame him for it at all. And he was right, he *did* have more class than Alex Delmore.

She got out of the car and closed the door behind her.

Jim was already halfway across the parking lot. Good. Let him go. She *wanted* him to be angry with her. She wanted him to hate her, remember?

Despite her intentions, she found herself running across the hot blacktop, chasing after him. "Jim!"

Jim stopped in his tracks. Damn it, every time she called him by his given name, his heart nearly stopped beating. It was as if he thought maybe this time she was ready to admit that the chemistry between them was undeniable. Of course, that was extremely unlikely right now, considering he'd just let her have a full dose of his notoriously hot temper. Still, he turned around to wait for her to catch up.

And then his heart nearly *did* stop beating. Emily was running. Toward him. Wearing that flimsy top. But what made him stand glued to the spot was the look in her eyes. She was scared. Unless he was reading her wrong, something had her really scared.

"Number one," he said gently when she reached him, "when we're out in public, you *have* to call me Dan. I'm your brother, remember? Don't forget it."

Emily nodded, out of breath.

"Number two," he deadpanned, "don't run in that halter top. This is Florida, remember? There're a lot of old guys around. You'll give 'em all heart attacks. I don't want to have to run you in for manslaughter."

That got a smile out of her. It was a rueful smile, but it was a smile just the same. "You'd be an accessory. It was your idea for me to wear this, remember?"

"Yeah, I remember," he said, walking backward toward the restaurant door, still watching her. "Come on. Let's go in there and wow Delmore, get invited onto his boat for a weekend cruise, and then have a great lunch, okay?"

"I'm not sure I'll be able to eat," Emily confessed.

"Sure you will," Jim said. His smile disappeared. "I'll be there with you, Em, the whole time. You're safe. You hear what I'm saying?"

He was dead serious, and Emily nodded slowly.

She was safe from Alex Delmore. But she didn't feel safe from Jim Keegan—because despite everything, even despite their wretched history, she was actually starting to like the man.

EMILY SAT BACK in her chair and calmly looked out at the magnificent view of the glistening Gulf waters. As she leaned forward to lift her ginger ale and take a sip, she looked at Jim.

"Has he seen us yet?" she asked quietly.

Alex Delmore was sitting slightly behind Emily and to her left. He was sitting with two other men in business suits. Jim glanced around the room again, not allowing his recognition of Delmore to show as he gave their table a cursory sweep with his eyes.

He smiled at Emily. "Yeah, I think maybe he has," he said. "Come on, smile. Remember, you're out to lunch with your favorite brother. Look happy, or Delmore's gonna think we come from a dysfunctional family."

Emily actually laughed.

Jim opened the menu. "What are you going to have?"

"A salad," Emily said.

"That's all?"

"Really," she said. "I'm not hungry."

"Well, I am," Jim said. "What do you suppose scallops meunière is?"

"Look, I'm sorry for what I said before," Emily said. Jim looked up from the menu, his eyes as vivid a blue as the water behind him. He almost looked surprised. "In the car," she explained. "I didn't mean what I said. And I can't believe you're not still mad at me."

He carefully closed his menu and glanced around the dining room to make sure Alex Delmore wasn't about to approach them. "We're both under a lot of stress right now," he said quietly. He took his time selecting a breadstick from the basket in the center of the table before he looked up at her again. "And you know, anyway, you were right. I don't know class from my—"

"Yes, you do."

Jim watched her across the table. His usually animated face was as serious as Emily had ever seen it. "Are you actually arguing in my defense?" he asked. "Correct me if I'm wrong, but it sounds like you're sticking up for me here."

"Yeah, I guess I am," Emily said.

Emily knew she'd set herself up. There were a thousand smartass quips Jim could make, and an equal number of possibilities for jokes, but he did neither.

"That's really nice," was all he said. He smiled at her, almost shyly, and Emily lowered her eyes, suddenly feeling self-conscious.

"Heads up," Jim said quietly. "Delmore's standing. He's going to come over here."

Emily closed her eyes briefly, but that was the only sign she gave that she was even slightly perturbed.

"Dan," Jim whispered. "Not Jim."

She smiled at him. "I know."

"Emily! What a surprise. No, please, stay in your seats." Delmore's smooth, refined voice made the hair on the back of Jim's neck stand up. God, two seconds into the game and he already hated the guy. No, not true. Jim had hated Alexander Delmore even before he set eyes on the millionaire. He'd hated him from the first moment he pictured Delmore making love to Emily.

Delmore was blond, with the kind of boyish good looks most often found at Ivy League colleges and in upscale fashion catalogs. Jim knew that the millionaire was probably nearing forty, but with a slight build on a six-foot frame he seemed much younger.

"I'm Alex," he said, offering his hand to Jim as he pulled over a chair from an empty table and sat down. "You must be Emily's brother." As he shook Jim's hand, he said in a loud aside to Emily, "Gee, I *hope* this guy's your brother," as if he were amused by the very idea that he might not be able to totally squash any kind of romantic competition.

The man positively reeked of confidence. Jim had to keep reminding himself to smile instead of snarl.

"This is my brother, Dan," Emily said. "Dan Marshall, Alex Delmore."

"Nice to meet you," Jim said, smiling broadly, thinking, *It'll be even nicer to throw your butt in jail, scumbag.*

"Likewise," Alex said. His attention swiveled over to Emily. "Don't *you* look terrific!"

"Thank you," Emily murmured.

Delmore launched into a description of the clients he was lunching with, filled with dropped names and six-digit figures with dollar signs in front of them. As the real estate mogul talked, his gaze traveled up and down Emily, settling more than once on the fullness of her breasts. Jim resisted the urge to grab the man by the neck and squeeze. And when Delmore reached out and lightly ran his fingers down Emily's arm from her shoulder to her hand, Jim made himself sit very still. He was afraid that if he moved even an inch, he would explode with jealousy.

Jealousy? No, please, not jealousy…

Emily sat and smiled at Delmore as he entwined his fingers with hers. There was nothing in her face or body language to give away her fear. Nothing that Jim noticed, anyway, except the pulse that beat at the base of her throat. He could see every beat of Emily's heart, and it was going way too fast.

Of course, Delmore, having an ego the size of a small planet, would merely assume that it was his touch that was making her heart pound.

Unless… Maybe Jim was wrong. Maybe Emily *was* turned on by this guy. After all, she'd been dating Alex for almost half a year. He had to assume they'd been lovers for nearly that long. It had been days since she'd seen Alex. And nearly a week since they would have had even a chance to make love…

"I've missed you," Alex said, in an intimate voice that was meant only for Emily's ears.

I'll bet, thought Jim. He watched Emily, waiting for her response.

But she said nothing. She only smiled as Delmore gazed into her eyes. What did it mean, that smile?

"I haven't called you in a few days," Delmore said, "because I wanted to give you some time alone with your brother." He smiled warmly at Jim.

This investigation wasn't set up to find out whether

Emily still had a thing for Alex Delmore, Jim reminded himself. He had work to do here.

"Emily's told me about your yacht, the *Home Free*," Jim said. "When I lived up north, I used to sail all the time. I don't get out on the water much anymore."

Delmore took the hint. "Well, you'll have to come out for a sail while you're in town," he said. "I don't have my calendar with me now, but we'll set something up for one of these coming weekends."

"That'd be terrific," Jim said. "I'm going to hold you to that."

"How long are you going to be in town?" Delmore asked.

"I'm not exactly sure," Jim said. "I've got the whole summer off."

"You'll probably be going down to Sanibel Island," Delmore said. "Your family owns a condo on the beach there, right?"

"Yeah." Jim nodded. "And, of course, I'll be spending some time up in Connecticut, visiting the folks."

Emily stifled a nervous laugh. It was strange, hearing Jim talk about Sanibel and Connecticut as if he'd lived part of her life with her, as if he really *were* her brother.

"Do you two have plans for tonight?" Delmore asked.

Jim met Emily's eyes across the table. She hesitated, so he answered. "No, we don't."

He was hoping that Delmore would invite them to dinner, or even over to his house for a drink.

"Have dinner with me tonight," Delmore said.

Bingo, thought Jim. But then he realized the man was speaking only to Emily.

"You don't mind if I steal Emily away from you, do you?" Delmore said to Jim. "Do you? After all, you've had her to yourself all week long."

For the first time in a long time, Jim was speechless. He honestly didn't know what to say. If he objected, he might come across as being selfish and petty. What kind of brother would object to his sister dating a millionaire? But, damn it, he *wanted* to object. He didn't want Emily to have to deal with Delmore on her own. He didn't want Emily to go.

The silence was stretching on way too long, so Jim did the only thing he could. He passed the ball to Emily. As her brother's hostess, she could graciously refuse. "I guess that decision's up to Em," he said.

"How about it?" Delmore said, turning to Emily. "I'll pick you up around seven?"

Say no, Jim silently willed Emily with his eyes. Come on, Em, turn him down.

"Seven sounds fine," she finally said, smiling at Delmore.

What the *hell* was she doing? Why on earth would she agree to have dinner with this scumbag? Why would she do something she didn't want to do?

Unless she *did* want to...

Jim looked at Emily, sitting there with Delmore. The guy was holding her hand, and he had his other arm wrapped loosely around her shoulders.

"I'll see you later, then," Delmore said, kissing Emily on the lips. Jim's blood pressure rose another notch.

Delmore stood up, offering his hand to Jim. "Nice meeting you, Dan."

Jim kept his face carefully bland, concentrating on not letting himself break all of Delmore's fingers as they shook hands.

And then Alexander Delmore was gone, back to his own table.

Jim's hand was shaking as he picked up his glass of water and took a sip. Emily glanced up at him. He smiled at her, but his eyes were unmistakably icy.

"Why did you agree to have dinner with him?" His voice was low, but rough with emotion. And he was still smiling, as if they were having a pleasant conversation.

"I thought you wanted me to," Emily said. Was he actually *angry* at her? She was mystified. With his words, Jim had clearly left the decision about whether or not to have dinner with Alex up to her. But his eyes had told her an entirely different story. She had been so sure he wanted her to accept Alex's invitation. Apparently she'd been wrong.

"Why the *hell* would I want you to?" Jim shot back. "I can't protect you when you're off somewhere, alone with him."

With one last wave in Emily and Jim's direction, Alex and his clients went out of the restaurant. As the door closed tightly behind them, Jim's smile vanished.

"Now I've got to call Salazar, arrange for surveillance," Jim said tightly as he glared at her. "Damn it, we don't even know where Delmore'll be taking you, so we'll have to set up a tail and—"

Emily's temper flared. "Sorry to inconvenience you," she said. "Maybe next time you could manage to tell me what you would like me to do and say *in advance,* rather than assume I'll be able to read your mind."

"I thought your avoiding a one-on-one situation with Delmore was the obvious choice," he countered. "But it seems you don't find him as much of a threat as I do. God knows you'll get a better dinner by going out with him than you would staying home with me. What I can't figure out is what else you'll get."

Jim stared across the table at Emily. Her cheeks were flushed, but was it from anger or embarrassment? There was no reason for her to feel embarrassed, was there? Unless, of course, he'd hit upon her real reason for having accepted Delmore's dinner invitation. Maybe, despite everything, she was still in love with the guy.

Next to the table, their waiter cleared his throat. "Are you ready to order?"

Jim stood up, throwing his napkin, a twenty-dollar bill and Emily's car keys on the table. "I'm not hungry anymore," he said, and walked out of the restaurant.

EMILY WAS DRESSED and ready for her date with Alex before Jim returned to the apartment.

As she let him in the door, she knew from his carefully neutral expression, and from the way he wouldn't hold her gaze, that he was still angry. What she couldn't figure out was why.

But why didn't matter, she tried to convince herself. What mattered was that he was giving her a healthy reminder of just how rude and childish he really was. This was a solid dose of reality. His kindness and concern were probably no more than an act. And his kisses… His kisses were pure fantasy, that was for sure. There was nothing even remotely permanent or real-life about them. Sure, they were nice while they lasted, but Emily wasn't interested in any kind of relationship that was based completely on sex.

Jim took a can of soda from the refrigerator and popped open the top. "Can you leave me your car keys, please?" he asked politely.

"They're on the table," Emily said, coolly but no less politely, checking her makeup in the front mirror.

"Phil's out in the parking lot right now," he told her, leaning against the wall and watching as she ran a brush through her hair. She was wearing it down tonight, and it hung in a full, rich sheet, ending just above her shoulders. "After Delmore picks you up, he's gonna follow you. When you get where you're going, he's gonna give me a call and tell me what restaurant you're at. I'm going to use your car to drive over and meet him. Then, together, we'll trail you for the rest of the evening."

Emily nodded and checked her watch. Ten minutes to seven. Alex would be here any second. Suddenly she was so nervous she could barely breathe. She sat down on the couch and closed her eyes, trying to regain her inner calm. What could happen? Nothing, really—right? The worst-case scenario was that Alex would have his hands all over her all night long, the way he had at lunch. And—oh, shoot, she was forgetting about having to kiss him good-night....

She was wearing one of her church dresses. It was a demure 1940s-retro thing in a tiny-flowered pink print. It had a sweetheart neckline, short capped sleeves and a long, sweeping skirt. It was a far cry from the blue sequined dress she'd worn the other night. It was also miles removed from the barely-there halter top she'd had on at lunch. Wearing this dress, she looked as if she could win the year's award for Miss Innocence. And that was the idea.

"Pretty dress," Jim said, and Emily opened her eyes.

He was sitting across from her in the rocking chair, watching her and drinking his soda.

"Thanks," she said. She closed her eyes again—and opened them quickly, sitting up as she suddenly imagined a new worst-case scenario. This one had Alex somehow finding out that she was working with the police. This one involved Alex turning her over to the organized-crime thugs that he worked alongside of. This one had Vincent Marino's boys disposing of her body in the darkest, densest part of the Everglades....

The doorbell rang, and Emily looked sharply over at Jim. The fear was back, screaming through her veins with every pounding beat of her heart.

But Jim wasn't looking at her. He'd already gotten to his feet and was opening the door.

"Hi, Dan, how are you?" Alex shook Jim's hand as he came into Emily's apartment.

Would they kill her quickly, or would she be alive when they took her into the alligator-infested swamp?

Emily took a deep breath, stood up and made herself smile at Alex.

"Ready to go?" he asked with an answering smile.

"Hey, you know, I intend to hold you to that offer to take me on a sail," Jim said. "Did you get a chance to check your calendar yet?"

It was amazing the way Jim sounded so easygoing. And with his wide, friendly smile, his reminder of Alex's invitation was not intrusive or at all offensive.

Alex shook his head. "Damn. No, I *knew* there was something I forgot to do when I left the yacht this afternoon." He shrugged sheepishly. "I'll have to get back to you with a date."

Would they put a bullet in her brain, or would they simply tie her up and leave her there—free lunch for the gators? She could imagine their yellow eyes, their razor-sharp teeth, the way their noses would break the water as they slowly swam toward her....

"I'm counting on it," Jim said.

"All right," Alex said. "Have a good evening."

"Don't keep Emily out too late," Jim said, his words softened by a smile. "We're planing to hit the beach pretty early in the morning." He turned to Emily. "See you later, Em."

She was smiling back at him, but as soon as she met his gaze, Jim saw that something was wrong. Was she *scared?* On impulse, he pulled her in for a quick hug that confirmed it for him. She *was* scared. She was actually shaking.

But Delmore took her by the hand and pulled her out the door before Jim could figure out what he could do to help her.

Then he saw it. Emily's purse. She'd forgotten it again. It was sitting on the table next to the front door.

Her bedroom looked out over the parking lot, and Jim dashed down the hall and quickly wound the casement window open. Delmore was just about to help Emily into his limousine.

"Yo, Em!" Jim shouted, and she looked up in surprise. "You forgot your purse!"

As he watched, Emily put her hand on Delmore's arm and shook her head, as if saying, *Stay here, I'll dash back to the apartment by myself.* Sure enough, she moved briskly away from the limo, while Alex leaned against it, waiting for her.

Jim met her at the door, but instead of handing her the purse, he took her by the arm and pulled her inside, shutting the door behind her.

"You okay?" he asked, looking down at her intently.

"Yeah."

"You're lying," he said, not unkindly. He held her shoulders to keep her from turning away. "This is scaring the hell out of you, isn't it?"

His eyes were so warm, and so full of concern. Emily couldn't seem to break free from his gaze. "Yes," she finally admitted in a whisper. "What if he finds out—?"

His grip on her shoulders tightened. "You don't have to do this," he said. "Em, you don't have to go—"

"Yes, I do," she said vehemently. "If Alex is running drugs, I want to see him rot in jail."

"There are other ways—"

"I can't wait for other ways!"

Her eyes were flashing with a passion she rarely let show. Jim had always known it was back there. Oh, yeah, he'd had the opportunity to see firsthand the power of the passion and spark she kept hidden behind her quiet calm. She'd looked at him with that same liquid fire in her eyes when they made love.

The memory rose with very little encouragement. She was naked, kneeling on his bed— Jim shook his head. This was *not* the time for erotic reminiscences. "Emily…" he said.

"I'll be okay," she said. "He's *not* going to find out, and besides, you're going to follow me, right?"

"Yeah, but—"

"Then I'll be fine," she said.

"God, I wasn't thinking," Jim said. "We should've had you wired for sound. Look, let me go down there and tell Delmore that you're sick, that you're not feeling well," he said, talking fast. Emily had already taken too much time. Delmore would be wondering what was keeping her. Soon he'd come to see what the problem was. "We can reschedule— Damn, this is making me *crazy*. I don't want you to do this if you're scared—"

Emily shook her head. "I'm okay. I've got to go—"

But he couldn't release her. Still holding her shoulders

tightly, he stared down into the swirling blue of her eyes, feeling again the loss of gravity, the absence of any solid ground. "Please," he heard himself say, his voice no more than a hoarse whisper. But please *what?* Please don't go? Or please kiss me?

"Jim, I'll be okay," she said again.

Perfect. He'd meant to reassure her, but she was the one doing the reassuring here.

Jim did the only thing he could think to do under the circumstances. He kissed her.

It was remarkable. One moment he was gazing into Emily's beautiful eyes, and the next he was locked with her in an embrace that told the truth about the fire that still burned between them. It was an explosion of desire, a chemical reaction between two highly volatile substances kept too long apart.

Jim heard himself groan as he kissed her again. She tasted sweet, so sweet, and she clung to him, returning his kisses with an equal desperation. Her body was so soft against his. He could feel her heart pounding, every beat an echo of his own drumming pulse.

And then the doorbell rang.

Emily sprang away from him guiltily, her eyes wide and her cheeks flushed as she stared at him.

"Don't go," he said. It wasn't a request, it was a demand, only there was something wrong with his voice. The words came out a mere whisper that made them sound more like a plea.

Emily's eyes filled with tears. *Don't go.* But she had to. She bent down to pick up her purse from where it had fallen on the floor. She was afraid to go, but the truth was, she was more afraid to stay. She turned and opened the door.

Alex surely noticed the tears that were still brimming in her eyes, and Jim's tight-lipped expression. But he politely didn't comment, at least not until he was helping her into the back seat of his limo.

"Isn't it strange how you can be apart from someone like a brother or a sister for years, but then, when you see them again, nothing has changed?" Alex said, with unexpected sensitivity. "Everything's exactly the same. It's as if you pick up right where you left off, with all of the old issues and emotions and arguments suddenly alive again."

Emily murmured her agreement.

He reached over and squeezed her hand. "This evening is perfect for you," he said with a smile. "What you need is a little time away from him." *Him* being Dan, who was, in reality, Jim.

Alex had no idea just how right he was.

As JIM WATCHED Delmore's limousine pull out of the driveway, he dialed the number of Felipe Salazar's car phone.

It rang once, twice, three times. Where the hell was he? God, was it possible that Salazar wasn't even in his car? And if he wasn't in his car, then he wasn't following Delmore and Emily—

Salazar didn't pick up the phone until after the fifth ring. *"Hola."*

"Answer the damn phone when it rings, damn it," Jim barked.

"Ah, Diego. I am fine, and how are you?" Salazar said, not one bit fazed.

"Are you following Delmore?"

"Yes, but it would be much easier if I were not distracted by the 'damn phone.' The limousine made a left turn across heavy traffic, and my choice was either to concentrate on following it or to lose them and answer the phone. I let it ring."

"I'm sorry. I'm just…" Jim took a deep breath, and let it out slowly. "Felipe, don't lose her," he said softly.

"You know I won't, man," Salazar said.

"When they get to their destination," Jim said, "go in, let Emily see that you're there. She was pretty nervous about being alone with Delmore."

"Got it," Salazar said. "I'll call you from inside."

"Thanks," Jim said.

"Later," Salazar said, and the line was cut.

Jim slowly hung up the phone. The silence in the apartment surrounded him, and he started to pace.

Emily was scared. He could still see the traces of fear in her eyes, could still feel her trembling as he held her in his arms. *What if he finds out—?* There was no doubt about it, she was scared. Of Delmore.

Jim stopped pacing. He stood in the middle of Emily's living room and stared sightlessly out the sliding glass door.

It was obvious now that Emily had dreaded this date with Delmore. Jim had been wrong, thinking that she might still be in love with the millionaire. No way could she be in love with a man she was so afraid of. Yeah, he'd been dead wrong about her reasons for accepting this dinner date with Delmore.

He couldn't remember the last time being wrong about something had made him feel so good.

CHAPTER TEN

As SALAZAR CRACKED OPEN another pistachio nut with his teeth, Jim glanced at his watch. Ten-thirty. Delmore and Emily had been inside Aquavia's restaurant for close to three hours now.

Salazar had been going inside every ten minutes to check on Emily. According to Jim's partner, Emily had ordered some kind of broiled whitefish for dinner, but she hadn't eaten much of the meal. She and Delmore had been sitting alone in a secluded corner of the harborside restaurant until about an hour ago, when another couple had motored up to the dock on their yacht. They were friends of Delmore's, and they'd joined him and Emily. Now they all sat at a bigger table, having dessert and drinks. Emily was drinking herbal tea, Salazar reported.

"This is driving me crazy," Jim muttered, staring at the back of Delmore's limousine. Salazar cracked open another nut, and Jim shot him a look. "And you're not helping any," he added.

"Sorry," Salazar said, crumpling up the paper bag that held the rest of the nuts and the discarded shells.

They sat for a moment in a silence broken only by the soft purr of the car's engine and air conditioner.

"Do you want to talk about it?" Salazar asked

suddenly. "You know, about what's going on between you and Emily?"

Jim turned to find his partner watching him. *Talk* about it? What could he possibly say? "There's nothing going on," he said flatly.

Salazar nodded slowly. He obviously didn't buy it. "You trust me with your life, Diego," he said. "You can trust me with this, too."

Jim raked his fingers through his hair. There was no way he could talk about what he was feeling. Hell, in order to put his thoughts into words, he'd have to figure out exactly what he *was* feeling. And that was way too frightening. "I'm sorry, Phil," he said. "It's not that I don't trust you, but…I can't…talk about it."

Salazar looked out the windshield at Delmore's limousine. "Me, I'm in too deep with that girl, Jewel," he said, as easily as if he were telling Jim what he had had for lunch that day. "You know, that friend of Emily's?"

Jim couldn't hide his astonishment. "The redhead?"

"Yes." Salazar smiled. "Jewel Hays. I have been going to visit her every day." He laughed and tapped his fingers on the steering wheel as he shot Jim a sidelong glance that was a mix of humor and despair. "Can you believe it? Me, Mr. Clean, getting involved with a crack addict."

Jim found his voice. "But…she's been through rehab."

"Three times," Salazar said. "Which means she has already slipped back twice." He sighed. "She looks like an angel—but I know she's not one. Far from it, in fact. She was on the street, turning tricks, before she was fifteen. *Fifteen.*" He broke off, muttering something in Spanish. Jim caught enough of it to know his partner was damning to hell everyone responsible for leading a child so far astray.

Another minute ticked by on Jim's watch as he stared out at the brightly lit parking lot. He'd been just a little bit older than Felipe Salazar when he first met Emily....

"Still," Salazar said, breaking the silence, "when she looks at me and smiles..." He shrugged and smiled ruefully. "You know, I'm not in love with her. I'm not crazy enough to let it go that far. But I can't control what *she's* feeling. I know she's got a crush on me. I know this attraction thing is very mutual, and way too strong, you know?"

Jim nodded. He knew. "What are you going to do?"

"What can I do?" Salazar sighed. "I'm going to keep visiting her. She needs *someone* to care, man, and it looks like I'm it."

Jim nodded again. He knew how *that* felt, too.

"And I'm going to pray that she stays away from the drugs," Salazar continued. "I know enough about addicts to know that keeping her drug-free is not something I can do for her. She has to do that herself. She seems to be doing okay, but, you know, she's still in the honeymoon phase."

The alarm on Jim's wristwatch beeped. As he turned it off, Salazar climbed out of the car. Ten minutes had passed. It was time to check on Emily.

Emily. Beautiful Emily, who deep down inside was nowhere near as cool and serene as she pretended to be. Emily, who had kissed him back as though there were no tomorrow. Emily, who was sitting in that restaurant right now, with another man's arm around her shoulders...

Big deal, Jim told himself sternly. Compared to Felipe Salazar's, his problems were nothing. At least the woman *Jim* was attracted to wasn't a recovering drug addict. Sure, it was true that Felipe didn't want any kind of lasting relationship with Jewel. He wasn't in love with Jewel, the way Jim was in love with—

The way he was in— No. Jim felt himself start to sweat, and he pushed the air conditioner's fan up a notch higher. He *wasn't* falling in love with Emily again. No way. Only a fool would set himself up for such total and absolute failure. Sure, Emily was still physically attracted to him. That was clear from the way she'd returned his kisses. But she'd damn near run out of the apartment afterward. Jim shook his head. She couldn't wait to get away from him. She'd told him, in plain English, that she didn't like him. Yeah, he had a screw coming loose if he thought falling in love with Emily again would bring him anything but pain.

So he wouldn't let himself fall. Easier said than done. Jim felt like a man clinging to the side of a rocky cliff, hanging on with his fingernails and the sheer force of his willpower. Every thought of Emily—which was damn near every thought—was like a strong wind, buffeting him, straining his tentative hold.

Felipe Salazar climbed back into the car. "They are all still sitting at the table," he reported. "I made eye contact with Emily. She's doing fine. She even smiled at me. That is one tough lady."

Jim murmured his agreement, wishing Salazar would change the subject. He wanted to know that Emily was all right—period, the end. He didn't want to know if she was smiling or if Delmore was holding her hand. He didn't want to remember her short but well-manicured fingernails, or her long, slender, cool fingers, or that only one touch of her graceful hands could drive him damn near wild....

"Jewel told me Emily teaches both remedial English

and honors AP English," Salazar went on. "Apparently remedial English is where they send the troublemakers in her school. According to Jewel, before Emily came along, that class was little more than baby-sitting the students the school's administration hoped would drop out when they reached age sixteen. But from the bits and pieces I've heard from Jewel, Emily wouldn't give up on those kids. She got them involved in creative writing. They published their own literary magazine—these kids who had never written anything that wasn't spray-painted on a wall. It was like magic. They were hooked. But from what I have heard from Jewel, I think it was more than the magazine that hooked the kids. I think it was Emily. I think she treats these kids like human beings. She respects them, and she gives them opportunities to gain her trust. And once she trusts them, she stands by them. She believes in them, so they can believe in themselves."

Jim knew what it felt like to have Emily believe in him. He could remember her eyes shining as she'd smiled up at him, back when they were dating. He could see her sitting by his bed in the hospital, believing that he would pull through, that his pain would soon ease, believing enough for both of them. He could remember her coming to his apartment, to his bed, giving herself to him, strong in her belief that he would not abuse her trust.

And then he had.

He'd destroyed everything between them.

And still she believed in him. He'd heard it in her voice, only a few hours ago. She'd said, "You're going to follow me, right? Then I'll be fine." She believed he would keep her safe.

As if his memory had been captured on film, lit by a

strobe light, Jim saw Emily's face as she stared up at him, as he bent his head to kiss her. Contact. Heat. Soft, sweet mouth. Fingers in his hair. Pulling him closer. Closer. His tongue against hers. Her body molding to his. A flash of pleasure so intense it was nearly pain.

And then it *was* pain.

Who the hell was he kidding here? He wasn't going to fall in love with Emily again. It just wasn't possible.

He wasn't going to fall in love with her again— because, damn it, he'd never stopped loving her in the first place.

EMILY HEARD the words, but they didn't register at first.

"It's still early," Alex's friend Marty was saying, swishing around the ice in her Long Island iced tea. "Why don't you and Emily sail back to the cottage with us?" She smiled. "I'm dying to show off the new pool we've just put in. What do you say? We can all go for a swim."

Sail? Across the harbor, to Marty and Ken's palatial "cottage"? Emily felt a flash of panic. If they sailed, if they didn't take the limo, Jim wouldn't be able to trail her. He'd have no idea where she'd gone, no way to find her.

"That sounds great," Alex said. He turned toward Emily. "I've been hearing about this new swimming pool for close to a year now."

"But…I didn't bring my bathing suit," Emily said.

Marty lit a cigarette and smiled at Emily from behind a cloud of smoke. "With a body like yours, you don't need one." She laughed, the lines around her eyes crinkling with genuine amusement. "On second thought, with a body like yours, we better keep you covered up. We don't want Ken's blood pressure to get *too* high. There're some extra suits in the boathouse. I'm sure there's something that would fit you."

"Great," Alex said again, as if it were settled. "Let me take care of this bill, and we'll get going."

"I should call...Dan," Emily said, "and tell him not to wait up for me."

"Emily's brother is in town," Alex explained to Ken and Marty, searching through his wallet for his credit card. "Use the phone at the bar," he said, glancing up at Emily. "Those public phones have lousy wiring."

Emily scooped her purse off the table, heading first toward the ladies' room. She had the phone number for Jim's cellular phone written on a piece of paper in her purse. But since she was supposedly calling her home, it would look strange for her to look up the phone number. She would quickly memorize it in the ladies' room.

But inside the ladies' room, in the privacy of one of the stalls, Emily realized that Jim's phone number was not in her purse. Too late, she remembered putting her wallet and her keys and the paper with Jim's phone number in her other purse, the white one—which was no doubt sitting on her dresser in her bedroom.

Silently she cursed her own stupidity. Jim was sitting in Felipe's car, not more than a few hundred yards away from her, yet he might as well be a thousand miles away.

She quickly searched through her purse. What did she have in here, anyway? A lipstick, an eyeliner pencil, a wide-toothed comb, a sticky pack of wildberry Lifesavers, about three dollars in change—mostly pennies—some gas receipts, last year's calendar datebook, a wrapped granola bar, a small packet of tissues, a tampon and an expired credit card.

She wasn't carrying a phone book. She didn't have any

obvious solutions. She didn't even have a pencil so that she could scribble a note to Jim telling him where they were going.

Come to think of it, even if she had Jim's phone number, she couldn't tell him where they were going. She had no idea what Marty and Ken's street address was. Shoot, she didn't even know their last name!

Emily closed her eyes, trying to imagine what would happen after she and Alex left the restaurant on Marty and Ken's yacht.

The limo driver would leave his seat at the bar, where he was drinking glass after glass of ginger ale. He would go out to the limo, get in and drive away.

Jim and Felipe would watch in astonishment. Felipe would come into the restaurant to find their table empty and Alex and Emily gone. It wouldn't take him long to figure out that they'd left by boat.

Jim would be mad as hell. And worried, too. Emily could still see the look in his eyes when she'd admitted that, yes, she was afraid to go to dinner with Alex. Jim had looked almost desperate. And then he'd kissed her…

Emily shook her head. She couldn't think about that kiss right now. She didn't *want* to think about it now. Or ever, for that matter. But it was hard not to. She could still feel the rough stubble of his beard against her face. She could still taste the too-familiar sweetness of his mouth. She could feel his arms around her, pulling her against the hard, lean length of his body….

Emily heard the water running in the sink, and smelled the unmistakable aroma of cigarette smoke that followed Marty around. She took a deep breath and left the illusion of safety and privacy that the bathroom stall had given her.

Marty was touching up her lipstick, looking into the long mirror that was on the wall above a line of sinks. She met Emily's eyes in the mirror and smiled.

Emily washed her hands. "Marty," she said, "I realized suddenly that I don't even know your last name."

This was normal, polite conversation. There was no reason Marty would suspect that Emily wanted to know her last name in order to inform the police of Alex Delmore's whereabouts....

Marty put her lipstick back in her purse and closed it with a snap. "Bevin," she said. "Martina Bevin. Your last name's Marshfield, right?"

"Marshall," Emily told the older woman, drying her hands on a paper towel.

Marty shrugged. "Oh, well," she said. "I'm lousy with names. But I won't need to remember Marshall much longer, right?" She smile slyly. "I've heard rumors you'll be changing your name to Delmore soon."

The woman was obviously fishing for gossip. If she only knew what Emily knew... Of course, maybe she did. Maybe Marty and Ken were as involved with running drugs as Alex was. The thought was chilling. They seemed so nice. Of course, before overhearing his conversation with Vincent Marino, Emily had considered Alex nice, too.

Emily murmured something polite, yet vague enough to neither confirm nor deny Marty's hint about wedding plans, and fled back into the restaurant. The day she married Alex would be the day the world stopped turning, that was for sure.

Once outside the ladies' room, she took a deep breath. Now what?

Ken and Marty *Bevin*. At least she had something to tell

Jim. But short of writing him a message on the ladies' room mirror in lipstick, she really had only one alternative.

She had to leave a message on her own answering machine. With any luck, Jim would think to call and check for messages. No, he'd get the message, and it wouldn't be because of luck. Jim was good at what he did. He was thorough. Checking her answering machine would be one of the first things he did after he realized he and Felipe had lost her.

The bartender already had the telephone out and waiting for her on the bar. "Just dial nine to get an outside line," he told her with a friendly smile. He was a big man with long hair pulled back into a ponytail. Something about the way he moved reminded her of Jim. Inwardly she made a face. It didn't take much these days for her to be reminded of Jim.

She quickly dialed her number. The telephone rang four times before the machine picked up.

"Hi, Dan," she said, in case anyone was listening in, "it's Emily. I wanted to let you know that I'm going to be back later than I thought. Alex and I are going over to Ken and Marty Bevin's house—I'm not sure of the address, but it's somewhere down here on the water." She lowered her voice. "Don't worry about me. Everything's fine. I'm okay. I'll see you later."

She pushed down the hook with one finger, cutting the connection. Taking one more deep breath, she plastered a smile on her face and went to the table where Alex was waiting for her.

"Ready?" he asked.

She nodded. She was as ready as she'd ever be.

DAMN IT, THIS WAS HELL.

Jim slammed down the telephone for the tenth time

in the past half hour. Where was she? Where the hell *was* she?

All his efforts at tracking down Ken and Marty Bevin had failed miserably. No such people existed. They didn't own property, they had no criminal records, no priors—not even a single parking ticket. They didn't have a telephone—listed or unlisted—they didn't file state income tax, they weren't even registered to vote, for crying out loud!

Each time a potential lead came up blank, Jim got more worried. Who were these people? Their name was obviously an alias. Damn it, it scared him that Emily was with them. It scared him that he didn't know where she was. She could be *anywhere*. She could be on a plane to God knows where. She could be handcuffed and unconscious, lying belowdecks on some boat, heading for South America. She could be dead—

With a growl, he pushed himself up and off the couch and started pacing again.

How could he have lost her? Why hadn't he been prepared for something like this to happen? He should have arranged for her to wear a listening device. He should have considered the fact that Aquavia's was on the waterfront. He should have realized that there would be nautical traffic to and from the wharf. He should have been prepared to follow Emily by boat.

Jim looked at his watch and cursed. It was nearly quarter to two in the morning. Where the *hell* was she?

Shortly after midnight, he and Salazar had split up. They had come back to Emily's apartment to see if maybe she'd returned. That was when Jim had found her other purse, the one that held her wallet, his cellular phone number—and her keys. That was perfect, just perfect.

Now he had to wonder if maybe she'd tried to come home but had been locked out.

Felipe had gone back to Delmore's house to watch for any sign of either him or Emily. Jim had stayed behind, hoping that she would call again, hoping that she would come home, praying that she was safe.

Praying. Jesus, when was the last time he'd actually prayed? He couldn't remember. But, God, he was making up for it now.

At one-fifty, the telephone rang.

Jim picked it up before it completed its first ring. But it wasn't Emily. It was Frank Gale, from the police station downtown. He had been searching computer files, trying to find any mention at all of Ken and Marty Bevin.

"I figured it out," he said. "Bevin's a stage name. Martina Bevin, remember? She used to have bit parts in those really cheap horror flicks back in the early seventies? She was always the girl with the big chest who took off her shirt and got killed early on in the movie. She keeps a low profile these days. Apparently some nutball fan stalked her, and she dropped out of the business. Back in '82, she married a local man—Ken Trudeau. Rich guy. He owns that resort out on the point."

Jim scribbled the name in his notebook. "You got an address on him?"

"Yeah—211 Flamingo Lane," Frank said. "It's off Ocean Avenue."

"Thanks, Frank."

"My pleasure, pal."

Jim hung up, then turned as the apartment door opened and Emily slipped inside.

Emily.

She closed the door, locked the dead bolt and leaned back as if she were exhausted.

Relief hit Jim like a punch in the stomach. She was alive. She was all right. She was… The relief soured instantly, turning to a rapidly growing disbelief.

Her hair was a mess, as if it had been wet, or windblown, or as if someone—Delmore—had touched it, run his fingers through it over and over. She was holding her high-heeled pumps in one hand, and he could see that she'd taken her panty hose off and stuck them into the toe of one shoe. Her legs were bare, and her dress looked rumpled, as if she'd taken it off and thrown it casually over a chair—

Jealousy knifed through him, hot and sharp and painful as hell.

"I'm sorry I couldn't call you," she said. "I didn't bring your phone number…."

"I know." He made an effort to keep his voice from shaking. "Are you all right?" What he really wanted to know was what she'd been doing all this time. Had she slept with Delmore? Had she made love to him? But he couldn't bring himself to ask.

Emily nodded. "I'm fine." She smiled, but it was tight, unnatural. "Better than fine. I got Alex to invite you to a party on his yacht. Next Saturday—a week from tomorrow. He's having a cocktail cruise on the *Home Free* from five-thirty until nine. We're both invited. He wanted to take the two of us out alone, another time, but I thought it would be better if there was a crowd. That way, you can sneak down to his office and not be missed."

"Yeah," Jim said. "That's good." Outwardly, he was calm. Inwardly, he was dying. She'd gotten Delmore to give him an invitation. He couldn't shake the picture of Emily doing her persuading in Delmore's bed.

"You'll need a tux," she said, meeting his eyes only briefly before she looked away.

What Jim was thinking was too terrible. Emily was afraid of Delmore. If she didn't want to go to dinner with him, she certainly wouldn't be eager to have sex with the man. But would she do it anyway? In an effort to hurry along the investigation, in an effort to find the information they needed to put Delmore in jail—and get Jim out of her life—would she force herself to make love to Alexander Delmore one more time?

Jim hated the fact that he didn't know. He hated the fact that he suspected not only that she would, but that she had. He wanted desperately to believe that she wouldn't prostitute herself that way, but he couldn't get past the obvious evidence. At some point during the evening, she'd taken off her clothes. He couldn't ignore that, and it was killing him. Despite all the danger and jeopardy he'd imagined her to be in over the past few hours, he hadn't let himself think about the possibility of Delmore making love to her. But he couldn't stop thinking about it now, and it made him feel sick.

"I need to take a shower," she said, and he realized he was blocking the hallway that led to the bathroom.

But he didn't want her to go. He knew that unless he stood and waited outside the bathroom door, she would slip quietly into her bedroom after her shower and he wouldn't see her again until morning. Then he'd be alone with his suspicions and his jealousy all night long.

He took a step toward her and motioned toward the couch. "Sit down and...tell me what happened," he said.

She glanced at the couch and shook her head. "Nothing suspicious happened." She looked down at the shoes she was holding in her hand. "We sailed out to Ken and Marty Bevin's—"

"Trudeau," Jim said, interrupting her, and she looked up at him, frowning slightly. "It's Ken and Marty *Trudeau.* It took my investigator until just a few minutes ago to figure out that Bevin is Marty's stage name. She used to be an actress."

Emily understood instantly. "Oh, shoot," she exclaimed. She dropped one of her shoes, but didn't bother to pick it up. She stared up at Jim, concern darkening her eyes. "So, all that time, you had no idea where I was or who I was with. Jim, I'm sorry—"

"No," he said, taking another step toward her and grasping her by the shoulders. "No, Emily, don't. I should be the one apologizing here. I told you I'd stay with you. I promised I'd follow you. Damn it, I should have made sure you were wired for sound—"

"Good thing you didn't," Emily said, then blushed. Jim froze.

She gently pulled free and stepped around him, heading toward the bathroom. He turned and caught her arm, stopping her.

"Why?" he asked. His voice was low, and Emily caught her breath when she saw the tension around his mouth and the dangerous light in his eyes. "What happened that you didn't want me to hear?"

She didn't answer, and his fingers tightened around her arm. "What did you do, Emily?" he asked. His voice got steadily louder. "Where did you go after you left the Trudeaus'? I know you didn't go back to Delmore's house. Salazar was staked out there all night. So where did you go? To Delmore's boat, right?"

Emily stared up at him. What was he implying? Oh,

God, was he implying—? He thought she'd slept with Alex. He actually thought she'd stoop that low. Angry tears burned her eyelids as she tried to wrench herself free. But his fingers tightened on her arm.

To her horror, she burst into tears.

He pulled her into his arms, instantly contrite. "God, I'm sorry," he said as he held her tightly. "I'm so sorry. I shouldn't have yelled at you. I...I lost it, and I shouldn't have, but I was so worried about you, and then... But what's important now is that you're here and you're safe. That's what I've got to focus on. You don't know how glad I was to see you walk in that door. God, I was so scared, and so damned helpless. But you're okay now. You're okay. That's what matters. That's all that matters."

Emily felt more than heard the catch in Jim's voice, and the sudden unevenness of his breathing. Jim was crying. He was actually crying, too.

She could feel his cheek pressed against the side of her head. She could feel his ragged breathing, warm against her ear. He was so solid as she leaned against him, enveloped by his powerful arms. For the first time all evening, she felt protected and safe.

And needed, she realized suddenly. He was clinging to her as tightly as she was holding him. This embrace was not one-sided. She was comforting him, too.

And that scared her to death.

She did the only thing she could. She let go of Jim and fled into the bathroom.

CHAPTER ELEVEN

JIM SAT IN EMILY'S LIVING ROOM, trying not to think about Emily and Delmore, alone on Delmore's yacht last night.

But, God, it was hard.

He tried to distract himself by watching the sun rise. The dawn sky was hazy and red. What was that old saying? Red sky at morning, sailors take warning. It was going to be another scorcher of a day—hot as hell, and muggy to boot, building up to violent late-afternoon thunderstorms. The storm would rid the air of this sticky humidity for only a few short moments. Before it even stopped raining, the puddles on the ground would begin to evaporate, creating more haze.

But hey—he shouldn't complain. This was Florida. It was summer. Heat and humidity came with the package. And he'd chosen to be here, right? He'd made a decision to leave the New York Police Department. He could have stayed up north. His boss had wanted him to stay. Even as a rookie detective, Jim had been good at what he did.

But he had had to leave. New York had already taken a solid chunk of his soul. His only hope of getting any of it back had been to get the hell out of there.

So then what had happened? He had moved to Tampa, not quite whole emotionally, but able to function, able to get the work done. But only a few months into the new job, he'd woken up to find he was missing a piece of his heart.

A piece? No. The whole damned thing. Emily had stolen the whole damned thing. He'd thought he'd gotten it back, but he'd realized last night that he was mistaken. Emily had possessed his heart all these long years. Nothing had changed. He loved her. He probably always would.

She was older now—they both were. God knows *he'd* grown up a hell of a lot in the past seven years. He'd come to terms with who he was and what he'd done. Yeah, he'd gotten at least some of his ravaged soul back. It was patched and uneven—not a pretty sight—but he'd come to realize that he wasn't as bad a person as he'd thought he was.

No, he wasn't that bad. But was he good enough for Emily?

He was a cop. He knew the risks he took every day when he went to work. His world and the people in it were brutal and ugly. And sometimes, in order to catch the bad guys, he had to be just as brutal and just as ugly. More than once, he'd pointed his gun at another human being and pulled the trigger. More than once he'd taken another's life. And in doing so he'd been dragged down to their despicable level.

No, he wasn't the kind of monster he'd imagined himself to be, but he was no golden prize, either.

As the sun gathered its strength and climbed higher in the sky, Jim pushed himself off the couch and went into the kitchen to brew another pot of coffee.

Whether or not Emily deserved a man better than him was a moot point. She didn't like him. There wasn't much he could do to make her like him—much less to make her *love* him again. He wasn't even sure he *wanted* her to love him again.

But he knew one thing that he had to do. He had to tell her the truth. He had to tell her why he'd hurt her, why he'd left her all those years ago. Maybe she wouldn't believe him. But maybe she would. Maybe at least she'd understand and forgive him.

And maybe that would be enough.

EMILY WOKE UP at ten-thirty, still exhausted.

She lay in bed, listening for the sounds from the living room that would let her know Jim was awake. She heard nothing. But she doubted he was sleeping. He never slept past eight.

She shivered, remembering the way he'd held her last night, remembering how he'd cried.

Having her disappear from the restaurant must have been a major shock for him. It certainly had had more of an impact on him than she would have imagined. But as she thought about it, his emotional reaction, his anger and upset, made sense. He had been assigned to protect her. He was responsible for her safety. Through no fault of his own, he'd found himself in a situation in which he was unable to do that. Added to that had been the stress of having failed. He was not a man who failed often—or took failure lightly.

She wouldn't allow herself to consider that his emotional upset had anything to do with her on a personal level. Thinking that way was dangerous.

Emily sighed. It had been one hell of an awful night.

Alex had asked her to marry him.

She'd been dreading that, and when he finally asked it had been both better and worse than she'd anticipated.

Better because he hadn't seemed at all surprised when she told him she'd need some time to think it over before she gave him an answer. And worse because, throughout the course of their entire discussion, not even once had Alex mentioned love. He wanted to marry her not because he loved her, but because he thought she would make the perfect little wife.

In a way, it was good. She would feel no guilt about betraying a man who didn't love her. But, despite that, she felt oddly depressed. She wanted to be loved. Jim hadn't loved her, either, and she was starting to wonder if anyone ever would.

She'd been *really* glad that she wasn't wearing some kind of bug that would have let Jim listen in on her conversation with Alex. *That* would have been too hard to take. It was going to be difficult enough to *tell* him about Alex's loveless marriage proposal.

Emily climbed out of bed and took her beach bag from the closet. She and Alex had purposely made no plans to see each other before next Saturday. That was a relief. She needed some time away. She needed it desperately.

All she really needed to pack was her bathing suit, a couple pairs of underwear, an extra pair of shorts and a T-shirt. She threw the clothes into the bag and hurriedly got dressed.

Carrying her bag with her, she went into the bathroom, washed her face, brushed her hair and teeth and packed up everything else she'd need for a few days away.

Taking a deep breath, she opened the bathroom door and went out into the living room.

Jim was sitting on the couch, staring down into a cup of coffee. He looked awful. Emily was willing to bet that he'd been awake all night, no doubt still kicking himself for failing to be a perfect cop. Still, when he glanced up at her, he forced a smile.

"Hey," he said. "Good morning. There's a fresh pot of coffee on."

Emily set her beach bag by the door and went into the kitchen. She poured herself a mug.

"Emily," Jim said, and she jumped, sloshing the hot coffee onto her hand.

He swore softly and put his own mug down on the counter. Moving toward the sink, he turned on the cold water.

"You startled me," Emily said. "I didn't hear you follow me."

"I'm sorry," Jim said. He reached for her hand, to pull it under the stream of cool water, but she shook her head.

"I'm all right."

He took her hand anyway. "Humor me."

The water was cold, and it contrasted oddly with the warmth of Jim's hand. She glanced up to find him watching her, and she quickly looked away. But he was standing way too close. She could smell traces of his shampoo in his still-damp hair. She could smell the fresh, tangy soap he'd used when he showered. He'd shaved this morning, too, and his lean face was smooth and seemingly vulnerable without his tough-guy stubble. Emily resisted the sudden urge to reach out and touch his cheek.

As he reached across the sink to turn off the tap, she risked another glance at him. He seemed preoccupied now, and his eyes were unfocused as he tore a paper towel from the roll and handed it to her.

"I need to tell you what happened last night," she said as she dried her hands.

Jim looked at her then, his gaze suddenly sharp and very, very blue. "No, you don't," he said quietly. He smiled then. It came out forced and a little shaky, but it was sweet just the same. His eyes held a glimmer of pain as he reached forward to push her hair back from her face. His fingers lingered briefly on the curve of her cheek. "Whatever happened last night is all right," he said. "It's over and done with, anyway."

Emily stood frozen by an icy wave of disbelief. "You still think I... You still think Alex and I..."

"Didn't you?" Jim shook his head, catching himself. "No, don't answer that. It doesn't matter."

But it did matter. "You think I let Alex have sex with me last night," Emily said. The icy cold turned suddenly to red-hot anger. "You think that's how I got that invitation onto his boat, don't you?"

Jim was looking away from her, down at the floor. He didn't answer, so Emily shoved him, hard. "You *do* think that, don't you?" she said.

He looked up at her in surprise. Her eyes were flashing, and she looked mad enough to spit. After the way she'd shoved him, he wouldn't be surprised if she did. Spit, that is. And right at him.

"Listen up, Detective," Emily said hotly, "because I'm only going to say this one more time. My relationship with Alex Delmore is *not,* nor has it *ever been,* nor will it *ever be,* sexual. I have never slept with the man. Not last night, not any night. Can you get that through your thick skull? Last night Alex and I went to Marty and Ken's house, we swam in their new pool and tried out their new hot tub. Then we went back to the *Home Free,* and Alex checked his calendar to see when he was available to take you for a sail. Then I came home."

Swam in their pool. Emily had gone swimming. That was why she'd looked so disheveled. She *hadn't* slept with Delmore. Jim started to laugh with relief. God, had he gotten it all wrong!

"What, you think this is funny?" Emily said. "You can go to hell, Keegan. I hear it's really funny there, too."

She was so mad, tears of anger blurred her vision as she spun toward the front door. How *dare* he think she would sleep with Alex, particularly now, when she suspected that the man was a criminal! How *dare* Jim assume such things!

Jim caught her arm as she bent down to pick up her beach bag. "Em, wait! Please—"

She pulled hard to get away from him and caught her foot in one of the large loop handles of the bag. She went down hard, with Jim following close behind. He twisted to avoid landing directly on top of her.

With the air knocked out of her, Emily couldn't protest as Jim pulled her onto his lap.

"Listen to me," he said, holding her tightly to keep her from squirming away. "Just listen, damn it! I thought you and Alex already were…you know…involved, because I couldn't…I *still* can't believe there's a man alive who could spend any time at all with you without falling in love with you—without wanting to make love to you."

Emily felt the fight drain from her. She felt her anger dissolve, leaving only hurt. No one loved her. *No one.* "You're wrong," she whispered.

"I spent half of last night trying not to imagine you making love to him," he said huskily, as if he hadn't heard her protest. Emily sat quietly now, listening to his soft voice, too worn-out to protest. "And I spent the other half trying to talk myself into believing that if you *had* made love to Delmore, it didn't matter. But it did matter. It *does* matter. I don't want him touching you."

Jim touched her bare arm, sliding his fingers along her smooth skin from her shoulder to her hand, much the same way Alex had done at lunch the other day. But while Alex's touch had repulsed her, Jim's sent arrows of sensation shooting through her body. Emily shivered as he gently entangled his fingers in her hair.

"I don't want him kissing you, either," Jim murmured, pulling her head back so that she was looking directly up at him through a shimmer of tears. The heat in his eyes was unmistakable, but Emily couldn't move, couldn't run away. He moistened his lips, and she closed her eyes as he lowered his mouth to hers in a tender kiss.

She heard his sudden intake of breath as she opened her mouth to him and willingly deepened the kiss. He tasted of coffee and desire, sweet and hot. His tongue filled her mouth, and she angled her head, wanting more, *more*. Maybe this was just a lie. Maybe she was only fooling herself, maybe this was make-believe, but damn it, when he kissed her, when he touched her, she felt loved. And she needed that right now. She needed him.

He shifted her weight on his lap, turning her so that she was facing him, and he kissed her again, even harder this time.

"I don't want him making love to you," Jim breathed as he trailed hot kisses down her throat.

He lowered her onto the floor, and she welcomed the weight of his muscular body on top of hers. She pulled him even closer, drawing him between her legs and pressing herself upward to meet the hard evidence of his arousal.

He groaned—it was a low, guttural sound, born half of ecstasy, half of despair. Emily gasped as his hand covered her breast, as he caught her hardened nipple between his thumb and forefinger. She clung to him, hot with desire and dizzy from a barrage of emotions so intense she could barely breathe. This game of make-believe they were playing wasn't all pretend. She loved him. After all this time, after all he'd done, after the way he'd hurt her, Emily had fallen in love with Jim Keegan all over again.

He pushed her T-shirt up and unfastened the front clasp of her bra. He caressed her breasts first with his hands, then with his mouth.

"So beautiful," he murmured. "You're so beautiful."

Emily was lost. As she ran her fingers through the silky dark waves of his hair, she knew that she was making a colossal mistake, but she was past caring. She needed him, here and now, and here and now was what James Keegan was best at.

She tugged at his T-shirt, and he pulled it off as she slipped her own shirt over her head.

Then Jim did the unexpected. He hesitated. Kneeling there between her legs, the heat in his eyes strong enough to burn her, a sheen of perspiration making his tanned chest glisten, the corded muscles standing out in his strong arms as he supported his weight above her, he actually hesitated. "Em, do you think—"

She reached up for him, answering him with the blazing heat of a kiss, with the shockingly intimate sensation of skin against skin, soft breasts against hard muscle. No, she didn't want to think. She wanted to feel, only to *feel*.

Jim was lost. Caught in the explosive passion of her

embrace, he didn't stand a chance. Something had happened to make Emily give in to the desire that sprang to life whenever they exchanged even a glance, but he didn't know what or why that something was. Finding out what had changed her mind mattered to him, and he knew he should stop kissing her, stop touching her, pull free from her arms. But her lips were so sweet, her body so soft, and God, it had been so long. His body was weak, and his heart was on fire. After seven years of the occasional poor substitute, and days and nights filled with a desperate loneliness he hadn't even recognized, he couldn't stop.

Her long, slender fingers were in his hair, touching him, stroking his back, his arms. Jim caught his breath as she reached between them and unfastened the top button of his shorts. The zipper stuck, and her touch was excruciatingly light as she attempted to pull it down. He took her hand and pressed it against him, against the hard bulge of his sex.

She gazed up at him, her beautiful eyes luminous, the rose-colored tips of her full breasts taut with desire. Her chest rose and fell with each ragged breath she took as she touched him.

"I need you," she whispered, and Jim felt a surge of heat so strong he had to close his eyes and pull back slightly to keep from losing his control.

And then he kissed her, returning her words with the urgency of his mouth against hers. He wished desperately that he could somehow make time stand still. He wanted this moment to last forever, this hot anticipation of knowing, of actually *knowing,* that he was going to make love to Emily. He wanted to be able to carry it with him always. He wanted to be able to look across a crowded room to meet Emily's eyes, and see a hint of this same liquid fire, to see this promise of paradise. He wanted to wear it like a bulletproof vest, protecting him from the pain and despair he was forced to face nearly every day out on the city's streets.

Except he wanted to know that there was something precious behind the desire in her eyes as she looked at him. He wanted more than lust to spark the flame of her need. He wanted Emily to love him.

He wanted more than he deserved.

She pulled again at his zipper, and this time it opened. And instead of time standing still, life went into fast-forward. Emily pushed him over onto his back, and together they pulled his shorts and his briefs down his legs. Her hand closed tightly around his shaft, and he reached for her. He pulled her onto his lap, burying his face in the exquisite softness of her breasts. His hands explored the smooth curve of her derriere as he noted with amazement that somehow, over the course of the past few seconds, the last of her clothes had disappeared.

Without a word of warning, she shifted her weight and, with one swift motion, ensheathed him with her smooth, moist heat.

Jim heard himself cry out as she set a rhythm that was too fast, too strong, a wild, furious, plunging movement that stripped him of the last of his control and drove him mercilessly to the edge.

But he wasn't wearing any protection. He was seconds from release, and he would have sold his soul to the devil for a chance to send his seed deep inside this woman he loved so fiercely. In less time than it took to blink an eye, Jim imagined Emily pregnant with his child. In less than a second, he saw a baby—*their* baby—growing into a child. He saw himself as he'd never imagined himself before—happy in a way he'd never known, happy with an inner peace, with a deep contentment, secure in his love for his family, secure in the warmth of their love for him.

He wanted that. Oh, how he wanted that.

But that was only a fantasy. Emily didn't love him. And he loved her way too much to risk burdening her with an unwanted pregnancy.

Jim took her by the hips and lifted her up and off him.

"No," she breathed, kissing his neck and his freshly shaven face. "I don't want to stop—"

"Let me get a condom, Em," Jim said hoarsely, straining to reach his shorts and the wallet that was still in his back pocket. His fingers fumbled, and his money spilled onto the floor, but even so, he doubted he'd ever put a condom on quite that quickly before.

Emily waited just long enough for him to finish covering himself before she straddled him again. But Jim picked her up and pressed her back against the floor.

"My turn," he whispered, gazing into her eyes as he entered her slowly.

He took his time. Each stroke lasted an eternity, filling her deeply and ending with a kiss that claimed her completely. It was exquisite torture, stripping her of the last of her defenses, leaving her vulnerable, all her feelings exposed.

Emily closed her eyes, afraid that if she continued to hold Jim's electric blue gaze, he'd see her for the fool that she was. He would know that she loved him.

She arched up toward him, pulling him down so that the full weight of his body was on top of her. She locked her legs around him, and he groaned, moving faster now, in sync with her every need.

"Em," he breathed, and she opened her eyes.

He was still watching her, his eyes bright, almost feverish, beneath his half-closed lids. His hair curled as it clung to his slick skin, and a bead of perspiration trailed down past his ear. Emily reached up to catch it with one finger, and he pressed his cheek into her palm.

"You're making me crazy," he said huskily. "We gotta slow down, or—"

But she didn't want to slow down. He might not love her, but she knew that when it came down to sex, she had power over him. Right now, as they made love, *she* was in control.

It was a sad consolation, an unfair trade-off, considering that the rest of the time Jim was running the show. He owned her heart, and Emily was forced to confront the truth: he'd probably own it for the rest of her life. She, on the other hand, owned only his body, and only for the next few minutes.

But if she had anything to say about it, it was going to be one hell of a next few minutes.

She pulled his mouth to hers and kissed him fiercely, increasing the slow rhythm of their bodies to a wild, primitive pace, each thrust harder and deeper than the last. She felt his arms tighten around her. She felt his body tense, then heard him cry out her name as he exploded inside of her.

And then she was no longer in control. Her body answered his, wave upon wave of exquisite pleasure surrounding her, lifting her, rocketing her to a height she'd only dreamed possible. She loved him. Absolutely. Completely. And unrequitedly.

It was over then, and tears stung Emily's eyes as she drifted back to earth.

Jim lifted his head, slowly becoming aware that he was still lying on top of Emily. She had her eyes tightly closed, and she only opened them very briefly as he rolled off her. He drew her into his arms, and she nestled against him, pressing her face into his neck, as if her body were cold, rather than slick with sweat and hot to the touch.

He kissed the top of her head, and slowly stroked her from her shoulder blades to her buttocks and up again.

Reality wormed its ugly way into the picture as Jim realized they were lying on the tan carpeting in front of the door. In front of the door, for crying out loud. He hadn't even had enough class to take her on the living room floor. He hadn't even taken the time to walk the few extra steps needed to make it to the couch. What a guy.

He sighed, wishing she would say something, *anything*. He wished she would tell him that she loved him. Of course, it was entirely possible that she was lying there next to him wishing the same damn wish, wasn't it?

Jim cleared his throat. "Hey, Em?"

She didn't move.

He cleared his throat again. "I gotta tell you, um…" This was a lot harder than he thought it would be. Come on, Keegan. Three words. Pronoun, verb, pronoun. Not that challenging. All he had to do was put them in the right order. Of course, he knew damn well it was what those three little words meant that made them so hard to say. But he meant it with all his heart. And he'd missed his chance to say it seven years ago. Besides, maybe, just maybe, she was wishing he'd say it….

"I, um…" Jim had to clear his throat one more time. Then he said it. He took a deep breath and just said it. "Emily, I love you."

Emily stiffened. Then she sat up, pulling away from him, and quickly gathered up her clothes. So much for thinking that she wanted to hear him say it… His heart sank, and he felt slightly sick. He had a bad feeling that things were going to start spiraling in a downward direction pretty damn fast.

But she didn't say a word to him. She simply pulled her shirt over her head, not bothering to take the time to put her bra on again, and quickly slipped into her underpants and shorts. She stood up then, without even giving him a second glance, and walked down the hall toward the bathroom.

"Hey!" Jim sat up, a burst of anger replacing the heartsick feeling. "You're not going to say anything? You're just going to walk away? Thanks a lot, it was fun?"

She didn't turn around.

Jim stood up in one quick motion and followed her down the hall. He caught the bathroom door before she closed it, bracing one hand on the door, the other on the frame.

"I believe the correct response should be 'Thanks a lot, it was a blast,'" she said. Her voice was cool, but she didn't meet his eyes. "So thanks a lot. It was a—"

Jim reeled. "Oh, *perfect.*"

She started to close the bathroom door, and he spun back, again forcing it to remain open. He was standing there naked, but he didn't care.

"Damn it, I just told you that I love you." His voice cracked with emotion, but Emily didn't seem to notice.

She bristled with anger. "Does it work better that

way?" she said. "It probably does. Women probably like it better when you pretend to love them. It makes the sex seem less cheap, I bet." She pushed past him, out of the bathroom. "Well, you blew it this time, Romeo. You forgot that I know you. I know how you operate. Love's not a part of your game. Don't insult my intelligence by pretending that it is."

"Emily, damn it, give me a chance to—"

"You had your chance seven years ago, Detective."

Emily scooped her beach bag from the floor, and her car keys from the table, and headed for the front door. But Jim got there first. He blocked it. It was clear he had no intention of letting her leave.

He was still naked, and still oblivious to that fact. But Emily wasn't oblivious. He was much too gorgeous. Every last inch of him was lean, well-toned muscle—muscle that rippled beneath his skin as he moved. It was distracting. Distracting and disturbing, because it made her realize she still wanted him. Despite the fact that they'd made love not more than a few minutes ago, despite the fact that he was making a mockery of her most treasured hope, despite the fact that she'd made a first-class fool of herself by giving in to his lust and her own wishful thinking… Despite all those things, she knew that if she stayed here much longer she'd end up back in his arms. Back down on the floor with him. Or on the dining table. Or up on the kitchen counter. Or wherever and whenever else he wanted her…

He gestured toward his clothes and his wallet, still scattered on the floor. "Then what just happened here?" he asked hotly. "If you weren't giving me a second chance, then what the hell were we just doing?"

Emily turned away, heading for the sliding glass doors that led to her tiny deck.

Jim followed, only a step behind. "Explain it to me, damn it!" he said, even louder. "What were we just doing?"

"We were having casual sex," Emily said, her voice shaking. "All right? That's all it was."

Jim shook his head. "No. No way. I know you. You don't have *casual* sex."

Emily laughed humorlessly as she slid open the glass door. "I'm not an eighteen-year-old virgin anymore," she said, going out onto the deck and looking over the rail. There was about a twelve-foot drop to the ground. She wouldn't get out of here *that* way.

She went back inside. Jim was frowning, staring at her as if she'd just announced she would be taking a trip to the moon.

"Wait a minute," he said. His voice was suddenly much softer, but no less intense. "Are you telling me—? When we first made love…you were a *virgin?*"

Emily stepped past him. He didn't block her route to the door. He didn't even move. He just turned and watched her, that incredulous look on his face, waiting for her to answer him.

But she didn't. She didn't say a word. She hadn't meant for him to find out. She hadn't talked about it seven years ago, and she had no intention of discussing it now. Emily opened the door and went out onto the landing, heading for the stairs that led down to the parking lot.

Jim moved then, sprinting after her. "Emily, *wait!* God, I didn't know—"

But she didn't stop. She didn't even slow down.

Halfway to the stairs, Jim realized he wasn't wearing any clothes. He swore, and dashed back into Emily's apartment. He jumped into his shorts and ran after her, taking the stairs two at a time as he fastened the top button.

But when he reached the parking lot, Emily's car was already gone.

Thanks a lot. It was a blast.

For the first time, the impact of what he'd done to Emily seven years ago hit him square in the face.

CHAPTER TWELVE

SANIBEL ISLAND was in an entirely different world, an entirely different Florida. Though it was only a few dozen miles down the Gulf Coast, it seemed to Emily as if it were a million light-years away. It was a tropical island, connected to the mainland by a toll bridge. Once over that bridge, everything moved more slowly, the air smelled mysterious and thick with tropical flowers, and the plants and underbrush seemed more green and lush, like a jungle on the verge of reclaiming the sidewalks and streets. Where the road wound between two particularly swampy areas, Alligator Crossing signs were posted.

When Emily first came to Sanibel, she had thought those signs were just a corny joke. But after seeing one or two of the giant reptiles at the side of the road, and after coming face-to-snout with one in her parents' backyard, she knew that Alligator Crossing *meant* Alligator Crossing.

The entire island was a throwback to Florida's past. Early in the island's development, rules had been set prohibiting the building of structures higher than a certain number of feet. The result was condos and hotels that were hidden from the beaches, instead of towering above the sand, blocking out the sun.

Emily sat in front of her parents' beach house,

watching the sun set across the Gulf of Mexico. It was beautiful. The sky was a blaze of oranges and pinks and reds, the colors swirling together and reflecting off the water. The beach had been close to empty for most of the day, due to the heat, but now it was totally deserted, as the few people who had braved the burning sun had gone inside for dinner.

This was Emily's favorite time to be on the beach. She was alone, save for the birds that floated overhead and occasionally dived after the fish that swam in the crystal stillness of the water. Shadows were long, and the brilliant blues of the sky and the sea were muted, softened by the red-orange shades of the sunset.

Emily sat there, on her favorite beach in the world, at her favorite time of day, and *still* she felt lousy.

And the depressing thing was, she didn't see herself feeling any better anytime in the near future.

She hadn't slept more than a few hours last night. Whenever she'd closed her eyes, she could feel Jim Keegan's touch, feel the heat of his mouth, the gentleness of his strong hands. When she finally fell asleep, she'd dreamed she was back in his arms, making love to him.

He'd hit the nail right on the head with his comment about casual sex. Emily *didn't* take sex lightly. She wouldn't make love to someone she didn't care deeply about. And she cared about Jim. Reprimanding herself and telling herself that she was a fool to be taken in by the same man twice was all well and good, but it didn't change the way she felt.

It had taken every ounce of her control not to cry yesterday morning after they made love, when Jim had told her so casually that he loved her. It had taken all her strength not to burst into tears at his words. How had he known to say that? Somehow he'd figured out the one thing to say that would hurt her the most. His lightly spoken words of love made a mockery of her own devastating feelings. She knew damn well that he didn't love her.

But she loved him. She really loved him. She'd set out to uncover the real James Keegan, hoping to find someone she would dislike, someone selfish and uncaring and cruel, someone more bad than good. Instead, she'd found this man. He wasn't the perfect superhero she'd thought him to be back when she was eighteen. He was human, with a whole array of human strengths and weaknesses, a curious mixture of good and bad, with the good often outweighing the bad. He was not perfect, and somehow his imperfections made her love him all the more.

If only he could mean it when he told her he loved her, too.

Emily pulled her knees in close to her chest, and rested her head on her arms, letting a tear escape. It trickled down her cheek to her chin, and plopped down into the sand between her feet. It was just one of a thousand tears she'd shed because of Jim Keegan. Emily sighed. One tear or an ocean of tears—it didn't matter. Crying wouldn't change the fact that she'd never have what she truly wanted. She'd never have Jim's love. She'd never have his real, true, honest love. Sure, she could have his automatic words, spoken in response to an intensely sensual physical joining, but those words were meaningless.

"Emily."

Startled, Emily lifted her head, then scrambled to her feet.

Jim.

He was standing only a few feet away from her, his lean face shadowed in the soft light of dusk. He looked different somehow, and Emily realized he was wearing his hair pulled austerely back in a ponytail. His face seemed more angular, more rugged.

He was wearing a short-sleeved button-down shirt carefully tucked into a clean pair of jeans. It was obvious that he'd taken some pains with his appearance. But why? Because he was nervous about seeing her again? If he was that nervous, why would he even bother to come?

"What are you doing here?" she asked, keeping her voice even.

"It didn't take much to track you down, you know?" he said, his familiar, husky voice blending with the gentle hush of the surf. "I figured you'd either head down here or fly up to Connecticut." He pushed his hands into his front pockets, kicking at the sand with the toe of one boot. He glanced up at her, his eyes catching the last of the light from the fading sky. "You scared me when you didn't come home last night, Em."

Home. The way he said it made it sound as if it were *their* home, as if they shared it together.

Emily didn't answer. What could she say? She had no intention of apologizing.

He sighed and took a step toward her. "Look, Em—"

She took a step back, away from him, and he stopped.

"You've found me," she said. "I'm safe, you can stop worrying." She looked out at the glistening ocean. "Now, if you don't mind, I came here to be alone."

"I *do* mind," Jim said, taking another step forward. Again she stepped away from him, and he gritted his teeth to keep from cursing. "*I* came here because we need to talk."

She stood there, so cool and serene. He only caught the slightest trace of something flickering in her eyes when she turned to look back at him. But it might've only been his imagination, or maybe a reflection of the sunset.

"I have nothing to say," she told him.

He tried to keep his hurt from showing in his voice, and instead his words came out with a sarcastic-sounding edge. "You have nothing to say to me at all?" he said. "*Nothing?* Well, that's just great. You make love to me as if the world were coming to an end. And if *that's* not enough to totally blow my mind, as you're walking out the door, you let slip the fact that seven years ago, I took your virginity." He exhaled loudly in disbelief. "Honey, we got truckloads to talk about here."

Her expression didn't change. "You took something from me far more valuable than my virginity," Emily said in a low voice. "But what happened between us seven years ago is over and done. Talking about it won't change anything."

He took another step toward her. "I need you to know why I...split up with you the way I did," Jim said.

This time she stood her ground. But anger and hurt flared in her eyes, cracking her calm facade. "Believe me, you made that more than clear at the time." She turned and started toward the house. "I'd like you to leave now."

Jim caught her arm just as she went up the steps to the wide wooden porch. "I thought you deserved someone better than me," he said, determined to make her listen. "I thought if we stayed together, I thought if you married me, you'd end up hurt."

"*Married?*" Emily laughed, then wrenched her arm free, her smile quickly fading. "You had no intention of marrying me, and you know it."

"You're right," Jim said. "I had no intention of marrying you."

She turned away again, and he reached for her, to stop her, but she jerked her hand out of his grasp. "Don't *touch* me!"

Jim held up his hands, as if in surrender. "I won't," he said. "I won't, all right? But you've got to *listen,* Em. Give me a chance here—"

"Why should I?" Her calm coolness was gone at last. She stood there, trembling with anger and emotion.

"Because even though I didn't marry you, even though I didn't ask you—God, Emily, I wanted to. It was crazy, you were only eighteen, but I wanted to *marry* you. I wanted you."

"Yeah, well, you got me," Emily said hotly. "Twice. So now you can just leave me *alone.*"

She reached for the screen door, but Jim was ahead of her. He pressed one palm against it, keeping it tightly shut.

"I was in *love* with you, damn it," he said between clenched teeth.

Again, Emily laughed, but she had tears in her eyes, angry tears that threatened to overflow. "You were in love with me," she repeated. "And because you loved me, you broke my heart?" She shook her head. "You are *so* full of—"

"You gotta let me explain—"

"You keep saying that! 'Give me a chance, let me explain….' Well, why? Give me just *one* good reason—"

"Because, damn it, seven years ago, you loved me, too."

He was standing there, his features shadowy and mysterious in the rapidly fading dusk. His mouth was a grim line, his jaw was stiff and unyielding. And his eyes... More gray than blue in the growing darkness, his eyes were filled with tears.

"Please," he whispered. He didn't seem to notice as one tear escaped and made a gleaming trail down his face. "Just hear me out. That's all I'm asking, Emily. Just listen to what I have to say. Then...I'll go."

She nodded, unable to speak.

Jim took a deep breath, relief making his knees suddenly feel weak. Emily was going to listen to him. She was giving him a chance to explain. He sat down on the porch, just sat right there on the wooden floor and leaned back against the house. He wiped his face in the crook of his arm, surprised to feel the moisture of his tears. God, had he actually been crying? Funny, he hadn't noticed. He must be in one hell of an emotional state, when the only way he could tell if he was crying or not was to check whether his face was wet.

He took another deep breath. "This story starts before I met you," he said, glancing up at Emily.

She was still standing, her arms crossed tightly in front of her.

"Are you just going to stand there?" he interrupted himself to ask.

"Yes."

He could barely make out her face in the darkness, but he knew enough not to argue. She was listening, and that was all he could ask for.

"Eight years ago," he said, trying to find the words that would explain, that would make her understand what he'd been carrying around all those years before—what he was *still* carrying around. "I was twenty-four years old, working for the New York Police Department. I'd just made detective, everything was perfect. I was living in Brooklyn, in an apartment in my brother Bob's house. Bob and Molly's house... He was, you know, married. They had a little baby, a little girl, Shannon. I was an uncle for the first time. Bob had a great job, and they really didn't need the rent from the apartment, but he was my big brother. Even though we were both grown-up, he was still looking out for me."

He was quiet for a moment. "Yeah, everything was perfect. The neighborhood wasn't the greatest, but that was okay, because, you know, I was a cop. Everyone knew I was with the twelfth precinct." He laughed. "I think everyone's property values went up just a little bit the minute I moved in. I'm not bragging—that's just the way those neighborhoods are." He laughed again. "Of course, Bob used to say that the property value would've gone up a whole lot higher if I'd been working for the mob."

Emily listened, staring out at where the ocean glimmered and gleamed, sparkling through the darkness like a living blanket of reflected light. Jim's husky New York accent seemed to thicken as he spoke, as if he had somehow been pulled back into the past.

"It was summer," he said, "and I was working with a team assigned to try to stop gang violence. Some of these kids were thirteen years old, walking around with automatic weapons, blowing away other kids because they were wearing the wrong colors. At the same time, there were members of the same gangs that were in their forties. I helped lock up some of the older members of this one gang, and they—"

Emily heard him shifting his position, and she glanced

toward him. She could barely see him as he ran his hands up through his hair. He cleared his throat—a sudden loud noise in the darkness.

"The gang retaliated," he said. "They found out where I lived. They drove by my house as I was getting home from work, and they blew me away. Except they made a mistake. It wasn't me they killed. No, those sons of bitches didn't kill *me*." His voice shook, but he didn't stop. "They killed Bob. They killed my brother. They gunned him down like a dog in the street."

Emily made a sound, a small sound from the shadows that told Jim he had her attention. She was listening. As he watched, she slowly sat down on the edge of a wooden lounge chair.

"Eight years, Em," he said quietly. "It happened eight years ago, and it still hurts as much as if it happened only yesterday."

Inside the beach house, an automatic light clicked on and shone out through the window, illuminating them. Emily was watching him, her eyes reflecting the pain that he knew was etched on his face.

"Molly never forgave me," he said. "She said she did, she said it wasn't my fault, but I knew she hated me for it. God, I hated myself. I couldn't look Molly—or my mother—in the eye. I still can't face my mother. I haven't talked to her in years. She calls me every few months, leaves a message on my answering machine, but I still can't bear to call her back."

Jim looked up, unable to hold Emily's gaze in the dim light. His eyes looked tortured, and his face was lined with despair. "I still sometimes hate myself," he whispered.

"I'm sorry," Emily murmured.

"There's more," Jim said, his voice harsh. "It gets worse."

Worse than his brother dying? Emily tried to imagine feeling responsible for her brother Danny's death, but she couldn't. She couldn't even imagine how awful that would be. The thought of Danny dead, his quick smile and his cheery "Hey, kiddo" gone forever, was awful enough.

"I wasn't assigned to the case," Jim said, "you know, to find Bob's killers. They wouldn't let me handle it, I was too involved. But I wanted to find those bastards. I wanted to find them and— So I kept on top of the investigation. There were witnesses who ID'd the shooter and the driver of the car. We knew who they were, we just had to find them. But New York's a big city, and these guys didn't want to be found."

Jim fell silent, leaning his head back against the wall and closing his eyes.

"What happened?" Emily asked softly.

He looked directly at her. All the sparkle and life was gone from his eyes, leaving them flat, devoid of expression.

"I found them," he said. "I found them, and I killed them. I shot them dead, like they shot Bob."

Silence. It surrounded them as completely as the night had closed in around them. But the darkness had been interrupted by the light coming on inside the house. In the same way, Emily broke the silence.

"I can't believe that," she said.

"Believe it," he said. "It happened."

Emily leaned forward. "Are you telling me that you went out after these guys, intending to kill them?"

"No!" he said, but his conviction soon faltered. "I

don't know." He swept his hands across his face. "Maybe, subconsciously, I did. After it was all over, everyone assumed I went out for revenge, and it made me wonder. You know, maybe I did plan to kill them. It all happened so fast...."

"How did you find them?"

"I was working the desk at the precinct," Jim said, "and a call came in. Everyone on the street knew we were looking for these guys, and one of our usual informers spotted them going into an apartment. While the lieutenant was organizing the raid, my partner and I went down to keep an eye on the place, make sure they didn't leave. We were supposed to sit outside in my car and just watch. But I went into the building. I couldn't just sit tight. I even went up the stairs— I don't know what I was thinking. I didn't have a warrant, I didn't have any backup, I only had this...this...*anger.* My partner was behind me and he kept telling me we had to go back to the car, that we were going to get in trouble doing this, but I didn't give a damn. And then it happened. The guys we were after came down the stairs. They recognized me, and they started shooting. When it was all over, two of them were dead, killed by bullets fired from my gun."

He was quiet for a moment, staring down at his boots. "They brought me down to their level, Emily," he said. "Killing them didn't bring Bob back. It only made me...a monster. By killing those bastards, I was no better than they were. It made me sick. I felt subhuman, I felt—" He took a deep breath. "It took me a long time to crawl out of that hell. I still don't know for sure if I went after those guys with the intent to kill, or if it just happened. But I *do* know now that I'm not a monster. I'm human. And, like all humans, I'm not perfect. I can forgive myself.

Sometimes, on really good days, I can even forgive myself for Bob's death. Sometimes.

"But when I first met you, I couldn't forgive myself for anything. I knew I didn't deserve someone like you. And I couldn't believe I would bring you anything but unhappiness." He looked up at her, meeting her eyes steadily for the first time in many long minutes. "So I staged that scene at the bar, to make you stop loving me. Everything I said, you know, about other women, about not sleeping alone, it was a lie. I loved you with all my heart, Em. There was never anyone but you."

Emily's eyes filled with tears. "Why didn't you tell me?" she whispered. "Why didn't you tell me about your brother, about everything you'd been through? How could you make a decision like that, about our future, without letting *me* have a say? Oh, Jim, I would've helped you. Don't you know I would've done *anything*—"

He shook his head. "I thought you'd be better off without me. And I thought—" His voice broke.

"What?" She moved toward him, kneeling next to him on the dry wooden floor.

"How could I have the life I wanted with you, knowing that Bob's life was over? He never got to watch his daughter grow up. He never got to hold his wife in his arms again. He was dead, Emily, so how could I let myself have you? How could I give myself that kind of happiness, when all he had was…nothing?"

Emily couldn't answer. She couldn't say a word.

"I still don't deserve you," he said in a low voice. "But, God help me, I want you." He didn't reach out toward her. He didn't take her in his arms the way he wanted to. Instead, he let his eyes caress her face, memorizing every last freckle, studying the way her eyelashes looked, matted with her tears. She was so beautiful, it hurt. "I know I...I had my chance with you, and I blew it seven years ago. I don't blame you for not believing me or trusting me, or even wanting me around. It's my own fault. That, and...bad timing."

She didn't say a word. She just sat there, watching him, her eyes luminous with unshed tears. Jim felt his own eyes start to sting. He felt the thick sensation of deep emotion tightening his chest. Another few minutes of this, and he was going to break down and cry like a baby....

"Em, I can't think straight anymore," he told her desperately. "I can't think at all, and it's driving me nuts. The way things are between us right now, I can't do my job. I can't take care of you the way I should, so unless you tell me otherwise, unless you want me to stick around, I'm going to have myself taken off this case. I just wanted you to know that I never meant to hurt you. I did what I did seven years ago only because I loved you."

There. He'd said it all. He'd gotten it all out in the open. He'd done everything he could, except maybe throwing himself on his knees and begging her to forgive him, to give him another chance.

But Emily still didn't speak. She didn't comment, didn't reply, didn't open her mouth.

Jim felt the tightness in his chest contract, making it hard for him to breathe. She didn't forgive him. She didn't want him to stay. In some ways, it made things easier. He knew he could live with the pain. He knew he could exist without her, doing the same kind of half living he'd been doing for the past seven years. And this way, he wouldn't have to wrestle with the daily knowledge that he had a life, while Bob's was gone.

Jim pulled himself to his feet, praying that the tears wouldn't come until he was in his car, until he'd had a chance to pull away from the front of the beach house. He moved toward the steps, his boots sounding too loud on the wooden planks.

Emily reached out and caught his hand.

Jim stopped, looking down first at their hands, their fingers intertwined, then at Emily.

"Don't go," she whispered. Her face was streaked with tears, and her eyes were so soft, so full of forgiveness. "Please?"

She scrambled to her feet and put her arms around him, holding him tight, giving him the comfort he'd denied himself for so long.

But the steel belt around Jim's chest didn't loosen. Instead, it got tighter. And, holding the woman he'd loved for so long in his arms, he wept.

Because, God help him, he still didn't deserve her.

CHAPTER THIRTEEN

EMILY WOKE UP alone in the big double bed. She wrapped the top sheet around her, using it as a makeshift robe, and went down the stairs and into the living room.

There was no sign of Jim.

She finally found him, sitting out on the back porch, watching the rising sun set fire to the ocean. He looked up at her and smiled, his eyes warm and welcoming, and she felt her pulse rate increase. This all still seemed so strange, so bizarre, so much like a dream. She hoped that if it was one she wouldn't wake up too soon.

"Couldn't you sleep?" she asked.

He reached for her, pulling her down onto his lap. "No."

"You should've woken me," she said.

He kissed her, running his fingers through her thick chestnut hair, then gently massaging the back of her neck and her shoulders. "I kept you up all night. It didn't seem fair to wake you so early this morning."

Emily closed her eyes, wondering if he knew that the soft touch of his hands had the power to make her heart pound—even at five-thirty in the morning. "*I* was the one who kept *you* up all night," she said, feeling the sheet slip farther off her shoulders. "That gives you the right to wake me up whenever you want."

Jim laughed. He had a rich, husky, sexy-sounding laugh that sent shivers up and down her spine. Or maybe it was the way he was kissing the base of her throat that felt so good.

"I have to tell you something," Emily said softly, and Jim sat up. He wanted to hear her say that she loved him. She hadn't said it—at least not in words—and, God, he needed to hear it.

She smiled at him uncertainly. "This is kind of weird," she said. "I mean, my telling you this after…what we spent last night doing…" She held his gaze, but a delicate tinge of pink covered her cheeks. She was actually blushing.

Jim felt an overpowering rush of love for her, and he held her tighter, pulling her mouth down to his for a lingering kiss.

"You're not making this any easier," she said, nestling against his shoulder, brushing her lips lightly against his bare skin. She felt his arms tighten around her, felt the unmistakable evidence of his desire for her, and she knew it wouldn't take much to table this discussion—at least temporarily. But she had to tell him about Alex. If she didn't tell him, it would feel as if she were keeping secrets from him, and she didn't want that. She closed her eyes—it was easier that way—and said, "The other night, Alex Delmore proposed."

Jim froze. "Marriage?" He knew as soon as he asked that of *course* it was marriage that Delmore had proposed. But Emily didn't comment on the stupidity of his question. He looked down into the deep blue of her eyes as she nodded.

"I told him I needed time to think it over," she said.

What the hell was this that he was feeling? What *was*

it? Jealousy? Outrage? Fear? Possessiveness? Hell, yes. All of it, yes. *You're mine,* he wanted to say. *You're mine now.*

He wanted her off the case, out of danger, away from Alexander Delmore. Fear that something would happen to Emily, some horrible, dangerous thing that he'd be powerless to prevent, lodged in his chest and made it hard for him to breathe.

"Em, let's not go back," he whispered.

"Not ever?" she said with a smile.

He shook his head and kissed her. *No, not ever.*

She didn't take him seriously. "Alex isn't expecting to see me until Saturday—until the party on his boat," Emily said. "We can stay here until then. If you want…"

Jim nodded. He wanted. "I have to call in, make sure it's all right," he said. His voice sounded huskier than usual, and he cleared his throat. "I think it will be—I'm supposed to be protecting you."

"*Protecting* me." Emily's smile nearly took his breath away. "Is that what you call this?"

He could see every one of last night's kisses, every one of last night's caresses, reflected on her face. The memory of making love to her was suddenly so strong, so vivid, that he ached, wanting to feel himself inside her again, surrounded by her, buried deep within her. God, would he never get enough of her?

From the slow burn of desire in her eyes, he knew she was remembering, too. Again the blush crept back on her cheeks. It was too charming, too sweet, too incredibly sexy.

"Are you real?" he murmured, his hands slipping down beneath the cotton sheet, stroking the satiny smoothness of her body. "Or have I died and gone to heaven?"

Emily answered him with a long, slow kiss.

She tasted so sweet, so warm, he could have gone on kissing her all morning long. But she pulled back to reposition herself on his lap, straddling him on the wooden lounge chair, so that they were face-to-face. The sheet fell away, and Jim caught his breath at the sight of her, naked in the silvery morning light.

She was beautiful. The creamy white of her full breasts contrasted with the rose-colored peaks of her nipples and the golden tan of the rest of her skin. Her stomach was flat, but wonderfully soft, flaring out into slender hips and strong thighs—thighs that gripped him in anticipation of pleasures to come.

Oh, yeah, she was beautiful. With her eyes half-closed, watching him watch her, with her hair mussed from sleep, with her lips slightly parted, the heat of her desire radiated from her. She wanted him. And it amazed him that she would sit here, out in the open like this, his shy, modest Emily, unmindful of the fact that she was naked for all the world to see. It was true that this house was secluded, and that this part of the beach was wide. But from time to time joggers *did* run past, and if they glanced up toward the house... Yeah, they'd certainly get an eyeful.

But it was one eyeful Jim didn't want to share with anyone. He sat up, sliding toward the end of the chair. As he stood up, he lifted Emily, too. She wrapped her arms around his neck and her long legs around his waist as he carried her into the house.

He didn't make it to the bedroom.

JIM SWAM in circles around Emily as she floated serenely in the warm ocean. He wondered how to bring up the subject of removing her from the investigation. The one time he'd brought it up over the past few days, she'd told him in no uncertain terms that she had absolutely no intention of quitting—not now that they were so close. The problem was, he had absolutely no intention of letting her put herself in further danger. But, short of flat-out forbidding her to continue with the investigation, he wasn't sure how to achieve his goal.

"Did you get in touch with Felipe?" Emily asked lazily, treading the water with the smallest of motions. She was wearing a high-waisted blue batik-print bikini that managed to be both modest and sexy as all hell. Just like Emily.

"Yeah," he said, standing up and shaking the water out of his ears. "He's been following Delmore all week. Nothing's out of the ordinary. According to Phil, the guy's been playing it clean. Hasn't even exceeded the speed limit."

"Did Felipe happen to mention Jewel Hays?" Emily asked, opening her eyes to look up at him. "He was visiting her regularly for a while there. Do you know if he's seen her lately?"

Jim squeezed the seawater out of his long hair. "Yeah," he said again.

Emily floated toward him. "Yeah what?" she asked, looping her arms around his neck and kissing his smoothly shaved chin. "Yeah, he mentioned her, or yeah, you know whether or not he's seen her lately?"

"Both," Jim said, smiling down into her sun-kissed face. She looked like some kind of wonderful sea creature, a mermaid or a sea sprite. "Jewel's doing really well. Her little boy, Billy, is, too. Phil was helping her study for her GED."

"But he's not anymore?" Emily asked.

Jim pulled her closer, fitting their bodies neatly together underneath the cover of the water. If only they weren't wearing these bathing suits…

"Mmm…" Emily said as he kissed her, but she was only temporarily distracted. "Something happened, didn't it? Jewel got too intense for Felipe, right?"

Jim sighed. "Felipe got too intense for Felipe," he said. "He's attracted to her, Em, but he says he's not ready for any kind of serious, strings-attached kind of relationship. And Jewel comes with all kinds of strings attached. He knows he's got a real weakness when it comes to women, and he also knows that a casual sexual relationship is *not* what Jewel needs right now. So he's keeping his distance."

"He's afraid he can't control himself, so Jewel loses a friend," Emily said.

"He's doing what he knows is best, Em."

"It still stinks," she said. "Jewel's got to be wondering what happened. She's probably hurt."

"This isn't easy for Felipe, either. What is he supposed to do?" Jim asked. "Whenever they're together, she starts coming on to him. He's a man, not a saint, Em."

"Maybe she's coming on to him because she doesn't know how to interact with a man in any other way," Emily said. "Maybe all she really wants is to be his friend."

Emily started wading to shore. "He could try talking to her," she said. "He could tell her what he's feeling, instead of leaving her completely in the dark." She stopped and turned to look back at him, hoping he'd realize that she was talking about more than Jewel and Felipe. "He could let her take part in the decision making."

Jim was looking down at the water, not meeting her eyes. He knew exactly what she was talking about. "Yeah, well…" he said. "That's not always easy, is it?"

He slipped underneath the water, ending the conversation. Emily went up to the beach alone.

"EXCUSE ME?" Emily said, crossing her arms tightly in front of her and leaning back against the kitchen counter. "I must not have heard you right. It sounded to me like you just told me that you weren't going to *allow* me to help catch Alex."

"Yeah, that's what I said," Jim said. He gripped her shoulders, begging her with his eyes to listen to what he was saying. "Em, if you're out there, something could happen. Anything could go wrong. You could be hurt— or worse. I can't take that risk. It's killing me. The only obvious solution is to take you off the case, so that's what I'm gonna do. I promise you, I'll find another way to get this guy—"

"You have no right—"

"Yeah, actually, I do," he countered. "I have both the right *and* the authority."

"I'm not talking about police procedures," Emily said hotly. "I'm talking about your macho male-chauvinist Y-chromosome-loaded assumption that as my lover you have the right to tell me what I can and cannot do. Didn't it occur to you to discuss this with me first, *master?*"

Well, no, actually, it hadn't. He went back to cutting vegetables for their salad. "Emily, stop. I'm not going to play games with your safety."

"I'm not talking about *games,* I'm talking about decision making. I'm talking about democracy, about a partnership, about equal give-and-take," she said, smacking the countertop with her hand to get his attention. "Don't I *matter* to you?"

He turned toward her, dropping the knife. "Of *course*—"

"Don't you respect my ability to come to my own conclusions, to make up my own mind?"

"Yeah, but—"

"I'm not quitting now," she said. "Not when we're so close. We're going to have a chance to get you onto Alex's boat *tomorrow,* Jim." She reached out to him, gripping the smooth muscles of his forearms, then letting her hands slide down to his wrists, to his hands. "It's not like I'll be alone with him. It's a society party. Dozens of people will be there. You'll be there, too."

Jim locked their fingers together to keep her from slipping away. He stared down at their intertwined hands.

"You'll be there, so I'll be safe," she said with total conviction.

Safe. Like the last time she'd gone out with Delmore, and he and Phil had lost her?

"What'll you do if he wants an answer to his marriage proposal?" he asked quietly.

She was ready for that. "I'll tell him I need more time."

No. Every nerve in his body was screaming no, he shouldn't let her talk him into this. But, damn it, she was making sense. They *were* so close. And what could Delmore do to Emily in the middle of a high-society cocktail party?

The problem was, with Jim's experience working on the streets, he could think of quite a few nasty things Delmore could do, party or no party. But Jim would be there, to watch over Emily, to protect her...

Emily slipped her arms around his waist, standing on

her toes to kiss him lightly. Her breath was warm against his face, her body fitting his perfectly. "If we don't find the evidence we need to catch Alex tomorrow, then I'll think about quitting, okay?" She kissed him again, longer this time.

"You're trying to distract me," he said.

She smiled into his eyes, running her fingers through the soft curls of his hair. "Is it working?"

"Yeah," he said, kissing her full on the mouth, pulling her in closer to him. It was working.

SATURDAY DAWNED bright and sunny—the perfect kind of day for a sail on a millionaire drug runner's yacht.

Jim woke up early and lay quietly in bed, watching Emily sleep beside him.

Tangled in the sheets, damp with perspiration from the relentless summer heat which even the air conditioners and the permanently turning ceiling fans couldn't relieve, Emily lay in the bed, her dark hair spread across the pillow. Her eyes were closed, and her lashes were long and dark against the soft curve of her cheeks. She looked so young and innocent, so pure and perfect. He loved her so much, he ached inside.

Was this the way Bob had loved Molly?

They'd been childhood sweethearts, his brother Bob and his wife, Molly. Bob had never even dated anyone else. He'd sworn up and down that he'd been in love with Molly since fourth grade. He'd always looked at Molly with such feeling in his eyes, declaring that they were two of the lucky ones to have found the kind of love they shared.

Molly had spent the past eight years alone, with only her little daughter, Shannon, by her side.

Molly was alone.

Bob was forever alone.

So what gave Jim the right to have Emily?

He climbed out of bed, careful not to wake her, exiling himself to the solitude and heat of the back porch.

CHAPTER FOURTEEN

EMILY SWIRLED the ice cubes around the bottom of her empty glass, aware of Jim's eyes on her from the other side of Alex's yacht.

Alex deftly took the glass from her hands and smoothed back her hair to place a well-aimed kiss underneath her ear. "I'll get you another drink," he said with a charming smile.

"Thanks." Emily made herself relax and return his smile. She glanced back across the deck as Alex walked toward the bar, but Jim wasn't there any longer.

"This is hell," a soft voice whispered in her ear, and she looked up to see him standing directly behind her.

Dressed the way he was, in a black tuxedo with a white shirt and black bow tie, with his hair pulled back into a ponytail at the nape of his neck, he looked incredible. His eyes glittered like blue ice—no, not ice, fire. As a matter of fact, she'd seen that same look in his eyes this morning, when they'd made love—after she'd woken up alone again, and gone out to find him sitting, again, on the back porch.

Something was wrong between them. But whenever she asked, he shrugged it off and wouldn't talk about it. It didn't have to do with the fact that he feared for her safety—he was more than willing to talk about *that*. No, there was something else bothering him, something eating away at him. But he wouldn't tell her what it was.

And that scared her.

Still, Emily had shut her eyes and played along this past week, pretending they were idyllic, blissful lovers, trying to believe Jim when he told her that he loved her. But the fact that he was holding something back kept her wary.

She hadn't told him that she loved him—at least not in words. She was afraid to. She was afraid saying it out loud would leave her vulnerable and unguarded. She was afraid of getting hurt again.

Emily knew Jim wanted to hear those words. She knew from the way he whispered of his own love for her, then watched her, waiting for some kind of response, some kind of reply. But she couldn't do it. Saying "I love you, too," would ring false. And to declare her emotions at any other time seemed too risky, too frightening.

But she *did* love him. Desperately. Just looking into his eyes like this could make her heart pound.

Emily quickly looked away, afraid that if she held his gaze too long people might notice the sensual flame that seemed to spark between them. Jim was playing the part of her brother, for crying out loud.

"Don't look at me like that," Emily murmured.

"I can't help it," he muttered. "You look too damn good. And it's driving me nuts, the way he's touching you all the time. Why'd I let you talk me into this?"

"Because stopping Alex is the right thing to do. When are you going to try to get into his office?" Emily asked quietly.

"I've already tried once," Jim answered. "There's too many people around. I need some kind of diversion."

"Like what?"

"I don't know—something big. A school of blue whales off the starboard bow," Jim said. "A meteor shower. A tidal wave. A falling UFO."

On the other side of the deck, Alex was talking to Marty Bevin and her husband.

"How about an engagement announcement?" Emily said.

"No," Jim said sharply. "Emily, don't do that."

If she went over to Alex now, in front of Marty, and told him she was accepting his marriage proposal, all hell would break loose. It wouldn't be quite as big as a falling UFO, but...

Jim caught her arm, trying hard to keep his voice low, glancing around to make sure they weren't being watched. "I don't want you even to pretend that you're gonna marry this guy."

"It would do the trick," she said. Emily forced herself to smile at a man and woman who were strolling a little too close to them.

Jim waited until the pair were out of earshot before he spoke. *"No."*

"Why *not?*"

"Because I want you to marry *me.*"

His words seemed to surprise himself as much as they surprised Emily. She stared at him staring back at her, both pairs of eyes widening in shock. Jim forced his face to relax and turned, leaning back on the railing with his elbows. To the casual observer, they were having a light-hearted chat.

Emily turned away, using the smooth wooden deck railing to support the weight that her knees suddenly couldn't hold. Jim wanted to *marry* her.

She looked out over the ocean. The water reflected the lights from the yacht. They sparkled and shimmered like diamonds in the darkness. He wanted to marry her. She felt tears sting her eyes, and she blinked hard to keep them back.

"Are you asking?" Emily finally said. Her voice was calm and cool, matching the poised set of her gaze. He would never know how she'd braced herself before looking up at him.

"No," he growled, his answer so abrupt and immediate that she actually flinched.

She started to turn away.

"Yes, damn it," he rasped. He turned his back on anyone who might have been watching them and closed his eyes briefly. "Yes, I'm asking."

A war of emotions was raging across his lean face. Terror fought exhilaration, shock went head-to-head with love and hope, as he pinned her to the spot with the intensity of his gaze.

"Say something," he breathed, then added, "No, don't. Em, you don't have to answer right away. You don't have to answer at all if you don't want—"

The battle was over—love had won, hands down. She could see it in the achingly desperate vulnerability in his eyes. He loved her. Whatever problems he was having, whatever it was that was tormenting him, whatever he was holding back from her, it wasn't that he didn't love her.

Jim forced himself to take a step back, to loosen the tightness in his shoulders. Damn it, this wasn't the time or the place to be having this conversation.

"Why wait to give you an answer," Emily said then, her voice shaking, "when I know I'd marry you in a split second?"

"You would?" he whispered, searching her face for the reasons, for the declaration he needed to hear.

On the off chance that he couldn't read it on her face, that he couldn't see it in the sheen of tears that glimmered in her eyes, Emily said it. Out loud. "I love you."

Jim turned away, afraid that if he didn't he'd give in to the temptation to take Emily into his arms. He gripped the deck railing so hard his knuckles turned white. He cleared his throat, glancing around to be sure he wouldn't be overheard. "What do you say we jump overboard, swim to land, and I make love to you for the next two weeks straight?"

He looked at her with such fire in his eyes that Emily nearly felt burned.

She took a deep breath. "What do you say I go create a diversion?" she whispered. "You go play James Bond and find the evidence we need to put Alex behind bars, and *then* we'll go home and make love for the next two weeks straight?"

Jim glanced over his shoulder at Alex Delmore, who was still deep in conversation with his friends. "I'm going to have to smile when I congratulate Delmore on catching you as his bride," he said, his mouth tight. He met Emily's eyes. "Later, you can give me an Oscar for my award-winning acting performance."

She smiled. "I'll give you *something* later," she said, almost inaudibly, "but it won't be an Oscar."

Jim smiled then, too—a quick flash of white teeth in the shadows. "Oh, baby."

"You better believe it," Emily said. "Now *go*. But be careful."

"You too, Em."

With one more look deep into her eyes, Jim disappeared toward the stern of the yacht. Emily took a steadying breath, plastered a smile on her face and headed toward Alex.

He looked up and smiled apologetically as she approached. "I'm sorry, were you getting thirsty?" Alex asked, handing her the drink he was holding in his left hand.

"You look radiant tonight, Emily," Marty commented, taking a long drag on her cigarette. "Who's the hunk you were talking to before?"

"Um…" Emily said. Dan, not Jim. God, she had to remember that. She'd almost called him Jim.

Marty's eyes narrowed, as if she'd somehow picked up on Emily's apprehension. "You're not playing around on our little Alex now, are you?" she said with mock outrage.

"That was my brother," Emily said, keeping her voice light. "Dan. He's here visiting for a few weeks. I told you about him, remember?"

"*That* was big brother Dan?" Marty said. "My, my… Good looks run in the family, don't they?"

Emily frowned at her drink, knowing with certainty that Alex, in his role as the impeccable host, would notice.

"Is there something wrong with your drink?" he asked.

Emily took a deep breath. Here goes. "Actually," she said with a smile, "I was thinking champagne might be more appropriate tonight."

Alex understood instantly—she could tell from the sudden smug satisfaction in his eyes. "I've got enough champagne on board to go around," he said. "How about I tell my crew to start opening it?"

"Are we celebrating something?" Marty asked eagerly.

"Emily's just agreed—" Alex broke off and turned back to Emily. "That *was* a yes, wasn't it?"

She forced herself to smile brightly. "Yes, it was."

Comprehension dawned in Marty's eyes. She screamed, loud and shrill and long, causing heads to turn. "Oh, my God! Oh, my God!" she shrieked. "Alex is getting *married!*"

Marty engulfed Emily in a smoky embrace as a crowd gathered around them. Partygoers came running from all ends of the yacht as the first bottle of champagne was popped open. Jim had his diversion.

"Congratulations," someone said, pumping her hand. "You must be very happy."

"Yes, thank you," Emily replied, able to say with heartfelt honesty, "I am."

Because she *was* getting married.

But not to Alex.

"I THINK," Alex said, trailing one finger along the line of the sapphire necklace that Emily had finally accepted, "now that you've consented to be my wife, we should celebrate."

Alex's pale eyes were heavy and reddened from wine and cigarette smoke. He'd finally taken his contact lenses out, and his nearsightedness made him squint at her slightly. Emily tried not to visibly back away, but she wanted to. Boy, she wanted to. And wearing this necklace was giving her the creeps. She couldn't wait to take it off. But after she agreed to marry Alex, there had been no way she could refuse it. The sapphire necklace had finally become an appropriate gift. At least she could be grateful Alex didn't have some enormous, even more expensive diamond ring ready to slip onto her finger.

She looked around the yacht. Most of the party guests were gone. The *Home Free* had been docked at the pier for close to two hours now, and only a few of Alex's friends lay sprawled on the lounge chairs that peppered the deck. Emily was well aware of Jim, not more than a few yards away, leaning against the wooden railing, grimly watching Alex touch her.

"We just had a party," Emily said lightly. "That was a great way to celebrate."

"I was thinking of something a little more…private," Alex said with a lopsided grin.

He was drunk. He kissed her—or he tried to, anyway. Emily moved her head so that his mouth landed on her cheek. Her eyes met Jim's. She could see the muscles working in his jaw. He stood up and walked toward them.

"It's late," he said. "Time to go."

Alex threw his arm around Emily's shoulders. "Well, hey, Dan," he said. "You heading out?"

"*We're* heading out," Jim said. "Emily and I."

"We were just discussing that," Alex said. "Emily's going to stay here tonight, so you can run on along home."

Jim shook his head. "Call me old-fashioned," he said, "but Emily's *not* staying with you. You're not married yet."

Alex laughed. "Is this guy for real?" he asked Emily.

She slipped free from his grip. "Oh, yeah," she said, with a smile at Jim—her first real smile in hours. "He's real."

JIM WAS SILENT in the car on the way home.

"Did you find out anything?" Emily finally asked.

He glanced up from the road and over at her. His face

was lit in a pattern of darkness and then light as they passed under the streetlights.

"Yeah," he said.

Silence.

"Aren't you going to tell me?"

He glanced at her again, his eyes colorless in the darkness. "I hated him kissing you," he said tightly.

"I'm sorry," Emily said softly.

"It's not your fault."

"It's over now," she said. She took off the sapphire necklace and dropped it into the bottom of her bag. She was going to donate it to the high school's drug education program as soon as this charade was over.

Jim laughed in exasperation. "Oh, yeah?" he said. "Wait'll you see what happens tomorrow. Your engagement to Delmore will make the morning society news, and by eleven-thirty every high-class department store in the state will be calling you, trying to get you signed up with their bridal whatchamacallit. You know, register you for wedding presents." He braked as they approached a red light. He put the car into first gear and turned to look at Emily as they waited for the light to change to green. "It'll be a different world if you marry me, you know? Hell, the way *my* friends buy presents, it'll be safest to register down at Wal-Mart."

"Do you really think I care?"

There were no other cars on the road, behind them or even in front of them. Jim ignored the light as it turned green. He touched Emily's face, gently skimming her lips with his thumb. "I want to give you all that stuff, Em," he said quietly. "I want to give you fancy jewelry, too, but I can't. Do you hear what I'm saying? There's a lot I can't give you, a lot you'll be missing."

"I don't care."

Right now, she didn't care. But how about in a year or two? How about in ten years? How about when they scraped and struggled to put their kids through college—if he even lived that long.

This was definitely a mistake. Emily didn't deserve this kind of future. And as far as what *he* deserved…

The light was red again. He went through it anyway, hoping that if they were moving, Emily would stop watching him that way, with her eyes so soft and gentle, as if she could see down deep within him. He didn't have to wonder if she saw all his scars and all the permanently torn and tattered places in his soul. He knew she did. And despite that, she still loved him. It was too damn amazing.

It made his chest feel tight and his eyes burn, and he changed the subject. He had to. If he continued even just *thinking* about the love in Emily's eyes, he'd lose control.

In another five minutes, they'd be back at Emily's apartment. Once they were inside, he *could* lose control. And he would. He'd do more than lose control—he'd lose himself, he'd bury himself deep inside Emily. He could let all these intense, crazy feelings loose when they made love. He could give in to his emotions, he could let himself be overwhelmed. And he'd be able to tell Emily all about the way he was feeling. He'd tell her with his mouth and his hands and his body. He'd tell her far more eloquently than he ever could with words.

But right now, he had to make it through the next five minutes. "Delmore's office was clean," he said, roughly clearing the thickness from his throat, "so I logged on to his computer."

"You're kidding." Emily was appalled. "Jim, what if someone had come in while you were online?"

"They didn't," Jim said shortly.

"But what if—"

"Em, it was cool. Nothing happened. No big deal."

"No big deal? If Alex had found you down there, with his computer on—"

"Look, you want to know what I found out?"

"*Yes*. But...I can't believe you."

"His records all looked perfect," Jim said, interrupting her. "At first. See, Delmore has all of his business transactions and records on his hard disk, and everything was very tidy. But I started thinking. If an honest, upstanding, tax-paying millionaire uses some of his millions to buy illegal drugs and sell them at an enormous profit, how's he gonna explain this enormous profit to Uncle Sam?"

He glanced at Emily. He knew she hadn't forgotten about being upset that he'd taken such a big risk by prying in Delmore's personal computer. He was going to hear about it, but not until later. Right now, she was listening intently, her eyes glued to his face.

"Good question," she said. "How *does* he explain it?"

"I figured he's got to have some sort of money-laundering operation," Jim said, "some way to report all that additional income. Because, you know, he can only keep so many millions in small bills under his mattress, right?"

"How does he do it? And how did you figure it out?"

"I didn't exactly figure it out," Jim admitted. "It was more like I stumbled onto it. See, one of Delmore's real estate transactions listed for last month was a condo at the same complex where I'm living. According to Delmore's records, he sold a one-bedroom unit for a hundred and twenty thousand dollars. On the surface, that's not so strange. There're plenty of condos around here that go for much more than that. But, see, I tried to sell *my* two-bedroom a few months ago, but I took it off the market when the agent told me I'd be lucky to get a whopping ninety-five thousand for it. Yet Delmore managed to make the sale of a *one*-bedroom for twenty-five thousand more? Either I want him to be *my* agent, too, or something pretty fishy's going on here. I bet my money on fishy, and dug deeper and found out that on top of the high price, Delmore's records show he's working for a twelve percent commission—almost twice as much as the fee other agents take. My guess is he's boosting both the sale price and his commission percentage on all his records—not by enough to make anyone notice, but enough to provide a supposedly legal source for all his extracurricular income."

"So now what?" Emily said. "Can you arrest him?"

Jim shook his head. "No. We can't bust him for accounting errors. We still need some hard evidence that proves he's bringing drugs into the country." He sighed in frustration. "It would be nice if we could catch him red-handed. I spent most of my time down in Delmore's office searching for some kind of sailing schedule or calendar—anything that would tell me the next time he plans to be out on his boat overnight."

"Monday night," Emily said. "Alex is going out late Monday afternoon, and he won't be back until Tuesday." At Jim's look of surprise, she explained. "He handed me his personal calendar and told me to pick a wedding date. He told me that anything he had written in pencil could be changed, but I'd have to work around the dates written in pen. I noticed that he had his sailing schedule marked off in pen, and that struck me as odd."

Jim was deep in thought as he pulled Emily's car into the parking lot of her apartment building. "I need to figure out a way to get onto Delmore's boat, to be there Monday night, when the shipment comes in."

"I can get us on board," Emily said.

He pulled up the parking brake and cut the engine, turning to give her an exasperated look. "What are you, nuts? No way am I going to let you near Delmore again—and especially not in a situation where you could be face-to-face with the people who are selling the stuff to him."

There was a dangerous glint in Emily's eyes. "That's strange. I *know* you wouldn't *dare* order me around, but that sure sounded more like an imperial command than a request to my ears."

"Emily—"

She leaned forward and kissed him. "Let's not argue about this now. Please? I'm exhausted. And I need a shower."

"I want you to catch a morning flight up to Connecti-cut," he said. "I want you to stay with your folks for a week or so, until we nail this guy."

"Jim—"

"Emily. You've got to let me keep you safe."

She kept her voice light. "I'm safe. After all, I'm living with a cop."

Jim didn't smile, the way she expected him to. Instead, his face became closed, shuttered. "Hell of a lot of good that did my brother," he said tightly, getting out of the car.

He came around and opened her door, standing stiffly, his anger evident in the set of his shoulders. All of a sudden, he seemed almost determined to fight with her. But Emily was just as determined *not* to argue. Not tonight.

She took his hand and pulled him gently toward the stairs that led up to the second-floor apartments.

"I'm serious about you going to your parents' house," he said as Emily unlocked her door. "I'm going to buy you a ticket tonight."

It was cool and dark inside Emily's apartment. She closed the door behind them and took off her high heels. The little red message light on her answering machine was flashing. But it was nearly 2:00 a.m. Whoever had called surely wouldn't mind if she waited until morning to listen to her messages. She went down the hall toward her bathroom without turning on a light.

"In fact, I'm going to call the airline right now," Jim said, switching on the lamp next to the couch, "and make a reservation."

Oh, no, you're not, Emily thought, turning on the shower. She took off her earrings and her necklace and put them in the jewelry box in the bedroom before going back down the hall to the living room.

Jim glanced up at her, the phone to his ear. He was obviously on hold. As she smiled at him, the muscle in his jaw jumped. He was more tense than she'd ever seen him before.

"Can you help me with my zipper?" she asked, turning around and pulling her hair up and off her neck.

She heard him stand up and move behind her, and felt his fingers fumble as he searched for the tiny zipper pull. He found it, and unzipped her dress slowly, careful not to catch the zipper's teeth in the delicate fabric.

Emily closed her eyes, allowing herself the luxury of remembering the way the world had seemed to tilt several hours earlier, when Jim had asked her to marry him. He wanted to marry her. As in forever. As in happily ever after.

They were finally alone together, after a grueling evening spent pretending they were something they weren't. She should be in his arms, he should be kissing her, loving her—they should be getting a head start on that happily ever after.

But Jim was still so stiff, so tense, so seemingly intentionally unhappy. It was as if he were making himself focus on all his fears about her safety, as if he didn't want to let himself be happy.

His hands fell away from her without touching her, without even the slightest caress. He was not going to be easily distracted—not this time. But Emily wouldn't accept defeat. She knew that he loved her. She *knew* that. And she was determined to see him smile again before the hour was out.

Turning, she reached for the base of the telephone, pushed the little buttons and cut Jim off.

"Damn it, Emily—"

With first a quick glance at the sliding glass door to be sure the curtains were closed, Emily pushed her dress off her shoulders. It pooled in a silky green pile at her feet. The sudden flare of heat in Jim's eyes was unmistakable as he took in her lacy black bra and matching panties, and all the smooth, tanned skin in between. But he stepped back, away from her, as if he were afraid to let her get too close.

He might be afraid, but she wasn't. She stepped out of her dress, toward him.

"Take a shower with me," she said, feeling her face heat slightly at the brazenness of her suggestion. "Please?" she added softly.

Jim's stomach twisted. She wanted to make love to him—she couldn't have made that any more obvious—

and yet he was just standing here, staring at her like an idiot.

What was wrong with him?

Ten minutes ago, back in the car, all he could think about was when would they get here, how many minutes would it be until they closed the door to her apartment behind them, and how many seconds after that would it take him to pull her into his arms? Damn, he'd wanted her so badly, he'd imagined himself unable to wait even the short amount of time it would take to walk down the hallway to her bedroom. He'd imagined picking her up, wrapping her incredible legs around his waist and taking her, right there, standing up in the middle of the hall.

But that had been before she reminded him of Bob.

Now he still wanted her that badly, but his desire was covered by a sticky blanket of guilt. What gave him the right to spend the rest of the night in Emily's sweet arms? What gave him the right to have the kind of nearly hedonistic pleasure that awaited him if he took her outstretched hand and let her lead him toward the bathroom, toward the sound of that steamy shower? What gave him the right to *marry* her, for God's sake, to spend the rest of his life surrounded by her beautiful smile and her generous, warm, wonderful love?

The fact that he loved her more than he loved life itself wasn't enough. And wanting her as badly as he did wasn't enough, either. Even the answering light of love and desire he could see in Emily's eyes didn't erase the guilt he felt deep in his soul.

But, God help him, if she so much as touched him, he'd surrender completely to the need to lose himself, to bury himself, within her passion. For a while, he'd forget. But the guilt and pain would return. It always did, sooner or later.

She took another step toward him, and again he backed away, afraid of the power she had over him.

"Emily, we need to talk," he said huskily.

"We can talk later, can't we?" she said, unhooking the front clasp of her bra and stepping out of her panties. "After we make love?"

She held out her hands to him, and he was rocked by how vulnerable she was, standing there totally naked, wonderfully, gorgeously naked, with him still fully clothed.

She was vulnerable, yet she didn't seem to care as she gave him the ultimate gift of her love. She was offering him her body, and he was well aware it was part of a package deal, tightly tied to the even more awesome gifts of her heart and soul.

He might have been able to resist the sexual temptation—although where Emily was concerned, he wasn't totally convinced of that—but the promise of such intense physical pleasure, combined with the pure strength of her love and trust, well, that was something he had no defenses against.

He couldn't have backed away from her again if his life had depended on it.

So he reached for her, *lunged* for her, and the universe exploded as he met her sweet lips in a piercing, soul-shattering kiss. Her skin was so soft, her body so supple beneath his hands. He heard himself cry out—all his anguish and frustration and pain drawn out in one long, wordless sound.

Help me, he wanted to say. *Save me.* But even Emily, with her pure, sweet, nonjudgmental love, couldn't rescue him.

He knew he was touching her too roughly, kissing her

too hard, and he tried to pull back, afraid that he would hurt her. But she kissed him just as savagely, welcoming the crushing strength of his arms and the fierce urgency of his hands.

Breaking free, she took his hand and pulled him toward the bathroom, toward the sound of the shower. The tiny room was thick with steam, and she pushed aside the shower curtain, then reached for Jim's bow tie.

One swift yank pulled it free, and as he reached for her again, as he kissed her, she peeled his jacket from his wide shoulders. The sleeves were inside out, but he didn't seem to notice or care as he threw it back behind him, out of the bathroom, onto the floor of the hall.

Emily unfastened the back catch of his cummerbund as he pressed his thigh between her legs, opening her to his searching fingers. *Yes.* She clung weakly to him as he explored her most intimate place, as he found her heat. This was what she wanted. This, and more, forever, for the rest of their lives. Her own fingers fumbled as she unfastened the button of his pants, as she pulled down his zipper and—

With a desperate-sounding groan, Jim picked her up and, stepping over the side of the tub and directly under the pounding stream of warm water, drove himself deep inside her.

The sensations were incredible—the cold tile at her back, the warm water pouring over them, and Jim plunging harder and deeper within her with each rhythmic thrust. Emily clutched the wet cotton of his shirt— He was still wearing his shirt and all the rest of his clothes, even his socks and shoes!

He didn't seem to notice that he was soaked. He didn't seem aware of anything but this incredible pleasure he was giving and taking. His eyes were tightly shut, and his face was a picture of intensity and emotion, made to seem even more so by the water dripping from his wet hair and running down his cheeks like tears.

"I love you," he whispered, his soft voice a gentle contrast to the physical onslaught of his body. "Emily, I love you so much...."

His words pushed her over the edge. True, the physical sensations were incredible, but it was hearing his confession of love that sent her rocketing toward a climax so exquisite it seemed otherworldly.

Waves of pleasure racked her body, and Emily cried out, in an explosion of sound that made Jim's eyes fly open. For several long seconds, he stared into her eyes, and time seemed to stand perfectly still as she felt a connection that was so much more than physical. They were one, two halves of a whole, made complete only by each other's love.

Unguarded, his dark blue eyes held such emotion, such love, such endless joy. All the dark clouds of worry, and all the sadness that had shadowed him were gone. He loved her, and nothing else mattered. Nothing else even existed.

She felt the tightening of his body as he was catapulted over the cliff of his own release. But still he looked into her eyes, holding her gaze as if he, too, wanted to share more than just his body with her, willingly letting her see that she had the power to touch his very soul.

He loved her. Endlessly, perfectly, truly.

Jim slowly became aware of the water running down past the collar of his shirt, soaking through the legs of his pants, dripping into his socks, making his shoes a sodden mess. He was still holding Emily. Her legs were still locked around him. Her head was resting on his shoulder, and he could feel the warmth of her breath against his neck as she clung to him.

He felt more than heard her laugh softly, felt her mouth curve up into a smile, felt her sigh with satisfaction. Then she lifted her head, and he helped her slide down.

Together, silently, they unbuttoned his tuxedo shirt and peeled it off him. Jim braced himself against the tile wall with one hand as he kicked off his shoes. His knees were wobbly, and from more than just the physical workout of their lovemaking. It was the emotion that made his legs feel weak, and he smiled wryly, thinking this was why so many men proposed marriage on their knees—their emotions were probably running so high, they couldn't have stood up if they'd wanted to. God knows right now it was taking all of his strength to stay vertical. Of course, he'd already done his proposing. He already knew that she wanted him forever, though what he'd done to deserve her love was beyond his knowledge.

A flicker of fear snuck through his sense of contentment, like the cold blade of a tiny knife, small but deadly. He shook his head, pushing it away, refusing it access. Don't think, he ordered himself. Just feel. Just *be*.

Emily threw his socks and his pants in the sink, and he gathered her into his arms, holding her under the stream of water, feeling her heart beating in sync with his own. Here, with the shower curtain drawn, the rest of the world seemed so far away, so remote. Here, in this dim, wet, tiny paradise, there was room only for two.

It was a crying shame they couldn't stay here forever.

CHAPTER FIFTEEN

REALITY STEPPED IN and, with a swift left hook, knocked Jim out of the warmth of the safe, make-believe world he had allowed himself to be lost in for a while.

"What's wrong?" Emily asked softly, using her fingers to comb through his wet hair as he rubbed her dry with a towel.

"I didn't use a condom, Em," he said. A muscle jumped in his cheek as he looked up at her from where he was sitting on her bed.

That glimmer of darkness, of sorrow or pain or whatever it was, was back in his eyes. But Emily pretended she hadn't seen it. "You're only realizing that now?" she teased. "And here I thought it was some kind of macho-male possessive thing. I thought you figured as long as we're getting married, it was worth the risk."

Jim shook his head. "No," he said. "I was… We… It was too intense. I wasn't thinking about birth control, and I should have been. I'm sorry. It's my fault."

Emily leaned forward and kissed him. "I'd love to have a baby with you," she said simply, then smiled. "Preferably not for a few years, but it wouldn't be the end of the world, would it? Provided the baby has your smile, of course."

But he didn't give her one of those smiles. Instead, he

pulled back, out of her arms. "Yeah, well," he said, clearing his throat. "I'm not ready for kids myself, you know? I think it would be a bad mistake right now."

That was a bald-faced lie, and Jim looked away, sure that if he met Emily's crystal-blue gaze she'd see through him to the truth. And the truth was, he would've killed for a chance to make a baby with her. Ever since Bob and Molly had had their baby, ever since he had watched Bob holding his tiny daughter in his arms, Jim had wanted a piece of that kind of happiness. And he wanted to share it with Emily. God, he wanted that more than he'd ever wanted anything.

"I mean, we should wait," he said. "You know, make sure we're right for each other, make sure it's going to work out. You hear what I'm saying?"

Emily's eyes dropped, and he knew his words had hurt her. She wanted words of love, promises of forever and happily ever after, not down-to-earth real-life warnings and cautions. But this *was* real life. And real life only rarely worked out. Real life usually sucker punched you, then kicked you when you were down and out. Real life was full of flat tires and broken dreams and forgotten promises. Real life meant getting gunned down in the street by punks out for revenge. Real life was Bob, bleeding to death, gasping his last words of love to Molly, without a prayer of survival.

Jim stood up, suddenly desperate for some fresh air.

He pulled on a pair of shorts and went out into the living room, pushing aside the curtains to open the sliding glass door to the deck.

The night air was humid, hot and thick. He closed the door behind him and sat down heavily on one of the lounge chairs, raking his still-wet hair back out of his face. Damn it, it was impossible to breathe, even out here.

The door slid open, and Emily slipped out onto the deck. She'd put on a sleeveless white cotton nightgown that made her look both impossibly innocent and gut-wrenchingly sexy. He wanted her again, Jim realized. He'd just had the most intense sexual experience of his life and yet, already, he wanted more.

He clenched his teeth and looked away from her, afraid to give himself away, afraid to let her see the power she had over him. Still, he heard her nightgown rustle softly as she sat down in the other chair. He felt her watching him.

"Do you want to talk about it?" she asked softly.

"Talk about what?" he asked huskily, not daring to meet her eyes.

"Whatever it is that's bothering you."

What was he supposed to say? I'm scared? Scared of what? He didn't know. Scared of being too happy, a small voice said, taunting him. Scared of having something you don't deserve, something you took away from Bob.

Jim stood up suddenly, gripping the wooden rail of the deck. "I've been trying to figure out a way to be on Delmore's boat when he sails on Monday night."

"I can get us there—"

"Me," he said, turning to face her. "Not you. You're done. I'm not letting you get within a hundred yards of Delmore again."

"Jim—"

"No." It came out too sharply, too harshly, and she flinched. But then she lifted her chin.

"If you're going to shout at me, we should go inside," she said.

"If you think that was shouting, you don't know what shouting is."

"I'm not fragile," Emily said evenly. "I *do* know what shouting is. Maybe you don't know this, but I've had kids pull knives on me—"

"Great. That's supposed to make me feel better?"

"Jim, I can get us onto that yacht," Emily said, leaning forward, as if maybe if she got close enough he'd start to understand.

"And I'm not letting you do it."

"Why not?"

"Why not doesn't matter," he said tightly. "This time I'm not going to let you talk me into—"

"You won't even discuss it?"

"There's nothing to discuss here. I've made up my mind."

A spark of real anger lit Emily's eyes. "Oh, you've made up your mind, have you? What about *my* mind? Or am I just supposed to bow to you?"

"This time, yes."

"What about next time?" Her voice was deceptively calm, deceptively cool. But her eyes couldn't hide her feelings.

Jim pushed himself out of the chair. "Look, if you want to marry me, then you gotta get used to me protecting you."

He pushed open the glass door and went into the living room. Emily followed. She was no longer trying to hide the anger in her eyes, and she closed the door with a little too much force. "*If* I want to marry you—? You're just going to say something like *that* and then walk away?"

"The conversation is over," Jim said. "I know what you're trying to do, and I'm not going to let you do it."

"Right now I'm trying to determine the bounds of this relationship," Emily said hotly. "I was under the impression that 'love, honor and *obey*' went out of style with…with…beehive hairdos. I thought our relationship was equal, that it was give-and-take. And by that I *don't* mean you give the orders and I take them."

"No way in *hell* am I letting you risk your life," he retorted. "And if you don't like it…"

He looked away, unable to meet her eyes.

"What?" she whispered, suddenly terribly afraid. "If I don't like it, what then?"

He was staring down at the floor, down at his bare feet. He wore only a pair of gray running shorts. They accentuated his tan and emphasized the long, muscular lengths of his legs. His hair was nearly dry now. It curled around his shoulders, thick and shiny and soft as silk. It was beautiful. *He* was beautiful. But when he finally looked up at her, his eyes were dull, almost lifeless, and pain was etched into the lines on his face.

"This isn't going to work," he said quietly. "You know. You and me."

With sudden clarity, like illumination from a tremendous lightning bolt out of the darkness of a storm, Emily understood. This argument they were having wasn't about whether or not Emily should risk putting herself in danger again to help catch Alex. Jim was an expert at subtly manipulating people. And it wouldn't have taken too much manipulation to make her give in. All he'd really have had to say was "I love you, and I don't want you to get hurt. Please, it's extremely important to me that you stay away from Alex Delmore," and she would have backed down. No, there was another reason he was arguing with her this way. There was another reason he'd picked a fight.

He didn't want to marry her. He was afraid.

"Oh, God," Emily said, as the realization hit her squarely in the stomach.

"I'm sorry," he said. "Em, I swear, I never meant to hurt you, but I can't... I...have to figure this all out."

Emily could feel the tears brimming in her eyes, but she followed him as he picked up his duffel bag and backpack and crossed toward the door. "Whatever the problem is, we can work it out," she said, and her voice shook with conviction. "You love me. I *know* you love me. And I love you."

"You shouldn't," he told her, his voice raspy. "I don't deserve it."

He opened the door.

"Jim, wait. Please. Talk to me."

He stopped and stood there, just outside her door, his head bowed.

"I need some time to think," he said, without turning around. His voice was so low Emily had to strain to hear his words. "I can't think at all when I'm around you, Em."

Emily held on to the doorframe, clinging to the memory of the joy she'd seen in Jim's eyes not more than an hour ago, when he made love to her. He hadn't been thinking then—only feeling. It hadn't been until later that the shadows and pain returned to cloud his view. It hadn't been until later that he tried to deny that their love for each other was enough to let them work through any problem.

But before she could tell him that, before she could beg him not to go, he had disappeared, fading into the darkness of the predawn.

THE PHONE RANG.

Emily leapt up from the couch, praying it was Jim.

He'd only been gone a half hour—one long, endless half hour—but maybe he was calling to tell her he'd been wrong. Maybe he was calling to say that he *did* want to spend the rest of his life with her, that he *did* love her, that he was coming back, that everything was going to be okay.

Who else could possibly be calling at four-thirty in the morning?

"Jim?"

"No, I'm sorry, Emily. It's Felipe Salazar," came Felipe's familiar voice. He sounded different—tighter, strained, his words almost clipped. "Are you awake? Take a minute to wake up, okay?"

Emily pushed her hair out of her face. "I'm awake," she said. "I was awake before you called. Is something wrong?"

Fear flickered in the pit of her stomach. Jim had only been gone thirty minutes. There wasn't possibly enough time for something bad to have happened to him. Was there?

"Yes," Felipe said. "I'm at the hospital—"

"No," Emily said, the fear freezing her in place. "Not Jim—"

"Diego is fine," Felipe said, and relief washed over her, making her legs weak. She carried the phone over and sat down on the couch. "It's…" He cleared his throat. "It's Jewel. She is here in surgery. They don't know, uh…" He cleared his throat again. "They don't know if she will…survive."

The relief was gone, replaced by new horror. "Oh, God," Emily said. "Felipe, how? What happened?"

"She was hit by a car—" His voice broke. "She was walking out on the exit ramp of the highway. She was higher than a kite. The doctor told me there are traces of both crack and LSD in her blood."

"Oh, no," Emily breathed. "Oh, Jewel. I thought she was doing so well. What happened?"

"I happened," Felipe said harshly. "I let her down. She needed me, and, damn it, I wasn't there for her."

He was silent then, but Emily knew from the sound of his ragged breathing how upset he was.

"Felipe, she's an addict," she said. "You know you can't hold yourself responsible."

"No," he said, interrupting her. "You don't understand."

"Where are you?" Emily asked. "I'm coming over."

FELIPE SALAZAR looked a wreck. His suit was creased and rumpled. His tie was long gone, and his usually pristine white shirt was wrinkled and partially unbuttoned. His gleaming black hair, usually neatly combed with not a lock out of place, was a wild jumble of curls.

He was sitting in the hospital waiting room, slumped over, elbows resting on his knees, head down, with his hands locked together on the back of his neck.

At the soft sound of Emily's sneakers on the tile floor, he looked up. His eyes were red and his face was tired, but he forced a smile and rose to his feet.

"Thanks for coming down here," he said.

Emily put her arms around him. "I'm so sorry," she said. "Is there anything I can do to help?"

Felipe pulled back. "You can help me pray," he said. "Man, I haven't prayed this hard since I was eight years old and my little brother had appendicitis." He shook his head. "It was the middle of the night, we were forty miles from the hospital, in the middle of nowhere, and my father's car broke down."

"What happened?" Emily asked softly.

"I prayed with all my heart for a miracle," he said. "Then a car came by, and the people stopped. They were college kids—hippies, you know, with long hair and headbands and everything. They'd gotten lost. They were looking for the highway. I remember they were happy to drive us to the hospital—one of them kept saying that their getting lost was a really groovy coincidence." He laughed softly. "But I knew it was no coincidence. It was my miracle. God had answered my prayers." He shook his head, and tears sprang into his eyes as he looked at Emily. "It has been at least fifteen years. Do you think I have a chance for another miracle today?"

Emily nodded, squeezing Felipe's hands, unable to speak.

"Phil, I got here as soon as I heard."

Jim.

Emily turned around to see Jim standing behind her. He met her eyes only very briefly before he returned his attention to his friend. She might as well have been a stranger or a mere acquaintance, for all the warmth—or lack of it—in his gaze. Could this possibly be the same man who had made love to her so passionately just a short time ago? Her stomach hurt, and she tried to convince herself that it was the gravity of the situation that was making him seem so cold. As soon as she had a chance to talk to him, she'd convince him that whatever problems he had could be worked out....

"What happened?" he asked Felipe.

"Jewel's aunt and uncle tracked her down, man," Felipe said. "They came to the shelter, insisted she was a runaway, proved she was underage. Did you know she was only seventeen?" he asked Emily.

Emily nodded her head. She hadn't realized that Felipe didn't know how young Jewel was.

"The aunt and uncle said that they were Billy's legal guardians, too," Felipe said. "They demanded she and Billy be returned to them. They told Jewel if she made a fuss, Billy would get taken away by the state."

He took several steps back, and sat down tiredly on the hard plastic bench. "She called me, Diego," he said, looking up at Jim. "She called me, man, yesterday, asking me to come to the shelter, telling me she needed me. I was home. I heard the answering machine take her message, but I didn't pick up. I didn't take the call, because I've been trying to keep my distance, you know? I've been staying away. I don't go and visit her every day like before. I figured that way it can't get out of hand. But she calls me all the time. I thought this was just another one of those calls. I thought she was trying to be dramatic, trying to get my attention. So I ignored her. *Madre de Dios,* she was in trouble, and I ignored her."

Jim didn't hesitate. He sat down next to Felipe and touched his shoulder. "You couldn't have known," he said softly. "Phil, you can't blame yourself for doing something you thought was best."

"She called me, too," Emily said, sitting down on Felipe's other side. "She left a message on my answering machine. I didn't call her back in time, either."

Felipe straightened up, trying hard to compose himself. Jim left his hand on his friend's shoulder, unembarrassed about offering what little warmth and comfort he could.

"How'd she get the drugs?" Jim asked.

"Her uncle made her take them," Felipe said. "He threatened Billy and forced her to shoot up. He wanted her hooked again, and back under his control." His face hardened, and his eyes glinted with a hatred so strong that Emily was taken aback. He turned to Jim. "Diego, I need you to help me, man. I need you to find that bastard and bring him in. So help me God, if I have to do it, I am afraid I will kill him. Please don't let me do that."

"I'll take care of it. Consider Hank Abbott already behind bars," Jim said, with a certainty in his voice that made Felipe relax slightly. "Where's Billy now?"

"With my mother," Felipe said. "I talked to Jewel before they took her into surgery. She was really out of it, but she was crazy with worry about Billy. She told me where he was hiding and asked me to get to him, to make sure he was safe—" His voice broke again. "She was bleeding internally, man, and her hip is fractured, both legs are broken, but all she could think about was her little boy." He closed his eyes. "God, please, give me another miracle. Give Jewel another chance— No, I was the one who let her down. Give *me* another chance. I know I don't deserve it…."

"You deserve it, Phil," Jim said softly. "You do deserve another chance, do you hear me? Everything's going to work out. Everything's going to be okay."

Emily looked up through the tears that were gathering in her eyes to find Jim watching her. But the instant their eyes met, he turned away and stood up.

"I'll call you from the station after I nail Uncle Hank," Jim told Felipe.

Felipe nodded. "Thanks, Diego."

"Be careful, Jim," Emily said.

He actually looked surprised at her words. How could he be surprised that she wanted him to take care? How could he not know that his safety was of the utmost importance to her?

He moved down the hall, and she stood up quickly, following him. "Jim, wait."

He stopped, turning slowly to face her.

"I love you," she said. "Will you come over later, so that we can talk?"

He jammed his hands into his pockets and looked down at the tile floor. "Nothing's changed, Em," he said softly.

"It can't hurt to talk," she said desperately.

He looked up at her then, his eyes dark with misery. "Yes, it can," he said. "It hurts like hell."

"Please—"

"I'm sorry."

He turned and walked away. Emily watched him go, too numb to move.

Everything's going to work out. You deserve another chance.

Deserve another chance.

I love you, Emily had told Jim before he walked out the door of her apartment.

You shouldn't, he'd said, his voice thick with emotion. *I don't deserve it.*

He didn't deserve her love. But why not?

Bob. It had to have something to do with Jim's brother, Bob.

He still felt responsible for Bob's death—so much so that he was determined to deny himself the chance to be happy. In a moment of weakness, he'd let his true hopes and desires come through, and he'd asked her to marry him. But long ago he'd painted himself into a guilt-ridden emotional corner, and he was trapped there, unable to break free. He couldn't marry her, because he didn't think he deserved more than the miserable, lonely life he'd purposely made for himself.

God, it was all so clear now.

Jim didn't think he deserved a chance to be happy, and Emily knew with stomach-wrenching certainty that talk alone wouldn't be enough to convince him that he was wrong. And if she couldn't convince him of that, everything was *not* going to work out.

At least not for her and Jim.

CHAPTER SIXTEEN

THE TELEPHONE was ringing when Emily opened the door to her apartment. But once again it wasn't Jim on the other end. It was Alex Delmore.

"Hey," he said, "you have plans for the next few days?"

"Um," Emily said, "I don't think so. Why?"

"I'm taking a few days off, sailing down the coast to Fort Myers," Alex told her. "We're lifting anchor in a few hours. Grab a bathing suit and your toothbrush and come along."

"I thought you weren't leaving until tomorrow," she said, her head awhirl. Alex wasn't supposed to go out sailing until tomorrow evening. What had made him change his plans?

There was sudden silence on the other end of the phone.

"You knew I was going sailing?" Alex finally said. "I don't remember mentioning it to you."

"I saw it in your calendar book last night," Emily said, the palms of her hands sweating. God, did he suspect her of spying on him?

But he laughed, and it seemed genuine. She felt a flood of relief. "Yeah, that's right," he said. "Of course. Well, my plans changed suddenly. I have to leave this afternoon."

Have to. Why else would he *have to,* unless he were meeting a shipment of drugs? Emily started sweating again.

She kept her voice light as she asked, "Going fishing again?"

"Fishing?" He was confused.

"Like you did last time," Emily said, trying hard to sound as if she didn't suspect him of being a drug smuggler. "In your dinghy, remember?"

"Oh, right, right," Alex said. "Fishing. Right. Yeah, I definitely will do some fishing."

Definitely.

The shipment must be coming in tonight.

"How about I have my driver pick you up in about two hours?" he asked.

What should she do? God, the police had wanted to plant a homing device that would help them track the *Home Free* by sending out a steady stream of beeps and blips over the radio waves. And Jim had talked about having a bug—a voice microphone—hidden on board the yacht. How were they going to do that in the next two hours, especially with Alex's crew preparing the ship for departure?

"Um…" she said, thinking hard and fast. "Dan's still in town, and I feel badly about going off without him."

Alex gave an exaggerated sigh. "He doesn't want us sleeping together, darling," he said. "I was hoping we could leave him home."

"He's very…protective," Emily said. "Please, may I ask him to join us?"

"Sure, why not?" Alex said, with a good-natured chuckle. "Bring him along. It'll be good practice for my self-control. Shall I have my driver get you?"

"No," Emily said. "No, I have...some errands to run. We'll meet you over at the *Home Free* by...what? Two o'clock?"

"Sounds good to me," Alex said. "See you then."

Emily slowly hung up the phone.

Jim was going to be mad as hell.

"I'M SORRY, DETECTIVE KEEGAN isn't here. He hasn't been in since early this morning." The large, unhappy-looking uniformed policeman behind the front desk barely even looked up at Emily as he answered her question.

She felt a rising wave of impatience—and fear. What if she couldn't find Jim? What if he wasn't available to come on the *Home Free* with her? Would she have to go by herself?

"Please, can you tell me when he'll be back," she said, "or how I can get in touch with him?"

"Nope. Sorry." The beefy man with the dour expression didn't sound one bit sorry. He turned away from the counter with his pile of papers and files.

"All right, then," Emily said evenly, "I'll talk to Lieutenant Bell instead."

That got him at least to focus his eyes in Emily's direction.

"The lieutenant's tied up at the moment," he said, and turned to walk out of the room.

"Excuse me," Emily said loudly, feeling her blood pressure shoot upward from frustration. "I'd like you to tell Lieutenant Bell that Emily Marshall is here to see her, and I'd like you to tell her that *now*, please."

"Sarge, Ms. Marshall is helping us with an important case," a familiar voice said. "I am sure the lieutenant will wish to be interrupted."

Emily turned around to see Felipe Salazar standing behind her. He'd buttoned his shirt and fixed his tie, but he still looked rumpled and weary.

"What are you doing here?" he said to Emily.

"How's Jewel?" Emily asked, searching his eyes, hoping he was bringing good news. "Is she out of danger?"

Felipe shook his head tiredly. "No." He took a deep breath. "They wouldn't let me near her. I was going crazy, sitting there in the waiting room. I had to do *something*, so…here I am. Has Diego brought that bastard in yet?"

That bastard—? He meant Jewel's uncle Hank. "I don't think so," she said.

"Lieutenant Bell will see you," the burly sergeant said, without a trace of apology in his voice. "Do you know where to go?"

"I'll walk her back," Felipe told the man, taking her elbow and steering her down the corridor.

Lieutenant Bell greeted Emily at the door to her office. "This morning Detective Keegan told me you wanted off this case," the older woman said, wasting no time on pleasantries, peering over the tops of her glasses at Emily.

"Well, Detective Keegan was wrong," Emily replied, unable to keep exasperation from showing in her voice. She could feel Felipe Salazar watching her curiously.

"Sit down." The lieutenant waved toward a pair of hard wooden chairs placed across from her desk. "I'd like you to come in, too, Detective."

As Emily and Felipe went into the room, Lieutenant Bell sat behind her desk. She was wearing pants today— loose-fitting khaki-colored slacks that had been tailored to fit her shorter-than-average height. "Keegan seemed to think that the situation had become too dangerous to allow a civilian—"

"Excuse me, Lieutenant," Emily said, leaning forward in her chair, "but a young girl I know is in the hospital, in intensive care, because of a nasty combination of crack and greed. I can't sit by and let Alex get away with bringing more cocaine into this city—especially not now. As dangerous as continuing with the investigation might be—and, to be perfectly honest, I believe this sudden higher level of danger is all in Jim Keegan's mind—I consider it *much* more dangerous to let Alex go on distributing illegal drugs."

Bell's pale eyes studied Emily steadily. Finally she shifted her position, crossing her legs and leaning back in her seat. "Okay, Ms. Marshall," she said coolly. "Tell me why you're here."

Quickly Emily told the lieutenant about Alex's phone call, and about his invitation for her to join him on the *Home Free*—and the implication that the drug shipment would be arriving sooner than they all had expected.

"Alex invited Jim along, too," Emily said. "You know, as Dan, my brother…" She glanced at her watch. It was already quarter past one. She took a deep breath, calming herself. "But I haven't been able to find Jim, and the ship's scheduled to sail in forty-five minutes."

Bell tapped a pencil on her desk. "There's no way I can get a court order to plant any kind of listening device on Delmore's yacht before two o'clock," she said. "But a signal transmitter, or homing device, is a different story. Emily, do you think you can get on the boat, plant the homing device and get off before Delmore sails?"

Get off—?

"I can do it," Felipe said. "Let me."

Emily glanced at him. "Alex's crew double as bodyguards," she said. "You won't get within ten yards of the yacht."

"And if you get on," Felipe said, "how will you get off?"

"Feigning a stomachache might do the trick," Bell suggested. "I can't think of anyone in their right mind who'd want to risk getting seasick on top of some kind of stomach virus. It shouldn't be too difficult."

"This is not a good idea, Lieutenant," Felipe said. "Jim wanted to keep Emily far away from Alexander Delmore."

"Do you have any alternative suggestions, Detective?" Bell asked acerbically.

"Yes," he said. "Wait until next time."

Emily turned to look at him. "And how many more young girls like Jewel will be hurt or—God help us— killed because of the drugs that'll be on the streets if we don't stop Alex today?"

She was playing hardball, and, as she'd known they would, her words hit him deeply.

"Wouldn't even just one be too many?" she added softly.

She knew from the look on his face that she'd won.

"I want her to wear a wire," he said tersely to Bell. "And I want to stay close by. I want to listen in. And I want Diego updated on the situation the moment he comes in or calls."

"Fine," Bell said shortly. "We don't have a whole lot of time. Take Ms. Marshall downstairs and get her set up."

JIM COULDN'T STOP thinking of Emily. He thought about her as he tracked down Jewel's scumbag of an uncle. He thought about her as he cuffed and Mirandaed the guy and stuffed him into the back seat of his car. He thought about her at every single traffic light. He thought about her as he drove, as he accelerated, as he braked, as he signaled for the turn into the precinct parking lot.

As he opened the back door of his car and motioned for Jewel's uncle to get out of the car, he thought about the welcoming warmth of Emily's smile. As he led Jewel's uncle up the steps and into the police station, he thought about the incredible blue of her eyes, and how with just one look she could make him forget everything and anything but the here and now.

And as he brought his prisoner to the desk to be booked, he thought of the way she had stood watching him in the waiting room at the hospital. He couldn't keep from thinking about the hurt in her eyes—hurt he alone was responsible for putting there. And that hurt wasn't going to disappear just because *he* disappeared.

He should have stayed away from her.

He should have, but he hadn't.

As Uncle Hank was led away to be fingerprinted and photographed, Jim closed his eyes, resting his head on his folded arms on top of the counter, for the first time all day allowing himself the luxury of imagining what it would be like to spend the rest of his life with Emily. Each night he'd sleep with her in his arms. Each morning he'd awaken to her soft smile. He'd never spend another moment alone, because even when she wasn't with him he'd carry her in his heart.

But that was only wishful thinking. Because no matter how much he wanted to turn that pipe dream into reality, the fact was, he couldn't escape the guilt and the blame.

All he could do now was stay the hell away from Emily, and hope to God that this time he hadn't hurt her beyond repair.

"Keegan."

Jim looked up to see Sergeant Curt Wolaski glaring at him from the other side of the counter. The big man tossed a folded piece of paper down in front of Jim. "Message from your pal Salazar," he said.

"Thanks," Jim said, but the sergeant had already turned away.

He unfolded the note and read it. And let out a stream of curses so pungent that heads turned in his direction from all over the room. Damn it, was Emily crazy? Did she *want* to get herself killed?

Fear hit him deep in his gut, and he turned and ran for the parking lot and his car.

His boots pounded the hot pavement, and his lungs strained as he pushed himself to the limit. He opened the car door and jumped in behind the wheel. He started the car with a roar, and threw it into gear before the engine had even finished turning over.

With a squeal of tires, Jim pulled out of the parking lot and onto the main road, heading toward the harbor—and Emily.

All his good intentions, all his plans to stay away from her, went right out the window. He wanted nothing more than to hold her in his arms and convince himself that she was safe.

EMILY HADN'T BEEN free from Alex's company since she'd come on board the *Home Free*. She was carrying the homing device in her purse, but she hadn't had even the smallest opportunity to plant it somewhere on the yacht.

"Are you *sure* your brother said he'd meet you here at the harbor?" Alex asked again, scanning the crowded docks impatiently.

"He *said* he'd be here," Emily lied, hoping against hope that Jim would suddenly appear. He still hadn't checked in at the precinct when Felipe dropped her off here, so there was no way he could have known to come down to the marina. Still, she couldn't help hoping.

"We really have to get going," Alex said.

Emily glanced at her watch—it was five after two. "Can't you give him another ten minutes?" she asked.

He didn't look happy. "Emily, to be perfectly honest, I've got a deadline…." His voice trailed off, and he looked uncomfortable, as if he were aware he'd said too much.

"Five minutes?" she said. "Please?"

She knew what she had to do. She had to go down to the head and use the privacy the tiny bathroom provided to hide the homing device in there. Then she'd come back on deck, the five minutes would have passed, Jim *still* wouldn't have appeared, and she'd regretfully tell Alex she couldn't desert her brother—she'd have to stay behind. She'd sadly wave goodbye as Alex sailed off down the coast, toward his illegal rendezvous, with the homing device signaling his every move to the police and the Coast Guard.

It just might work.

Alex cursed under his breath, and Emily looked up at him, surprised. She followed his line of vision to the end of the dock, where a familiar-looking dark-haired man, followed by several large men who looked like bodyguards, was walking toward them.

Emily felt a wave of panic, and she took a steadying breath. "Isn't that Vincent Marino?" she asked for Felipe's benefit, knowing he was listening in via the tiny radio microphone that was hidden in the delicate metal petals of the rose-shaped silver pin he'd given her to wear.

"Yeah," Alex said shortly. "It sure is."

"Were you expecting him?" Emily asked.

"Nope," Alex said. He looked scared. He looked the way she felt—like he wanted nothing more than to start running and not look back.

For one brief, crazy moment, Emily actually considered leaping over the side of the boat into the murky waters of the harbor. But before she could move, Marino was climbing on board the *Home Free* to stand right beside her, and her opportunity was gone.

"Mr. Delmore," Marino said with feigned politeness. He turned to look at Emily. "And Miss Marshall. A pleasure, as always. News of your upcoming nuptials was in the morning paper. May I offer my congratulations?"

"Get the hell off my yacht," Alex snarled. His hands were shaking, and he didn't look half as confident as he sounded.

Marino shook his head, making soft *tsk*ing sounds. "Such manners," he said. "It's a wonder you got anywhere in the business world."

"Get off," Alex said again, "or I'll have you thrown off."

There was sweat on his upper lip.

Emily was in way over her head. Jim had been right. She was foolish to have tried this.

Marino laughed at Alex. It was a harsh, ugly sound.

"Cast off," he ordered Alex's crew. "We're going for a little sail. A little pleasure cruise. That all right with you, Delmore?"

It was not all right. Alex snapped his fingers. "Throw

them over the side," he ordered his crew. But no one came to his aid. They all just continued preparing the yacht for departure. His voice rose with outrage and fear. "I said, get them out of here. Protect me. Do your jobs!"

Marino just kept laughing. "They *are* doing their jobs," he said. "They work for me now. You really should pay higher wages, Delmore. Didn't you know loyalty is directly related to the size of a paycheck?"

The sky was a hazy blue, and the sun glared off the gleaming wooden deck. The harbor was bustling with activity—there were people walking not five yards from the *Home Free*. It was the middle of the day, in a public place. It didn't seem possible that they were being kidnapped or hijacked or yacht-jacked, or whatever this was. But the hard-edged glint in Vincent Marino's eyes was frightening. Emily had an awful feeling that if she didn't get off here and now, she wasn't ever going to get off the yacht—at least not alive.

She walked calmly toward the gangplank. "Alex, it looks like Dan isn't going to make it," she said, unable to hide the breathlessness of fear in her voice, "so I better stay home. Call me when you get back—"

Marino grabbed her by the arm and pushed her none too gently toward one of the lounge chairs that were open on the deck. He shoved her down into it.

"Sorry, babe," he said. "But you're coming along for the ride."

Emily opened her mouth and screamed, but Marino was next to her in a flash, silencing her by covering her mouth with his beefy hand. He pressed a deadly-looking knife against her side, down where no one on the dock or the other ships could see it, and she felt the tip prick her.

"Next time you scream," he told her, almost matter-of-factly, "I'll give you something to scream about, you understand?"

Emily nodded slowly.

FELIPE SALAZAR shouted into the radio.

"I *know* we didn't think we'd need the boat until later, but we need it *now,* damn it," he said. "I called three hours ago, and you said you had a powerboat. You didn't say anything about the fact that its engine was lying in pieces on the dock—"

"We've got the Coast Guard and the harbormaster ready to move in and intercept at the edge of the breakwater," the dispatcher told him.

"No!" Felipe said, adding several choice comments about *that* suggestion in Spanish. "Marino's got a small army of men on that ship. We have to assume they're armed with semiautomatics. And what do the Coast Guard have? Small handguns, and maybe a tranquilizer rifle? No way do I want to see the outcome of *that* gun battle, *muchas gracias.* Besides, we've got a civilian on board the *Home Free.* We don't want to risk a potential hostage situation."

"We can get you one of the Coast Guard's speedboats," the dispatcher suggested.

Felipe gritted his teeth. "Oh, that would be most inconspicuous," he said. "No, I need an *unmarked* boat, and I need it thirty minutes ago!"

JIM RECOGNIZED the nondescript olive-green police surveillance van on the far side of the parking lot, and he pulled up to it, his tires sending a spray of little pebbles into the air as he stopped.

Leaping from his car, he hammered on the back door of the van until it opened.

The interior was dimly lit and crowded. Two other detectives sat with Phil Salazar in the glow from the high-tech equipment. The tape deck was whirring, and the receive signal lights were lit. Emily wasn't there, and Jim felt a stab of panic.

"Where is she?" he demanded harshly. "Delmore's boat isn't at its mooring, and it's not at the dock, and I *know* you'd never let her sail with that son of a bitch so where is she— Oh, God."

The look on Salazar's face said everything Jim didn't want to hear.

"Jim, you have got to stay calm," Felipe said. "Going ballistic on me will not help this situation."

Jim took a deep breath. "Situation," he repeated. "So. We have a situation, do we?" He could feel his blood pounding angrily through his veins. So help him God, if anything happened to Emily…

"She was going to plant the homing device and get off the ship," Felipe said. "But then…Marino came on board."

Vincent Marino. The organized-crime boss who was nicknamed the Shark, due to his lack of mercy. Oh, God, no.

"From the conversations that we've overheard, Marino and Delmore are not on friendly terms," Felipe said. His jaw tightened. "It's my guess that Marino means to abscond with Delmore's arriving shipment of drugs. And it would not surprise me if Marino also intends to use the opportunity to remove Delmore from the crack market—permanently."

Jim felt dizzy. Jesus, this was worse than he'd

imagined. "Get me a helicopter," he ordered huskily. "I've gotta get her out of there."

But Salazar was shaking his head. "*Think,* Diego," he said emphatically. "If you go after the *Home Free* in a police helicopter, what do you think is going to happen? You're gonna get her killed, man, and yourself, too."

Jim took a deep breath. Phil was right. He was right. Going after Emily, guns blazing, wasn't the solution. He had to slow down for a minute. He had to *think.*

"Where are we going?" Emily's voice said clearly via the surveillance microphone she was wearing. "Where are you taking us?"

She sounded so cool, so in control, but Jim knew better. He knew she was scared to death. God, he was scared to death for her. His throat tightened.

"We're gonna have a little party with a few of your fiancé's buddies," Marino answered. "I hate to break it to you, but you may not want to marry your little Alex after you meet these guys."

Emily didn't answer. Jim closed his eyes, wishing the microphone she was wearing could receive, as well as send. He wanted to talk to her, to tell her to play along with Marino, to tell her not to antagonize him.

Listening in like this was torture. If he'd ever experienced payback for what he'd done to Bob, this had to be it. God, if something happened to Emily, if Marino killed her... He loved her with his life, and without her his life would be over. Just like Bob's.

Except not more than a few hours ago, Jim had been willing to spend the rest of his life without Emily—a life that would have been cold and lonely and bleak as hell. He had been willing to do voluntarily what Marino could do permanently with a single bullet. He'd assumed that life without Emily was what he deserved.

"Oh, and if you're thinking about jumping overboard," Marino said, his voice getting louder as he leaned closer to Emily, "it's nearly two miles to shore. *And* I hear there're sharks in these waters."

"Apparently there are sharks out of the water, too," Emily said quietly. Jim held his breath. Was Marino going to get angry? But he only laughed, and Jim exhaled noisily.

"Ever hear of survival of the fittest, sweetheart?" Marino said. "I'd much rather be a shark than a blowfish like little Alex. You, you're more like a flounder—soft and delicious, and totally defenseless. One bite and you're history, you read me?"

"Yes," Emily said softly.

Jim read him, too, loud and clear. He swallowed, listening intently to the silence. Then Emily spoke again, almost inaudibly, and one of the detectives leapt forward to turn up the volume on the receiver.

"He's gone," she breathed. "Felipe, I'm not sure what to do. The homing device is still in my purse. I never had a chance to plant it anywhere. It's turned on, though, and you should be receiving its signal." She took a long, shaky breath.

"I'm not sure if I should try to jump overboard, or if I should just wait and see what's going to happen," she continued. "They have Alex down below. I think Marino's men beat him up." She was quiet for a moment. "I honestly can't imagine that Marino's going let me stay alive after everything I've seen and heard here."

Another pause. "Felipe, I need you to tell Jim that I love him. And make sure he doesn't come out here and

get himself killed because of me. This was my mistake—
Please, I don't want him to die because I made a bad
decision."

"Hold on, Em," Jim whispered, even though Emily
couldn't possibly hear him. "Don't give up. I'm on my
way." He turned to Felipe. "We need a boat. Something
big enough to hide all this stuff down below," he said,
gesturing at the equipment that was receiving the signals
from both Emily's surveillance microphone and the
homing device.

"We're working on that," Felipe told him.

Jim's eyes flashed, and his voice rose dangerously.
"What, am I hearing you tell me that Lieutenant Bell set
this thing up and she didn't make damn sure you had a
boat?"

"I'm sorry, man. There was a snafu and—"

"Get this equipment ready to travel and meet me down
at the dock," Jim snapped, pushing his way out of the van.

Felipe jumped to work. The other two detectives exchanged a long look, glad as hell that *they* weren't
wearing Lieutenant Bell's shoes.

IT TOOK EMILY several moments to understand what the
commotion was about. She sidled closer to the naviga-
tor's station, trying to eavesdrop.

Marino was arguing with one of his crew about some
problem they were having with the ship's radio.

The vessel they were to rendezvous with had contacted them via radio. But they were having some diffi-
culty communicating. They were picking up strange
interference.

It was the transmission from the homing device that
was in her purse, Emily realized with a wave of fear. The

scratchy interference faded in and out with the same pulsating beat as the homing device's signal.

How soon would it be before Vincent Marino figured that out? How soon until he searched the ship and found the homing device in her handbag?

The handbag, Emily realized with dread, that she had unwittingly left over on the other side of the deck, next to the lounge chairs...

"Turn that damn thing off," she heard Marino say. "It's annoying the hell out of me."

The static was shut off, and Marino came out on deck, followed by one of his bodyguards.

"Could be the result of another radio signal," Emily heard the bodyguard say.

Marino stopped and turned toward the man, his foot mere inches from her handbag. Emily felt the palms of her hands start to sweat.

"Bring Delmore up here," Marino commanded. "We'll find out soon enough if he's got another radio on board."

He stepped back, and his foot bumped the handbag.

Emily could feel her heart pounding.

He looked down and noticed it.

Kick it to the side, she silently implored him. Don't pick it up....

He bent over and picked it up.

"Whoa, this weighs a ton. What do you have in here?" he said to Emily. "Your bowling ball?"

Her throat was so dry, she couldn't speak. She shook her head no. Please, God, don't let him look inside....

"Your nose is getting sunburned," he said. It was obvious from his mocking tone that he was toying with her. He was trying to make her squirm, and getting pleasure from it. "You might want to put some sunblock on."

Emily couldn't answer. She couldn't move.

"You got some sunblock in here?" he asked, opening her bag. "Jeez, you got everything else, don't you?"

This was it. It was all over. He was going to find the homing device, and he was going to kill her.

"Yep, here it is, right on top," Marino said, pulling out a bottle of number fifteen sunblock and waving it at her. He put it back inside, closed the zipper and tossed the bag to her.

Instinctively Emily reached for it, to catch it. But she didn't want to catch it. She didn't want it on this ship. So, when the canvas fabric hit her fingers, she fumbled.

The handbag—and the homing device—went over the side of the *Home Free,* and into the dark blue Gulf waters.

"Damn," Marino said with disgust. "Didn't anyone ever teach you to catch?"

Emily stared down into the water. Her handbag had already disappeared from view.

Vincent Marino would never find the homing device now.

Of course, it was also true that without that homing device, Jim and Felipe would probably never find *her.*

"COME ON, COME ON," Jim said, taking an armload of equipment from Felipe and hurrying his partner and the other two detectives onto a sleek white powerboat.

He opened the throttle and headed away from the dock at a speed that made the other boat owners shake their fists.

"Where did you get this thing?" Felipe shouted over the roar of the powerful engine.

Jim slipped his sunglasses over his eyes as he rounded the buoy that marked the exit from the harbor. "I hot-wired it," he shouted back matter-of-factly.

"You *stole* it?"

"Borrowed," Jim replied. "For official police business."

"Whatever you call it, what you did is illegal. I oughta arrest you, man," Felipe said.

"Why don't you go below instead," Jim shouted, "and make sure Winstead and Harper are setting that equipment up right?"

As Felipe started down, Winstead stuck his head up through the companionway. "We have a potential problem," he announced. "The signal from the homing device just went dead."

Jim's knuckles whitened as he gripped the steering wheel tighter. "Phil, take over for me," he said, pulling the throttle back. The boat still skimmed across the water, but no longer at a breakneck speed. The noise of the engine dropped considerably.

"Are you going to call for a helicopter?" Felipe asked as the two men switched places.

Jim nodded tersely. "I want one warmed up and ready to go at a moment's notice."

"When you radio in," Felipe said, squinting out across the glare on the water, "ask if the hospital called with any word about Jewel."

Jim had damn near forgotten about Jewel. He nodded again, touching Felipe briefly on the shoulder, then turned to go below.

Winstead and Harper both had headphones on and were listening intently to the conversation coming in from Emily's radio microphone.

Winstead glanced up at Jim, handing him a third pair of headphones. "They've made physical contact with the second ship," he told him. "Vincent Marino is on a first-name basis with these guys. It appears that he's intending to take his men and Delmore's drug money and depart on this other ship."

"What about Delmore and Emily?" Jim asked, slipping on the headphones.

"Oh, my God! Alex!" he heard Emily say. In a lower voice, surely for their benefit, she added, "He's been beaten up. His face is a mess, and I think his arm's been broken. He can't even stand up."

"See what you get for screwing with me?" Marino's voice said. "See what you get?"

"I'm sorry," Delmore sobbed. "I'm sorry. Please… please, I'll cut you in from now on, I promise."

"Too late," Marino declared. "You had your chance to do business with me. Now I'm doing business with you, and it's in my best interest to cut you out of the picture entirely. You get my drift here?"

"Oh, God," Emily breathed, and Delmore began to cry in earnest. "They're rigging some kind of bomb to the yacht's engine."

Jim pushed the headphones off one ear, reached for the radio and keyed the mike that connected him directly to St. Simone's police headquarters. Briefly he explained about the bomb, and how they'd lost the signal from the homing device. "I need a chopper," he said, "up and over these waters, helping us find the *Home Free*."

"We've got a chopper standing by," the dispatcher replied over the squawky radio speaker.

Jim passed the microphone to Harper. "Give them the last known reading and heading of the vessel, so at least they'll know where to start looking."

Over the headphones, he could hear Marino say, "Take

care of the shortwave radio. We don't want them sending
out any SOSs."

"You're just going to leave us here to die?" Emily asked.

CHAPTER SEVENTEEN

"ACTUALLY, NO," Vincent Marino said. "I'm going to leave you and your fiancé already dead."

His words came as an icy shock, even though Emily had been waiting for them ever since Marino had come aboard the yacht. She hadn't been thinking about *whether* he was going to kill them, she'd been thinking in terms of *when*.

Now all of the crew were on the other boat, an enormous speedboat, with the exception of Marino and one other man. And Alex and Emily.

Alex had crumpled into a pile on the deck. At Marino's words, he cried even harder.

"Looks like you didn't really need that sunblock after all, did you?" Marino said to Emily with a laugh, ignoring Alex's pleas for mercy. He turned to the man standing next to him. "Waste them."

Emily had never faced death before, but she knew right now she was looking at it dead-on, straight in the eye.

Death wore sunglasses and a conservative dark suit. Death had a long, dangerous-looking gun that he pulled from the holster nestled under his right arm. Death was left-handed, Emily thought inanely.

But he wasn't death. He was a man. He was human.

The man turned his head slightly and looked from her to Alex, and Emily knew in that flash of a moment that he was squeamish about shooting a woman. As he pointed his gun at Alex, Emily dived for the companion-way doors and threw herself down the stairs into the yacht's cabin. She tripped and hit the wall with her shoulder and chest. The pin that held the microphone and the miniature radio dug painfully through her shirt and into her skin.

She heard the gunshot, felt the recoil, and heard Alex scream in pain. God, they'd shot Alex, and she was next.

"Go after her!" she heard Marino say as she scrambled down the hall and into the room Alex used as an office.

"The clock's running, Mr. M.," she heard the other man say. "We have less than ten minutes. She's not going anywhere. Let's get out of here."

Were his words a trick to make her relax, to make her believe he wasn't coming after her?

Alex kept a gun in his office. Emily knew he kept a gun in here. And, by God, if they were going to kill her, she was going to go down fighting.

Her breath came in sobs as she searched Alex's desk. The front drawer was locked, and she used a letter opener and a paperweight to pry it open.

And there was Alex's gun, small but deadly, lying amid the paper clips and pencils.

It felt cold and hard in her hands.

She held it up, supporting her right hand with her left, aiming it at the office door, praying it was loaded.

But then she heard the hum of an engine, and felt the *Home Free* rock slightly in the other boat's wake. She peeked out one of the portholes.

They were leaving!

Still holding the gun, she opened the door and slowly went out into the corridor. The yacht was silent. But not dead silent. There was a hissing sound, the sound of white noise, or interference. It was coming from the shortwave radio.

The yacht's radio had been smashed, hit with some kind of heavy object, the microphone pulverized. But it was receiving *something*. She turned the knob marked Volume, and the hissing got louder. She tried to adjust the tuning, but nothing happened. The hiss didn't subside, and the needle didn't move.

JIM'S HANDS WERE SHAKING. He was going on faith here, purely on faith. He'd heard only one gunshot. He'd heard someone try to talk Marino into leaving. But all he'd heard from Emily in the past two grueling minutes was silence.

"Come on, Em," he muttered. "Tell me what you're doing. Tell me you're okay. Tell me you're not lying somewhere on that boat, wounded…." Or worse.

"The chopper pilot is leaving the airport," Harper said. "He'll be over the harbor in about ten minutes."

"That's not soon enough," Jim said.

"He's fighting winds coming in from the west," Harper said apologetically. "He's doing the best he can."

"Emily, talk to me, damn it!" Jim growled. Adrenaline was surging through him, but there wasn't one damned thing he could do to help her. She was out there, some-where, on a boat wired to explode any minute, any time.

"Jim? Felipe? Are you receiving me?"

Emily was alive.

Both Harper and Winstead cheered. Jim closed his

eyes briefly. Thank God. Her signal wasn't the greatest—
it was as if she were speaking from a long way away,
rather than into a microphone that was located just underneath her chin.

"I fell and landed on the mike," she said, her voice
shaking slightly, "and I don't even know if it's still
working, but I'm hoping that it is. Marino and his men
are gone, Alex was shot in the chest. He's bleeding all
over the place. He's still alive, but just barely."

The signal from her mike faded slightly, and Winstead
worked furiously to bring it back in.

"There's a digital clock on the bomb," Emily reported,
"and it's counting down by seconds. Right now it says
seven minutes and forty-eight seconds. Forty-seven.
Forty-six."

Jim synchronized his watch to the sound of her voice.

"The shortwave radio is receiving *something*," she
said, "but there's a lot of interference. It seems to be
stuck somewhere around the 20."

Jim quickly flipped the shortwave to that frequency
and keyed the mike. "Emily, can you hear me?" he said.

"Jim! Oh, God, you're there! You're really out there! I
can hear you! The reception's not great, but I can hear you!"

"Emily, we're more than ten minutes away from you.
We're not going to reach you before the bomb is set to
blow. Does the *Home Free* still have a dinghy? Or a
lifeboat?"

"Oh, Jim, I'm so sorry about this—"

"Em, we don't have a lot of time here," Jim said. "I
need you to stay calm and fill me in on the situation."

"Jim, I love you—" Emily's voice broke. "For a while,
I didn't think I'd get a chance to tell you that ever again."

"Yeah, I know," he said hoarsely. "I didn't think I'd

get a chance to tell you that I love you, too. And I do, Em. I love you so much that it's killing me. I don't think I can live without you, Emily, so help me out here, please. Is there a lifeboat?"

"No," she said. "There was a dinghy, but they took it with them."

"Okay," Jim said. "Listen carefully, Em. I want you to find a life preserver, put it on, and swim as hard and as fast as you can, away from the ship. Do you hear me?"

"And just leave Alex to die? Jim, I can't do that."

"Emily, damn it, save yourself," Jim rasped. "You can't take Delmore into the water with you. If he's bleeding the way you said he was, you'll be shark bait. Hell, if he's bleeding the way you said he was, he doesn't have a chance. So *save yourself.* Don't die for a man who's already as good as dead."

"You don't know his condition," Emily said. "Maybe he is going to die. But maybe he's not. Maybe he'll make it. He deserves—"

"He deserves *nothing.*"

"You're wrong," Emily said. "Everyone deserves a second chance. Even Alex. Maybe…maybe I can disarm the bomb."

Fear made the hair stand up on the back of Jim's neck. "Don't touch that bomb!"

"Isn't there someone who can talk me through it?" Emily asked. "Don't the police have a specialist or someone who can tell me what to do?"

Seven minutes and two seconds. One second. Seven minutes even.

"Emily, get away from the boat. Do it *now.*"

Harper leaned over to Jim. "We have the bomb squad team leader standing by at police headquarters."

Six minutes fifty-four seconds.

"Em, please," Jim said desperately. "Delmore doesn't deserve the effort."

Emily didn't answer.

"Emily? Are you there?"

"I'm here," she said. "And I disagree. Are you going to let me talk to the bomb expert or not?"

Jim gritted his teeth. "Connect them," he ordered Harper.

EMILY LEANED over the engine, staring down at the bomb. The digital clock read six minutes and three seconds. She'd spent thirty of her precious seconds describing the bomb to the demolitions expert, a man with a slight French accent, named Jean Dumont.

"Carefully remove the housing," Dumont said in his elegant voice, over the crackling interference of the radio, "but don't touch any of the wires."

"Okay," Emily said, brushing the sweat out of her eyes. "I did it."

"Emily, are you there?" Dumont said. "Your last transmission was breaking up."

Emily tapped at the microphone in the pin she was wearing. "Hello?" she said. "Do you read me now?"

Jim's voice broke in over the radio receiver. "Emily, we've lost your signal. Dumont is going to continue to give you instructions, but he can't hear your reply. None of us can—the mike has gone dead. Please, I'm begging you. Get off the yacht. I love you. Do you hear what I'm saying? Now get *out* of there."

"I love you, too," Emily whispered, feeling her eyes fill with tears.

Dumont's voice came back on. "Emily, inside the

housing you will see four wires. Red, green, blue and yellow. Do not touch the red or the yellow, do you understand?"

Emily stared at the bomb. Yes, there were four wires.

But they were all blue.

JIM STOOD ON DECK with his legs spread, braced against the up-and-down motion of the powerboat. He scanned the horizon with a pair of field glasses, searching for any sign of the *Home Free.*

The numbers on his watch ticked down, faster and faster now, heading toward zero.

Forty-seven seconds. Forty-six. Forty-five. Forty-four...

In the distance, he could hear the sound of the approaching chopper. He swung his binoculars back toward the east, and he could see it, still too far away, coming in low to the water, and fast. But not fast enough.

Felipe doggedly held the powerboat in a southwesterly direction, following the course heading that the location signal on board the *Home Free* had indicated before it had gone dead.

Harper stuck his head up from the companionway. "Dumont's finished," he said. "If Emily was disarming the bomb, and if she did everything Dumont told her to do correctly, they've got the job done in time. Oh, and Salazar, the hospital called the precinct, looking for you. Your friend's condition's improved."

Felipe said a quick prayer of thanks in Spanish, and Jim glanced over at him.

"Send an extra word or two up there for Emily, while you're at it," Jim said.

"I have been," Felipe said.

Jim looked at his watch. Seventeen seconds. Sixteen. Fifteen. Fourteen.

Out on the horizon, farther south than west, Jim caught sight of what might have been the tip of a mast. He shouted at Felipe, pointing in the mast's direction.

Ten. Nine. Eight.

As they roared toward the ship, more and more of it appeared above the line of the horizon, as if the sea were opening up and spitting it out.

Seven.

Please...

Six.

...God...

Five.

...let...

Four.

...her...

Three.

...be...

Two.

...safe.

One.

The *Home Free*—and it was definitely Delmore's yacht that Jim had spotted—sat at the edge of the horizon, facing into the wind, perfectly still, perfectly calm, perfectly—

The yacht exploded, sending a column of fire up into the air. The sound followed several seconds later, a rumbling roar of noise that echoed across the water.

Jim slowly lowered the binoculars and stared numbly at the thick black smoke that poured from the debris where the ship had once been.

Harper and Winstead came up on deck and stood there silently.

Felipe was the first to speak. "Do you think she got off in time, man?"

Jim shook his head. "I don't know," he said quietly. "God, I honestly don't know."

The thought of Emily dead was overwhelming. Jim felt shockingly empty, totally bereft.

How could the sun be shining so brightly? How could the sky be such a deep shade of blue? Without Emily, colors couldn't possibly exist. Without Emily, life was a single shade of gray.

The powerboat bounced higher over a large swell, and Jim stumbled. His legs felt useless and weak, so he sat down heavily on the bench that lined the deck.

"Hey!" Felipe said. "Are you giving up on me, man? Come on, get those field glasses working. We're getting closer. I know she's out here somewhere. I feel it in my bones, Diego. God's gonna give us a two-miracle day."

Overhead, the chopper made ever-widening circles around the smoking debris. Harper went back down into the cabin to talk with the pilot on the radio.

Jim stood up as Felipe slowed the boat to a crawl.

A two-miracle day? Why not try for three? Because if Emily was still alive, Jim was going to make damn sure he never walked away from her again.

He had told her not to throw her life away for a man who was as good as dead. But wasn't that exactly what he himself had been doing all these years? Because Bob was dead, Jim had been depriving himself of happiness. He'd been walking around more dead than alive himself, letting his guilt control him.

But that hadn't brought Bob back. He could spend the next four hundred years in hell, and that *still* wouldn't bring Bob back.

Bob was dead. End of story. End of Bob's story, anyway. It didn't have to be the end of Jim's.

"Come on, Emily," Jim murmured, using the binoculars to search the water. "Where are you?"

Harper burst up from down below. "The chopper pilot says he's spotted something to the south."

Felipe gunned the boat, turning sharply toward where the helicopter was hovering.

Jim's mouth was dry. Through the binoculars he could see *something* in the water. Something orange and brown. Was it a life jacket? Was it Emily? Or was it just some debris from the explosion?

Everyone deserves a second chance, Emily had said. Please, God, Jim thought, let me have mine. Prove to me you think I'm worth it....

"Can't you make this thing go any faster?" he shouted at Felipe.

"Hang on." His partner rode the throttle, giving the boat surges of even greater speed, and creating a very rocky ride. Jim steadied himself against the railing, focusing and refocusing the binoculars on that floating splotch of orange.

There was definitely something brown in the middle. No, now it wasn't brown, it was lighter. Skin colored. A flick of his finger brought it sharply into focus.

It was Emily's face. She was looking directly at the powerboat.

"She's alive!" Jim grabbed Winstead and kissed him on the top of his shiny bald head.

"All right!" Felipe shouted, holding up one hand to Jim for a high five. "All *right!*"

Jim leaned down and shouted into the cabin, "Harper, we found her! She's alive!"

He no longer needed the binoculars to see her. He leaned over the rail toward her, as if those few extra inches would get him to her faster.

As they drew nearer and Felipe slowed the boat, Jim dived over the side and swam under the water, toward Emily. He surfaced four feet away from her and flicked his wet hair back, out of his eyes.

"I knew you'd come," she said.

He swam closer. "I love you," he said.

Her hair was wet and lank against her pale face. She had smudges of soot on her forehead and her cheeks. But her eyes were the color of heaven, and Jim had never seen her look so beautiful.

She met his eyes steadily. "Do you love me enough to forgive yourself?"

Jim didn't hesitate. "I sure as hell am going to try. Will you help me?"

Emily nodded. "Every day, for as long as you need me to."

He moved even closer. "How about every night?"

She smiled at him then, with her pure, sweet, sexy-as-hell smile. "You don't need any help there, Detective."

The powerboat drifted closer, and Jim reached up and grabbed the side. Pulling Emily close with his other arm, he kissed her.

BY THE TIME Jim drove Emily home, it was sunset. With his arm around her shoulders, they climbed the stairs to the second-floor landing—and nearly got run over by Carly Wilson.

"Oops! Sorry," she said. "I'm in a real rush. Mac's waiting for me downstairs."

A truck horn sounded, as if emphasizing her words.

Carly rolled her eyes. "What a romantic guy. He couldn't even get out of his damned pickup truck and walk me upstairs—tonight of all nights."

"What's happening tonight?" Emily asked.

Carly sighed dramatically. "I know I said I wasn't going to do it, but...Mac and I got married today," she said. "Isn't that the stupidest thing you've ever heard? We're driving down to Key West for a two-week honeymoon." She laughed. "At least I know the marriage will last *that* long."

"Maybe this time it'll work out," Emily said.

"Yeah, sure," Carly said with a laugh. She looked from Emily to Jim and back. "Well, look at you two." Carly crossed her arms and leaned against the railing, apparently forgetting that she was supposed to be in a hurry. "Aren't *you* friendly? Jeez, my sister and I still can't get within six feet of each other."

"He's not my brother," Emily said.

Carly leaned forward. "Come again?"

"Carly, meet Jim Keegan," Emily said. "He's a detective on the St. Simone police force. When you met him before, he was undercover. He was only pretending to be my brother."

Carly looked from Jim to Emily. "What's he pretending to be now?"

"I intend to be Emily's husband," Jim said. "And I'm not pretending."

Carly nodded slowly. "When I get back from Key West, you're going to have to tell me the whole story," she said to Emily. "I have a feeling it's going to be a *real* good one."

The horn beeped again, and with a wave Carly was gone.

"She doesn't honestly think her marriage is only going

to last a few weeks, does she?" Jim asked as Emily unlocked her door and pushed it open.

Emily shrugged. "With Carly, you never know. Her average for a marriage is only about fifteen months."

Jim closed the door behind them, then led Emily over to the couch. He sat down, pulling her onto his lap. "When *we* get married," he said, tracing her lips with his thumb, "I intend for it to be forever."

Emily smiled. "That sounds just about long enough." She leaned forward and kissed him.

His smile faded, and his eyes became serious. "I was really glad that you got off the *Home Free* when you did."

Emily laced her fingers in his hair. "Alex died," she told him quietly, "while I was talking to Dumont, the bomb expert." She met his eyes. "After my microphone stopped working, and I realized I wasn't going to be able to defuse the bomb, I was going to put Alex into a wet suit and take him over the side with me, but…he was already dead."

"Four SWAT teams intercepted Marino and his men," Jim said. "He resisted and was killed. The boat they were in was loaded with cocaine. The other men are going to get sent away for years."

"So it's over," Emily said. She smiled ruefully. "Until the next drug lord comes to town."

"The fight goes on," Jim said. "We do the best we can. And today we did one hell of a lot. Thanks to you." He smiled at her. "Of course, thanks to you, I've also got one hell of an ulcer starting."

"I'm sorry," she murmured.

"It's okay," he said, kissing her gently. "But next time you decide to make a major decision that involves risking your life, I'd appreciate it if you'd at least talk to me first. This relationship *is* a partnership. Do you hear what I'm saying?"

Emily laughed. "Loud and clear."

Jim leaned his head back, nestling her head underneath his chin. He closed his eyes and sighed. "Did we sleep last night? I don't think we slept last night. I'm exhausted."

Emily kissed his neck, then stood up. She held out her hand to him. "Let's go to bed."

Jim took her hand and kissed it lightly. "I'll be in in a second," he said. "I have to make a quick phone call."

The pain was back in his eyes, and Emily felt a wild burst of frustration. Was she going to wake up in the middle of the night and find him sitting out here again, all alone, in the dark?

She went into the bedroom and, leaving the door ajar, began to undress. If that happened again, she vowed, she was going to get up and sit with him. She was going to hold him and love him and...

From the living room, she heard Jim's voice as he spoke on the telephone. "Hi, uh, Ma? It's Jimmy," she heard him say, and she froze.

"Yeah, *Jimmy*," he said huskily. "Surprise, huh? Yeah, look, I, um...I'm getting married." There was a long pause, and then he laughed. "Yeah, *married*. Can you believe it? Her name's Emily, and you're gonna love her, Ma. God knows I do. Look, I was wondering if, um, if you'd maybe want to come to the wedding— You *would?* That's *great*. That's really great. And Molly and Shannon, too? You really think they'd— They'd want to come, too, huh? That's...that's great. Look, Ma, we had a really rough day, and I've got to go, but I'll call you in a few days, okay?" Another pause. Then Jim's voice caught slightly as he said, "I love you, too, Ma."

Emily slipped quietly into bed, using the sheet to wipe away the tears of happiness that had suddenly filled her eyes.

And when Jim came into the room and climbed into bed beside her, she welcomed him with a kiss and an embrace.

The healing had begun.

* * * * *

A MAN TO DIE FOR

CHAPTER ONE

July

IT WAS QUARTER PAST MIDNIGHT before Carrie Brooks turned off the computer in the Sea Circus office, twenty past before she turned off the lights.

With the laser printout of her environmental coastal report safely tucked in her backpack, Carrie stopped only to pick up the tranquilizer rifle she was borrowing for tomorrow's expedition to the edge of the Everglades. She was leading one of her well-known wildlife preserve tours for a group of college professors from Ohio. The rifle wasn't really necessary. She wasn't planning on using it, but it made for good show, and it *would* be pleasant to have on hand should any of the gators get nasty, or should one of the professors get careless.

One of the rifle's double barrels was loaded, she realized as she locked the office door behind her and headed down the rickety wooden steps into the hot, humid summer night. That wastecase, Simon, had no doubt left the gun loaded, and returned it to the Sea Circus office without even putting the safety on. Didn't he realize it was a weapon? Just because it shot tranquilizer darts meant for sharks or gators didn't mean it couldn't hurt or even kill a human.

Carrie put the safety on, locking it into place as she started across the Sea Circus grounds.

She had to be up and alert and at the marina by six in the morning. By the time she got to her car, drove to the gate, punched in her security code, opened the gate, drove her car out, closed the car, restarted the alarm system and drove all the way home to her little apartment on the other side of town, she'd stand a chance at getting four solid hours of sleep.

Four wasn't too bad, she thought as she cut across the lawn next to the main aquarium tank. She'd be able to nap tomorrow afternoon, maybe take the boat back out and just let it drift. She'd close her eyes in the soft sunshine and work on her tan....

Carrie froze. Was that the sound of laughter that had floated across the sandy grounds, or had it been some lonely seabird, or the sound of the surf?

Listening hard, Carrie heard it again. Laughter. Laughter, followed by a stream of rapid-fire Spanish, then a plaintive voice, complaining clearly in English, "Yo, man, talk American, wouldja?"

Teenagers on the beach, she decided. No one could have gotten onto the Sea Circus grounds without triggering the alarm system. And even if they had somehow managed to get in without setting off all the bells and whistles and bright flashing lights, the fail-safe silent alarm would ring down at police headquarters, and a patrol car would be out in a matter of minutes.

Carrie rounded the corner of the main aquarium tank, heading to her parked car.

And came face-to-face with a group of men.

Good Lord! How the hell had they gotten in?

The scientist that she was, quickly assessed the facts.

There were four of them—that she could see any-way—and they were *not* teenagers. They were grown men in their mid-twenties. Several of them may have been even older.

The take-no-bull Montana rancher's daughter that she'd been for the first eighteen years of her life planted her feet firmly on the ground and cradled the rifle in her arms, making sure they could see it clearly.

"I believe you gentlemen are trespassing," she said coolly. "I suggest you allow me to escort you off Sea Circus property before the police arrive."

One of the men wore a red bandanna tied around his head. On closer examination, he looked to be in his late thirties, with deep-set eyes and gaunt, hollow cheek-bones. He merely smiled at her words.

"But we're not ready to leave," he said with a thick Cuban accent.

Another of the men had a nose ring the size of a quarter. He was tall, taller than the rest of them by a good six inches, and he towered over Carrie. He had greasy blond hair pulled back into a messy ponytail at his nape. He kept his eyes carefully hidden behind a pair of mirrored sunglasses despite the fact that it was the middle of the night.

A third man was standing slightly to the left of Bandanna. He had short red hair in a crew cut and a face that still bore the scars of teenage acne. He was wearing a faded Nirvana T-shirt and a pair of cutoff jeans that revealed a pair of skinny legs. "Yeah, baby," he said, leering at her. "Iceman wants to look at the fishies."

"Then he should come back tomorrow," Carrie said tartly, "when Sea Circus is open to the general public."

"We ain't the general public," Nose Ring sneered.

The men seemed undaunted by the rifle she was holding. They moved slowly, spreading out around her, and Carrie realized in another few seconds she'd be completely surrounded. She slipped the safety off the rifle and took several steps backward until her shoulder blades hit the rough concrete of the main aquarium building. Better to have a wall behind her than God-knows-who and his even uglier brother.

In one quick movement, she hoisted the solid barrel of the rifle to her shoulder and cocked the trigger, closing one eye and squinting to aim directly at Bandanna—the man who was clearly the leader. At this proximity, shooting the tranquilizer dart at his head would probably kill him. The dart would shatter the bones in his skull, then penetrate his brain. He'd be tranquilized—permanently.

Bandanna seemed to realize this, too, and he gave a brief command in Spanish.

"Back off," another man translated, a man who had been standing slightly out of Carrie's sight, in the shadows behind Bandanna.

Carrie glanced in his direction.

He was the only one of the four who looked as if he might actually be nice to stand downwind of. He was more than average height—which meant that he stood a good nine inches taller than Carrie—and his clothes were pure American Urban. Despite the heat, he was wearing a black leather biker's jacket over a white T-shirt, and a pair of faded blue jeans that fitted him like a second skin. Snakeskin cowboy boots with pointy toes and silver-chained boot bracelets added the final touch.

His hair was long and thick, curling down around and past his shoulders. He had wide, angular cheekbones that spoke as clearly of his Latin heritage as did his gentle Hispanic accent.

He was a handsome man. No, forget handsome. He wasn't handsome. He was drop-dead gorgeous, Carrie realized as he stepped out into the light—but not because of his cheekbones or his shiny hair or his trim, muscular body.

It was his eyes.

Soft and black, his eyes were incredible—the color of the midnight sky—surrounded by a fringe of thick, dark, almost femininely long lashes. They held a gentle serenity, a quiet confidence, like that of a priest or a minister, that contradicted his macho leather-and-chains getup. But then that look shifted, and there was something else in his eyes, too—a glint of excitement, a flare of fire and power, a sense of very real danger. Part priest maybe, but also part devil.

This was not a man to mess with.

Holding Carrie's gaze, he stepped in front of Bandanna, shielding the older man from her rifle. But he didn't stop there. He kept going, slowly moving closer and closer to her.

"We were only cutting through. We *will* leave, but first you must give me the gun," he said. He smiled at her, showing a set of white, perfect teeth, and added, "Please?"

"Pwetty pwease?" Crew-cut said, then laughed loudly. "Yo, Carlos, man, you forgot to say 'Mother, may I.'"

Carlos. The man with the midnight eyes was named Carlos.

"Freeze, Carlos," Carrie ordered him, training the gun on the center of his forehead.

But he just kept coming. "Give me the gun, miss," he said again, "so that no one gets hurt."

"You don't want anyone to get hurt?" she asked, her anger making her sound breathless and afraid. "Then turn around right now and leave."

Bandanna spoke again in Spanish.

"Iceman says we will," Carlos said, translating. "But only when we are ready." Was that genuine remorse that flashed in his eyes? Or was it amusement?

He was almost within an arm's reach of her rifle. Carrie moved the barrel down slightly, so it was aimed steadily at his stomach. He smiled, and she knew *he* knew she didn't have the nerve to kill him. But if he came any closer, she *would* pull the trigger. And God only knows how the human body would react to the fast-acting tranquilizer intended for a four-hundred-pound marine mammal.

"Take another step and I'll shoot," she warned him.

He stopped. And laughed. "You would, too, wouldn't you?"

"Damn straight," she said grimly.

"And then what?" Carlos asked his eyes glittering, reflecting the dim glow of the floodlights that lit the park grounds. "I fall." He shrugged. "But there are three others. And I doubt that my friends will wait patiently while you reload your gun. No, if you shoot me, you will be in serious trouble. I cannot recommend it."

"Let's skip the trouble, shall we?" Carrie said. "Now, you boys just hop back over that fence and clear on out of here, and we'll call it a night."

"You sound like one of them thar Western movies," Crew-cut said, mimicking and exaggerating Carrie's drawl. "Like a cute little cowgirl." He smiled, revealing a variety of cracked and broken teeth. "Come on, baby, why don't you show us your spurs and whips?"

Carrie glanced at Crew-cut for only a fraction of a second, but that was all it took to give Carlos an edge.

He moved, faster than she thought it was possible for a man of his size to move, quickly closing the gap between his hands and her gun.

She squeezed the trigger, but it was too late. He knocked the barrel of the gun up, and the dart shot harmlessly into the night sky.

The recoil caught her off-balance, and Carrie went down, hard, into the sandy dirt. She scrambled quickly to her feet, straining her ears for the sound of police sirens. But there was only silence.

Bandanna, Crew-cut and Nose Ring stood in a semicircle around her, just watching. Carlos was looking at her gun, releasing the spent cartridge and making sure there wasn't another round in the second barrel.

"She was gonna shoot ya, man," Crew-cut said to Carlos.

Carlos just smiled serenely.

Now what? Carrie was still breathing hard, trying to control the crazy hammering of her heart. The situation wasn't looking very good. She was unarmed, in a deserted spot, in the middle of the night, with four scary-looking men. Could things get much worse?

Bandanna said something to Carlos in Spanish.

Carlos answered evenly.

Bandanna spoke again, gesturing toward Carrie.

Carlos smiled at Bandanna, smiled at Carrie and nodded his head. *"Sí,"* he said. *That* she understood. *"Sí"* meant yes. But yes *what?*

A police siren wailed faintly in the distance, and Carrie held her breath. But it was moving away from her, getting softer and softer until she couldn't hear it anymore. Dammit, where *were* those police?

And still the conversation in Spanish went on.

Crew-cut finally exploded, voicing all of Carrie's frustration, letting out a stream of foul language. "I'm feeling left out here," he added. "If you guys aren't discussing the balmy weather, then translate, for chrissake."

"Iceman said he wants to see the dolphins now," Carlos said, clearly tongue in cheek.

Nose Ring scowled. "Cut the crap, Carlos."

"Time to go," Carlos said evenly.

"What about her?" Crew-cut asked, pointing to Carrie with his chin. "We can't just leave her here."

"Sure you can," Carrie lied. "You clear out of here, I'll forget I ever saw you. No harm done, right?"

Carlos laughed, humor lighting his face.

"What?" Carrie said defensively. But she could tell from his eyes that he knew if they simply left her here, she'd run up to the office and call the police faster than they could sneeze.

"I'll take care of her," he said to Crew-cut. "You go with Iceman. I'll catch up."

Bandanna and Nose Ring were already walking away, heading for the other side of the park.

"No way, man," Crew-cut said, his voice cracking. "Why do I want to go on ahead when *you're* having all the fun?"

Carlos shrugged. "Suit yourself." He turned to Carrie. "Do you have a car?" he asked.

Her blood felt icy cold despite the evening's heat. Take care of her? How was Carlos going to "take care of" her? Still, she stuck out her chin. "Maybe."

"Please give me the car keys."

"I don't have 'em," she lied.

He leaned the rifle against the side of the aquarium and

stepped toward her. "Give me the keys, please," he said, "or I'll have to take them from you."

"And I'll help," Crew-cut said with an ugly smile.

Carrie crossed her arms. "You boys planning to steal my car now, too? Aren't breaking-and-entering charges good enough for the lot of you?"

One arm. That's all it took for Carlos to hold her while he quickly searched her pockets for her car keys. Both her arms were pinned and her face was pressed against the sweet-smelling leather of his jacket. If he hadn't been wearing that jacket, she would've bitten him, but she didn't even try, since all she would've gotten was a mouthful of cowhide. She pulled back her leg to kick him, but he found the keys in the front pocket of her shorts and let her go before her boot connected with his shin.

Carrie was gasping indignantly, but Carlos was unruffled.

"Thank you," he said politely, as if she'd handed him the keys. He slipped them into his own pocket.

A strand of her long blond hair had come free from her ponytail, and she pushed it back off her face, looping it behind her ear. "I have three more payments on that car," she said hotly. "If you think I'm just going to let you steal it—"

"No one's going to steal your car," Carlos told her.

"Wait a minute, man." Crew-cut looked at Carrie. "What kind is it?"

Even Carlos looked exasperated. "Get lost, man," he said to Crew-cut. "You're cramping my style, you know?"

But Crew-cut didn't budge. "If *you* get to have fun," he said with a petulant set to his square jaw, "*I* get to watch."

Watch? Watch what? The fear was back, fear for her personal safety, fear for her very life. But the fear brought a new wave of anger—anger that her father and brothers were going to be proven right. She *couldn't* take care of herself. She had had no right to leave the safety of their isolated Montana ranch and move to a crime-riddled Florida city. Dammit, she could just imagine them saying "We told her so," as they morosely gathered around to identify her body at the St. Simone morgue.

Carlos took her gently by the arm, but she pulled free, glaring at him.

"Where are you taking me?" she asked.

He countered with a question. "Where's your car parked?"

She didn't answer, so he answered for her.

"Not in the parking lot outside the gate," he said, "or I would have seen it there. It's probably somewhere inside the fence, no?"

She stared at him silently. If he so much as touched her, she'd throw up on him. That's what she'd always been told to do in the event of a sexual assault, right? It sure wouldn't take much effort on her part. She was already feeling queasy.

"Are you going to walk?" Carlos said patiently, "or perhaps I should carry you?"

"Yo, Carlos, *I'll* carry her," Crew-cut volunteered.

"I'll walk," Carrie said quickly.

"Oh, man," Crew-cut said, exaggerating his whine. "I don't think she likes me." He pretended to pout. "But, baby, you know, I like *you*...."

He reached out to touch her, and Carrie jerked back out of his grasp. "Don't you come near me," she said sharply, including Carlos in her glare.

What were her options here? She could stand passively by and wait to see what they were going to do with her. Or she could run. She could dart away into the shadows and hide. She could slip into the seal tank and swim to the covered hutch that could only be accessed underwater.

She glanced toward the seal tank. It was more than a hundred yards away. If she was smart, she'd run in the other direction first, lose these jerks in the shadows underneath the main aquarium bleachers, and then head back to the seal tank. Once she was under the water, they'd never find her. Not in a million years.

"Don't even think about it," Carlos murmured, as if he could read her mind.

"Think about what?" she asked innocently. And bolted toward the bleachers.

Seven steps. That's all it took before Carlos tackled her, pulling her down onto the hard sand with him. He pinned her to the ground, her hands above her head, the full weight of his body pressing against her.

Carrie struggled to get away, struggled to bring her knee up to kick him, but she couldn't move. Her heart was pounding and she was nearly blind with panic.

"Madre de Dios," Carlos said. "You are a handful and a half, aren't you?" He brought his mouth closer to her ear, lowering his voice. "Look, I'm not going to hurt you. I'm a—"

Carrie bit him between his shoulder and his neck, right through the white cotton of his T-shirt collar.

He swore sharply, and pulled away from her. She scrambled into a sitting position and tried to back away, but he grabbed her ankle with one hand. With the other he rubbed his neck.

"A biter, huh?" Crew-cut said, crouching down next to them. "Oh, baby, you can bite *me* anytime."

Carrie was shaking uncontrollably, and she couldn't stop the tears that had flooded her eyes. One spilled down her cheek and she wiped it fiercely away. She'd be damned if she was going to let these bastards see her cry.

Carlos muttered something in Spanish, pushing his hair out of his face. One dark, curly lock caught on his eyelashes, but he didn't seem to notice. The priest look was back in his eyes, making his entire face seem warm and compassionate and full of remorse. Would he look at her that way after the devil took over again, after he'd forced himself on her?

Carrie spit at him, and he closed his eyes as the spittle hit him full in the face.

"Oh, gross," Crew-cut exclaimed. "Slap her, man. Don't let the bitch get away with that. Hell, I'll slap her for you."

"No, thank you."

"Aw, come on—"

"I said, *no.*" Carlos kept his eyes closed until he'd wiped his face clean with his hand. When he opened his eyes again, Carrie could see no anger there—only patience. He smiled apologetically at Carrie. "I'm sorry," he said. "I didn't mean to frighten you."

"You're telling her you're *sorry?*" Crew-cut said. "*She's* the one who should be apologizing."

Carlos exchanged his hold on Carrie's leg for a steady grip on her arm and got to his feet, pulling her up with him.

She tried to pull free, but he wouldn't let go. "If I let you go, you'll just run again," he said, "so I'm not going to do it."

"You're hurting me," Carrie said.

"Don't pull, and I won't have to hold you so tightly," Carlos said.

He led her around the corner of the main aquarium, and there was her little sports car, bright red and very shiny, even in the dimly powered floodlights.

Crew-cut gave a low whistle. "Nice wheels."

The trunk was open, the way she'd left it when she'd come to the office that evening. She'd been airing out the fishy smell that seemed to follow her around.

"I guess I didn't need those keys after all," Carlos said, pulling her around to the back of the car. He was still holding her arm with his right hand, so he gestured grandly toward the trunk with his left. "Get in."

Carrie stared at him, not understanding. What did he want her to do?

"That's it?" Crew-cut sputtered, disappointed. "You're just going to lock her in the trunk? Man, if it was me, I'd've taken her right here, in the front seat of her car."

Carlos was going to lock her in the trunk of her car. He wasn't going to force himself on her; he was just going to make sure she couldn't call the police. He *wasn't* going to hurt her; she was going to be all right. Except, Lord, that trunk was awfully tiny, and with the hood down, it would be incredibly dark and hot and...

Crew-cut reached out and ran one grubby finger down the side of Carrie's face. She pulled away, slapping at his hand, disgusted by his touch. On further thought, maybe being locked in the trunk wasn't such a bad idea.

Crew-cut drew back his hand to slap her, but Carlos caught his wrist.

"Rumor has it," he said dryly, "that sex is more pleasurable when the woman is willing."

"Yeah, well, this would be better than nothing," Crew-cut said with a shrug, jerking his hand free.

"No," Carlos said firmly. "In a case like this, *nothing* is best."

"Aw, come on, man," Crew-cut said. "I think she's kind of cute, so little and pretty. Look at all this blond hair."

Her hair had come free from its ponytail, and it hung around her face in a smooth blond sheet. Crew-cut ran his fingers through it, and Carrie yanked her head back, nearly toppling over. Carlos steadied her, and she realized she was grateful for his presence, grateful for the warmth of his body behind her. Crew-cut was the one she was afraid of. Carlos didn't want to hurt her. At least she *hoped* he didn't.

"Come on," Crew-cut said again. "Take me five minutes, ten minutes tops. I bet she's a real screamer." He leered at Carrie. "I bet you'd like to sink those sharp little teeth in me, huh, baby?"

"If you so much as touch me," Carrie snapped, "I'll kick your family jewels through the roof of your mouth."

"And that's after *I* get finished kicking your family jewels through the roof of your mouth," Carlos said mildly. "Back off, T.J."

"Why? You don't want her—"

"I didn't say that," Carlos corrected him. "On the contrary. You're right. She *is* very pretty. And I like her spirit. Very much so. No, I didn't say I didn't want her."

Carrie's eyes flew to Carlos's face. Her heart was pounding so loudly she could barely hear. She searched his eyes, looking to see if he was serious, or if he was joking— or if he'd been joking all along and he really meant to force himself on her, and then let his horrible friend take a turn.

"Shh," he said softly, as if he could see the sudden flare of panic in her eyes. "No one's going to hurt you."

His eyes were unreadable, an odd mix of heat, excitement and...*kindness?* Carrie was confused, and terribly frightened again. If this was some kind of head game Carlos was playing with her, he was winning, hands down.

"Just do her, man," Crew-cut urged. "You know you want to."

"But the real question is, does *she* want to?"

"Try it, and I'll kill you," Carrie whispered.

"Unlike you," Carlos said to Crew-cut, "I am quick to recognize a no when I hear one, and that sounded like a very definite no to me." He turned to Carrie. "Get in the trunk, please."

But Carrie couldn't do it. She couldn't move. As much as she wanted to be away from Crew-cut and Carlos, she couldn't bring herself to climb into that tiny, dark, airless trunk. Never mind her childhood claustrophobic fears of being locked in a closet or trapped in her parents' camper's tiny bathroom. Lord, in a few hours, the hot Florida sun would rise, and that trunk would turn into an oven. She'd bake. She'd dehydrate. Her body temperature would soar, and she'd be dead in a matter of hours.

Carlos scooped her up, holding her, one arm behind her shoulders, the other supporting her knees, and lifted her easily into the trunk.

"No!" She clung to his neck, afraid to let go, afraid that his would be the last face she'd ever see, afraid of the hood closing down on her, trapping her, entombing her.

"You'll be safest here, *cara,*" Carlos murmured, prying her fingers loose. "Trust me," Carlos said to Carrie, his dark brown eyes so gentle, so kind. "You have to trust me."

The hood of the trunk closed with a frightening finality. She was alone, alone in the dark.

"C'MON, MAN, we're going to be late," T.J. said, running his hand anxiously across his crew cut as he looked across the dark marine park. "Iceman's gonna start the meeting without us."

"I'm not ready to go," the man known as Carlos said calmly, stopping at a row of pay phones near the closed and shuttered concession stand.

"This ain't the time to call your girlfriend," T.J. said, watching him dial. "911? What the hell…?"

"Someone's got to get the girl out of the trunk before the sun comes up," Carlos said in his gentle Hispanic accent.

"Yo, we can let her out on the way back." T.J. smiled. "*I'll* come back this way and—"

"Yeah," Carlos said into the phone. "I'd like to report a woman locked in the trunk of a red Miata inside the grounds of Sea Circus. Yeah, that's Sea Circus—down on Ocean and Florida Streets? The car's *inside* the park, not out in the lot."

T.J. shook his head. "You're a stupid sonuva—"

"No, I wish to remain anonymous," Carlos said.

"We gotta go," T.J. growled.

Carlos put his finger in his ear, blocking the sound of T.J.'s voice. "How do I know there's a woman in the trunk of a red Miata?" He laughed. "Because I put her there. Just send a patrol car down to let her out, okay?" There was a pause. "Good," he said.

He hung up the phone and smiled at T.J. "Now I'm ready to go."

CHAPTER TWO

January—six months later

FELIPE SALAZAR adjusted his bow tie in the mirror of his furnished suite at the ritzy Harbor's Gate Apartments, then wiped imaginary dust from the shoulder of his tuxedo.

It was a very nice tuxedo, carefully tailored so that his shoulder holster and gun didn't disrupt the lines of his jacket.

This penthouse suite was very nice, too. It was four times bigger than his tiny one-bedroom apartment on the other side of town. Of course, the monthly rent was much higher than four times that of his little, airless apartment. But luckily for him, he wasn't paying it.

In fact, he wasn't paying for anything these days. The hotel, his expensive clothes, his meals, the two thousand dollars in spending money he carried around in fifties and one hundreds were all courtesy of the St. Simone Police Department.

It was one of the perks of working a round-the-clock dangerous job. In fact, it was the only perk most people would understand. Very few people would call the danger, the risk, the *thrill* of being an undercover police detective a perk.

But Felipe Salazar wasn't most people.

And tonight, he wasn't even Felipe Salazar.

Tonight, as he'd been for the past five months, he was Raoul Tomás Garcia Vasquez. Raoul Tomás Garcia Vasquez had quite good taste in clothes. He wore expensive suits and Italian shoes and underwear that cost more than a police detective's daily salary.

Felipe looked at himself again in the mirror. Yes, the tux fitted him very nicely. It was a far cry from the leather jacket and worn-out blue jeans he'd worn on his last assignment. He'd been called Carlos for that one, and he'd infiltrated an uneasy alliance of street-gang leaders out to make a fortune in the world of illegal drugs. As Carlos, he'd come face-to-face with Caroline Brooks, that intriguing blonde at Sea Circus and…

He shook his head. This was no time to think about blondes, particularly about *this* blonde. Unfortunately, there was never any time. He'd gone straight from being Carlos to being Raoul Vasquez. He couldn't remember the last time someone had actually called him Felipe. But such was the nature of his job. Felipe glanced into the mirror again, and Raoul Vasquez looked back at him.

Raoul was fresh out of prison, and ready to start over. He'd come to St. Simone—or so his story went—after cashing in some favors, some *big* favors. His old boss, Joseph Halstad, the head of a minor crime syndicate in Washington, D.C., had offered him his old job back, but Raoul wanted a fresh start, someplace new, someplace where the police didn't recognize his face.

So Halstad had phoned Lawrence Richter, the man who ran Western Florida's organized-crime outfit, and called in a few favors of his own.

Of course, Richter didn't know that Halstad had made

that phone call as part of a deal struck with the Washington D.A. over certain racketeering charges.

And Richter *wouldn't* know—at least not until Felipe had gathered all the proof he needed to cement this case shut and send Richter and all the men and women in his syndicate to jail for a long, long time.

After five months, Felipe was immersed in Richter's organization deeply enough to put Richter and many of his underlings away. Strangely enough, even with all the drug and weapons sales, the prostitution, gambling and racketeering that went on, it was the importation of illegal aliens that was going to bring Richter down.

On the surface, it seemed innocent enough, benevolent even. Lawrence Richter, humanitarian, was helping the poor and impoverished into America. He was helping them get a start, helping them find that American Dream.

Felipe knew all about the American Dream. His own parents had made the move from Puerto Rico to Miami, searching for a better life for themselves and their five children. But Miami had been hot and angry, and they'd moved on, across to the west coast of Florida, to the city of St. Simone.

Some American Dream.

Felipe's father had worked himself into an early grave, trying to keep his floundering auto shop afloat. Raphael, Felipe's older brother, had run with the wrong crowd, nearly overdosed on drugs and ended up doing time in a state maximum security prison. His oldest sister, Catalina, had married a man who'd been killed in a car accident by a drunk driver, leaving her alone to raise their two small children. His other sister, Marisela, had given up her own dream of going to college and had taken over their father's garage with the help of Roberto, their youngest brother, who was still in high school.

And Felipe? Felipe had become a cop.

He smiled wryly at himself in the mirror. His father, the dreamer, had been disappointed in Felipe's choice of profession. Yet it was Felipe who was most like the old man. Out of all his brothers and sisters, it was Felipe who was the idealist. It was Felipe who still believed in good versus evil, in right over wrong. It was Felipe who still believed in the criminal justice system and the rule of law. It was Felipe who was keeping alive the American Dream.

And that meant putting away Lawrence Richter, who was bringing entire families of illegal immigrants into the country and turning them into little more than slaves. In exchange for safe passage into America, the land of opportunity, Richter would squeeze years of indentured servitude from these people. He'd contract them out to work in factories and sweatshops at much lower than the legal minimum wage. Then he'd keep most of their paycheck, giving them only barely enough to get by. If they complained, they'd get delivered into the hands of the immigration department, speaking hardly any English and knowing only the assumed names of the men who had brought them into the country.

Felipe had seen many of these people, trapped into working sixty-hour weeks for money that they would never see, money that would line Lawrence Richter's pockets. Felipe had looked into their eyes and seen the despair and desperation—and utter hopelessness.

For them, the American Dream had become a nightmare.

Shutting Richter's operation down would mean deportation for many of them. But some would slip through the cracks, free at last to pursue that elusive American Dream.

Still, as close as Felipe was to nailing Richter, he had to wait. Because last week, something he'd suspected for quite some time had become more than a mere suspicion.

Richter had a partner.

And Richter's partner was someone relatively high up in St. Simone's government. He was someone with power, someone with clout, someone who, it seemed, could make the entire police force turn their heads and look the other way if need be.

And before he took Richter down, Felipe Salazar, faithful believer in right over wrong and staunch defender of his father's American Dream, was going to make sure that this other man, this man Richter had nicknamed "Captain Rat," whoever he was, fell, too.

BOBBY PENFIELD III was *the* most boring man Carrie Brooks had ever met in her twenty-five years of life.

Yet she sat across from him at their table in Schroedinger's, St. Simone's most elegant restaurant, located on the ground floor of the glamorous Reef Hotel, and tried to smile. *This* was why she didn't go out on dates, she reminded herself sternly. The next time some relatively nice-looking man that she didn't know asked her to dinner, she would definitely find some excuse to stay home.

Sure, some women might have found Bobby Penfield III and his endless stories about the ad agency wars exciting. But frankly, Carrie couldn't see how choosing a man over a woman to plug some paper towel on TV could really make that much difference in the future sales of those paper towels. And it certainly didn't warrant nearly an hour of dinner conversation. Besides, as an avid environmentalist, she'd prefer it if the entire world stopped using paper and turned to reusable cloth towels instead.

Carrie wished that he'd change the subject. She wished that he'd talk about *any*thing else. Hell, she'd rather discuss last week's sensational mob-related killings—the "Sandlot Murders," the press had so cleverly dubbed them. Everyone across the state was talking about it. It had even made the national news. Two mobsters, Tony Mareidas and Steve Dupree, had been executed in a vacant lot downtown—a vacant lot that happened to be next to an elementary school. Children had discovered the bodies, and the city was in an uproar, searching for the man or men responsible for the bloody crime.

But Bobby Penfield III rambled on about his paper products, and Carrie was forced to smile cheerfully back at him. She was here because Bobby's ad agency was going to produce a series of commercials and print ads about Sea Circus, at quite a discount off their regular rates. Or so Hal Tompkins, the aquarium's business manager had told her. And when Hal had brought Bobby over to see the dolphins run through their afternoon training session with Carrie, and when Bobby had asked Carrie to dinner and Hal had widened his eyes at Carrie in a silent plea to be nice to Bobby, Carrie had stupidly accepted the date.

So here she was in her own personal level of hell, in a much too posh restaurant, underdressed in the fanciest dress she owned—a simple blue-flowered sleeveless dress with a short, swingy skirt—sitting across the table from a man she had nothing, absolutely *nothing* in common with. Except maybe for the fact that they both liked the new two-piece bathing suit Carrie had been wearing during that afternoon's dolphin training session.

Across the restaurant, a long banquet table caught Carrie's eye. It was filled with men in tuxedos and their beautiful wives. Or dates. Dates, Carrie decided cynically. Their wives were probably all home with the children.

A silver-haired man sat at one end of the table, smiling benevolently at his guests. Yes, this was his party, Carrie decided. Silver-hair was definitely the man who'd be picking up tonight's check.

Bobby Penfield droned on about marketing disposable diapers, unaware that Carrie's attention had long since wandered. As she watched, across the room, Silver-hair stood up and made a toast. Another man, a man who had his back to her, stood also and bowed graciously to polite applause.

Carrie leaned forward, trying to get a closer look. Something about this man, something about the set of his shoulders—or maybe the way his tuxedo fit those broad shoulders—was oddly familiar. She studied the back of his head, silently willing him to turn around.

But he didn't. He sat back down without giving her a chance to see his face. Whoever he was, he wore his long, dark hair pulled tightly into a ponytail at his nape.

Carrie knew plenty of men with long, dark hair that they wore in a ponytail. But none of the men *she* knew had ever worn a tuxedo—let alone a tuxedo that had so obviously been altered to give its wearer such an incredibly precise fit.

Carrie looked up, startled, suddenly aware that Bobby

had stopped talking. He was looking at her as if he was waiting for her to answer a question.

She did the only thing she could. She smiled at him. And asked him where he went to college.

Bobby was only too happy to keep talking about himself. He didn't even notice she'd never answered his question. Carrie wasn't sure he'd heard a single thing she'd said all night—except the questions she'd asked about him.

Lord, somewhere, someplace in the world, there had to exist a man who actually listened to the words another person spoke. But whoever he was, he sure as all hell wasn't named Bobby Penfield III.

Of course, she wasn't exactly listening to *him*, either. She sighed. She'd known from the moment she'd gotten into his car that this entire evening was going to be a disaster. She'd picked up on their incompatibility that early and wished now that she'd had the nerve to bow out gracefully.

Except Bobby still seemed to harbor hopes that Carrie would go home with him after dinner. She could see it in his eyes, in the way his gaze lingered on her breasts and on her mouth.

Carrie sighed again. This was truly the pits.

But it sure wasn't as bad as being trapped in the trunk of her car for two endless, nightmarish hours, the way she'd been back in July.

It still haunted her, even after all these months.

Those two hours had seemed more like two years.

Carrie had gone ballistic at first, flashing temporarily back to the time she was locked in the tiny bathroom of her parents' camper when she was nine years old. Just as she'd done when she was nine, she'd cried as if the world were coming to an end. She'd cried, and kept crying, until she'd groped around and found the old flashlight she kept in the trunk of her car for emergencies. The main bulb was out, but it was one of those big box flashlights with a bullet-shaped red light attached to the handle, and *that* light was working.

The trunk had been absurdly tiny and terrifyingly confining in the red glow from the flashlight. But at least the darkness hadn't pressed in on her anymore, suffocating her. And there had been fresh air—or at least there had been after she'd pulled the foam sealing strip from between the trunk hood and the frame. Her trunk would probably never be watertight again, but fresh air had been her immediate concern.

Then, lying on her back with her legs scrunched up and her face only a few inches from the inside of the hood, Carrie sang. She sang to keep herself from losing her mind. She sang every song she'd ever learned, and some she hadn't. She sang all of the top forty hits from the year she'd entered eighth grade. She sang all of those annoying Broadway musical show tunes that her mother had loved so much. She sang every song from Patty Loveless's two most recent compact discs. She sang until her throat was raw.

It truly had been hell, lying there, sweating, trying to keep the panic from engulfing her, feeling the walls closing in even tighter….

Carlos.

Her thoughts continued to return to him every now and then, even after all this time. In the first few weeks after he'd locked her in the trunk, she'd thought about him often.

Oddly enough, he still sometimes showed up in her

dreams, too. Even odder, those dreams were steamy and erotic, filled with entangled legs, and cool, smooth, muscular skin, and long, dark hair hanging down around her face as he slowly bent to kiss her, as he sensuously, languorously, exquisitely moved inside of her—

She'd wake up with a start, surprised and sometimes a little disappointed to find that she'd only been dreaming.

Six months ago, she'd gone to the police station and sworn out a complaint, but the man named Carlos and his three friends still hadn't been caught.

Lucky for them, she told herself fiercely. If she so much as set eyes on any of those sons of bitches again...

Across the room, Silver-hair's guests stood up, stretching their legs. The women moved off, almost in one body, toward the ladies' room. The men shook hands and—

No.

It couldn't be.

Could it?

Carrie had gotten only the briefest glimpse of the man's face, but those exotic cheekbones were unmistakable.

She wouldn't be absolutely positive until she saw his eyes, but either she was going crazy or the man with the long dark ponytail, the man in the well-tailored tuxedo, was *Carlos.*

Of course, it was entirely possible that she *was* going crazy.

It had been six months, and Carrie *still* thought she spotted Carlos everywhere—in the mall, in the grocery store, at the movies, and even in the crowd at Sea Circus. She'd see a tall man with long, dark hair and she'd stare and take a closer look. But then the man would turn his head and she'd realize it wasn't Carlos after all. It was just someone who looked a little bit like him.

But *this* man didn't turn around and give her a second chance to see his face. He stared toward the lobby door with his back to her.

"Excuse me," Carrie said to Bobby Penfield as he paused to take a much-needed breath. She folded her napkin and set it down next to her salad plate. "Excuse me for just one minute. I'll be right back."

She pushed back her chair and hurried toward the lobby after the tuxedo-clad men.

Schroedinger's lobby was splendorous, with lots of plants and high ceilings and chandeliers and big wall mirrors that seemed to make the room twice the size it really was. The man who might be Carlos was standing near the checkroom, talking to Silver-hair. Several of the other men stood nearby.

Carrie stopped short at the sight of the long-haired man's face in one of the mirrors.

It *was* Carlos. Lord in heaven, it really was him.

He was smiling, with that gentle, priestly smile, at something Silver-hair had said to him. Silver-hair said something else, and the smile exploded into a devilish laugh, complete with a full view of perfect white teeth.

Despite all her dreams and various pseudo-Carlos sightings, Carrie had forgotten exactly how handsome this man was.

At that exact instant, his gaze flickered in her direction, then landed squarely on her face. For the briefest second, Carlos froze, recognition darkening his eyes as he looked at Carrie.

She'd known him six months ago for all of half an hour, but during that time, even when she aimed her rifle directly at his head, she'd not seen anything besides confidence and calm control in his eyes. But now, suddenly, she could see panic. Sheer, total panic. It flared for an instant, and then it was gone, and his face and eyes were oddly expressionless.

He was afraid of something. Afraid of *her,* probably.

Damn straight he had a reason to be. He'd locked her in the trunk of her car, for Pete's sake. All she had to do was point her finger and scream loud enough, and the entire St. Simone police force would be down upon his head.

Slowly, deliberately, Carrie started toward him.

CHAPTER THREE

HE WAS LOOKING at the cause of his death.

Felipe Salazar was standing in the lobby of Schroedinger's, and looking directly at the cause of his certain death.

It was the dolphin-riding cowgirl from Sea Circus, and she was heading toward him, a small, tight smile on her perfect lips, and the fires of hell gleaming in her pretty blue-green eyes.

She'd traded her clunky boots for a pair of brown leather sandals, and her grungy shorts and T-shirt for a sleeveless, short, blue-flowered dress that would have sent his heart into his throat—if it hadn't already been there for an entirely different reason.

Her blond hair was longer than it had been six months ago, and she wore it down around her shoulders, parted on the side, a straight sheet of gold that shimmered in the light from the chandeliers.

She wasn't wearing much makeup, just a hint of eye shadow and lipstick, maybe a touch of rouge. She hadn't tried to hide the charming splash of freckles that dotted her delicate nose and softly rounded cheekbones.

Madre de Dios, but she was even lovelier than he remembered. And dear God, he'd spent an awful lot of time remembering, those first few weeks after the showdown with Iceman and the rest of his gang. Felipe had even gone back to Sea Circus, just to see for himself that the girl was really all right.

Her name was Caroline Brooks, nickname Carrie.

He'd caught most of her dolphin show, and seeing her dive into the huge tank with the enormous sea creatures, seeing her actually ride on their backs, seeing the gentle way she treated them, seeing her smile and laugh without that tinge of panic on her pretty face, and yes, seeing her in that amazing red, form-fitting Speedo bathing suit, he'd almost approached her. He'd almost gone up to her and finished that sentence he'd started, that sentence she'd interrupted with a bite from her sharp teeth.

I'm a cop.

So why hadn't he told her?

Because he liked her way, *way* too much. Because in his heart, he knew that even if he were able to seduce her, one or two nights simply wouldn't be enough. Because he knew in a matter of days, he'd be gone, deep under cover, infiltrating Lawrence Richter's crime syndicate as Raoul Tomás Garcia Vasquez. And, most of all, because he knew that any romantic involvement with him would place her in potential danger.

So he'd made himself forget about her.

Or at least he'd tried.

At the very least, he'd stayed far, far away from Sea Circus and pretty Caroline Brooks.

How very ironic to realize now that *not* approaching her, *not* telling her he was a cop, *not* revealing his true identity to her, was going to result in his own death. And, dear God, probably her death, too.

Because, coming over here the way she was, with that bright light of justice and retribution in her eyes, Felipe had no doubt that she was going to blow his cover to kingdom come.

And if Lawrence Richter had the slightest reason to believe that Felipe was a cop, then Felipe was soon going to be a very dead cop. There was no way—not knowing what Felipe knew—that Richter would let him live.

Felipe hadn't spoken to his best friend, Jim Keegan, in more than four weeks. That thought flashed crazily into his head and he wondered briefly how Jim—or Diego, the Spanish version of James, as Felipe was fond of calling him—would take the news of his friend's death.

The best defense is a strong offense. That's what Jim always used to say back when they were partners on the vice squad, before Jim took a coveted spot on the force as a homicide detective. *There's always a way out. You've just got to find it,* and *Keegan's Rule Number One: Nothing is impossible.*

If there was a way out of this mess, it would involve somehow keeping Caroline's smart mouth tightly shut.

And that wasn't going to be easy.

"Excuse me, please," Felipe murmured to Lawrence Richter. "I have to head off an…old girlfriend."

If the older man saw the bead of sweat drip down the side of Felipe's face, he didn't mention it. He merely looked from Felipe to Caroline and back, and smiled.

"Of course," Richter said.

Felipe moved quickly then, intercepting Caroline Brooks a good ten feet away from Richter. Maybe, just maybe, they were far enough away to keep him from overhearing their conversation….

"Well, what do you know?" the tiny blond woman said, gazing coolly up at Felipe as if she were the one who was almost ten inches taller. "We meet again, C—"

Carlos. She was going to call him Carlos, in a voice loud enough to carry around the entire lobby. But he wasn't Carlos now. He was supposed to be Raoul Vasquez.

Felipe shut her up the only way he could.

He covered her mouth with his and kissed her.

She tasted like the house salad dressing, fresh and spicy and delicious. She drew her breath in sharply, pulling back to look him in the eye, and Felipe knew in that one fraction of a second he hadn't imagined the electricity that had sparked between them that night at Sea Circus. It was still there, still fierce and hot. And he also knew without the slightest doubt that if he'd gone to her the way he'd longed to, if he'd told her the truth, told her he was a cop and apologized for treating her so roughly, he would've been able to seduce her. Or, *Madre de Dios,* maybe she would've seduced him.

Regret coursed through him, regret that he'd missed his chance, regret that he'd probably never have another opportunity to kiss Caroline Brooks, let alone make love to her. Because unless Felipe took her arm and dragged her away from Lawrence Richter and his right-hand triggerman, Tommy Walsh, his life was about to end.

"Darling," he said smoothly, while she was temporarily silenced, "how nice to see you again. Come, let's step outside where we can talk privately."

He took her by the arm and drew her toward the main entrance.

But she wasn't having any of it. She pulled her arm free and laughed. "You're crazier than I thought if you think I'd go *any*where with you," she said coldly in her Western twang.

Felipe could feel Richter's eyes on him, watching.

Richter was always watching, always aware of every little thing that went on around him. It was one of the reasons he was so successful, and one of the reasons he'd never been apprehended.

"I know you've missed me," Felipe said, loudly enough for Richter to overhear. "And I'm sorry I haven't called you, but I've been busy. Please don't be angry—"

"*Missed* you?" She laughed in disbelief. "You locked me in the tr—"

Near desperation, Felipe kissed her again. Anything, *any*thing, to make her stop talking. He kissed her harder this time, drawing her body completely against his and holding her tightly in his arms.

Again she was temporarily silenced, and he took advantage of those few precious seconds.

"Please," he said, again loudly enough for Richter to hear. "I know you'll find this difficult to believe, but I've stayed away because I care for you so very much and—"

She hit him. She pulled her right arm free and hauled off and punched him, hard, in the stomach. Felipe saw it coming and tightened his stomach muscles. She probably hurt her fist more than she hurt him. But it was enough to catch the attention of the restaurant staff.

"Mister, you are *so* full of crap," Carrie said, her coolness gone. She was livid with anger.

"Is there a problem here?" the maître d' said, smoothly sidling up.

"No, no," Felipe said almost desperately. "Everything is fine—"

"Yes, there most certainly *is* a problem," Carrie said. "This…this…*con* man is trying to make it seem as if he and I have known each other for longer than the thirty minutes we spent together over at—"

"Caroline," he said quickly, interrupting her. Con man. Better than cop, but not by much. One glance at Richter told Felipe that the older man was still watching him. Watching and listening. "I think the gentleman would like us to continue this discussion outside and—"

Carrie's eyes narrowed. "How do you know my name?"

"She gets like this sometimes," Felipe said in a low voice to the maître d'. "Too much to drink. Will you help me take her outside?"

"Touch me again and I swear I'll scream," Carrie warned him, glaring at both men.

The maître d' backed off, eager to keep the young woman from having a fit in the lobby of his four-star restaurant.

Richter nodded once and Tommy Walsh stepped forward, his pale blue eyes bored and flat. "Raoul," he said in his thick Brooklyn accent, "you need some kind of help here?"

Carrie turned her wide blue-green gaze back on Felipe. *"Raoul?"* she said in disbelief. She turned indignantly to Tommy. "Funny, six months ago I knew him as Carlos."

Six months ago, Raoul Vasquez was supposedly in prison.

"Oh, really?" Tommy said to Carrie. "Is that right?"

"It was August," Felipe said, talking fast and low. "I was just out on parole. It had been eighteen months, man. I didn't want to get married. I just wanted a little relief, you know? I told her my name was Carlos and—"

"It was *not* August. It was July," Carrie said sharply. "And you didn't touch me. You locked me in the trunk of my car, remember?"

She sounded loco. The way she said it, it sounded as if Felipe—or Raoul or Carlos or whoever he was—had turned down an opportunity to spend the night with her. And standing there in that enticingly simple blue-flowered dress that accented her near-perfect figure, with her slender, tanned arms and shapely legs, her shining golden hair, her eyes the color of the ocean and her sweetly pretty face, it didn't seem possible that any man in his right mind would have turned her down.

So Felipe laughed, praying hard that Tommy would get the joke.

He did. Tommy's beefy boxer's face crinkled slightly in a tight smile that didn't reach his eyes. But then again, Felipe had never seen Tommy truly smile.

"She's crazy, man," he said to Tommy, grateful at least for that half smile. He turned back to Carrie. "Sweetheart, I know you must've been upset when I was gone in the morning but—"

Carrie crossed her arms and turned her imperious gaze on the maître d'. "Call the police. I want this man arrested."

"You must be confusing me with someone else," Felipe said, in a last-ditch effort to keep her from revealing his true identity. But he knew it was too late. Yes, Tommy was smiling, but he was smiling as if the joke was on Felipe.

"Oh, no," Carrie said with certainty. "You're Carlos, all right. And it wasn't August. It was July. July 22. You were with that son of a bitch you called T.J. And that other guy you called Iceman and—"

Carrie kept talking, but Felipe didn't hear her. He didn't hear her because she'd just told Richter clear as day that he was a cop.

Iceman. Her mention of Iceman had given him away.

Iceman had been one of St. Simone's hardest-working drug pushers.

And Iceman had owed Richter a cool quarter million at the time of his death. The money had been borrowed in order to make an investment in what was quite possibly the biggest small-time drug shipment to hit the west coast of Florida. The money had been borrowed and never paid back, because when Iceman and T. J. Cerrone and big, nose-ring-bedecked Randall Page, aka Mule, went to pick up the shipment of cocaine, the police went, too.

Although surrounded and clearly outgunned, Iceman had pulled his weapon and started a gun battle that had injured four police officers and left himself and his two business associates dead.

It had happened last summer, on the night of July 22, to be precise. And if Felipe had been with Iceman on July 22 before his death, it could only mean one thing.

Richter was a smart man. Tommy Walsh, despite the fact that he looked like an aging boxer, was a smart man, too. They could add one plus one, and in this case, one plus one equaled cop.

Richter looked at Tommy and Tommy looked at Richter, and Felipe knew that they'd come to the obvious conclusion.

"You were good," Tommy said quietly to Felipe, speaking to him in the past tense as if he were already dead. "You just weren't lucky enough."

Tommy's pale blue eyes flickered once toward Caroline, and Felipe knew with dreadful certainty that Richter's right-hand man was going to use the petite blonde to make sure Felipe cooperated. Tommy was going to threaten to blow Caroline's brains across

Schroedinger's lobby if Felipe didn't go quietly with him out to the parking lot and Richter's waiting limo.

But if Felipe went along for the ride, it would be his last ride. He had no doubts that Tommy would take him into the Everglades and kill him. And then he'd kill Caroline, too, because by then, *she'd* have seen and heard too much. Dear God, she'd probably already witnessed enough to warrant her death in Tommy's mind.

From the corner of his eye, Felipe could see the big glass doors that led out of the restaurant. Outside, a valet pulled an expensive-looking car under the brightly lit awning.

As if in slow motion, Tommy reached under his jacket for his gun.

The valet got out of the car, leaving the door open. He crossed to the other side and opened the front passenger door as the owners of the car, a middle-aged couple, started out into the Florida night.

It was now or never.

Felipe turned, scooped Caroline into his arms and ran for the door.

She screamed in outrage, just as he knew she would. He prayed that drawing attention to themselves this way would keep Tommy from pulling out his gun right there in the lobby and shooting Felipe in the back.

Felipe heard the muffled thud of a gunshot, then a bullet whizzed by his left ear, and he knew with a sinking heart that Tommy wanted him dead badly enough to risk going to prison himself. He shielded Caroline Brooks with his body and moved even faster, hoping desperately that Tommy would miss again. But Tommy didn't often miss, and Felipe knew without a doubt that the gunman's next shot was going to hit him.

The car's owner was still holding the glass door open for his wife, and Felipe knocked them both aside, praying they wouldn't get caught in the cross fire.

Tommy was using some kind of silencing device— most of the people around them were unaware of the gun, unaware of the danger.

"Get down," Felipe shouted, shifting Caroline easily into one arm, drawing and brandishing his own gun. "Everyone down!"

The valets scattered.

As Felipe threw Caroline into the front seat of the waiting car, slamming the door behind her, he felt a slap hit the back of his leg. He scrambled up and over the hood of the car and into the driver's seat. The keys were in the ignition and the motor was idling, and he threw it into gear.

The tires squealed on the pavement as the powerful engine responded. Felipe knew he'd been shot. He knew his leg was bleeding, but the pain hadn't registered yet. It was masked by the adrenaline surging through his veins. Besides, a bullet in the leg was nothing compared to what might have been.

He was alive. He was still alive.

Tommy's aim was usually unerringly accurate, and Felipe knew that it had only been good fortune that had kept the bullets from slamming first into the back of his head, and then into the small of his back. Or maybe somebody was listening to his prayers.

But that somebody wasn't listening to all of them.

In the rearview mirror, Felipe could see Richter's limousine leave the parking lot, bouncing as it took the slope of the driveway too quickly. Tommy was following them. This wasn't over yet.

Next to him in the car, Caroline Brooks had stopped screaming. One glance in her direction told Felipe that she was watching him. Her face was pale and her eyes were big. That and her rapid breathing revealed the fear she was trying so hard to hide.

"Fasten your seat belt," he told her curtly over the roar of the engine.

"Just let me out of the car," she said, talking low and fast, working hard to keep fear from raising the pitch of her voice. "I don't know what your game is, mister, but you don't need me to play it."

"I don't need you," Felipe agreed, taking a hard right turn that took an inch of rubber off the tires. Caroline lost her balance and was thrown across the seat nearly onto his lap. "But you need me."

"Like hell I do." She scrambled back, away from him, and quickly fastened her seat belt.

Sixty miles an hour. He was going sixty miles an hour on shadowy back streets. His mind was going even faster.

Tommy was right behind them. It would take quick thinking and a great deal of luck to lose him—Tommy Walsh was one of the best when it came to pursuit. And even if Felipe *did* lose him, he couldn't be sure he'd actually succeeded. He couldn't be certain that Tommy hadn't simply faded into the background, unseen but ready to blow Felipe away the moment he stepped out of the car.

Even if Felipe drove directly to police headquarters, Tommy would gun him and Caroline down in the parking lot.

There wasn't too much Felipe could do short of driving this expensive car up the front steps and through the double doors of the St. Simone Police Department's Fourth Precinct.

No. He had only one option here. And that was to lead Tommy to a place where Felipe would at least have a fighting chance at defending himself.

Felipe went through a red light, swerving to avoid hitting a pickup truck, and Caroline yelped in fear.

"Look," she said sharply. "Just pull over and let me out."

"I can't do that," Felipe said.

"Whatever you're wanted for," Caroline said sharply, "kidnapping me will only make it worse."

Felipe took a sharp left at Ocean Street, leaving more of the car's tires behind on the street. There was heavier traffic in this part of town, and he kept his eyes on the road, praying that no cars would pull out in front of him.

"I'm not wanted for anything," he told her matter-of-factly. "I'm a cop."

CARRIE STARED at the man sitting so calmly next to her.

He was a cop?

He'd stolen a car and kidnapped her and now was driving like a lunatic, violating every traffic law in the book. And she was supposed to believe that he was a cop?

She laughed, but it had nothing to do with humor. "Try another one, Carlos. Or Raoul—or whoever you are."

"Felipe," he said in his gentle Hispanic accent, raising his voice only very slightly to be heard over the sound of the racing engine. "Salazar. I'm an undercover detective with the Fourth Precinct. You blew my cover back there, Miss Brooks. Those men I was with, they're very dangerous. We're lucky we're still alive."

Carrie stared at him as she braced herself against the dashboard. "Just pull over to the side and let me out," she said tightly. "And then you can get back to whatever little fantasy you've got going here, okay?"

He glanced at her with those deep chocolate brown eyes, those dark, penetrating eyes she'd seen so many times in her dreams, then looked back at the road ahead of them. His face was glazed with perspiration, and his hair curled damply around his face where it had come free from his ponytail. A bead of sweat traveled down past his ear and plopped onto the lapel of his tuxedo jacket.

"I'm sorry," he said apologetically. His eyes flickered up to the rearview mirror. "I can't do that. I can't stop. There's a man—Tommy Walsh—chasing us. He's not a very nice man. He wants me dead, and I think he's going to try to kill you, too."

Carrie loosened her hold on the dashboard and turned around. She looked over the back of the plush leather seat, through the rear window.

There *was* a car following behind them. It, too, was driving at breakneck speed. Tommy Walsh. He must be the balding man with pale eyes and a boxer's scarred face and muscular build who had approached them in the lobby.

"Well, I think *he's* the cop and *you're* the bad guy," she said. "That's usually how these chases work, isn't it?"

"Not this time," Felipe told her. "I've been under cover for five months and I've witnessed some things that would put Walsh—and his boss—into prison for years. They aren't going to let me get away without a fight."

Carrie looked at the car that was following them, at Mr. Muscles, and then at Felipe. How could she possibly believe *any*thing this man told her?

"All right," she said abruptly. "Show me your ID. If you're a cop, prove it."

But he shook his head, still watching the road. "Do you know what it means to be deep under cover?"

They were rapidly approaching a red light. Carrie could see the traffic crossing the intersection in front of them, but Felipe didn't hit the brakes.

"Lord in heaven," she gasped. "Slow down!"

"Hold on," Felipe said, and gunned the car even faster.

They were going to die. Forget about Mr. Muscles in the car behind them. Forget Mr. Muscles, who Carlos— or Felipe or whoever he was—said wanted to kill them. They were going to die all by themselves, without anyone's help.

Carrie shrieked and held on as they roared through the red light, but her voice was drowned out by the sound of squealing tires and blaring horns as first one, then another and another car swerved. Then one vehicle went into a skid and slid sideways into them. Metal scraped against metal, creating a chilling, awful, screeching sound.

And then it was over. They were through the intersection, once more going sixty down Ocean Street.

Carrie glanced back through the rear window. Unbelievably, the big, dark limousine was still behind them.

"When a detective goes deep under cover," the dark-eyed man said calmly, as if nothing were wrong, as if they hadn't just nearly been killed in a car accident, as if he hadn't just removed all the paint from one side of this expensive car—this *stolen* car, "when he intends to infiltrate an organized-crime outfit, he does not bring any police identification with him. Hold on again, please."

Felipe yanked the steering wheel hard to the left, cutting across the oncoming traffic to pull into a narrow side street. The car skidded on loose gravel and dirt, hitting a metal garbage can with a bang and a crunch. The windshield was instantly covered with a layer of rotten vegetables.

"Oh, Lord," Carrie breathed, and for the first time since she'd seen the panic in Felipe's eyes at the restaurant, the man seemed unsettled.

He muttered in Spanish, alternately searching the dashboard for the controls to the windshield wipers and peering at the narrow road through a tiny hole in the muck.

Carrie saw it first. Loosening her grip on the dashboard, she reached over next to the steering wheel and switched on the wipers.

"Gracias," Felipe said. "Thanks."

"Don't bother," Carrie said tersely. "It was pure self-preservation."

"I'm sorry you had to become involved in this," Felipe said, glancing at her, then back in the rearview mirror at the car still following them. "It was an unfortunate coincidence that we were both at that same restaurant."

The neighborhood they were roaring through was run-down and unkempt, with crumbling stuccoed apartment buildings, their wooden porches sagging and rotten. The road, too, had seen far better days. Carrie's teeth rattled as they hit another pothole.

"I *had to* become involved?" Carrie said skeptically. "You really expect me to believe that Mr. Muscles would *kill* me simply for talking to you at Schroedinger's?"

"You were a witness," Felipe said.

"A witness to *what?* A conversation?"

"When I turn up dead or missing," Felipe said, taking another sharp right turn, "there'll be a great deal of publicity. You're the only one who can place me in that restaurant lobby with Tommy Walsh—Mr. Muscles, if you will—and Lawrence Richter. It's not enough to base a murder case on, but Walsh is known for his caution."

Carrie glared at him. "There were twenty other people in that lobby," she said. "Is Muscles going to kill them, too? That is, assuming he really does want to murder you."

"Hold on," Felipe said.

"Lord, I hate when you say that," Carrie muttered, bracing herself by bending her knees and putting her feet up against the dashboard.

They were coming to the end of the side street. Felipe could turn either left or right onto Clark Road. For once, the light was green.

Felipe took a left, and then an immediate right, going the wrong way down a one-way street.

Carrie bit back a shout. There was no need to point out his mistake. Because it was no mistake. He knew exactly what he was doing.

"With the exception of the maître d'," Felipe said calmly as if their conversation hadn't been interrupted, "who's probably on Richter's payroll, you were the only one in that lobby who knew me well enough to make a positive ID."

"Know you?" Carrie said. "I don't know you at all. And there's no reason for anyone to think that I do."

"But you're wrong," he said.

He glanced at her again, and in a flash, Carrie remembered those kisses. He had kissed her—twice—there in Schroedinger's lobby, and she knew just from looking at him, that he was remembering it, too. His gaze dropped to her legs, to where her ungainly position had caused her skirt to fall away from the tops of her thighs.

They were barreling, sixty miles an hour, the wrong

way down a one-way street, and he was sneaking looks at her legs?

No, not sneaking. He wasn't sneaking anything. There was nothing even remotely clandestine about the way he looked at her legs. His gaze was almost leisurely, appreciative and very, *very* male. And he glanced up and met her eyes afterward, as if he wanted to make sure she knew that he'd been looking at her legs.

That's when she saw it. The car phone. It was in a special case between their seats. Carrie pointed at it. "If you're a cop," she said, "why don't you call for backup?"

"Because I don't have the telephone's access code," Felipe said. "I've already checked. It's got a valet lock. You know, so the parking-lot attendant doesn't make a hundred dollars' worth of long-distance phone calls while the owner's having dinner?"

"You have an answer for everything, don't you?" Carrie observed tartly.

"Unfortunately, no," Felipe said. "I haven't figured out a way to get rid of Tommy Walsh without putting you in real danger."

Real danger? *Real* danger? Their current situation wasn't *really* dangerous? If this wasn't real danger, then what was?

The rear window shattered with a crash.

"Get down!" Felipe shouted, grabbing Carrie and pushing her onto the seat.

The right passenger mirror was blown completely off the car door.

He was shooting at them.

Mr. Muscles, the guy in the car behind them—Tommy Walsh or whoever he was—was *shooting* at them.

With a gun.

With bullets.

Real bullets.

The kind that could kill you.

"Hold on!" Felipe shouted again, and for the first time, Carrie was glad to hear him say those words. For the first time, she actually *wanted* him to drive even faster.

But the way she was down on the seat, there was no place to hold on to, nowhere to get a good grip.

The tires squealed as Felipe turned another corner and Carrie started to slide.

Felipe reached out with one hand and held her tightly, pulling her against him, anchoring her in place.

"He must've stopped and picked up a shooter," he said. "I saw him slow down, but I didn't see him stop."

Another bullet made a hole in the windshield and Felipe ducked.

And then the car phone rang.

CHAPTER FOUR

CAROLINE BROOKS turned to look up at Felipe from her rather indelicate position, sprawled out on the seat across his legs, her head down. Normally, the sight of long, fine hair like spun gold fanned out across his lap would trigger rather powerful sexual fantasies. But at the moment, Felipe could allow himself only the very briefest possible flash of pleasure. And even if he had allowed himself to dwell on the possibilities, the fear and alarm in Caroline's blue-green eyes would have quickly brought him back to the task at hand.

Somewhere underneath beautiful Caroline Brooks, the car phone was ringing and Felipe knew exactly who was on the other end.

Caroline scrambled off him, her head carefully kept down behind the protective barrier of the seat back. Gunning the car to over seventy, Felipe picked up the phone.

"*Hola,* Tomás," he said.

There was a brief moment of silence. Then Tommy Walsh spoke.

"Give it up, Vasquez," he said. "Or should I call you *Detective Salazar?*"

Felipe's hand tightened on the phone. He wanted desperately to swear. He wanted to let loose a long stream of the blackest curses, but instead he kept his mouth tightly shut. By knowing his real identity, Tommy Walsh was already one giant step ahead of him. If Felipe vented his frustration by swearing, that would only reveal to Walsh just how badly he was rattled.

Before the silence stretched on too much longer, Felipe made himself laugh.

"Very good, Tomás," he said, taking the entrance ramp to the interstate and pushing the car even faster. Seventy-five. Eighty. "Please extend my admiration to Mr. Richter. His efficiency is—as usual—quite remarkable. Of course, it helps to have an inside man in the police force, does it not?"

It was Tommy Walsh's turn to let the silence turn stale.

"Here's how it's gonna work," Walsh finally said. "You give up and pull over, and I'll make it quick and painless. One bullet in the back of the girl's head, nice and neat."

Felipe glanced at Carrie. She was watching him, her eyes wide in the light from the dashboard, listening only to his side of the conversation.

"I recommend you stop and pick up a dictionary, Tomás," Felipe told Walsh, "and look up the definitions for both *nice* and *neat*. A bullet in the head is neither. It's ugly, in fact."

"No," Tommy Walsh said. "Ugly is what happens when I have to chase you all over kingdom come. Ugly is when I make you spend the last few hours of your life listening to your little girlfriend scream."

Eighty-five. Felipe shot past a row of semis that were themselves going well above the sixty-five miles-per-hour speed limit.

"So that's it," he said. "Option A or option B?"

"That's what it boils down to," Walsh replied.

Ninety.

"You know, man, there's always option C," Felipe said. "You give yourself up to me and plea bargain for your freedom in return for testifying against Richter—"

"Three more miles," Walsh interrupted him. "You pass the next exit, and we do it the ugly way."

The phone line was cut as Walsh hung up.

Carrie was still watching him. Felipe smiled ruefully. "I don't think he liked option C," he said, reaching over to put down the telephone.

"I want to get out," she said. "Just pull over and let me out. I'd rather take my chances with him." She gestured with her head back toward the car that was still following them.

One hundred. How much faster could this car go? Or a better question—how much faster could the limo Walsh was in go?

"I'd reconsider," Felipe said. "He just offered to put a bullet into your brain."

"That's what *you* say," Carrie said. "And we both know I have absolutely no reason to trust *you*."

Felipe nodded. "That's right," he said. "You don't. But if I were you, I'd test this situation with something smaller and less important than my life."

One hundred and five. One hundred and ten.

The exit was approaching, the green sign reflecting their headlights in the darkness. It was the point of no return. *Madre de Dios,* don't let him regret this. The thought of having to watch and listen as Walsh tortured Caroline Brooks was excruciating. But to simply pull over and quit… No. If they were going to die, they'd die fighting.

They shot past the exit, and sure enough, the shooter in the limo opened fire, trying for one of their tires.

At nearly one hundred and twenty, if they lost a tire, they'd be smeared across the road. But at nearly one hundred and twenty, the limo was hard-pressed to keep up. If only this car could go a little faster, they'd lose Walsh. Unfortunately, Felipe, too, had maxed out, with the gas pedal to the floor. Now all he could do was pray.

Pray, and turn off the headlights and rear running lights. Why give them a lighted target?

They were barreling into the darkness, with only the lights from the other cars and trucks to guide them.

But then, suddenly, the shooting stopped.

Felipe glanced into what was left of his rearview mirror.

He could see inside the limousine. The interior lights were on and Tommy Walsh was on the phone again. Walsh hung up and the limo began to slow.

As Felipe watched, Walsh moved into the right lane. As he raced up to the crest of a hill, he looked back and saw the limo's headlights turn away as the car exited the highway.

What the hell...? Was Tommy Walsh giving up? Man, what just happened here?

Felipe had a sudden bad feeling in the pit of his stomach as he lifted his foot from the accelerator and the car began to slow. Something was wrong. Something was *seriously* wrong. The only time he'd ever seen Walsh back away was when his prey was dead. The implication was that in Walsh's eyes, Felipe and Caroline were already dead.

Still, Felipe hit the brakes and turned his lights back on. He could feel Caroline's eyes on his face as he searched the rearview mirror, watching for some sign of a trap. But there was nothing. There was no sign of the limousine, no sign they were being followed by anyone else.

He exited at a rest stop, pulling onto the ramp at the last instant, keeping his signal light off.

Caroline peeked over the back of the seat. "Did we lose them?"

"No," Felipe said tersely. "They lost us. Something's wrong."

"Something's *wrong?*" she echoed. "They're not shooting at us anymore. I'd consider that to be something *right.*"

"Tommy Walsh shouldn't have given up so easily," Felipe said, glancing at her. He had to make a phone call, find out what the hell was going on.

He saw a row of pay and credit-card telephones that could be accessed without leaving the car. That was good, because now that the immediate danger had passed, Felipe's leg was starting to hurt like hell. He parked next to one of the phones, leaving the car engine idling.

But even before the car had stopped moving, Carrie was out the door like a shot.

Felipe swore. He'd pulled up to these phones because he hadn't wanted to get out of the car. His pants were wet with blood and his leg was throbbing with an unholy pain. Despite the agony, he slid across the bench seat, leaving a smear of blood on the fancy leather upholstery. Carrie hadn't closed the door, and as he left the car after her, he hit the pavement running. *Man!* His leg hurt like a *bitch,* but he ran after her anyway. If he didn't catch her, she was as good as dead. Worse, he thought, remembering Walsh's threats.

The parking lot was mostly empty. There were a few cars but no people around. She headed toward a brightly lit fast-food restaurant.

"Caroline, wait!" Felipe called, but she only ran faster, harder.

She was fast, but she was small, and her stride was only three-quarters the size of his, even with a bullet in his leg.

He caught her before she reached the wheelchair ramp up to the front door of the restaurant, and pulled her down with him onto the soft grass that lined the sidewalk.

"No!" she cried. "Let me *go!*"

She took in a deep breath to scream and he covered her mouth with his hand, trying desperately to ignore the fire of pain shooting up and down his thigh.

"Stop it!" he hissed into her ear. "I'm not going to hurt you, but Tommy Walsh will. By now, he and Richter know who you are and where you live. You go home, you're *dead.*"

There was fear in her eyes as she looked up at him. But was it his words, or was it he, himself, that frightened her?

He realized with a sudden stab of awareness that he was on top of her, covering her with the full weight of his body. Mother of God, she was so very female, so very soft, and he was crushing her.

Keeping a tight hold on her arm, he rolled off her.

"I'm sorry," he said. "I didn't mean to…"

But now she was looking at him with new horror in her eyes. "Are you bleeding?" she breathed. "My Lord, you *are.*"

Her dress and part of her leg were streaked bright red with his blood.

Still holding her with one hand, Felipe pulled himself to his feet before helping her up. "I need to make a phone call," he said, "and then we need to get out of here. We're not out of danger yet, Caroline."

He winced as he put his weight on his wounded leg. But he tried not to limp as he led her back across the parking lot toward the car. On the off chance someone was watching, he didn't want them to know he was injured.

"Lord above," Carrie said, "you were *shot*."

He glanced at her. The expression in her eyes begged him to tell her otherwise, but Felipe nodded his head. "Yes," he said. He had her full attention, and he pressed his advantage. "This is not a game we're playing here. The bullets are very real, and Tommy Walsh is saving one or two of them especially for you, do you understand?"

He watched her steadily, seeing the doubt and mistrust on her face. What he would have given simply for her to trust him. But she didn't believe him. She didn't buy into what he was telling her. Even so, behind all that mistrust, he could see her concern.

In her mind, he was the enemy, yet she was concerned for his health. Felipe found himself smiling as he gazed at her. Despite her tough-guy exterior, she was soft-hearted. She was as sweet as she looked. Dear heaven, even with her dress rumpled and stained, and her hair windblown and messy, she still managed to look incredibly sweet.

"You better do something to stop the bleeding," she said, glancing up at him. She quickly looked away, but not before Felipe caught the answering heat of attraction in her eyes. Maybe sweet wasn't quite the right word....

"You know," he said softly, "instinctively, you want to

trust me, Caroline. Instinctively, there is this powerful attraction between us—"

Carrie laughed. "I'd be willing to bet that instinctively, there's a powerful attraction between you and every woman on earth," she said, carefully not meeting his eyes.

He smiled again. "Not like this," he said. "Never like this." He closed the car door and led her around to the other side. He opened that door and, still holding her wrist, shrugged out of his tuxedo jacket. He handed it to Carrie. "Use this to wipe off the seat, please, and then get in."

To his surprise, she took it and tore it cleanly down the middle. She handed him back one of the halves. "Use this to tie around your leg to try to stop the bleeding," she said. "It *is* your leg that's hurt, isn't it?"

Felipe nodded, once again touched by her concern. Still, she wouldn't meet his eyes. "Yes," he said. "Thanks."

But he wouldn't let go of her wrist to tie the jacket around his leg.

"I won't run away," Carrie said.

Felipe just laughed.

In frustration, she took the torn fabric from him and tied it herself, folding a piece of the sleeve against the gash on his upper thigh, forming a bandage that applied pressure to the wound. Damn, it hurt. He had to grit his teeth to keep from crying out. He must have made some sort of sound, though, because she glanced up at him.

"Sorry," she whispered.

And she was. She was tending to him with as much compassion as she'd give a wounded manatee—or shark. Yes, Felipe could imagine her coming to the aid of an injured shark and disregarding its sharp, deadly teeth in the name of compassion.

Her hands were unquestionably gentle, but there was a hole in his leg where the bullet had entered. A hole, with a bullet still inside, that hurt like *hell*.

If she noticed the new layer of sweat that was glazing his face, she didn't mention it. "I've never been shot," she said, tying the bandage into place, "but my brother has— in a hunting accident. It was barely a scratch, but my other brothers had to carry him down from the mountains on a stretcher."

Brothers. Felipe realized in a flash just where they could go to hide. To his brother's. Of course. He'd cut himself off so thoroughly from Raphael, no one in the police force, including Jim Keegan, knew he had an older brother. Not even Richter would be able to track him there.

The pain had subsided to a dull, throbbing ache. Felipe forced his face to relax, then even managed to smile at Caroline. "Well, my brothers are not here right now," he said, "so I'll have to carry myself."

"You should go to the hospital," she said. "I didn't get a really good look at your leg in this light. I can't tell if the bullet's still in there. If it is, you're risking serious infection. If it's not, you still need stitches."

"The hospital can't treat a bullet wound without reporting it to the police," Felipe said. "I can't go in yet. Not until I know that it's safe for both of us."

"Please," she said, still looking up at him. "Just turn yourself in. You're clearly a man of integrity—"

"I'm so glad you've recognized that," Felipe said with a wry laugh.

"I'll go with you," she said. "I'll make sure no one hurts you. I'll help you get an attorney—"

"Caroline, I'm a cop," he said. "I don't need a lawyer."

"If you let me go right now," Carrie said as if she hadn't heard him, "I'll ask them to dismiss any kidnapping charges."

"I'm cop, a police detective," Felipe said again, looking down at her. "There will be no kidnapping charges. I wish you would believe me."

She still gazed up at him. "If you're a police detective, then let's go to the police station," she said beseechingly. "Right now. Let's just get in the car and drive over—"

"I can't."

She stood up. "Because you're not a cop."

Felipe shook his head. "No, because we're dealing with organized crime," he explained, "and they've bought someone in the department. Neither of us would last a day in local protective custody. Richter would be tipped off as to our every move, and he'd bring in a hit man to finish the job. And God knows how many good men and women would die trying to protect us."

Caroline didn't buy it—he could tell from the set of her mouth. "That's a convenient excuse," she said.

They were standing so close, she was forced to tilt her head to look up at him.

"I'm telling you the truth," he said.

She only laughed. "Are you sure you even remember the truth?" she asked. "Or maybe you simply change it with your name, Carlos. Or should I call you Raoul? No, wait, it's Felipe, isn't it? Yeah, Felipe Salazar, undercover cop."

"If you would get in the car, please, and sit down," Felipe said, feeling his patience start to slip, "then I could sit down, too. And I really, *really* would like to sit down."

She climbed into the car, and still holding tightly to her wrist, he followed her, closing the door behind him.

It was cool inside. With the engine running, the air conditioner kept the temperature down to a comfortable level. Caroline was silent as Felipe pushed the button that lowered the window, then reached outside the car for the telephone. He dialed Jim's direct number, glancing over at her.

It was so easy to imagine this woman sitting next to him in his own subcompact car, smiling instead of looking at him with this mixed expression of wariness and mistrust. He could imagine the sound of her laughter; he could picture amusement dancing in her beautiful eyes. And he could imagine bending to kiss her smiling mouth, her face upturned in anticipation of his lips.

"Jim Keegan, Homicide," said a familiar, husky voice on the other end of the line.

Felipe pulled his gaze away from Caroline's face. "Diego, it's me."

"Phil! Jesus! Thank God you're alive."

"Look, man, I need—"

"I'm sure you realize that this line's tapped," Jim said, cutting Felipe off and talking fast, "and that I've got to try to keep you on as long as possible so we can track you."

"Of course," Felipe said. My God, he'd had no idea. His heart sank. Obviously, Jim wasn't in any position to help him.

"An APB came in just a few minutes ago," Jim said. "All available men are looking for you and a stolen car, New York plate HTD-761."

In other words, ditch the car.

Jim Keegan was one of the few people who knew that Felipe had been trying to infiltrate Richter's organization. Why would he make hints for Felipe to stay away, to keep running, to stay hidden?

"You're wanted for the Sandlot Murders, pal," Jim said. "It's not my case, but the word is we've got evidence that ties you to the crime scene."

The Sandlot Murders? They'd happened less than a week ago. Two men with mob connections had been killed in a vigilante-style execution after they'd been released from prosecution on a technicality. Word on the street was that they'd been prepared to deal with the D.A. Now they were DOA and a very obvious warning to the other underlings who worked for the crime bosses.

The media had sunk their teeth into the case because the murders were committed in a vacant lot next to an inner-city elementary school. The children were traumatized, the parents were in an uproar and the newspapers and TV stations were searching for someone to blame.

The triggerman could've been any one of a number of hired assassins. It was a high-profile case with virtually no chance of being solved.

It was the perfect case to use to create a frame.

It was so obvious. Richter's man in the police department, this partner of his, this "Captain Rat," had worked hard and fast to set Felipe up. It was such an obvious frame, it was almost laughable.

Almost.

But maybe, if he could stay alive long enough, the last laugh could be Felipe's. He may not know exactly who Captain Rat was, but he *did* know that there was a planned meeting between this man and Richter in less than three days, at three-thirty in the afternoon. But he couldn't tell Jim about it—not with the line being tapped and God only knows who listening in.

"I'm supposed to try to talk you into turning yourself

in," Keegan said. "Just stay where you are, stay on the line and we'll come to you, you hear me?"

In other words, get out of there fast.

"I hear you, man," Felipe said. "Loud and clear." He hung up the phone.

Caroline Brooks watched him in silence.

"Diego can't help us," he told her, even though she had no idea who Diego was.

Diego couldn't help him, but maybe Raphael could.

It was time for a Salazar family reunion.

CHAPTER FIVE

CARRIE HEARD THE SIRENS in the distance at the same time Felipe did.

But instead of starting the car the way she expected, he opened the door.

"You're wearing sandals, not heels, am I right?" he asked, looking down the length of her legs to her feet. "Good," he added, not even waiting for her to answer. "Come on."

He was still holding on to her wrist, and he tugged her gently out of the car.

"Where are we going?" she asked.

"The police are looking for this car," he answered, leading her across the parking lot toward a grove of trees, beyond which shone the lights of a suburban street. "We're better off on foot."

"The police," she said. "I thought you *were* the police."

"I am," he said.

"Then how come they're looking for this car?" she asked. "And you, too, I assume?"

"Because they don't know that I'm one of the good guys, and that one of the bad guys is in the department," Felipe said.

His hair had come free from his ponytail, and it curled around the shoulders of his snowy white tuxedo shirt.

He'd untied his bow tie and unbuttoned the top few buttons of the shirt, its perfection now marred by darkening stains of blood. He was still shockingly handsome, despite the lines of pain Carrie could see on his face.

His eyes were as soft and as dark as the night sky above her, and equally mysterious. If she could suspend all disbelief, it would be easy to see him as one of the good guys. In a more perfect world, no criminal could possibly have eyes so kind, so warm. If she looked at him for too long, she felt as if she were being pulled into some kind of vortex—spinning, imprisoning, consuming.

She looked away, and from the corner of her eye, she saw him smile at her confusion.

"You really don't want to like anything about me, do you?" he asked as he led her into the cover of the trees. "Careful where you step," he added.

"Let me go," Carrie countered, "and I'll be your best friend."

It was dark in among the trees, away from the lights of the parking lot. The ground was spongy and wet. Mud squished up over the soles of Carrie's sandals and between her toes.

He'd slid his hand down so that he was no longer holding her wrist. Instead, he was holding her hand, their fingers interlocked as if they were lovers rather than captor and hostage.

She could no longer see his face in the darkness, but she could hear his ragged breathing. His leg must hurt him. He stumbled slightly, and his grip on her hand tightened and she heard his quick inhale. He was clearly in serious pain.

But when he spoke, his voice was even. "I can't let you go, Caroline. I'm sorry."

"Then I can't be your best friend," she said.

"That's too bad," he murmured.

Yes, oddly enough, it was.

The sirens were louder now, and despite his injury, Felipe picked up the pace. Together they half ran, half skidded down an embankment to the street below.

One dim street lamp illuminated a row of shabby houses, blue television light flickering from most of the windows. In one of them the volume was up too high. Canned laughter echoed among the cars parked along the side of the road. Farther down the street, a dog barked, but other than that, nothing moved.

Here in the darkness, Felipe didn't try to hide his limp. Still, he moved quickly along the line of cars.

"What are you looking for?" Carrie asked.

He turned toward her, putting one finger to his lips. "Shh." Bringing his mouth up close to her ear, he said very softly, "We need transportation. I'm afraid I'm not up to walking back to St. Simone."

She pulled back to stare at him. "You're going to *steal* a car...?"

"Shh," he said again. "Not steal. Borrow."

Carrie nodded. "Right. Tell that to the guy who owns the car."

Felipe ran his hand across his face. "If there was another way, I wouldn't do this," he said. "But I believe a life—*your* life—is worth more than a 1979 Subaru, don't you?"

He tugged at her arm, and she knelt next to him as he opened the driver's-side door and quickly turned off the interior light. He pulled her in front of him, pinning her between the car and his body so he could use both of his hands.

"I'm worth a vintage Ford Mustang convertible," Carrie said. "Preferably from 1966 and cherry-red."

He glanced at her and smiled, his teeth a flash of white in the darkness.

"I'm glad your sense of humor is back," he said, disconnecting a panel from the steering column.

"It's hard for me to keep my sense of humor when I'm being held hostage," Carrie said.

It was also hard to keep her sense of humor with his body pressed against hers the way it was. As he worked to hot-wire the car, his arms were on either side of her, his weight against her. Carrie tried to shift away, but only succeeded in wedging herself more firmly against him.

He pulled back slightly to look down at her. "You're not a hostage," he said.

"Are you sure?"

He didn't hesitate. "Yes. You're in protective custody."

"Assuming you are who you say you are, Carlos-Raoul-Felipe," she said.

Felipe shifted his position, then winced as his weight came down more fully on his injured leg. He wiped the sweat from his upper lip. "I'm tempted to take you to my apartment in St. Simone, just to show you my police identification," he said.

"But no doubt you've got some dramatic excuse to keep us from going there, too," Carrie said, trying to ignore the fact that his face was mere inches from her own. If he leaned forward another four inches, he'd be kissing her.

"They're looking for me. My apartment is one of the first places they'll stake out," he said. "It's no dramatic excuse. It's a fact."

"They who?" Carrie asked. "The police?"

"The police and Richter's men," Felipe said. "They'll both send someone around to watch my apartment, assuming I'd be stupid enough to show up there." The car started with a roar. "Quick, get in."

Carrie scrambled across the stick shift and into the passenger seat. She reached for the opposite door and was about to throw it open, when Felipe firmly put his hand on her left knee.

"Give me a break," he said.

"Let me go," she countered.

"Haven't you been listening to *any*thing I've told you?" Felipe said. "Put the car in first gear, please."

With her left hand, Carrie pushed the stick shift up into first position.

With a jerk, Felipe pulled away from the curb.

"If I let you go," he said, trying hard to be patient, "you're dead. Second, please."

Carrie shifted into second gear as Felipe rounded a corner onto a secondary road heading south toward St. Simone.

"I do not want you to be dead," Felipe said, "therefore, I will not let you go. As long as you're with me, I'll keep you safe. Third gear, please."

Carrie snorted, shifting gears. "Oh, you've kept me really safe so far."

Felipe turned to look at her. His eyes were dead serious. "A lot of it's been luck, and circumstance," he said, "but yes, so far, I have."

His hand was still resting on her knee. She looked down at it pointedly. "You can have your hand back," she said. "I'm not going to jump out of a car going forty."

He glanced at her and grinned. "Thirty-five, you'd try it, but not forty, huh?" He squeezed her knee slightly, then put his hand on the stick, shifting into fourth gear. "Short of driving to the precinct or going to my apartment to get my ID, what can I do to make you believe me, Caroline?"

Nothing. Carrie shook her head. "If Silver-hair—this Richter guy—if he's such a threat, how come I haven't heard about him before?"

"He's very low-key," Felipe said. "Some mob bosses, they get off on people knowing who they are and how powerful they are, you know? But not Lawrence Richter. Instead of taking a seat on the city finance committee, or some position where the media would check into his background, Richter joined the public library's volunteer board of directors. The papers and TV reporters don't pay him any mind—he's not paid after all—and, through the contacts he's made, he has the ears of some of St. Simone's most powerful politicians."

"Lawrence Richter," Carrie mused. "Doesn't exactly sound like he's Old-World Mafia."

"The Mafia controls only a portion of organized crime," Felipe said. "These days, organized crime is an equal-opportunity employer."

He used the back of his arm to wipe the sweat from his face. This car's air conditioner wasn't anything to write home about. He glanced at her and tried to smile, but she could tell it was getting harder for him to hide his pain. His face was pale—it looked almost gray in the headlights from the oncoming traffic. She wondered how much blood he'd lost.

"Do you want me to drive?" she asked.

He looked at her in surprise. "No," he said. "I'm okay. Thanks."

She studied his face in the dim light from the dash-board. With his exotic cheekbones and liquid brown eyes, with his elegantly shaped mouth and sensuous lips, with that trim, athletic body, he could have made a fortune modeling for perfume ads or loose-fitting-jeans ads or, hell, even underwear ads. Maybe especially for underwear ads. Or, if he could dance even just a little bit, he could surely have made a bundle every night over at the Chippendale's club at the corner of Gulf and Garden Streets. But he didn't even seem aware of his striking looks—well, except for the fact that somewhere down the line, he'd learned that women responded to his smile. Or maybe that wasn't learned. Maybe it was instinctive.

He could have slid along in life, getting by with that smile and those warm, expressive eyes. Instead—so he claimed—he'd chosen to become a cop.

"What made you decide to join the police force?" Carrie asked.

He glanced at her again. "Is this a test?" he asked. "If I don't have an answer ready, that proves that I'm lying?"

"You're stalling," she returned. "Do you need more time to make up your story?"

"I became a cop," Felipe said without further hesitation, "because of my brother, Rafe. Raphael. He was a robber. I figured someone had to go in the other direction and balance the family out."

"That's it?" Carrie asked. "You just woke up one morning and decided that you had to be Wyatt Earp because your brother was Jesse James?"

He looked over at her. "You really want to hear the whole story?"

She pushed her hair back behind her ear. "Yeah," she said. Oddly enough, she did. "Is Rafe older or younger?"

"Older, by about five years," Felipe said. "He first started using when he was fourteen—I was nine."

"Using?"

"Drugs."

He stared at the road. Carrie could see the sudden tension in his jaw.

"We shared a bedroom," Felipe continued, "and he used to come in wasted and tell me not to tell our parents. He was my hero—how could I tell? Besides, it was a laugh at first. He was funny when he drank or when he got stoned. But then it stopped being funny when he started using the hard stuff.

"It happened real fast—he was an addict at fifteen. By the time I realized what was happening, I couldn't stop him. I don't know how many times I tried to talk sense into him, but you can't reason with an addict.

"I could only pick him up off the street when he was too high to walk, and carry him home. I could only hide his stash from my father. I could only give him the money from my paper route when he was broke and hurting and needing drugs to ease his pain. And I could keep my mouth shut when he started stealing."

Felipe glanced at Carrie, but she didn't speak. She simply waited for him to continue.

"Rafe didn't know it," he said, "but I gave back most of the stuff he stole. He thought he was getting ripped off by some of the other guys in the 'hood, but it was just me, covering his ass." He laughed, but the sound was devoid of humor. "Man, I was the perfect little enabler but I didn't even know the definition of the word. I was Rafe's worst enemy, second only to himself." He turned to glance at her again. "You sure you want to hear more?"

Carrie nodded. His words rang with a certain bitter truth. She actually wanted to believe him.

"Rafe and I did the addict-enabler dance for eight

years," Felipe said, his gentle accent like music accompanying the soft hiss of the car's tires against the road. "Then, the summer I turned seventeen, one of the detectives in the local precinct started an outreach program designed to help kids like me—and indirectly, help kids like Rafe.

"By that time, Rafe had a few priors, nothing too big, and no punishment bigger than a reprimand. Still, this detective, Jorge Gamos, added up Rafe's record with what he saw going on in the neighborhood. Gamos actually came out on the street and hung with the kids. He got to know us. He saw that Rafe had a habit, and he also saw my stress levels, which were pretty high by that time. I was seventeen—going on forty-five. I hadn't been a kid since Rafe lit his first crack pipe. Anyway, Jorge Gamos saw what was going on, and he figured out—correctly—that my brother couldn't have lasted so long on the street if it hadn't been for me.

"It took Gamos nearly a year, but he finally talked me into going to a meeting that he helped run—a counseling session for kids who'd lost a brother or sister to drugs. It was…eye-opening, particularly when he told me that I was going to end up right there, with those kids, talking about my brother Rafe. My *dead* brother Rafe."

Carrie wanted to believe him, but his story was probably fictional. Still, it was one hell of a good tale. "Did Rafe die?" Carrie found herself asking, as if Rafe were a real person, as if Felipe really had been a kid who'd lost his childhood to drugs.

He glanced at her, a fleeting smile touching his lips. "Not yet," he said. "I virtually turned him in. He came to me for an alibi, but I wouldn't lie anymore. He was convicted and served an eight-month sentence. During that time, he detoxed. When I went to see him in the jail, he thanked me for helping him, and he swore he'd never touch crack again. He was clean and he was going to stay clean. I was attending the police academy by that time. I was going to be a cop. With Jorge Gamos's help, I got Rafe an early release."

Felipe shook his head. "Raphael hit the streets and in a matter of weeks, he was using again. It nearly broke my heart. He'd conned me into getting him out of prison. His apology, everything he'd told me had been nothing but crap. None of it had been sincere. *None* of it." He laughed bitterly. "He ended up back in prison, but after he scammed me, I washed my hands of him. I haven't seen him in years. Apparently, Rafe's been out of jail for a while now. Jorge tells me he's really clean these days, that he runs a halfway house and works as a counselor for addicts and ex-cons. I've heard that counselors who've been addicts and ex-cons themselves are the most compassionate. Man, I guess he's got that covered because he's been there and back." He leaned over and tried to turn the air conditioner's fan higher. "That's where we're heading, by the way."

Carrie blinked. "You mean…right now?"

"Yes. To Raphael's halfway house." Felipe glanced at her, his dark eyes even more mysterious. "It's time for my brother to pay some old debts."

BY THE TIME Felipe pulled up in front of the A Street Halfway House, his left leg was on fire. He should have ripped off a car with an automatic transmission. Borrowed, he corrected himself. The car was only borrowed. And he'd memorized the plates so that when this was over, he could track down the owner and give him or her money for the mileage, gas and inconvenience.

If he was still alive when this was over....

He looked over at Caroline Brooks who sat quietly in the passenger seat, gazing back at him, unmindful of the fact that they were parked in the most run-down, dangerous part of the city.

"Are you all right?" she asked quietly.

Her blue eyes were colorless in the shadowy darkness. Her hair looked silvery, reflecting what little light there was. He could smell her perfume—no, that wasn't perfume. It was sun block that he smelled. Carrie wasn't the type to wear perfume. The fresh tang of the lotion suited her better than any flowery fragrance could have. She smelled like blue skies and white sand and warm gulf water. She smelled like paradise.

He'd had a bigger whiff when he'd kissed her back at the restaurant. He thought back to the way her lithe body had fitted against his.... Paradise indeed. Oh, what he would give to kiss her again.

"I must be all right," he said, finally answering her question. "The thoughts I am thinking are those of a healthy man."

She turned away. It was too dark for him to see the blush tingeing her cheeks, but he knew it was there.

She was such a contradiction, this Caroline Brooks. Part of her was a tough-talking, rifle-wielding, no-nonsense fighter. But another part of her blushed at his sweet talk.

Felipe reached over and took her hand, and she nearly jumped out of her seat.

"I know it's an inconvenience to hop over the stick shift," he said, "but I need you to come out of the car this way. I can't risk your running again."

Still holding tightly to her hand, he opened the car

door and stiffly pulled himself to his feet. Pain hit him in one solid wave and that, with his light-headedness, nearly made him black out. But Caroline was right behind him, and she held him up, looping his arm around her neck and supporting most of his body weight.

"Can you make it inside?" she asked, "or should I get help?"

Felipe tried to straighten up. "No way in *hell* am I going to face my brother on anything but my own two feet," he declared, then realized he had spoken in Spanish. God, he was losing it fast. The concern in Caroline's eyes was growing. "I can make it," he said, this time in English. He forced a smile. "Thanks for not running away."

Regret passed briefly across her eyes. "Yeah, well, I should have," she said, helping him around the car and onto the cracked sidewalk. "I'm leaving as soon as I get you inside."

"No, you're not," he countered. "I can't let you."

"Watch it," she said sharply, "or I'll drop you right here and run."

"If you do," he said, "somehow, someway, I will find the strength to follow you."

She turned to look up into his eyes, and he knew that she believed him. She may not have believed his story about his brother, she may not have believed that he was a cop investigating Lawrence Richter, she may not have believed that Tommy Walsh would kill her as easily as blinking, but she *did* believe that he would follow her.

It was a start.

CHAPTER SIX

RAPHAEL SALAZAR was bigger than his brother. He was older, harder, leaner to the point of being wiry, and several inches taller. His hair wasn't quite as long, though he, too, wore it pulled severely back from his face in a ponytail at his nape. But the biggest difference was in his eyes. Unlike Felipe's, Rafe's eyes were flat, cold and expressionless.

He didn't bother to greet his brother but simply came into the linoleum-tiled waiting room. Two other men, the two who had answered the door, stood slightly behind him. One was almost as broad as he was tall, his Bugs Bunny T-shirt stretched tight across his belly; the other was just a kid, looking barely even eighteen years old.

Rafe didn't move, didn't even blink. He just stared at Felipe, who was sitting on a hard bench against the far wall, Carrie at his side.

"Yes," Felipe said. "That's right, man. It's me."

Rafe took in the bloodstains and the makeshift bandage on Felipe's leg. Then his cold eyes flickered toward Carrie. He spoke softly, but in rapid-fire Spanish.

"In English, please," Felipe said. "Or she won't understand."

"Figures you'd get a gringa girlfriend," Rafe said. His voice was raspier, harsher than Felipe's. "Our kind's not good enough for you, eh, little brother?"

"My kind is human," Felipe said evenly. "Besides, she's not a girlfriend. She's in my protective custody."

"Does she have a name?" Rafe asked, looking back at Carrie.

His face was similar to Felipe's in shape, but because he was older, or maybe because he was thinner, his cheekbones looked angular, his nose sharp. He was dangerous-looking, like a wolf or an attack dog.

"She has one," Felipe said pleasantly. "But you don't need to know it. The fewer people who know her name, the fewer who can spread the word on the street that she was here, no?"

Carrie looked from Rafe to Felipe. "*She* doesn't like people talking about her as if she wasn't in the room, *if* you boys don't mind."

Rafe said something to Felipe in Spanish.

Felipe shook his head. "Stop," he said quietly.

Rafe turned again to Carrie. "Even though you are not one of our kind, I was pointing out your obvious physical attributes to my little brother," he said. "Sometimes he gets so caught up in being superhuman, he forgets that the people he's dealing with are mere flesh and blood."

Carrie looked at Felipe, but he was staring down at the floor. Even though this building was air-conditioned, he was still perspiring. His face was expressionless but his jaw was tightly clenched. Whether it was from his brother's harsh words or the pain from his bullet wound, Carrie couldn't tell.

As if he felt her eyes on him, Felipe glanced up. There was sadness in his eyes. He tried to force a smile, but failed miserably.

"I don't think I've ever seen him with his hair this long," Rafe continued. "He usually wears it well above his ears, you know? And I'm certain I've never seen him with his jacket off and trousers torn. What's the deal with my little brother? He under cover?"

"I don't know." Carrie stood up. "I'd like to leave," she said, lifting her chin and staring straight into Rafe's peculiar, lifeless eyes.

Felipe reached out and took her arm. Rafe, of course, didn't miss the move.

"But you're in 'protective custody,' no?" he said. "Maybe you don't think you need to be? Ah, but Felipe, he always knows what's best for everyone else. Felipe, he's always right. Except..." Rafe's gaze flickered back to the bandage on Felipe's leg, and all the blood that covered what was left of his tuxedo. "Maybe this time Felipe was a little *too* right, huh? And maybe someone with a gun doesn't like being wrong. Was it anyone I know, *niño?* One of our other brothers and sisters perhaps? Maybe you've betrayed one of them lately, the way you've betrayed me, huh?"

That one hurt. Even though Felipe's expression didn't change, his fingers tightened around her wrist, and Carrie knew that the barbs from Rafe's sarcastic comment had struck hard.

Still, when Felipe spoke, his voice was even. "You don't know the man who shot me," he said. "But you probably know *of* him."

Rafe laughed, but it was humorless. "I know of half a dozen men who'd probably like very much to shoot you or any one of the men in blue you work with," he said, "and that's without thinking very hard."

"This one's real trouble, man," Felipe said.

He spoke quietly, but there was something in his tone that made Rafe pause. He turned to the two men who were standing behind him and spoke to them in Spanish. They went out of the room, closing the door behind him.

"Tommy Walsh," Felipe said. He glanced at Carrie. "He wants us both dead."

"Walsh," Rafe said. His thin face became even more wary and aloof.

Carrie felt fear flicker in the pit of her stomach. Rafe's quiet response to Walsh's name told her more than any louder reaction could've done.

"I need help," Felipe said quietly. "I'm in deep, man. I've been shot, Walsh is after us and Richter's got a man in my department, ready to get rid of me the minute I resurface at the precinct."

"So you come to me," Rafe said softly, sarcastically. "I'm touched."

"All I want is to get cleaned up," Felipe said. "A shower, and maybe some clean clothes for both me and…" He looked at Carrie. "Her."

Rafe smiled, a bitter twist of his lips that attempted to hide his anger. "You don't even trust *me* with her name, huh?"

"I'm sorry," Felipe said. "I don't."

Rafe's temper exploded. "You're not sorry, you self-righteous, holier-than-thou son of a—"

"You're wrong," Felipe interrupted him, his cool vanishing, too. His voice shook with passion and he pulled himself clumsily to his feet. "I spent more years sorry than you even have memories of. Sorry for *your* mistakes, sorry for *your* pain. Sorry for you, and sorry for myself, too, because your mistakes and your pain were mine to share. They were *my* burden, too. I *am* sorry I don't trust you, but I don't. That's one thing you taught me well, Raphael—that you were not to be fully trusted, *never* to be fully trusted."

"If you don't trust me," Rafe snarled, "why the hell did you bother to come here? How do you know I'm not going to run out and tip Walsh off that you and little Miss No-name are here?"

"I don't know that you're not going to," Felipe said. "I can only hope that you won't. I can only pray you'll remember everything I've done for you—"

"You kept me from hitting bottom on my own," Rafe countered hotly. "Because of you, it took me another three years to come clean."

"When some people hit bottom, they hit with enough force to kill themselves," Felipe said. "I knew you were going to hate me for doing it, but I loved you and I didn't want you to *die*." He shook his head in resignation and turned to Carrie. "Come on, we're getting out of here. He's not going to help."

"I don't hate you," Rafe said, suddenly quiet.

To Carrie's surprise, his eyes were filled with tears, tears and a depth of emotion that made his eyes look so much more like Felipe's. But then he blinked, and both the tears and the emotion were gone, leaving his eyes oddly flat again.

"My apartment's on the second floor," Rafe continued, his voice still quiet. "You can take a shower there. There're clothes in the closet. Help yourself. I'll have Highboy show you up."

And with that, Rafe turned and walked out of the room.

RAPHAEL SALAZAR'S apartment consisted of one small room with a tiny attached bathroom. He had a sofa bed with a small coffee table in front of it and a cheap television set and a VCR on a stand in front of that. There was nothing on the walls—no pictures, no photos, nothing to personalize the room.

A dresser stood in the corner, with shaving supplies and a brush and comb neatly arranged on top, a small mirror attached to the wall above it. Several days' worth of newspapers were on the coffee table, but they, too, were neatly stacked.

In the other corner was a makeshift kitchen area, with a tiny sink built into an equally tiny counter area. A small table and a pair of cheap kitchen chairs sat nearby. On top of the table was a hot plate and a plastic sugar bowl. Underneath the table was a small, square refrigerator.

There was one window, with bars both on the inside and the outside.

Felipe locked the door behind the man in the Bugs Bunny shirt—Rafe had called him Highboy. He limped to the window and pulled down the shade.

"So, you see? My brother Rafe's real," he said to Carrie. "Any chance you're starting to believe what I've told you about Walsh and Richter?"

Carrie could see herself in the mirror over the dresser. Her hair was tangled and limp. She had a smudge of blood—Felipe's blood—across her cheek. *Was* she starting to believe him? She didn't know what to think anymore.

Felipe sat down on one of the kitchen chairs. He didn't wait for her to answer. "Why don't you take a shower?" he suggested gently. "You'll feel better. It'll clear your head."

"We need to—*you* need to get your leg cleaned up," Carrie said. "You should go first."

His eyes were warm as he looked up at her. "Thanks," he said. Then he peered at his roughly bandaged leg and grimaced. "But it's going to take me a while to get undressed. So go ahead. Just don't use up all the hot water, okay?"

He started unfastening the mother-of-pearl buttons of his tuxedo shirt, and Carrie turned away. A shower seemed like an especially good idea—particularly since the alternative was to stand and watch Felipe strip down to his underwear. Or beyond.

Carrie quickly went into the bathroom.

It was as Spartan as the rest of the apartment. The white tile floor was spotless. The sink, tub and toilet were gleaming white porcelain. The shower curtain looked fairly new. It was clear plastic, and it hadn't yet been fogged up by mildew and age. The room was devoid of any personal items—with the exception of a copy of *Off Road Cycle* magazine on the top of the toilet tank. A small cabinet held clean white towels in a neatly folded stack.

There was no window for her to climb out of and escape.

Carrie wasn't quite sure whether to feel disappointed or relieved. Because the truth was, Rafe's reaction to the name Tommy Walsh *had* made her start to wonder if Felipe's story wasn't true.

Lord above, maybe Felipe *was* a cop.

Carrie locked the door securely behind her and quickly stripped off her clothes.

The shower felt good, and she washed her hair with Rafe's inexpensive shampoo, wondering if maybe everything Felipe Salazar had told her was the truth.

If that was the case, he'd saved her life more than once tonight. And with no thanks from her.

She came out of the shower and toweled herself dry.

She didn't want to put her bloodstained dress back on, but she had no choice.

She also had no comb, so she ran her fingers through her wet hair, trying to untangle it. When she'd done the best she could, she put her hand on the doorknob.

Taking a deep breath, Carrie opened the door. She opened it slowly, then peeked around to see if Felipe had moved from his seat in the far corner of the room.

He had. He was standing in front of the tiny kitchen sink, his back to her. He'd undressed down to an expensive-looking pair of dark green and navy blue paisley silk boxer shorts and a white tank undershirt that contrasted with the rich darkness of his tanned skin. He was wearing more than he would have had she run into him on the beach. Still, he was in his underwear, and Carrie felt uncomfortable—possibly because she had dreamed about him wearing even less.

His body was as trim and athletic as she'd imagined. The sleek muscles in his shoulders and arms rippled as he supported his weight on the kitchen counter. The water was running, and he didn't hear her as she approached.

Without his pants on, she could clearly see the wound that the bullet had made on the side of his thigh, just under the edge of his shorts. He was lucky that the bullet hadn't hit an artery. The wound was still bleeding slightly, or maybe it was bleeding again from his attempts to clean threads of tuxedo fabric from the gash. Bright red blood trickled slowly down his leg.

As she watched, he reached into the sink to wring water and blood from a washcloth he was rinsing out. He swayed slightly and caught himself on the edge of the sink, closing his eyes and trying to breathe deeply.

"Why don't you sit down?" Carrie said. "I'll do that."

He opened his eyes and turned to look at her. "Ah," he said, "you're out of the shower."

"Sit down," she said again. She took the washcloth from his hands and finished rinsing it in the sink.

Felipe didn't move. He stood there, inches away from her, so close she could feel the heat from his body.

"So," she said, turning off the water and wringing the cloth out, "what on earth made you decide to be a detective in the vice squad? I figure you're vice, right? That's where organized crime fits in, doesn't it?"

She looked steadily up into the warmth of his brown eyes. He looked back searchingly, and then he smiled, a real genuine smile despite his pain. It softened his face and made him seem so much younger.

But he *was* young, Carrie realized. He probably wasn't much older than she was—twenty-five. He was twenty-six or twenty-seven at the most.

"You believe me." It was a statement, but his eyes were full of questions.

"God help me," Carrie said. "I think I'm starting to. But…" She shook her head, pulling away from the hypnotizing heat of his eyes, turning back to the sink.

"What?"

He touched her. It was just a light hand on her shoulder, just the gentlest of caresses.

"You have a question?" he asked. "I'll answer anything you want to know, if I can."

Carrie moved out of reach, crossing her arms in front of her, afraid of the way that touch made her feel. "I still can't believe anyone would want to kill *me*," she said. "I didn't even get a good look at that muscle man—you know, Tommy Walsh." She shook her head. "I probably wouldn't even be able to pick him out in a lineup."

"Probably," Felipe said. "Probably's not good enough for Tommy. He'd kill a blind man at a crime scene simply on the off chance that the man caught a whiff of his cologne. Promise me something, Caroline."

She looked up at him, and once again was sucked into the intensity of his gaze.

"Promise me you'll ask Rafe—or anyone else here—about Tommy Walsh," Felipe said. "Please don't leave until you hear what the word on the street is about him. Promise me you won't leave."

Carrie swallowed. He was so serious, so intense. His hair was slick with perspiration and several stray curls clung to the side of his handsome face. With his midnight eyes, he was willing her to agree.

"Promise me," he whispered again.

She nodded, not sure whether or not she was lying. "All right."

But he believed her and relief made him sag. She moved quickly beside him, holding him up.

"Come on," she said. "You better sit down."

"Part of my problem," Felipe said ruefully, "is that I've got a bullet where I sit down."

He did, too. Still have a bullet in his leg, that is. There was an entry wound, but no exit wound. That was bad. That was *really* bad, especially since he refused to go to the hospital. Carrie helped him into one of the kitchen chairs.

He swore softly in Spanish. The change in his position must've hurt like hell. Carrie knelt next to him.

"You're going to need to get that bullet out," she said, examining the back of his leg. "This already looks infected."

He nodded slowly. "Unfortunately, I can't do it myself."

"You need a doctor," Carrie said.

"That's going to have to wait," Felipe said.

"Until when?" Carrie asked. "Until after you get so sick you can't even stand, or until after you die?"

Felipe pushed himself up off the chair. "I need a shower," he said. "Then I'll figure out what to do."

"You'll need antibiotics, too," Carrie said. "Where are you going to get them?"

"I don't know." Painfully, he reached down to where he'd thrown his pants onto the floor, and dug through his pockets. He pulled out a key.

"Since you trust me," he said, handing her the key, "it's only fair that I trust you." He gestured to the key. "It's for the dead bolt on the apartment door."

Carrie glanced at the door, then back at the shiny key in her hand.

"You promised me you wouldn't leave," Felipe reminded her.

He turned, carrying his bloody clothes and his shoulder holster and gun with him to the bathroom. He pushed the door shut behind him, but didn't latch it.

Carrie heard the water turn on. Slowly, she sat down on the sofa.

Felipe needed a doctor. They both needed some kind of protection from this Tommy Walsh. And—if Felipe's story really was true—Felipe needed to figure out exactly who in the police department was on Lawrence Richter's payroll.

Carrie shook her head. It was too much. A few hours ago, her biggest problem had been how to ditch her date without hurting his feelings. Now she was neck-deep in intrigue and murder attempts...and undercover police detectives with charming smiles that could make her melt.

It was getting more and more difficult *not* to believe Felipe. Was his story really becoming more convincing, or was she simply falling victim to his persuasive eyes?

Still, if she truly were his hostage, he wouldn't have given her a key to the door. He wouldn't have risked the possibility of her running away.

A sharp knock on the door broke into her thoughts and made her jump up.

"Who's there?" she asked, aware once again that she was holding the key. She could actually unlock the door if she wanted to.

"Rafe," Felipe's brother's voice replied. "I've brought something for you to eat. Open up."

Carrie slipped the key into the dead bolt's lock, but it didn't fit. She tried again. No, it was definitely the wrong key. "They key doesn't work," she said.

"There are two keys," Rafe said impatiently. "One has a round head, the other is square. The round one opens the dead bolt. The square is for the bathroom door."

Carrie looked down at the key in her hand. The head was square. Felipe hadn't given her the key to unlock the apartment door after all.

"The food's outside the door," Rafe said, his voice already fading as he walked away.

So much for Felipe trusting her...

Carrie turned and looked at the bathroom door. It was ajar, and she could clearly hear the shower still running.

Lord, maybe she *was* his hostage. Maybe everything he'd told her was one great big lie.

Angrily, she marched to the bathroom door and pushed it open.

Felipe was in the shower, eyes closed, hands braced against the tile wall as he let the water stream down onto his head. She could see him clearly through the plastic shower curtain. He was naked, of course. He was very, *very* naked.

Which made sense, again of course, because he was in the shower.

The bathroom door slowly swung all the way open and hit the wall with a thud.

Felipe looked up and directly into Carrie's eyes.

For one heart-stopping moment, the rest of the world ceased to exist. Tommy Walsh and Lawrence Richter and all the car chases and gunfire and anger and mistrust vanished, swirling down the drain with the blood-tinged water. Carrie was all that was left behind—Carrie, and this incredible-looking man, with his seemingly perfect, gentle smile and kind brown eyes.

But he wasn't smiling now, and his eyes couldn't possibly be described as kind. Hot, yes. Intense, definitely. Passionate, absolutely.

He made no effort to cover himself. Clearly, he was comfortable with his body—and why shouldn't he be, with a body like that? He had muscular legs, narrow hips, a flat stomach with a full array of washboardlike muscles. His chest was wide, his shoulders were broad and his arms were powerful-looking.

His skin was smooth and slick with water, accentuating the planes and angles and curves of his muscles. He didn't have a tan line—either he sunbathed nude, or his skin was naturally a beautiful golden brown.

Felipe slicked his hair back out of his face and turned off the water. With one movement of his hand, he pushed the shower curtains open. Steam billowed into the tiny bathroom, following him as he stepped out of the tub, making him seem mystical and savage.

He reached for a towel and wrapped it around his waist, careful of his injured leg. "Is there a problem?" he asked in his gentle, musical accent.

For heaven's sake, she was standing there like a ninny, with her mouth hanging open, just staring at him as if she'd never seen a naked man before in her life.

She'd never seen one like Felipe, that was for sure.

"You gave me the wrong key," she said. Her voice came out sounding squeaky, not accusing or outraged the way she'd intended.

Water ran in tiny rivulets from his shoulders, down his neatly sculpted chest, up and down the ripples of his abdominal muscles and into the towel, knotted casually beneath his belly button. He had an exceptionally nice-looking belly button.

"You promised you wouldn't leave," Felipe said.

Carrie jerked her eyes up from where she'd been staring at his smooth, perfect stomach. "I didn't promise I wouldn't let your brother in," she said. "He brought up some food, and I couldn't unlock the door."

"You couldn't?" He sounded surprised.

"You knew perfectly well I couldn't," she said. He took another towel and began drying his dripping hair. "There were two keys—you purposely gave me the wrong one."

He was watching her. His eyes didn't give away either his guilt or his innocence. "My mistake," he said quietly.

A mistake? Carrie wasn't so sure. She couldn't believe this man ever made *any* mistakes.

Felipe had hung his torn and dirty tuxedo pants on the back of the bathroom door, along with his holster and gun. He reached into the pants pocket and took out another key.

"I'm sorry," he said, handing it to Carrie. "Please don't mistrust me because of this."

The key in her hand had a round head. It would unlock the dead bolt and let her out of Rafe's apartment.

"You're going to let me walk out of here?" she asked.

"You promised not to leave," he said. "You're a smart lady, Caroline. I don't think you will leave—not after you hear what my brother and his friends have to say about Tommy Walsh. And if you do decide you have to leave, I hope you'll be smart enough to go home to Montana."

"How did you know I'm from Montana?" she asked suspiciously.

He looped the second towel around his neck and sat gingerly on top of the closed toilet. He was hurting, but he still managed to smile at her. "After our first meeting at Sea Circus," he said, "I was…intrigued, shall we say? I went back—and not just to make sure you were all right, although I went back for that reason, too."

"If you're really a cop," Carrie said, searching his eyes for something, *any*thing that would convince her he was telling the truth, "why didn't you say something? Why didn't you introduce yourself to me?"

"I should have," he said simply. There were pages of meaning compressed into those three little words. His eyes caressed her face and Carrie had to look away. "I loved watching you with the dolphins," he added. "I've always wanted to swim with dolphins, but I think I'd draw the line at getting into the tank with the killer whales—what were their names? Biffy and Louise?"

She looked back up at him. "You really *were* there," she said. "Weren't you?"

Felipe nodded. "I came more than once," he said, "although I tried not to. I thought knowing me would be dangerous for you." He smiled ruefully. "Looks like I was right."

"Nothing at Sea Circus mentions that I'm from Montana," Carrie said. "Was that just a good guess?"

"No," he said. "Don't be angry, but I looked you up in the police computer. I also found out that you have the habit of driving too fast on I-75. Two speeding tickets in the course of one week. Eighty-one one day, seventy-nine the next." He shook his head, making tsking sounds. "Shame on you, Miss Brooks."

He was hiding a smile, but that smile finally slipped out. Carrie found herself smiling back at him.

"I have no excuse," she said, "and obviously I didn't learn my lesson, did I? I slowed down, but not by much."

"I took care of the tickets for you," Felipe said. "It was the least I could do after locking you in your trunk."

Carrie's smile faded. "Was that really necessary?" she asked. "I mean, assuming you really are a police detective, and assuming you really were under cover that night at Sea Circus. What do you really think would have happened if you hadn't locked me in the trunk of my car?"

Felipe sighed. "I *am* a police detective," he said, clearly disappointed that she still doubted him. "I *was* under cover that night. And if I hadn't put you in the trunk where you were safe, well, those men I was with? They were not very nice men. I would have had to hurt them. Or worse. Because I would not have let them hurt you."

It was very hard not to believe him, not when he sat there, gazing up at her with that protective light in his eyes.

I would not have let them hurt you.

Carrie could almost believe it. She *wanted* to believe it.

"Talk to Rafe," Felipe said. "Talk to some of the other

men who live here. Ask them about Tommy Walsh. Then come back and talk to me. Okay?"

Carrie nodded. Okay.

She turned and walked out of the bathroom. She could feel his eyes watching her as she crossed to the apartment door. She could feel him watching as she turned the key, unlocking the bolt. She glanced back once, then slipped out the door.

FELIPE SCRAMBLED for the living room, searching for a clock. There was one on the VCR—it read 9:36 p.m.

Thank God.

The halfway house was locked up tight from nine-thirty every night until six in the morning.

Carrie wouldn't be able to leave the building even if she wanted to—not without a great deal of trouble anyway. She certainly wouldn't be able to simply walk away.

And that was good, because Felipe couldn't let her leave. He would not let her get killed, even if that meant locking her up, holding her prisoner. Even if it meant that she would hate him.

Better that she hated him and stayed alive, than loved him and died.

CHAPTER SEVEN

CARRIE HADN'T REALLY NOTICED when she'd first come in, but now she realized the entire halfway house was as spotlessly clean and orderly as Rafe's apartment. The halls and stairway were swept and brightly lit, and the walls wore a fresh coat of paint.

She wandered down past a large common room and into the kitchen. Highboy was cleaning the stove, an apron tied carefully around his wide expanse.

Rafe was sitting at the kitchen table, drinking a diet cola straight from the can. He looked up as Carrie lingered in the doorway.

"Is he okay?" Rafe asked without greeting. They both knew who he was talking about. Felipe.

Carrie shook her head. "He's still got a bullet in his leg," she said. "Not only does it hurt him, but it's going to make him sick."

Rafe blinked. "I know what a bullet does, what it can do," he said. He turned to the man cleaning the stove, and spoke to him in Spanish.

The man nodded and left the room, squeezing past Carrie, who still stood in the doorway.

"Gracias," Rafe called after him. He looked at Carrie. "We have a former medical doctor in residence. He spent about four years in service in 'Nam. He'll know how to

take care of a bullet wound. He owes me, big time. This will make us even."

"May I sit down?" Carrie asked.

Rafe shrugged. "It's a free country. Sit where you want."

Carrie came into the kitchen and sat down at the table across from him. The kitchen was as immaculate as the rest of the house—maybe even more so. From somewhere, maybe the common room down the hall, came the sound of canned TV laughter.

"This is a nice place," Carrie said.

Rafe laughed derisively. "That surprises you," he said. "No, don't deny it, I know it does. You think, ex-cons, recovering addicts and alcoholics, and you automatically think dump, right? Yeah." He laughed again. "The problem is, some of the time you're right. But not here." He sat forward, leaning toward her across the table, his flat brown eyes oddly alight. "One of the things you need to learn when you're an addict is self-respect. You think anyone who truly respects themselves would shoot themselves full of crap? No way. So how do you learn to respect yourself? One of the things you do is take pride in where you live. You *don't* live in a dump. You keep your place clean. And then you look around and you say, 'Hey, I live in this nice place, so maybe I'm worth something after all. What do you know?'"

Carrie didn't speak. She wasn't sure what to say. She could feel Rafe Salazar's eyes studying her.

"Forty-eight hours," he said suddenly.

She looked up at him. "Excuse me?"

"That's my prediction," he said with a wolfish grin. "My little brother's gonna get you into bed with him in the next forty-eight hours."

Carrie felt herself blush, but she held her chin up and looked him straight in the eye. "You're wrong," she said. "But wrong or right, I really don't think that it's any of your business."

"You look like one of those little blond angels we used to hang on our Christmas tree," Rafe mused. "Even when he was a kid, Felipe liked the little blond angels. He's not going to be able to resist you, angel. If you don't want him in your bed, you're gonna have to work hard at keeping your distance."

"Thanks for the tip," Carrie said dryly. "You have any additional words of wisdom to share with me about this Tommy Walsh guy?"

"Why's he after you?" Rafe asked.

Good question. "I was there when Felipe's cover was blown," Carrie said. "I think your brother had infiltrated some crime boss's organization—"

"Lawrence Richter," Rafe broke in, supplying the name.

"That's right," Carrie said. "Felipe says he has enough information to put both Walsh and Richter away."

"And you were there when Felipe's cover was blown?" Rafe repeated. "How much 'there'?"

Carrie made herself steadily meet his eyes as she confessed, "I, um, blew his cover."

Rafe didn't say anything for several long moments. He took a sip from his can of soda and put it carefully down on the table, turning it so that the label was directly in front of him.

"Well, angel," he finally said, "if I were you, I'd think about getting my personal effects and last will and testament in order."

Carrie had been holding her breath, but now she let it out in a ragged swoosh of air. "That bad, huh?"

"You have two options," Rafe said. "Either you change your identity and disappear, or...Walsh finds you and you die."

"Even though I'm not positive I could ID him?" Carrie asked.

"Walsh wasted a six-year-old for witnessing a hit," Rafe said. "He's got to do Felipe—he's got no choice, not if Felipe can put Richter in jail. But my little brother's a cop. Killing him's a capital offense. We're talking mandatory death sentence. You'd be able to tie Walsh to Felipe's death. Walsh probably doesn't like the idea of the electric chair, so he's got to do you, too."

"But Felipe's not dead," Carrie said.

"Yet," Rafe finished grimly. "I knew the *estúpido* sonuvabitch would get himself into something like this someday. I swear to God—" He looked up at Carrie, stopping abruptly. "There's something that you should know about my little brother."

Carrie waited for him to explain.

"He expects everybody to be the same kind of saint that he is," Rafe said. "It's impossible to live up to his expectations." He smiled, but it was humorless. "No doubt you'll disappoint him too, angel, when he finds out you're just human, a mere mortal like the rest of us."

"Can you really blame him for being disappointed and mistrustful of you?" Carrie asked Rafe quietly.

Her words struck home. She could see it in the tension in his face and shoulders, but Rafe shook his head. "He scorns me because I am an addict. A recovering addict, but an addict just the same. But you know what?" Rafe added. "Felipe, he's an addict, too. He's addicted to living on the edge. He's addicted to danger. Either that, or he's got some kind of sick death wish, no? What kind of man would try to bring Richter and Walsh down? What kind of man would put himself eyeball-deep in that kind of danger?"

"A brave man," Carrie answered. "A man who wants to help and protect innocent people."

As she spoke those words defending Felipe, Carrie realized that she believed him. She believed he was a cop. She believed what he'd said about Richter and Walsh. She believed everything Felipe had told her.

Rafe laughed and laughed. "Ah, angel, you've already bought into the saint story, huh?"

It was something of a relief, believing Felipe. She could rely on him to protect her from Tommy Walsh. She could quit fighting him, quit searching for a way to escape. She could let herself trust him. And she could stop worrying so much about the powerful attraction that sparked between them every time their eyes met....

"You're not so different from your brother," Carrie observed. "You help people, too."

"Felipe doesn't see it that way," Rafe said. "To him, I'm just a time bomb, ready to explode and start smoking crack again. He can't see past what I was."

"That's because you hurt and disappointed him when he was a child," Carrie said. "You can't expect him just to forget that."

"He'll never forget," Rafe said bitterly. "He'll never forgive me."

Exasperated, Carrie stood up, shoving her chair away from the table with a screech. "If you really want him to forgive you, you might try being a little nicer to him," she said sharply. "Good Lord, Felipe walks in here with a bullet in his leg, needing help, and you insult him and argue with him and are downright *mean* to him. Maybe *you're* the one who won't forgive and forget."

She pushed her chair back under the table and strode out of the room.

Rafe's harsh laughter followed her down the hall. "An angel for the saint," he said. "It's perfect. Did I say forty-eight hours? I'm gonna change that prediction to twenty-four."

Carrie ignored him, hurrying up the stairs.

FELIPE'S LEG was throbbing, and he was so nauseated he was sure he must look green. But the bullet was out of his leg, thanks to a tall, heavyset man who called himself Doc Bird.

He'd given Felipe something to bite down on as he dug for the bullet. It had been a grueling two minutes, but only two minutes. One hundred and twenty seconds of hell. It could've been far worse.

Once more, Felipe was drenched with sweat. But he doubted he could stand up and take another shower. Besides, the stitches Doc Bird had put into his leg had come with instructions not to get them wet for at least a day if not two.

He pushed the hair out of his eyes and tried to focus on the clock on the VCR. It was nearly ten o'clock. Where was Caroline?

Another ten minutes, and pain or no pain, nausea or no nausea, he was going to go looking for her. Until then, he had to find something to distract himself.

He checked out the pile of newspapers on the coffee table. The top paper had a headline about St. Simone's newly appointed chief of police, a man named Earley.

Felipe knew him. He'd met him at least half a dozen

times, maybe more. He was a little too conservative, a little too old-fashioned and probably exactly what the city needed in a police chief.

He picked up the paper, but the tiny print made his eyes swim and he threw it back on the table. Instead, he picked up the remote control and switched on the television.

The Fox affiliate carried a ten o'clock news program. Curious to see if the news had been released about his so-called connection to the Sandlot Murders, he switched to that station.

The program was just starting. The lead story concerned an outbreak of salmonella poisoning at a local nursing home. Three elderly people had already died, dozens more were ill.

Next came the story about newly appointed Chief Earley. Felipe was surprised. He'd been almost positive that the fact that he was suspected of committing the Sandlot Murders would've been leaked to the media. But there was no mention of it. Nothing at all.

There was a brief interview with Earley, then a background profile. The police chief had served in Vietnam as a demolitions expert. Felipe hadn't known that. Apparently, Earley had worked clearing booby traps from the labyrinth of underground tunnels that Vietcong guerrillas hid in during the daytime. His was one of the most dangerous and terrifying jobs in the marines. It was not a job for the faint of heart or the claustrophobic, that was for sure.

Felipe heard a sound in the hallway, and pushed the mute button on the TV remote control. The apartment door swung open, and...thank you, Lord.

Caroline was standing there.

She came into the apartment, closing the door behind her.

She seemed embarrassed, almost shy, and Felipe realized that he was wearing only his boxer shorts. He hadn't had the energy to make it over to Rafe's closet to find a pair of jeans or a T-shirt to put on.

Still, she crossed over to the sofa, looking down at him. "You look awful," she said.

He tried to smile. *"Gracias,"* he said. "I *feel* awful. But the bullet's out. My brother sent someone up, someone who I think was a doctor at one time."

Carrie nodded. "I know," she said. She knelt on the floor next to the sofa. "It must really hurt. I'm sorry."

"I'm not," Felipe said. He took a deep breath in and released it slowly. He found that now he *could* smile at her. "I don't mind the pain. In fact, I like it. It reminds me that I'm alive. And I really like being alive—particularly after an evening like this one."

Carrie smiled tentatively back at him. How beautiful she was. Felipe had to hold on tightly to the remote control to keep himself from reaching out and drawing her into his arms. What he would have given for one small, comforting embrace. Except there was no way on earth an embrace between them would have remained either small or comforting for long.

"I don't think you realize how close we both came to being killed tonight," Felipe said quietly, searching the depths of her sea-green eyes.

But she didn't look away. She didn't turn her head. She didn't shut him out. Instead, she nodded. Yes.

"Yes, I do," she said. "I talked to your brother about Walsh."

"And…?"

"I believe you," she said.

"About Walsh?"

"About everything."

Heat coursed through him at her words. She believed him. Even though he knew that he shouldn't, Felipe let go of the remote and reached for Carrie. He touched the side of her face and her skin was so smooth, so soft. And she didn't pull away.

He could see her pulse beating at the delicate base of her neck, he could see her chest rising and falling with each breath she took, he could see her lips, parted slightly and moistened with the tip of her tongue, and still she didn't pull away.

She looked the very way he felt—hypnotized.

Knowing quite well that he shouldn't, but unable to stop himself, he leaned forward to kiss her. How he wanted to kiss her! He truly didn't have a choice.

He brushed his lips against hers in the smallest, gentlest, most delicate of kisses.

Her eyelids fluttered, and she looked up at him. She looked scared to death, terrified, but she still didn't pull away.

So he kissed her again, knowing that he shouldn't, knowing absolutely that kissing this woman was a gigantic mistake. He liked her too much—*way* too much. He couldn't afford to have any kind of relationship with her. He couldn't bear the fact that just *knowing* him would put her in danger. And, maybe for the first time in his entire life, he knew that he wouldn't be able to keep the physical, sexual side of a relationship with Caroline from becoming entangled with the emotional. And that truly frightened him.

No, Caroline was not the only one who was scared to

death. But he couldn't stop himself. And this time, she met him halfway. She reached up and threaded her arms around his neck and kissed him as if there were no tomorrow.

And maybe, just maybe, she was right.

But the danger they were in, the risk of impending death, wasn't the real reason Felipe pulled her even closer and deepened the kiss. He did it for one reason only—because he so desperately wanted to. He could no sooner resist Caroline Brooks than he could stop breathing.

Her mouth was so sweet, her lips so inviting. Her hair was like silk as he ran his fingers through it. And her soft, fragile body was neither entirely fragile nor entirely soft. She was slight and slender, yes, but still quite strong. He slid one hand down her back to the curve of her firm derriere and pulled her toward him.

Man, five minutes ago, he'd been lying here on the sofa, feeling like death warmed over, uncertain whether or not he'd even be able to stand. It was funny what desire could do to a man. Because now he knew without a doubt that he could stand. He could stand. He could walk. Man, he could run laps if he needed to.

His fingers found the edge of Caroline's dress, and the soft, smooth warmth of her thigh. Felipe heard himself groan, and she pulled back, alarmed.

"Did I hurt you?" she whispered, her voice husky. Her hair was tousled and her cheeks were flushed. It didn't take much imagination to picture her amid the rumpled sheets of a bed....

"Oh, yes," he said, barely hiding his smile. "You can't imagine my pain. Although it has nothing to do with my leg."

She blushed and laughed, then leaned forward to kiss him again.

And then the door burst open.

Felipe reacted. He found his gun almost instinctively, remembering he had thrown the holster over the back of the sofa. As he drew it out, he pulled himself off the sofa so that his body was shielding Carrie's.

"Jesus, it's only me," Rafe said. "Put that thing away, Superman. Lois Lane's still safe."

Felipe sagged with relief. It was only his brother. Relief turned sharply to annoyance. "Didn't our mother teach you to knock?" he asked, dragging himself back onto the sofa.

Rafe smiled humorlessly at his brother. He looked pointedly at Carrie, who was running her fingers through her disheveled hair. "Yeah," he said. "She also taught us not to play with fire—a rule you've obviously forgotten, little brother."

Felipe reached down to help Carrie onto the sofa next to him. He kept his arm behind her, his fingers lightly touching her shoulder. She glanced at him, and he nearly felt burned. Rafe was right. He *was* playing with fire. But what a way to go.

He looked up at Rafe. "Was there something you needed?"

Rafe looked at the television, which was still on, but muted. A commercial for a dishwashing liquid was showing.

"Were you watching the news—no, obviously not," Rafe said, answering his own question.

Felipe sat up a little straighter. "Why?" he asked.

Rafe glanced at him. "I think you know why," he said. He bent down and picked the remote control off the floor. As the commercial ended, he pressed the mute button.

"To recount a story just in," the news anchor said, looking seriously out from the television screen, "police sources have revealed that they are searching for a suspect in the controversial Sandlot Murders case."

A rather grainy picture of Felipe appeared at the top right of the screen, with the words Rogue Cop in jagged letters underneath.

"Police Detective Felipe Salazar," the anchor reported, her voice still solemn, "being labeled a rogue cop by the supervisors in his department…"

"Good Lord!" Carrie cried, leaning forward to look more closely at the screen. Felipe's hand fell away from her shoulder.

"…is wanted in connection with last week's double slaying in a downtown sandlot, next to the East 43rd Street Elementary School. Salazar, described in the official police statement as being a twenty-five-year-old Latino male, is six feet tall, one hundred seventy pounds, with dark hair and eyes. He is believed to be armed and extremely dangerous."

Caroline was staring at the television, clearly aghast. She looked up at Felipe, and he knew with a sinking heart that all her doubts about him had come flooding back.

"It's a frame," Felipe told her, but the news broadcast had once again caught her attention.

"We're going to the Fourth Precinct where we have a reporter standing by," the anchor said, reaching up to adjust a tiny speaker in her ear. "Hello, Walt, are you there?"

The picture switched to that of a man standing in the brightly lit lobby of the police station.

"This is Walter Myers reporting from downtown at the

Fourth Precinct, where Felipe Salazar is a member of the police force," the man said, staring into the camera. "Newly appointed Police Chief Jack Earley will be arriving shortly to hold a press conference. We'll be breaking into regular programming to bring you that live report."

The camera followed Walter Myers down the corridor.

A man stepped into camera range. "Gentlemen, I'm going to have to ask you to leave," he said.

"That's Diego," Felipe said. His friend and former partner had gotten a haircut since he'd seen him last. But other than that, Jim Keegan looked the same. He was wearing his standard uniform—jeans and rumpled button-down shirt, with a loosened tie around his neck to make it look a little more businesslike.

Carrie glanced at him. "That's the man you called?"

"Yeah."

"And you are...?" the reporter asked.

"Detective James Keegan," Jim replied patiently. "I'm afraid you're going to have to continue your news report outside, sir."

"His name's not Diego, it's James," Carrie said, her eyes still glued to the screen.

"Diego's Spanish for James," Rafe told her.

"Can you comment on the latest suspect in the Sandlot Murders?" the reporter asked Jim.

"No, I cannot," he replied firmly, herding them back to the door.

"Do you know Salazar?" the reporter asked.

"Yes, I do," Jim said.

"Do you believe he committed this crime?"

Jim was about to respond, then he glanced toward the camera. It was almost as if he'd decided to change his answer. "You never know," he told the reporter. "That's one thing I've learned in all my years on the force. You just never know."

The reporter looked into the camera. "Back to you, Mary."

The news anchor reappeared with another story, and Rafe reached over and turned off the television.

Carrie didn't move. "You don't seem surprised by this," she said tightly to Felipe.

"It's a setup," he said again. "A frame. And yes, you're right. I'm not surprised. I knew they were going to try to pin these murders on me."

She turned and looked at him. He could see anger in her eyes. Anger and hurt. "You knew," she said. "And you didn't tell me. This is really why you can't go to the police, isn't it? Because you're wanted for *murder.*"

"I didn't do it," Felipe said. How could she think that he would kill someone in cold blood? "I wouldn't kill anyone."

"Not anyone who didn't deserve it," Rafe cut in. "But a vigilante-style execution…? Maybe."

"Stop it," Felipe said sharply. "You know damn well—"

"I only know you're a big fan of justice," Rafe retorted. "You'd send your own brother back to prison, two years hard labor. You're probably capable of delivering this kind of justice, no?"

Carrie was looking at Felipe as if he'd just been accused of slaying infants. "Even your friend, what's his name—Keegan—wouldn't stand up for you," she said.

Felipe reached for her hand. She didn't pull away fast enough, so he held it, wishing that she could somehow get inside his head and see for herself that he was telling the truth.

"Caroline, don't you see?" he said quietly, intensely. "This is why Walsh let us get away. Richter's man in the police department set up this frame, somehow making me look like a suspect in this murder case. They may not even have any evidence against me, I don't know. If they *do* have anything, it's trumped up or fake. But the case is never going to go to court, because as soon as they find me and bring me in, Walsh will be tipped off. He'll wait until I'm being transported and then he'll put a bullet in my head. Everyone will assume my death was some kind of mob counterhit, and the case will be closed."

Carrie didn't look convinced. She was staring down at her hand, entrapped by Felipe's larger hand.

"I need you to leave," Rafe said. "Your being here is jeopardizing everything I've worked hard for—including my own freedom. I won't serve time for aiding and abetting. Not even for you, little brother."

Caroline pulled her hand free.

Felipe looked up at Rafe. "Don't you mean *especially* not for me?" he asked bitterly, then ran his hand across his face. "I'm sorry. I didn't mean that."

"Yes, you did," Rafe said. He sighed. "Look, I had one of my staff get rid of the car you drove over here. I can't risk giving you one of my vans, but I'm going to tell you where I keep the keys, do you follow?"

Felipe nodded.

"They're in the kitchen, top cabinet, left of the microwave. I'll give you seventy-two hours, then I'm going to report the van stolen," Rafe continued.

"Do you have a tape recorder I can borrow, too?" Felipe asked.

"There's a tape deck in the van," Rafe told him,

"though this is hardly the time to be thinking about tunes, little brother."

Felipe ran a hand back through his hair. "No," he said, "I need to make a recording, to make a tape telling what I know about Richter and Walsh. You know. In case…"

Rafe nodded curtly. "I'll find you something," he said. "The bastard's gonna blow you away, least you can do is leave behind incriminating evidence, right?"

"Wrong," Felipe said. "It wouldn't be evidence. A taped statement wouldn't hold up in court. No, it would just be information to help the next guys nail Richter."

"You mean…" Rafe stared at him. "If you're dead, that's it? No case against Richter?"

"That's why he's so hot to waste me," Felipe said.

"Jesus," Rafe said. "You don't stand a chance."

Carrie was silent. She stared down sightlessly at the floor.

Rafe crossed to the closet and pulled out a pair of jeans and some worn-out black leather boots. "Here," he said, handing them to Felipe. He took a T-shirt and a clean pair of socks from his dresser and tossed them onto the sofa. He gestured toward Carrie. "I don't have anything in her size," he said. "But she can put a shirt on over that dress. And you, you probably need something to cover up that holster and gun," he added, crossing back to the closet.

He took out a black leather biker's jacket.

Felipe shook his head. "I can't take that," he said. "That's your jacket, man."

Rafe looked down at the jacket in his hands. When he looked up again, the lines in his face seemed deeper, the seat of his mouth even tighter than normal. "I don't have anything else to give you, Felipe," he said, for once all the sarcasm gone from his voice. "I *am* sorry that I can't let you stay. Do you have somewhere to go?"

Felipe nodded. "Yeah. I've got someplace in mind, someplace to lie low for a day or two until I feel like running again."

"Then what?"

"Then I find out who Richter's mysterious partner is," Felipe said. "Richter called him Captain Rat. I thought there was some connection to the wharf, the harbor authority, maybe the Coast Guard, but now I think this 'Rat' is a captain in the police department. Who else could have engineered this kind of a frame-up so quickly?"

Stiffly, gingerly, Felipe pulled on the jeans. They were a little loose—his brother was taller than he was—but they fitted just fine over his bandaged leg. He pulled the T-shirt over his head and slipped on his shoulder holster.

That little bit of movement exhausted him, and he had to stop and gather his strength. Only God could help them if Walsh came after them now.

He opened his eyes and found Caroline watching him, wariness still on her face. She looked away, unable to hold his gaze.

She didn't trust him, didn't believe him again.

They were back to square one.

CHAPTER EIGHT

CARRIE STOOD in the hallway with Rafe, waiting while Felipe limped into the kitchen. He was taking the keys to one of the halfway house's vans, with Rafe supposedly unaware.

She still couldn't believe the news report they'd just seen on the television.

The man she was with was indeed Felipe Salazar— that much had been established without a doubt. He *was* a detective with St. Simone's Fourth Precinct—that was true, too. And he could kiss exactly as she'd imagined in her dreams—better, in fact.

Good grief, one kiss, and she'd been ready... Well, she wasn't sure exactly *what* she'd been ready for, but she certainly hadn't been ready to find out that this handsome, charismatic man who could kiss like a dream was wanted for murder.

Felipe was wanted for *murder.*

He said he didn't do it. He said it was a setup, a frame. Carrie wanted to believe him, but she couldn't ignore the fact that if the man was a cold-blooded killer, he certainly wouldn't balk at lying.

Rafe was watching her, his flat, expressionless eyes studying her face.

"Do you believe Felipe?" she asked him.

He shrugged, holding his arms out wide. "I don't know," he said. "Used to be my brother couldn't even fib. He was the straightest kid you ever met, you know? He was the kind of kid who'd break something and then stick around to face the music. No running or hiding." He glanced toward the kitchen door, but there was no sign of Felipe. "But working under cover, he's had to learn to lie. I mean, when you think about it, an undercover cop does nothing *but* lie, huh?"

Carrie nodded.

"Do *you* believe him?" Rafe asked.

But Carrie didn't have a chance to answer. Felipe came out of the kitchen.

Part of her *did* believe him. When he told her he'd been set up, his words had been very persuasive. And the look in his eyes had begged her to trust him. She ought to trust him, considering the way they'd connected. And they had really connected—the proof was in that kiss they'd shared.

Hoo boy, what a kiss....

But just because Felipe Salazar had the power to knock her socks off with a kiss didn't mean that she should simply trust him. And the truth was, her belief in him was based on instinct, on gut reaction alone. It had nothing to do with logic or provable facts.

And that scared her. How could she believe him when there was no proof to back his words? How could she trust him when all of the data implied that he was not to be trusted?

She couldn't. Despite her gut reaction, despite their obvious attraction, she couldn't let herself trust him. It was that simple.

"You get what you need?" Rafe asked Felipe, leading them to the front door.

Felipe nodded. His expression was almost as guarded as Rafe's. Carrie thought he was trying to hide the pain in his leg until he glanced at her. But with one look at his eyes, she could see that his pain wasn't from the bullet wound. It was from his disappointment. In her.

Rafe had stopped in the entry hall. He held a key, but he didn't attempt to unlock the front door.

Felipe looked incredible in those blue jeans and that black leather jacket, with his hair loose and flowing around his shoulders. It was different from the way he'd looked in his tuxedo, but no less commanding.

"Highboy's got the other key," Rafe explained. "Until he gets down here, we're locked in."

Locked in?

Felipe was studying the tips of his borrowed boots, his hands jammed deep into the pockets of his jeans as he leaned against the wall.

"Locked in?" Carrie asked.

Felipe still didn't look up, so she turned questioningly to his brother.

"Yeah," Rafe said. "That's the way the halfway house operates. Door doesn't open unless both guys who hold the keys can be talked into opening it. See, night can be the worst time for some of the addicts. I know it always was for me—still is sometimes. If the door is locked, and you can't get out of the house, you can't give in to the devil. We keep the door locked tight from nine-thirty at night until six in the morning. It helps everyone stay clean. No one comes in or goes out unless it's an emergency. And it has to be one mother of an emergency."

The doors were locked after nine-thirty. Carrie looked at Felipe, who was still studying his boots as Highboy came down the stairs carrying the key.

Felipe had given her the key to get out of Rafe's apartment—but only after nine-thirty. She'd thought that he'd set her free, but she had still been a prisoner. She simply hadn't realized it at the time.

Highboy unlocked the top bolt; Rafe undid the bottom. The door swung open and Felipe and Carrie stepped outside.

Carrie's head was spinning. She took a deep breath, trying to clear it, but the night was warm and the air was tainted with the smell of trash.

"Raphael," Felipe said, turning back to his brother. *"Gracias."* He held out his hand, but Rafe turned away.

"Dejame," Rafe said flatly, closing the door in Felipe's face.

The hurt that flashed in Felipe's eyes was heartbreaking. But Carrie didn't have time to feel bad. If ever there was an opportunity to get away, it was right at this very moment.

She started down the sidewalk at a brisk pace, hoping Felipe wouldn't even notice that she was walking away. But he caught up with her before she'd gone ten yards. He took hold of her arm. "The van's parked in the alley," he said. "It's the other direction."

"That's real nice," Carrie said, "but I'm not going in the van with you."

"Yes," he said, "you are." His patience was wearing thin—she could hear it in his voice. He led her around the side of the house to the alley where the van was waiting.

"So I *am* your hostage," she said, steadily meeting his eyes and refusing to be seduced by the heat she could see there. "I have been all along, haven't I?"

"Caroline, you're not a hostage."

She looked pointedly down at his hand holding her arm. "Coulda fooled me," she said.

Something snapped. She could see it in his eyes, in the tenseness of his jaw.

"You believed me a half hour ago," he said tightly.

"You should have told me you were wanted for murder," she countered.

"I didn't really think they could pull off a frame-up this big—not until I saw it myself," he said. He laughed harshly. "Ah, the power of television. You'd rather believe what you see on the screen than believe me, no?"

"How can I believe you?" Carrie asked, "when I don't even know you?"

"You know me," Felipe said, his voice suddenly soft. His dark eyes glittered in the moonlight. "I think you know me quite well, in fact. Trust your heart, Caroline."

She closed her eyes, afraid of the hypnotizing power of his gaze, afraid of the magnetic pull of this man, afraid of the way his hold on her arm suddenly felt like a caress.

But then he let her go. "Okay," he said, still quietly. "You're free to go."

Carrie opened her eyes in surprise, and he dropped the keys to the van into her hand.

"There's one condition," he said. "You have to get on the interstate heading north. You have to go directly to your father's home in Montana, tell your father and your brothers everything that's happened here tonight, and then ask them to protect you. If you won't let me do it, you've got to let them."

"I'm just supposed to leave you here?" Carrie asked incredulously. "With a bullet wound in your leg?"

He shook his head. "I don't have time to argue with you," he said. "Especially not out here in the open like this, where anyone can see me. I've got an awful lot to do tonight. My first priority is to make sure you're safe. My second is to stay alive so that tomorrow I can get to my third priority—clearing my name. So kiss me goodbye and get the hell out of here."

Carrie looked from the keys in her hand, to the van, then back to Felipe. His number-one priority was her safety. In fact, he'd given up his one means of escape for her. Without the van, he'd be forced to take public transportation and risk being spotted by some vigilant citizen who'd seen the evening news. Of course, he could always travel by foot—although how far he'd get on his injured leg was uncertain.

He looked pale in the moonlight, and she could see that he was perspiring again. The pain from his bullet wound had to have been excruciating. He was just barely standing on his feet. How could she just drive away from him?

His eyes held no reproach, no recriminations. She could see only gentleness and warmth.

"Go," he whispered. "Godspeed, Caroline Brooks."

But Carrie didn't want to go. She wanted to stay. She didn't want to have to rely on her family for protection— not when she had the best possible protection right here in St. Simone.

Her feelings weren't scientific. They weren't based on fact or data or any kind of proof. For the first time in years, Carrie was rejecting the obvious and trusting her heart.

She took several steps forward, closing the gap between them, stood on her toes and kissed him.

She could taste his surprise. Nevertheless, he pulled her to him and kissed her, too. It was a long, slow, deep kiss, a sweet kiss, perhaps the sweetest she'd ever known.

He was kissing her goodbye, Carrie realized suddenly. He was giving her a kiss to last a lifetime, a kiss to remember him by.

He held her close, as if gathering his strength to push her away. "Don't stop for anything until you're out of state," he said, his voice husky.

She looked up at him and could actually see tears in his eyes.

"After you're out of Florida," he continued, "get rid of the van—leave it in some neighborhood just parked on the street. Then take a bus. Pay in cash and don't use your real name." He released her, digging into the back pocket of his jeans for his wallet. "I'm going to give you some money—"

"No," Carrie said. There were tears in her own eyes now. He was giving her the van *and* some money, too? She wiped at her eyes fiercely with the back of her hand.

Felipe shook his head. "Caroline, you're going to need—"

"Get in the van," she said, unlocking the passenger-side door. "I'm driving."

He stepped forward and touched the side of her face. "As much as I'd like to, I can't go to Montana with you."

"I'm not going to Montana," she said, then smiled at the hope that sprang into his eyes. He was trying to control it, trying not to allow himself to assume anything. "I'm safer with you," she added. "My brothers are lousy shots."

He nodded slowly, as if he was taking her words very seriously. "You've decided to believe me?" he said.

"Is there anything else that you've neglected to tell me?" she asked. "Any other sensational murders or maybe a kidnapped child or two in your basement? Or maybe you've been keeping secrets from me about your health. Any brain tumors or terminal illnesses you've been hiding?"

He smiled and shook his head. "Nothing of that great a magnitude."

"Then get in the van," she said, hoping to hell that she wasn't going to regret this.

FELIPE SAT LOW in the passenger seat of the cargo van so that no one could see him. He didn't like that he wasn't driving. In fact, he couldn't remember the last time he'd been in a car but not behind the wheel—excluding rides in Richter's limousine, of course.

He watched Carrie as she drove. She'd had to shift the driver's seat way up close to the steering wheel, but she drove the oversize vehicle with all the confidence and skill of an experienced truck driver.

This was a far cry from the little red sports car she'd had all those months ago at Sea Circus, when they'd first met. Still, someone who owned a precision automobile like Carrie's had to care about her car. And, in Felipe's experience, people who cared about their cars tended to know how to drive, and drive well. And usually fast. Her two speeding tickets verified that fact—although at the moment she was keeping their speed slightly below the limit. The time they'd save by going faster wasn't worth the risk of getting pulled over.

Carrie glanced over at him. He tried to smile, but the muscles in his face weren't working quite the way they should have been.

"You okay?" she asked, concern thickening her already husky voice, accentuating her slight Western drawl. She sounded a little bit—just a *little* bit—like

Lauren Bacall trying to imitate John Wayne. On a woman of her less-than-imposing size, with all that silky blond hair and those enormous blue eyes, the effect was utterly charming.

"My leg hurts," Felipe admitted. *Hurts* was an enormous understatement. The damn thing throbbed steadily with a knifelike pain. And, as a bonus, he felt nauseated from the antibiotic Doc Bird had given him. He was supposed to take one of the capsules four times a day to keep his wound from becoming infected. Doc Bird had given him a ten-day supply of the medicine.

Ten days. He could only hope he lived that long.

Man, he was exhausted.

"Is there anything I can do?" Carrie asked quietly. She glanced at him again, and this time he managed to smile.

"You're doing it," he said.

"Where are we going?" she asked. "Besides south?"

"Sanibel Island," he told her. "Diego's in-laws own a beach house out there. It's empty at this time of year. We can hide there, at least overnight."

She nodded, her eyes carefully on the highway.

He took out the tape recorder that Rafe had given him. It was small and cheap and at least twenty-five years old. But it would get the job done.

"If you don't mind," Felipe said, "I'd like to record that information about Richter's operation."

"In case you're not around to do it in person," Carrie said, glancing over at him.

He nodded. "Yeah."

"But you will be," she said.

"Yes," he said with more certainty in his voice than he felt. "But I would hate not to make this tape, and then be wrong."

"Rafe thinks we don't stand a chance, doesn't he?"

We. Felipe liked the sound of that. She was on his side. "My brother is a pessimist," he said.

"But you're not," she answered back.

"We're still alive, aren't we?" he declared. "Against all odds, our hearts are still beating. Either we're lucky, or God's got a reason for keeping us around."

"God?" she said, turning to look at him in the darkness.

"Don't you believe in God?" he asked. "Some god, any god? Some force bigger than we are?"

She turned her head away from him as if she was embarrassed. "Gee, I don't know."

"Too bad," Felipe said, studying her profile as she drove. He adored the way her nose turned up very slightly at the end. "I've found believing is helpful in times like this."

She glanced back at him again. "I'm...surprised," she said.

Felipe smiled. "That's good," he said. "I'd hate to be boring."

Caroline laughed, a low, husky sound that hit him low in the gut and spread all the way out to his fingers and toes. Man, bullet wound or not, he would have sold his soul right at that moment for a chance to finish what they'd started with a kiss back in Rafe's apartment. His borrowed blue jeans were getting tighter and more uncomfortable by the second. But at least it took his mind off the pain in his leg.

"Believe me," she said. "You're not boring." She looked over at him, but quickly focused on the road again, as if she could see his desire simmering in his eyes. She probably could. He wasn't very good at hiding that sort of thing. "Go on and make your tape," she added. "I'd like to know why someone's trying to kill you—and me."

Felipe looked down at the tape recorder, and ejected the tape that his brother had put inside. It needed to be rewound to the beginning, so he put it back in and pushed the rewind button. Then he pressed Record and Play and silently counted to five to let the leader run out.

"My name is Felipe Ricardo Salazar, and I am a police detective with the Fourth Precinct in St. Simone," he said, speaking clearly into the machine's built-in microphone, still watching Caroline as he talked. "Today is January 17, 11:45 p.m.

"Early August of last year, I went under cover to infiltrate Lawrence Richter's crime syndicate. Posing as Raoul Tomás Garcia Vasquez, I have spent the past five months winning both Tommy Walsh's and Lawrence Richter's confidence."

Felipe took a deep breath. "Two months ago, I learned of a scam that I believe Richter has been operating for nearly a decade here in Florida. He imports illegal aliens from Cuba and Haiti and other Caribbean islands, and even from as far away as Mexico, charging them exorbitant prices for a so-called safe passage and entry into the United States. After they arrive, having spent every penny of their life savings, they are told of other, equally exorbitant fees for forged green cards that will enable them to stay. Richter's men sign a contract with these people, trading their future wages for these coveted—and counterfeit, therefore worthless—green cards."

Carrie drew in a sharp breath, again glancing over at Felipe.

"In short," he said, nodding grimly at her, "it's a form of indentured servitude, or should I say slavery? Richter currently has a work force of over twenty-two hundred illegal aliens—including children. Child labour laws don't apply to children who technically don't exist."

"That's awful," Carrie murmured.

"I've seen the below-poverty conditions that these people live in," Felipe continued, watching the impact his words had on her through the expressions on her face. "Most of them are housed in run-down buildings that Richter has bought in the worst neighborhoods in the city. These buildings have no running water, no electricity and no hope of ever being renovated. They are scheduled to be torn down, but Richter has orchestrated a series of delays in the legal proceedings surrounding their con-demnation. It could be literally years before the buildings are destroyed, and by that time, Richter will have pur-chased—dirt cheap—other equally squalid buildings.

"Most of these apartment buildings are between Howard and Stern Streets, on First and Second Avenues." He sighed. "Although by the time you hear this tape, all the illegal tenants will probably have been moved.

"Garrett Hedford and Stuart Tiffler are two of Richter's men who use intimidation to keep the work force in line," he continued. "They also schedule the arrival of additional boatloads of people. In the past two months, I've seen ships arriving in both Miami and Fort Myers." Quickly, he rattled off the information on the ships' names and ports of call.

"I've seen copies of Richter's books," he said, shifting in his seat, trying to ease the endless throbbing in his leg. "He grosses over two hundred thousand dollars each *month* from these people, his *slaves*. I've witnessed him giving orders to both Hedford and Tiffler, as well as Tommy Walsh. I've witnessed the production of the counterfeit green cards, and their distribution to the illegal aliens. I've witnessed the signing of contracts, indenturing these people to Richter— although his name is not used. A corporate front, called L&R Co. is used, and it virtually cannot be traced to Lawrence Richter. At least not without me around. I've witnessed Richter transferring funds from the L&R account to his Swiss bank account."

"Felipe."

He turned off the tape recorder, looking up at Caroline. "Yes?"

"If you know all this," she asked, "what were you waiting for? You'd seen enough to put Richter away."

"His partner," he reminded her. "I found out that Richter wasn't working alone. The more I found out, the more I wanted to catch this other man, too." He smiled ruefully. "The more I found out, the more I realized I *had* to nail this guy. I'd guessed he was someone in St. Simone's government, someone who'd have access to my whereabouts after I went into protective custody while awaiting Richter's trial. I was the chief witness against Richter—the *only* witness. If I didn't bring a case against this other guy, too, this inside guy, I'd end up dead. I'm lucky I found out about this Captain Rat. If I hadn't, I probably never would have heard the bullet coming."

Caroline swallowed. "You say that so casually."

"It's my job," he replied.

"It's an awful job," she said.

"No, it's not," he returned gently.

"In my opinion it is," she said. She looked at him. "And I'm entitled to my own opinion."

Felipe leaned back against the headrest, just watching her. She believed him. Oh, she didn't believe him one hundred percent, but she believed him enough to stick around. And that was what counted.

Is there anything else that you've neglected to tell me? Her words echoed in his mind as he watched her drive.

Nothing of that great a magnitude.

But his answer had been a lie. And not just because there was something that he hadn't told her. It was true, there *was* something, but he couldn't possibly have told her about it, because he wasn't sure yet himself exactly what it was. It was difficult to pinpoint, harder even to define, these feelings, this *emotion* that seemed to swirl around him, enveloping him in a chaos both perfect and terrible whenever she looked in his direction, whenever he caught her eye.

What was it? He didn't know. Man, he didn't *want* to know.

But whatever it was, something told him it was of a far greater magnitude than he could ever imagine.

"I WANT TO TELL YOU...why I didn't come back and explain who I was and what I was doing that night at Sea Circus," Felipe said softly.

Carrie glanced at him, startled. He'd been quiet for so long, she was certain he'd been asleep.

"You know I went under cover as part of the Richter investigation back in August," he said. "One week I was pretending to be Carlos and running with some of the leaders of the most powerful gangs in St. Simone, and the next I was Raoul, driving a Jaguar and living in a penthouse at the Harbor's Gate. I had maybe three days between the two assignments. It...wasn't long enough."

"Long enough for what?" Carrie asked, looking over at him again. "It was certainly long enough for you to come and apologize."

He shifted in his seat. "It wasn't long enough for what I wanted," he said bluntly. "And I didn't think you deserved to be a one-night stand."

Carrie laughed, afraid to look at him, afraid of what she knew she'd see in his eyes. Desire. He'd stopped trying to hide it from her ever since they'd shared that kiss. "How gallant of you," she said. "You were saving me from my own lack of control, huh?"

"At the risk of sounding conceited," he said, "you would not have been able to resist me."

Coming from any other man's lips, his words would have been outrageous and disgustingly egomaniacal. But when Felipe said them, those words, combined with the rueful look in his eyes, were merely a statement of fact.

It was, however, no less disconcerting.

"Your brother thinks I'm going to sleep with you within the next twenty-four hours," Carrie said tightly. "But that's not why I'm here, and I intend to prove him wrong. In fact, I think we should ignore this… this…physical attraction until after you clear your name and Lawrence Richter and Tommy Walsh are in jail."

Felipe was silent. One mile, then two, sped by under their wheels before he spoke. "That's probably best," he agreed quietly.

It was. It was best. Still, Carrie couldn't help but remember the power of his kisses. If Rafe hadn't interrupted them, she very likely would have made love to Felipe right there on the sofa, injured leg and all. No, forget twenty-four hours. It would have been more like four hours. Four hours after they'd met—not counting the half hour or so at Sea Circus six months ago, and the dozens of dreams she'd had about him since then—and she would have had sex with this man. Did he have some special power over her specifically, she wondered, or did he experience this phenomenon with every woman he met?

"I'm sorry if Rafe offended you," Felipe said. He shook his head. "He had no business saying that to you." His dark eyes were lit with anger and embarrassment. "I *am* sorry, Caroline."

"It's okay," she said. "He was just trying to rattle me." She laughed. "It worked, too."

"I don't understand him," Felipe said, shaking his head again. He ran one hand across his forehead, applying pressure, as if he had a headache. "Sometimes I think I never will." He looked up at her. "It's not as if he didn't know that crack was addictive. It's not as if he didn't know it could kill him. So what the hell made him do it? What pushed him over the edge? And what kind of man cares more about getting a rush than he does about his life?"

"Rafe seems to think you get a similar rush from being an undercover cop," Carrie said.

His gaze sharpened. "You talked to him about me?"

"Only a little," Carrie said. "He wants you to forgive him."

"He sure as hell has a funny way of showing that," Felipe muttered. "And I *do* forgive him," he added. "I just don't trust him. How do I know he's going to stay clean? How can I be sure he won't start using again?"

All his frustration and anger and hurt—deep, deep hurt—showed on his face. He was speaking to her from his heart, sharing his darkest fears and innermost secrets with her.

She liked him, Carrie realized suddenly. There were so many sides to him, so much more than a handsome face, more than those exotic cheekbones and the long, curly hair.

Who would've guessed that such a powerful, independent, self-sufficient man would believe so firmly in the idea of a god? And in this day and age, when religion was a low priority in most people's busy lives?

Who would've guessed that talk of his brother could reduce him in part to the little boy that he'd once been, badly hurt, and afraid of being hurt again?

And who would've guessed that he'd let her see that pain, rather than try to conceal it from her?

Yeah, she liked him, despite the fact that he'd locked her in the trunk of her car, despite the fact that he'd put her life in jeopardy.

He was waiting for her to say something, watching her with those liquid eyes.

"Sometimes," Carrie said softly, her eyes on the highway, talking about more than Rafe—*much* more than Rafe, "you've just got to have faith."

CHAPTER NINE

CARRIE DROVE PAST the darkened beach house three times before Felipe nodded his head.

"Okay, no one's there," he said, his gentle Hispanic accent like velvet in the darkness. "Let's park over on the next block. I don't want to leave the van out front, or even in the driveway."

"Maybe I should drop you off," Carrie said, "so you don't have to walk that far."

He didn't say anything. He just looked at her, one eyebrow slightly raised.

"Bad idea?" she asked.

"Bad idea. I can't protect you if I'm here and you're a block away."

You can't protect either of us if you're too tired and in too much pain to walk, she wanted to say. But then she thought better of it, remembering the way he'd run after her when he'd stopped to make that phone call. He'd had a bullet in his leg, yet he'd still managed to chase her across the parking lot. And he'd caught her—with a flying tackle and total disregard for his injury.

Yes, dropping him off *was* a bad idea. If mobsters with guns wanted her dead, then maybe it was a good idea if Felipe Salazar stayed near her at all times, healthy or injured, awake or asleep.

Awake or…

The image of Felipe asleep next to her in the clean white sheets of a cozy double bed was a powerful one. His wavy black hair spread out across the snow-white pillow, his eyes closed, his long, dark eyelashes like fans against his tanned cheeks, his body relaxed but his muscles still hard as steel under silky smooth skin….

Thinking this way wasn't going to help her one bit. And sleeping with him would be rash and reckless—and possibly a knee-jerk reaction to the danger they were in. Yes, he was sexy as hell. Yes, he was sensitive and compassionate and he seemed to know exactly what she was thinking when he looked deeply into her eyes. Yes, he was quite possibly the most complicated, interesting and exciting man she'd ever met.

But imagine what would happen if—heaven forbid— she let herself fall in love with this man. Could she imagine them together, having breakfast every morning for the rest of their lives?

Actually, the image was not as difficult to conjure up as she'd thought. In fact, it was a nice picture, a comfortable picture. He'd be sitting at the kitchen table, drinking a glass of orange juice and eating a bowl of cereal. She'd be sitting across from him, spreading jam on her toast. He'd look up, meet her eyes and smile and…

Carrie shook her head, trying to dispel the warm feeling that had somehow invaded her body. So, okay, the thought of Felipe Salazar eating breakfast with her every morning wasn't such an alien one.

But imagine her taking him home to meet her father. Imagine Felipe Salazar in the mountains of Montana. Well, actually, that wasn't such an incongruous picture, either. She could imagine teaching him to ride a horse, imagine him loving it, imagine them riding up into that meadow above the house and sharing a picnic lunch spread out on a blanket. A picnic lunch and a whole lot more....

As for her dad, well, he'd be put off at first by Felipe's accent, by his long hair and the diamond stud he wore in his left ear. But her father was a fair man, and he'd quickly see that Felipe was everything he could want for his only daughter—

Good grief. What was she doing? One kiss, and she was daydreaming about happily-ever-after.

Happily-ever-after could end permanently and quite abruptly in a matter of days, considering the danger they were in. And even if it didn't, even if Walsh didn't find them and kill them...well, Felipe Salazar wasn't exactly the happily-ever-after kind.

Sure, he had a certain steadiness, a certain serenity about him that counteracted the risks he took. But he *did* take risks, and it was clear that he loved the danger and excitement. What had Rafe said? He'd said that Felipe was addicted to danger.

No, if she wanted to dream up some image to help keep her resolve to stay away from this man, all she had to do was picture his being led away from her in handcuffs. *That* was a much more likely scenario than any she'd imagined. Yes, she had no doubt that he would make love to her exquisitely. It would be desperately exciting, incredibly thrilling, considering both their adrenaline levels were already quite high. But the reality was, this man was wanted by the police. For murder.

He said he didn't commit the crime.

She wanted to believe him. She *did* believe him.

But what if she was wrong? What if he *was* a cold-blooded killer? What if he wanted her around only as a hostage, not for her protection? What if…?

Carrie parked the car and turned off the engine. He was watching her as if he could read her mind, as if he knew her every thought. She handed him the keys, which he pocketed.

Carrie cleared her throat. "Do we have a way to get into the house?" she asked.

"I know where a key is hidden," Felipe said, opening his door and swinging his legs out.

He winced as his feet hit the ground, and Carrie quickly got out of the van and went around the front to help him.

"I'm okay," he insisted. But he swayed slightly, and she slipped his arm around her shoulders.

He surely outweighed her by more than sixty pounds, and the leather jacket he was wearing added even more to that. But Carrie was strong. Besides, she didn't try to carry him; she merely offered support.

Slowly, they moved down the street and around the corner toward the beach house.

Carrie's head was tucked up almost underneath Felipe's arm, and her own arm went around his waist under his jacket. As they walked, his thigh brushed against hers.

She tried to ignore the heat that coursed through her. After all, it had been her idea to suppress the physical attraction they both obviously felt toward each other. And *he* seemed to have no trouble doing just that.

But then she stumbled slightly, and he reached for her to keep her from falling. The movement made his T-shirt go up, and all of a sudden her fingers were against the smoothness of his bare back. He inhaled sharply, and she quickly pulled her hand away.

"Sorry," she said, not certain which she was apologizing for—nearly tripping and taking him down with her, or touching him that way.

He didn't say a word, he just looked at her, the moonlight failing to fully light his face. His eyes were in shadows, not that she could have deciphered the mysteries in his hooded gaze even if they hadn't been. But one thing was very clear. He wasn't finding it easy to keep his distance from her. He was simply better at hiding it.

But he wasn't hiding it now. She could hear him breathing, smell his warm, masculine scent, feel his heart beating—racing, really—in his chest.

Her own pulse was pounding just as hard and fast. Soon they were going to be inside the beach house. Soon they'd be behind the closed door. Alone. Together. With the world and all of its threats and dangers and realities carefully shut outside.

She could do anything, *any*thing, and no one would ever know. Except…*she* would know. She could make love to this man whom she wanted to trust and believe in, and then hope beyond hope that he *wasn't* the man the police were looking for.

But if he was…

Carrie walked down the driveway around to the rear of the house with her arm still tightly encircling Felipe's waist. He stopped at the bottom of the stairs leading up to the back porch, pulling her more fully into his arms, turning what might have been called support into an undeniable embrace.

"Caroline," he said, his mouth a whisper away from hers. He touched her hair, moving it back from her face in the gentlest of caresses.

Carrie stood staring up into the darkness of his eyes,

unable to move, unable to speak. He was going to kiss her. He was going to…

Instead, he released her, stepping away and using the stair railing for support.

"The key's under the flowerpot next to the back door," Felipe said, his voice husky. He cleared his throat. "We must remember not to turn on any lights inside. We don't want to catch the neighbors' attention."

As Carrie watched, he pulled himself up the stairs. He found the key exactly where he'd said it was and unlocked the door. Motioning for her to be quiet, he went inside first.

She followed him into the dark house and stood silently in the coolness. He stood several feet in front of her, his black jacket and jeans making him little more than a dark shape. He was listening intently, and Carrie found herself listening, too.

There was a clock somewhere in the room, and the sound of it ticking seemed thunderously loud. Outside the closed windows, the surf murmured, but other than that and the clock, the house was silent.

The air-conditioning unit came on with a hum, and Carrie nearly jumped out of her skin.

Felipe vanished, his dark shape moving out of the room they were in—the kitchen, Carrie saw as her eyes became more accustomed to the dark. But he reappeared a moment later.

"It's all right," he said, still whispering even though he had no need to. "There's no one here."

He opened one of the drawers and rummaged around, coming up with a box of matches. He lit one, and the tiny light seemed unnaturally bright.

The beach house was gorgeous—at least the kitchen

was. The shiny finish of blond pine cabinets gleamed in the match's glow. White and blue Mexican tile made up the countertops and floor.

A candle stood on the windowsill, and as Carrie watched, Felipe lighted it. "Come," he said, leading the way into the living room, shielding the candle's flame with his hand.

The living room was as splendid as the kitchen. More so. A huge fan hung from a beamed cathedral ceiling. Big glass windows and sliding doors covered nearly one entire wall. A huge stone fireplace was in the corner. White wicker furniture had been grouped around the room, creating an airy, spacious feeling.

Perfect. The beach house, the candlelight—it was all incredibly romantic. In fact, she couldn't remember anything quite so utterly romantic. And she was here, alone, with the most charismatic, attractive, *irresistible* man she'd ever met.

Absolutely perfect.

But Felipe didn't stop in the living room. He led her down a hallway, toward a trio of bedrooms. He stopped outside of one of them. "Check to make sure the shades are pulled down," he said, still speaking softly in the hush of the quiet house.

Carrie went into the room and crossed toward the windows. She pulled first one and then the other shade down.

"Those windows face the neighbor's," Felipe said.

Carrie nodded, not daring to meet his gaze. Instead, she looked around.

This was the master bedroom. It was big, with the same high ceiling as the living room. A king-size bed with a heavy oak frame was set against one wall. There were two doors in the far wall. One led to an open walk-in closet that was nearly as big as her entire apartment. The other opened into an adjoining bathroom. Carrie could see the gleam of tile and mirrors, shiny and clean and new.

The other wall, the same wall that in the living room held all those windows, was covered by curtains. She was willing to bet there were sliding glass doors behind them, doors leading out onto a private deck, with maybe a hot tub overlooking the backyard, which was in fact the moonlight-kissed beach.

It was too much. It was all way too much.

She wasn't going to be able to resist him. She was going to turn around, and he would be watching her with those black velvet eyes. And then she would fall headlong, with no hope of landing on her feet, off the dizzying cliff of desire and need.

She turned to look at Felipe. He stood in the doorway holding out the candle, offering it to her.

Carrie crossed toward him and took it. Their fingers brushed, and she jerked her hand away as if she'd been burned.

Holding her gaze, he backed away from her into the hallway. "Good night," he said, and closed the door.

He was gone.

Carrie stood there for a moment, staring at the rich wood of the door.

He was gone.

Obviously, he'd taken seriously her request to keep their relationship platonic.

Carrie looked around the room—at that enormous bed, at the luxurious plush carpeting, at the rich fabric of the draperies.

It wouldn't have taken much effort on Felipe's part to change her mind. In fact, another one of his high-powered kisses would've surely done the trick.

But he hadn't tried. He'd respected her decision.

Carrie wasn't sure whether to feel happy or sad.

Happy, she told herself fiercely as she went into the bathroom. She was happy.

Happily, she washed her face. Happily, she brushed her teeth with her finger and some borrowed toothpaste. And happily, she climbed into that great big bed all by herself and blew out the candle.

And lay there.

FELIPE STARED at the ceiling, listening to the sounds of the house, wishing he could fall asleep.

From his bed, he heard the sound of water running as Caroline Brooks drew herself a bath. It was one in the morning. She'd been quiet for a while, but now she was up and moving around. He guessed she couldn't sleep, either.

It wasn't hard to imagine her lying back and soaking in that bathtub. He'd stayed here at this beach house before, slept in the master bedroom. He'd soaked in that tub himself.

He'd been alone at the time. Come to think of it, he'd never brought any of his lady friends here to Sanibel Island. He'd never wanted to share either the peaceful solitude when he was alone, or the friendly atmosphere that prevailed when Diego and Emily Keegan were also here.

True, he'd once or twice brought Jewel Hays and her little boy, Billy. But Jewel was like a sister to him. They were old friends, nothing more.

But Caroline...

He closed his eyes, remembering the taste of her, the feel of her in his arms, the touch of her fingers on his neck and in his hair. Truthfully, his wounded leg wasn't the only thing that was throbbing.

He could go to her. Right now. He could stand up and walk the few feet down the hall and into the master bedroom. He could push open the bathroom door and she would look up at him in the candlelight, her huge blue-green eyes wide with surprise.

He would move closer and look down at the graceful lines of her body through the clear, warm water of the tub. She would sit up, water falling off her in a sheet, her small, firm breasts like some delicious, exotic, mouth-watering fruit.

Please, he'd say. It would be all he'd have to say, and she'd hold out her arms to him. He'd slip off his boxer shorts and join her in the water...

Felipe's eyes opened. No, he wouldn't. He wasn't supposed to get his stitches wet—at least not with more than a quick shower. Certainly he wasn't supposed to soak them in a tub.

He smiled ruefully at his overactive imagination. Like hell she would hold out her arms to him and welcome him. Like hell she would urge him to make love to her. She'd told him in no uncertain terms that she didn't want their relationship to become sexual.

Sure, he could seduce her. He knew that was a fact from looking into her eyes earlier tonight. He could kiss her and ignite the rocket fuel of their mutual attraction, and the earsplitting roar would drown out her protests. He'd kiss her again, and those protests would fade away. It wouldn't take long before she'd help him undress her, before she'd undress him, all her reservations forgotten.

At least temporarily.

And therein lay the reason he didn't stand up and go into the master bedroom, he thought with another smile. Caroline had asked him specifically to back off. She'd said no, quite distinctly and directly to his unspoken question, to the look she'd surely seen in his eyes. No. And no didn't mean maybe. No didn't mean catch me later when I'm more vulnerable. No meant no.

In the other room, on the other side of the wall, came the sound of water swirling around and then the pipes thumped as the water was turned back on. Caroline was adding hot water to the tub. Too bad. Felipe could think of a dozen or so ways to warm her up. He shifted his position in the bed, trying desperately to get comfortable.

He couldn't blame her for wanting to keep her distance. Until just a few hours ago, she'd thought he was some kind of criminal, some gang leader named Carlos who ran with an ugly bunch of friends. And just when she finally believed that he was who he said he was, she found out that he was wanted for murder. No, he couldn't blame her.

Quite honestly, Felipe was amazed she'd come here with him. He was grateful and relieved that she had. Because as he'd watched that news broadcast, as he'd watched her face as *she'd* watched it, he had been certain that she would never trust him again. And if he hadn't talked her into going to Montana, he *would* have had to make her his prisoner, his hostage, just the way she feared. And God, what a mess *that* would have been. But no way was he going to let her walk around without protection. No way was he going to let Tommy Walsh kill her. No way. No *way*.

The savage rush, the intensity of his feelings, made him grip the bedsheet like a rope that kept him from falling into some terrible abyss. Dear God, what was wrong with him?

He tried to tell himself he'd feel the same about any woman, about any *person* who was in danger of being killed, who was a target for Tommy Walsh's bullets.

But that wasn't true.

Caroline Brooks was special. If she died, he'd more than mourn the loss of a human life. He'd grieve deeply for himself, for his own loss. And he would miss her desperately, even though he'd only known her for a short time.

She fit. In his arms, she fit perfectly. And she fit in his heart. *His* heart? Heaven help him, he realized with a sudden flash of icy fear, it wasn't his heart anymore. Sure, it still beat in his chest, but it was hers. She had stolen it. She'd stolen it all those months ago during that night at Sea Circus. Why else had he gone back all those times to watch her from a distance? Why had he told Diego and Emily about her? Why had she haunted his dreams for months?

No, he tried to tell himself. That had been attraction. Nothing more. Attraction, simple lust. Well, maybe not simple. But it was entirely sexual. Wasn't it? Just a case of raw sexual attraction. Just as this…this…odd feeling in his chest was nothing more than a case of being overtired. Or it was heartburn, from the antibiotic. Sure. That was probably it.

He closed his eyes, willing himself to sleep. In the morning, in the light of day, he'd feel better. He'd be back on track.

From the other room he heard the sound of water

going down the drain. With sudden clarity, he could picture Caroline Brooks, stepping from the bathtub, reaching for a towel, her lithe body wet and shivering with cold and…

Felipe stared at the ceiling, listening to the sounds of the house, wishing he could fall asleep.

CHAPTER TEN

A CAR PULLED into the driveway, and Felipe was instantly awake and reaching for his gun.

He sat up and threw the sheet from his legs before the engine was turned off.

It was morning. Daylight seeped in around the shades. He hit the well-polished floorboards running, his mind racing even faster. Hide. They had to hide. But where? He remembered a crawl space underneath the house with an access door on the floor of the closet in the master bedroom. *Yes.*

Felipe ignored the sudden pain in his injured leg as he scooped his jeans, his shirt and his holster off the chair he'd thrown them over the night before, and snatched his boots from the floor.

He could hear the sound of a car door—one car door—as he moved swiftly and silently down the hall toward the master bedroom and Caroline.

He could hear the sound of footsteps—one set of footsteps—on the back porch as he pushed the bedroom door open.

Caroline was fast asleep, sprawled diagonally across the king-size bed. She'd kicked one tanned leg free from the sheets and her face was partially hidden under a cloud of golden hair. Her arms were spread wide as if she were embracing the world. She was wearing blue cotton high-cut panties and an old white tank top she must've found in one of Emily's father's dresser drawers.

His body began to tighten, an instant reaction to her state of dishabille, or maybe just a reaction to her presence. But he had no time to consider this, no time to do more than get them out of there, to keep them safely hidden from whoever was coming inside.

Felipe jammed his gun into the holster that was over his shoulder. With one hand, he swept Caroline's hair back from her face. The other he clamped firmly down over her mouth.

She woke up immediately. Her eyes were wide as she stared at him for a moment, a scream at the back of her throat securely stopped by his hand.

"It's okay," he whispered. "It's me. Someone's outside—they're coming in."

Instant understanding filled her eyes and he helped her sit up. She untangled herself from the sheets as he searched in vain for her clothes. Damn, he couldn't find them. Where had she put her dress and sandals?

But then there was no time. As a key turned in the back door, there was no time for anything but hiding.

Still carrying his own clothes, Felipe took Carrie's hand and tugged her toward the big walk-in closet. Motioning for her to be silent, he pulled back the carpet, revealing the access to the crawl space. He pulled up the inset brass ring, and the small trapdoor opened with a squeak.

"Go on," he whispered to Caroline. "It's a crawl space. It's not deep—it's less than three feet down. Just climb in."

But she didn't move. She stared down into the

darkness, her eyes wider than ever, her hair a golden tangle around her face. She heard the back door open, and she turned, glancing over her shoulder toward the sound, then looked at Felipe.

He threw his clothes and holster into the crawl space, keeping his gun in his hand.

"Quickly," he urged. "I'll be right behind you."

Wordlessly, she shook her head.

The back door closed behind whoever had come inside.

Felipe grabbed Caroline around the waist and pulled her down with him into the crawl space.

It was dark and damp and tight and hot and filled with cobwebs and other things he didn't want to think about. He closed the access door over their heads, taking care to flip the carpet back over it.

And then it was *really* dark.

There was barely enough room for him to lie on his side without his shoulder brushing the support beams for the floor above. Gingerly, Felipe shifted around, one arm still encircling Caroline's waist, the gun in his other hand pointed up through the blackness at where he knew the access door to be. Carrie's back was against his chest, her head tightly nestled below his chin. He could feel her heart pounding and hear her ragged breathing in the pitch darkness.

And then he could hear footsteps.

In his arms, Caroline held her breath as if she was afraid whoever was up there might be able to hear her.

She was terrified. Her entire body was trembling. But she tried to stop herself from shaking, entwining her smooth legs with his as if to anchor herself. It didn't help.

It certainly didn't help him.

Her round little bottom was pressed intimately up against him, and now his thigh was wedged firmly between her legs. His left hand was up underneath her shirt, and his thumb rested against the swell of her breast.

Felipe felt many trickles of sweat begin their journeys. One traveled down his back, others slid past his ear, another rolled down his collarbone.

The footsteps moved across the floor again. Whoever was up there was not overhead. The sound was coming from the other side of the house—where the kitchen and living room were located.

Caroline seemed to realize that, too, and she let herself breathe again. She took short, fast breaths as if she were running a marathon—or as if she were nearing sexual release.

That particular image was nearly too much for Felipe to bear. He tried to concentrate on the concentric waves of pain that were radiating from his wounded leg rather than his growing arousal.

But it was no use. Despite the imminent danger, despite his pain, he couldn't stop himself from being turned on. Afraid of offending Caroline, knowing his silk boxers did little to hide his state, he tried to loosen his hold on her and back away from her just an inch or two.

But she wouldn't let him go. "No," she breathed almost inaudibly in the silence, turning her head toward him. "Felipe, please, stay with me!"

There was such desperation in her voice, such fear— and such total trust that his presence could make it all okay. He stopped trying to pull away.

"I'm here, sweetheart," he whispered. He was experiencing a jumble of emotions he could barely recognize. Protectiveness—he felt fierce, almost savage protectiveness. And he felt possessiveness, yes, there was plenty of that, too. Only God could help Tommy Walsh, or whoever else tried to take this woman away from him. And gluing everything together was sort of an odd tenderness, making all these powerful emotions stick like a painful lump high up in his chest, making his eyes burn and his heart hurt.

And the really loco part of it was, despite the fact that he wanted her so badly, these things he was feeling had absolutely nothing to do with sex, with the desire that was making his blood boil.

Above their heads the telephone rang.

The footsteps moved rapidly toward the kitchen.

In the total darkness of the crawl space, Felipe strained to listen.

"Hello?" a faint voice said. "No, who's callin'?"

Female. Southern belle accent. Anywhere from thirty to sixty years old. Not Tommy Walsh. Not a threat.

"No, I'm sorry," the voice said. "The Marshalls aren't here right now. They'll be down in February. I can take a message and call the daughter if you wish. She and her husband are in and out all the time." There was a pause, and then the gentle tinkling of a delicate laugh. "No, no. I live next door. I'm just over to water the plants. Uh-huh. That's right." Another laugh. "Bye now."

Felipe lowered his gun to the floor, suddenly aware how much his arm ached from holding it up for so long. He let himself relax slightly, twisting his head to get the kinks out of his neck.

But in his arms, Caroline still shook.

"Hey," he said softly, putting the safety on his gun. He set it down, away from them on the hard dirt floor and wrapped his other arm around her. Maybe in her fear she hadn't heard the phone conversation; maybe it hadn't sunk in. "It's all right— we're all right. We're not in any danger. Even if she sees the unmade beds, even if she calls the police, we'll still have time to get away."

Carrie took in a deep breath and tried to let it slowly out of her mouth. But that still didn't stop her trembling. "It's so dark," she whispered, her husky voice cutting through the pitch black. "I can't see anything."

"But that's good," Felipe said soothingly. "If we can't see anything, then no one can see us, right?"

"No," she said. Her voice sounded choked, unnatural, her breath still coming in sobs. God in heaven, was she crying? Felipe reached up and felt the tears on her face. She *was*. She was crying. His heart lurched.

"Caroline," he whispered, his voice nearly cracking with his concern. "*Cara,* my God, are you hurt? What's wrong?"

"I'm okay," she whispered. But it sounded as if she was trying to convince herself as well as him. "It's okay. See, I'm claustrophobic, but I'm okay."

Claustrophobic?

Man, to a claustrophobic, the past ten minutes had to have been a total nightmare, a living hell. And she was still living it. Squeezed tightly together in a narrow crawl space, without any light…

"My God," he said, hardly aware he was speaking aloud. "My *God*—"

"Shh," she said, turning toward him, trying to comfort *him*. "It's all right. I'm all right. It's okay, because you're with me. I'm not alone. Really, it's not so bad."

Not so bad? She was still trembling. He could feel her

heart drumming in her chest. And she couldn't stop the tears that were flowing down her face, wetting his neck.

And, oh, God, give him strength! At Sea Circus, he'd locked Caroline in the trunk of her car. He'd locked her in the tiny, dark airless trunk of her little sports car, all by herself.

Felipe felt sick. His stomach churned and tears burned his eyes. Two hours. She'd been in there for two hours, she'd told him. He knew 911 calls were often dangerously backed up, but *two hours!* What he'd done to her was tantamount to torture.

"Oh, Caroline," he whispered raggedly, holding her tightly. "I'm so sorry."

The footsteps upstairs had been silent for a while. From outside the house, Felipe heard the sound of a car engine. The voice, the neighbor, had left.

He found his gun in the darkness, then moved toward the access door. He was careful to bring Caroline with him, careful to keep as much of his body in contact with hers as he possibly could, aware that such obvious proof of his presence helped her.

With a heave, he pushed the trapdoor open, and light—brilliant, glorious, golden light flooded down on top of them.

Caroline scrambled toward the light, and Felipe helped her up and out. Gathering his clothes and holster from where he'd thrown them, he climbed stiffly after her.

She lay on the floor of the master bedroom. Her eyes were closed and her hair had tumbled forward to hide her face.

Felipe holstered his gun and tossed aside the pile of clothes he'd been holding. He knelt next to her and brushed her hair back from her face.

"I'm sorry," he said again. "At Sea Circus, when I put you in your trunk... God help me, I had no idea."

She opened her startlingly sea green eyes and looked directly up at him. "I know that," she said, still breathing hard. "How could you have known? Besides, you did what you had to do to save me."

He was miserable, and he realized that every bit of his misery showed clearly on his face. No wonder she had been so angry with him at Schroedinger's restaurant. No wonder she was adamant about keeping her distance. "How you must hate me," he said.

She pushed herself up off the floor. Reaching out with one hand, she touched the side of his face. "No," she said quietly. She took a deep breath in, then let it slowly out. "No, I don't."

The tears that were in Felipe's eyes threatened to overflow. He reached up, pressing her hand tightly to his cheek. "I'd never do anything to hurt you," he said. "Please believe that."

She nodded, her own eyes luminous. Her face was smudged with dirt, and her tears had made clean tracks through it. Still, she looked beautiful. Lord, the torment he'd put her through...

She tried to smile and actually succeeded. "That was a heck of a way to wake up," she said. "A hand over my mouth to scare me to death, and then a trip to my own personal hell. Tomorrow you might try something a little lower key—maybe like this."

And then she kissed him.

She kissed *him.*

It started out feather light, the gentlest of butterfly kisses.

Felipe pulled back, surprised and even embarrassed.

Had she really kissed him? Or maybe he'd kissed her, and maybe—certainly—he shouldn't have.

But she leaned forward again, and this time there was no mistaking. She *did* kiss him.

Her mouth was warm and soft, her lips opening under his, pliant and willing and...oh, *yes*.

He pulled her against him, turning his head to kiss her deeper, harder, longer. She molded her body against his and wrapped her arms around him.

Dizzy with desire, Felipe sank down onto the floor, pulling her with him. Their legs intertwined, and this time, he let himself truly enjoy the sensation of her smooth, silky skin against his. He kissed her again and again, exploring her mouth with his tongue, taking his time, content just to kiss her for hours and hours.

But then she moved against him, the softness of her belly against him. Her legs tightened around his thigh and he heard himself groan.

Her heart was beating as fast and hard as it had been down in the crawl space—faster, even. She tugged at him, and he rolled over so that he was on top of her.

This was not a case of him seducing her. This was not a case of him taking advantage...or was it?

Felipe pulled back. "Caroline," he said, shaking his head, unable to speak.

She looked up at him, fire in her sea-green eyes. He reached for her hand, pulling her so that she was sitting up. Confusion and then trepidation replaced the fire in her eyes.

"You don't want to...?" she whispered.

"*You* don't want to," he replied, hardly believing he was saying those words, hardly believing he was denying himself what would surely be a first-class trip to heaven. "You told me that yesterday, *cara*, remember?"

She looked at the obvious sign of his arousal. He couldn't hide it, so he didn't bother to try. He could feel her eyes studying him, searching his face. He looked back at her, steadily meeting her gaze.

"Is it okay if I changed my mind?" she asked softly, and his heart leaped.

"Oh, yes," he said huskily. "It's very okay."

"I changed my mind," she said.

He wanted to touch her. But right at this moment, it was enough to look, knowing that soon, very soon, he would be touching her.

For the first time, he let himself really see her in that ridiculous excuse for a shirt. The thin material was nearly transparent as it hung loosely on her slight frame. The armholes dipped down almost to her waist, revealing the soft, round sides of her breasts. Her nipples were dark, tight points that the shirt did little to conceal. It was sexy as hell and her smile told him that she knew it. She liked knowing that she turned him on. That was good, because he couldn't have hidden his attraction to her even if he had wanted to.

She was beautiful, and she was to be his. That knowledge made his body nearly hum with desire.

"Do you have any protection?" she asked. "A condom?"

"I keep one in my wallet." He smiled. "I kept it there in hopes that I'd meet up with you."

She laughed. "I know that's supposed to be romantic," she said, her eyes dancing with amusement. "But, really, Felipe, that's *such* a total crock of—"

"Do you know for sure it's not true?" he countered, his eyes sliding down her body, across those perfect breasts, down her shapely legs then up again to meet her eyes. "I've met you in my dreams quite often these past six months, Caroline Brooks."

Her smile faded, leaving only heat in her eyes. She moistened her lips with a nervous flick of her tongue. "Why don't you call me Carrie?" she asked.

"Because Caroline is more beautiful," he said. "It suits you."

She rolled her eyes. "Ease up on the B.S., Salazar," she said, "or I might change my mind again."

He watched her steadily. "It's not bull," he said serenely. "And, you know, if you change your mind again, that's okay, too."

She smiled at his words, but then stopped as she realized he wasn't kidding. It *was* okay. *Every*thing was okay.

"There is more to the way I feel about you than sex," Felipe said quietly. His words were true but purposely vague. He couldn't get more specific. He was afraid to delve more deeply into his own feelings. But even though it scared him—both the words he spoke and the feelings that prompted those words—she had the right to know.

She looked down, away from him, and he was struck by how sweet, how young and innocent she looked. She was only twenty-five—that was his age, too, he realized. But she was still young and he was not. He'd grown up a lot faster, a lot harder. They came from different neighborhoods, he and Caroline. The mountains of her father's ranch couldn't be compared to the rough, unforgiving city streets where he'd spent his childhood—what little of it he'd had. He'd been twenty-five for the past fifteen years. She'd been twenty-five only since last October 16—at least that was what had been listed on her driver's license.

But then she glanced up at him from underneath her long eyelashes and smiled. It was a smile that promised paradise, a dazzling contrast to her seeming shyness moments before. She was full of surprises, full of contradictions, a living kaleidoscope of mercurial energy and emotion. He liked that. He liked *her*.

He leaned forward to kiss her and she met him halfway.

The explosion of passion was nearly instantaneous. He heard her moan as he pulled her, hard, against him. As he kissed her again, he felt her hands in his hair, on his back, touching, caressing, drawing him yet closer.

They were back exactly where they'd been several minutes earlier. Only this time, when Caroline pulled him down on top of her, she opened her legs, pressing the heat of her most intimate self against him.

Oh, *yes*.

The pain in his leg no longer existed. St. Simone and Lawrence Richter and Tommy Walsh and this whole damned mess they were in no longer existed. The world—the entire *universe*—no longer existed.

There was only Caroline.

Felipe rolled over onto his back, pulling her along so that she was straddling him. She kissed him, her tongue dancing with his, mimicking the movement of their bodies as she slowly, sensuously moved on top of him. Her hair fell around his face, a curtain of gold, as his hands cupped her buttocks, fixing her more tightly against him. Only the silk of his shorts and the cotton of her panties kept him from entering her.

"Oh, Caroline," he breathed. "This is…" He couldn't find the words. But he didn't have to.

She stopped kissing him long enough to gaze down

into his eyes and he knew that whatever it was he was feeling—this euphoria, this sense of perfection, of completeness—she was feeling it, too.

He found the edge of her shirt and pushed it up and over her head. Her breasts were small and round and perfectly proportioned to the rest of her body. He covered them with his hands, groaning at the pleasure of touching her soft flesh. She moaned, too, pressing herself forward.

With one swift move, he flipped her onto her back, moving to touch one taut, pink nipple with his lips. Gently, so gently, he kissed her, then touched her lightly with his tongue.

Her skin smelled fresh and clean and ever so slightly of sun block. Yes, now more than ever, he would associate that scent with paradise.

Felipe could feel his pulse racing. He tried to bring it under control, to slow down his breathing and ease this feeling of an imminent explosion that tightened his throat and his gut and made him ache even lower. He wanted to rip off her panties and his boxer shorts and plunge himself deep inside her.

Instead, he forced himself to move deliberately, unhurriedly. He drew languid circles around her nipple with his tongue while his hands swept slowly up and down her tanned, flat stomach to the edge of her panties and then up and across her other breast. She touched him the same way, too, almost reverently, as if she couldn't believe she was finally getting her heart's desire.

Her fingers felt cool and delicate against the burning heat of his skin. Could she feel his heartbeat? he wondered. Did she know that the gentleness of her touch had the power to make him tremble? As he drew her more fully into his mouth, pulling, sucking, laving her with his tongue, she gripped his shoulders with a strength that surprised him. She arched her back, wanting more. Her response nearly did him in, nearly pushed him over the edge.

By sheer willpower, he managed to hang on to his sanity and his control. He closed his eyes, counting slowly to ten. When he opened them, she was watching him. She smiled and his heart nearly burst. If it wasn't one part of him ready to explode, it was another.

She pushed his hair back from his face in a gentle, loving caress. It warmed him and he smiled back at her, whispering words of endearment in Spanish—words he wouldn't have dared say to her in a language she could understand.

He broke away from the spell her ocean-colored eyes had cast over him, gazing down at her beautiful body, clad only in those blue panties.

She was tanned all over, he realized. At least on the top. She did have a tan line where she'd worn bathing-suit bottoms, and another line of shading where she'd worn shorts, but her breasts had the same perfect, golden tan as her shoulders and arms and stomach.

More contradictions. Somehow he couldn't imagine Caroline driving south down the coast from St. Simone to hang out at Tamiami Beach, the area's only topless sunbathing spot. Still, she'd obviously spent some time— quite a bit of time—in the sun without her top on.

"Nice tan," he murmured, and she blushed. More con-tradictions. But then he lowered his mouth to her other breast, and she forgot her embarrassment. He felt her hands in his hair as she ran her fingers through his dark curls. He ran his hand down her stomach again, and when he would've stopped short of her panties, she lifted her hips, pressing herself up and into his hand. She couldn't have been any clearer about what she wanted if she'd announced it through a megaphone.

So he slipped his hand beneath the elastic waistband of her panties, lifting his head to gaze into her eyes as he touched first the nest of her curls and then her soft heat. The light of pleasure on her face was sinfully delicious as he explored her most intimately.

This would be enough, he realized. Even though he was straining against his shorts, even though he wanted to be inside this woman more than he'd ever wanted anything in his life, simply giving her pleasure would truly be enough.

She closed her eyes, moving against him as he stroked her harder, deeper.

He murmured to her in Spanish, telling her of the strange sensations in his heart, urging her on, right there, right now, as he held her in his arms.

But Caroline had an entirely different idea.

She reached for him, encircling his shaft with her hand right through the silk of his shorts. "This is what I want," she whispered. She moved her hand along his length and he bit back a cry of pleasure.

She reached for the waistband of his boxers, pulling them down, freeing him from their restraint. And then she was touching him, her fingers against his hardness, and once again he fought for self-control.

But she wasn't going to let him get it back.

She sat up, pulling away from him, getting up on her knees to drag his shorts down his legs, careful to lift them over the bandage that covered his stitches, touching him all the while. Feverishly, he reached for his jeans, for the wallet that was still in the back pocket, and for the condom that was stored there.

His hands shook as he tore open the foil package. She pushed off her panties—how beautiful she was!—then quickly helped him cover himself. Helped? Not really. She stroked him, squeezed him, caressed him as he blindly tried to put on the damned condom.

All of his English had left him, every single blasted word of it. He tried to tell her that he wanted to make love to her this first time in the traditional way. The first time, the man should be on top, giving the pleasure.

But she didn't understand. She murmured something to him about his leg, something about not wanting him to hurt himself, something he didn't understand because he wasn't hurting—he was feeling absolutely no pain. She kissed him, still straddling him, moving her hips so that she touched him with her moistness and heat. Oh, man, at this rate, he'd be finished in seven seconds. Felipe lifted her up, about to turn her and lay her down on her back, wincing when all at once the pain from his leg cut through. And, then, "No."

The single word penetrated and he froze.

No?

He looked into her eyes through the fog of desire, and she shook her head.

Yes, that was definitely a no.

Stopping like this was going to kill him, but if she'd changed her mind, then he'd stop. He was holding his breath, he realized, and he let it out with a long, ragged sigh, trying desperately to regain his equilibrium. What had happened? Had he done something wrong?

Slowly he lowered her back down, but instead of moving away from him, she moved toward him. With one smooth thrust, she unsheathed him.

Oh, *yes*.

It was a lot like being thrown a surprise birthday party. He was caught totally off guard, but instantly able to adjust to the shock. And just as quickly, he understood what she had been saying no to. She wanted to be on top.

It went against the grain of everything he believed about making love to a woman. The man gave and took the pleasure. The man was in control.

And he was not in control here.

But as she moved on top of him, as she rode him, her eyes half-closed with pleasure, her long, blond hair loose around her shoulders, covering all but the tantalizing tips of her breasts, Felipe realized an awful truth.

When it came to making love to Caroline Brooks, he would never truly be in control.

The only consolation was that she was not in control, either.

He moved his hips, thrusting up to meet her downward movement, driving himself deep into her. Her eyes widened, then shut tightly, and she threw her head back, crying out her pleasure at the sensation.

He was lost, swept away by passion and pleasure and an ache in his heart he was beginning to fear would never let up.

Time blurred, and he pulled her down to kiss him as they moved together. *Together.* He wasn't making love to Caroline, he was making love *with* her. The thought exploded in his head as clearly as the flash of light from fireworks. Suddenly, all of his previous beliefs about making love seemed old-fashioned and obsolete. Because as sure as he was born, he'd never in his life felt anything even remotely like what he was feeling right now. It was delicious ecstasy, wild abandon, pure pleasure. And he was sharing it with Caroline. It was dizzying, consuming, terrifying. Could he actually feel this way for more than the briefest moment and not disintegrate?

And still they moved together.

She pulled away from his kiss to sit up, still atop him, and the movement sent him plunging harder and deeper into her again and again. Her head went back and she clutched at his arms, and feeling something close to disbelief, Felipe fell over the side of a cliff.

He felt the last shred of his ragged control dissolve as his body took full command. He exploded with a violent rush as, for the only time since he'd first made love at age sixteen, he finished before his lover.

He heard the hoarse sound of his voice crying out her name, heard her answering cry, felt her shudder of pleasure as she, too, found her release.

His ears were ringing as she slumped on top of him, her hair covering his face. He closed his eyes, breathing in the sweet scent of her shampoo, feeling their two hearts racing, pounding a syncopated tattoo.

His breathing slowed, and his pulse finally returned to near normal. But the dizzying, consuming emotions that had been let loose in his mind and in his heart at their coupling wouldn't fade away.

Perhaps they never would.

That thought scared him to death.

What could it mean? Why was he feeling this way?

They swirled around him like a tornado, those almost palpable emotions, forming a pattern of words that repeated over and over in his mind.

Te amo. Te adoro.

I love you.

His eyes opened and he stared at the ceiling through a haze of golden hair.

He was in love with Caroline Brooks.

No. He couldn't be. He wouldn't let himself be. It was not possible. Not now. Especially not now. But not later, either. There was no room in his life for such a thing.

And there was no room in *her* life for both him and the danger he would bring with him. How many gang members, mobsters and crime lords had he angered over the past few years? How many contracts were there on his life right now? And how many people wouldn't think twice about ripping the life from an innocent young woman, simply to get back at the undercover police detective who had given them their due?

No.

If he cared about her at all, after this was over and he knew that she was safe, he would walk away. And if he loved her, he'd run.

Te amo. Te adoro.

No. It wasn't true. And even if it was, he couldn't tell her. He'd never tell her.

Never.

CHAPTER ELEVEN

"I'M SORRY," Felipe said quietly, his mouth up against her ear.

Carrie turned her head to look at him, pushing her hair back off her face.

He gazed up at her, his dark eyes mysterious and unreadable.

"Sorry?" she asked.

She could have sworn she saw a flash of embarrassment in those eyes. He looked away from her, but then forced his gaze back up, steadily meeting her inquisitive stare.

He moistened his lips. "I, uh…" he said, then he cleared his throat. "Usually…I'm not so…inconsiderate. Usually…I allow my partner to…reach, uh, satisfaction first."

Carrie felt herself start to smile as the meaning of his words penetrated. She couldn't hide a laugh. "Are you *apologizing* for the way you just made love to me?" she asked, her voice dripping with disbelief.

He *was* embarrassed. He closed his eyes briefly, then nodded his head.

Carrie couldn't keep from laughing. "Mister, are you telling me that this is just an off day—that you've done that even *better?*"

"I came before you," he said. He wasn't laughing.

"Was it a race?" she asked. "And were you trying to let me win?"

Unblinkingly serious, he gazed up at her. "It's important to me," he said. And then he blushed slightly, looking away, unable to meet her eyes. "This hasn't happened since… It hasn't happened ever."

Carrie's heart flip-flopped in her chest. The tinge of red across his high cheekbones was utterly charming, despite the slightly archaic and macho tinge to his words.

He was still inside her and she didn't move off him. She didn't want to. The glow from the perfection of their joining still surrounded her. She nestled her head on his shoulder, careful that her hair didn't fall across his face, marveling at how well they fit together, even now, even after.

He stroked her back almost absentmindedly, his fingers trailing lightly from her neck to her derriere and up again.

"Do you know," she murmured, lifting her chin so that her breath touched his ear, "what it felt like to me just now?"

His hand stopped moving. He swallowed, then shook his head once slightly. He'd closed his eyes, but he was listening to her very carefully, absorbing each of her words.

"Do you know," she asked, stopping for a moment to brush her lips lightly along the line of his jaw, "what a turn-on it is when the man you're making love to loses control like that?"

Again, he shook his head.

"It's unlike anything you can imagine," she said, her voice husky with the memory and the emotion. "At the risk of feeding your ego, I've never been made love to like that before. *And* as far as I'm concerned, we were together. You started first. Big deal. I was a millisecond behind you. Who's counting?"

He opened his eyes and turned his head to look at her. "You're very sweet," he said, pressing a kiss to her forehead.

"You don't believe me?" Carrie shook her head, feeling impatience rising in her. Impatience, and something else. Hurt? How could he not think that the love they'd just shared was anything but sensational? "I can't believe we're arguing about this. Can you honestly tell me that that entire experience gets stamped *rejected* because of one minute detail that didn't happen exactly the way you'd planned? Or are you telling me that the whole thing was lousy—and if that's the case, I better take a good long look at my sex life, because if *that* was lousy, I've been missing something all these years!"

"Caroline—"

"And if that's the case, we're on very different wavelengths, Detective, with you thinking that was lousy sex, and me thinking…" She took a deep breath and let it slowly out. "And me thinking it's never been so perfect, so complete," she finished miserably.

She rolled off him, wishing she could crawl away and hide. How had this happened? Two minutes ago, she'd been laughing, euphoric. Then this man whom she thought she was finally beginning to know and understand, this man who had been so amazingly in tune with her every want and need as he'd made love to her, this man had mutated into some kind of rigid caveman who needed to follow an extremely macho set of rules when making love. She began to search almost frantically for her clothes.

Felipe caught her arm. "Please," he said. "I was being stupid." He pulled her close to him and cradled her in his arms. "I was being *really* stupid. You were right. I was…stupid."

"Damn straight you were," Carrie muttered.

He gently moved her chin so that she was facing him. "I was frightened," he murmured. "The power of the feelings… It still frightens me. Forgive me, Caroline."

And then he kissed her.

He may have voiced some very old-fashioned ideas about male and female roles in bed, but his apology sounded sincere, and he could kiss like no one else in the world.

Most men that Carrie had known had kissed her for a reason. To placate or apologize. To get on her good side. To get her into bed.

But even though Felipe had just apologized to her, his kiss was very separate from his words. He kissed her purely for the sake of kissing her, for the pleasure of her mouth against his.

He kissed her slowly, lazily, his tongue sweeping possessively into her mouth, claiming her, staking out his territory.

Carrie heard herself sigh, felt herself melt, felt the world tilt and disappear. Maybe having a lover who could be an absolute caveman at times *wasn't* such a terrible thing. She laced her fingers up through his long, gorgeous hair, slanting her head to grant him easier access to her mouth.

He drew in a breath and murmured to her in Spanish. She couldn't understand the words, but his voice sounded like poetry in the hush of the quiet room. And still he kissed her.

She felt dizzying heat pooling in her stomach. Was it really possible that she wanted him again? Already?

He lifted his head, supporting his upper body with one elbow as he looked down at her. "I love kissing you," he said.

Carrie's heart pounded in her chest. For a moment, when he'd started that sentence, she had been so sure he was about to tell her something else. *I love you.* But how could she expect him to say that? He barely knew her.

They were undeniably compatible—especially physically. They'd certainly proved that. And despite Felipe's momentary slip revealing his old-fashioned beliefs, she honestly liked him more and more with each passing moment. Heck, she liked him more *because* of his slip. Before she'd seen that side of him, he'd been too damn perfect. She liked him better because now she knew that he was human and that he had his weaknesses and doubts.

He was stroking her, his strong, warm hand sliding up her hip and over the curve of her waist. His eyes were hooded as he looked at her. Carrie felt the tips of her breasts harden into tight little beads under the weight of his gaze. He glanced into her eyes and smiled.

"Do you really go out to Tamiami Beach?" he asked.

Tamiami…? Where…? The nude beach, Carrie remembered. No, not nude, topless. He was referring to her nearly allover tan. She felt her face heat with a blush.

"No," she said, shaking her head. "No. I…do a lot of research work out on my boat, all by myself." Did he really want to hear the entire story? He was listening, waiting for her to continue, so she did.

"I always used to just wear my bathing suit, but one day I was out doing some work along the coast near one of the swamps, and I forgot to bring my suit or even a change of clothes. I was bringing in a sampling of the marine life that had died as a result of an oil spill, and I ended up with tar all over my T-shirt." An angry alligator had surprised her near an illegal garbage dump and she'd tripped in her haste to get back into her boat. "It was hotter than hell that day, and the sun was heating the tar on my shirt. Obviously, it wouldn't rinse out, and I was actually afraid it was going to burn me. My options were to take off the shirt, or turn and head for home. I figured if I were a man, I'd have had my shirt off hours earlier, so...I took off the shirt and put in five more hours of work. And got a great tan."

She smiled up into his eyes. "I also got a...certain sense of liberation. Ever since then, when I'm alone on my boat, I go topless. No one knows but me. And now you."

He leaned forward to touch the peak of her breast with the tip of his tongue. "The thought of you working like this is...stimulating," he murmured. "Someday, will you let me come and help?" But then he shook his head, as if he thought better of his words. "Or maybe that's not such a good idea," he added. "It would be too distracting, at least for me."

He pulled back from her, no longer meeting her eyes. He ran his fingers through his hair, then rubbed his forehead as if he had a headache. She could see the sudden tension in his neck and shoulders. Even the well-defined muscles in his arms seemed tighter. He hadn't moved an inch, but mentally he was stepping back, away from her. Was he doing that because he thought she wanted him to? Did he think she still wanted him to keep his distance?

"I'd love for you to come out on my boat someday," Carrie said quietly, trying to read his reaction.

But Felipe shook his head, still looking away from her. "We don't have someday, *cara*," he said just as quietly. "We only have right here and right now." He looked up at her then. The deep sadness was back in his eyes.

"Walsh and Richter aren't going to be looking for us forever," Carrie said. "And you're going to prove that you didn't kill those men in the sandlot—"

"Even then," he said, interrupting her. "Even if this ends and we're both still alive…" He took a deep breath. "I can't make you any promises, Caroline. I probably should have told you this before we made love, but…I can't fall in love with you."

His words filled her with a disappointment that was a great deal stronger than she'd expected. And his words proved how deceptive good sex could be. She'd interpreted his caresses, his sighs, those long looks he gave her, and especially the way he'd clung to her and called out her name, as a measure of his feelings. In truth, those things were merely a measure of *what* he was feeling. Physical sensations, not love in any way, shape or form.

But what the heck, she told herself, she hadn't *really* thought Felipe Salazar would fall in love with her, had she?

Yes. The word rose in her throat like a bubble that had to break free.

No, she told herself harshly. No, she hadn't. And it was good he'd told her this, because now that she knew, she'd make damn sure she wouldn't fall in love with him.

She forced her mouth into a smile. "Well, that's fine," she said to Felipe. "Because I have no intention of falling in love with you, either. You know, I don't even really trust you entirely."

Now, why the hell had she said that? She saw the flash

of hurt leap into his eyes, and knew that her words had stung. She *knew* that his innocence was a sticky subject for Felipe, that he wanted her to trust him.

But what she'd said was true, she told herself. For all she knew, he really had killed those men. Or maybe he hadn't actually pulled the trigger himself. Maybe he was just involved in some other awful way. She had seen no proof that he wasn't involved. She only had his word.

You said it because you wanted to hurt him. You said it because you want him to fall in love with you, because you've already fallen in love with him.

"You must trust me on some level," Felipe said, "or you wouldn't have made love to me."

Carrie lifted her arms over her head and stretched, pretending desperately to be casual and noncommittal while her brain and her heart were going in twenty different directions. He followed her movement with heat in his eyes, like a cat watching a bird and ready to pounce. Was it desire or anger glowing there?

"I trusted that sex with you would be great," she said, keeping her voice light. Inside, she felt heavier than lead. She *wasn't* in love with him. She *wasn't*... "I wasn't wrong, was I?" She pushed herself off the floor and stood. "I'm going to take a shower, maybe take another soak in that tub." She stopped at the bathroom door, looking back at him. "Too bad you can't get your stitches wet for another day or so."

Then it was all desire that flared in his eyes. "Maybe I can—"

"You told me nothing but a quick shower until tomorrow," Carrie said, pretending that she actually *wanted* him to shower with her, pretending that his admission that he didn't love her, would *never* love her, was something that she took casually in stride, pretending that her heart wasn't breaking. "And if you get in the shower with me, it won't be quick. You better wait out here."

He smiled at her, a smile that held a promise of paradise. But no, he'd said he couldn't promise her anything. Nothing but sexual pleasure anyway, and certainly not paradise. Paradise was more than pure, raw sex. Paradise was murmured words of love, promises of forever. He wasn't even going to pretend to give her that.

Carrie supposed she should be grateful that he wasn't trying to deceive her. At least he'd been up-front and honest about his feelings—or lack of feelings in this case.

He was so utterly handsome, lying there on the floor buck naked, his long, muscular legs stretched out in front of him. His hips were narrow, leading up to his equally narrow waist and the washboard muscles of his stomach. He didn't have much hair on his chest. He didn't need it; it would have hidden the near perfection of his pecs and other steel-hard muscles. His skin was smooth and golden brown, his nipples a darker shade of that same delicious color. A line of dark hair started at his belly button and spread downward toward the thick thatch of black curls between his legs and...

He was fully aroused.

She did that to him, Carrie knew. With her talk of showering together, her stories of working on her boat without a top, and with the way she'd just looked at him—as if she were starving and he was a five-course gourmet meal....

He was more than willing to let himself make love to her. *Make* love, yet not love her. He wouldn't let himself love her.

It didn't seem fair.

It *wasn't* fair.

Carrie went into the bathroom and turned on the shower. Stepping under the rush of water, she closed her eyes.

He *could* be a killer, she reminded herself. Maybe if she repeated that over and over, she'd stop loving him. Maybe she should take precautions against further hurt and take care not to make love to Felipe again.

Yeah, right. And maybe alligators could fly.

Rafe's prediction had come true, she realized ruefully. Less than twenty-four hours had passed since she'd sat with Felipe's brother in the kitchen of the halfway house, and sure enough, she'd gone and slept with Felipe. Slept with. It was a funny expression, considering neither of them had ever had the slightest intention of sleeping. Gone to bed with? That wasn't true, either, since they'd made love on the plush carpeting on the bedroom floor. Made love to. Only half-true—her half, not his. Still, a half truth was better than none, wasn't it?

Any predictions for the next twenty-four hours? she wondered as she turned her face up to the stream of water. Where was Rafe when she needed him? Too bad he hadn't warned her she was going to fall in love with his little brother. Of course, if he'd as much as suggested the possibility, she would've laughed that off, too.

The water falling on her face hid her tears. As long as she stood there in the shower, Carrie could pretend that she wasn't crying.

Predictions for the next twenty-four hours? She had one that she knew so damn well to be true, it would make Nostradamus look like a cheap carnival palm reader.

Sometime in the next twenty-four hours or less—and

probably many, many hours less—she was going to make love again to that man, that beautiful, exciting, charismatic, dangerous man that she'd so foolishly, and against all her better judgment, fallen in love with.

CHAPTER TWELVE

UNTANGLING HER WET HAIR with a brush she'd found in
the bathroom, and dressed in a too-big pair of cutoffs and
a man's dress shirt that nearly covered the legs of the
shorts, Carrie walked down the hall toward the living
room. Felipe was nowhere in sight.

She stood looking out through the big glass doors at
the turquoise blue ocean. The private beach was deserted
and picture postcard perfect. She could see why someone
would want to build a beach house on this spot. The sun
reflecting off the white sand filtered in through the tinted
glass of the windows, illuminating the living room with
an unearthly golden light.

A sound from behind her made her turn around.

Felipe stood in the doorway that led to the kitchen. His
hair, too, was wet from his own quick shower, and he ran
his fingers through the tight curls, loosening them and
letting the air dry them. His eyes were gentle, so soft and
serene as he looked at her. There was no sign of the fire
that had threatened to consume her only an hour or so
earlier. But then his gaze traveled down her body, grazing
her breasts, taking in the fact that she wasn't wearing a
bra underneath her shirt, reminding her that both her bra
and panties were hanging in the bathroom, drying. His
eyes caressed the length of her legs, lingering, heating her
with just a look.

The fire was still there, Carrie realized as he glanced back into her eyes. He was just very, very good at keeping it hidden.

"Are you hungry?" he asked, his soft accent like velvet in the quiet room.

Carrie's stomach clenched with a sudden rush of desire, and inwardly she kicked herself for her body's blatant reaction to this man. Hungry? Yes, sir, but not for food.

He was wearing only a pair of dark blue, knee-length shorts. A size or more too large, they hung low around his waist. He looked as if he were on vacation at the beach, as if he'd just come in from a morning of swimming in the surf. His muscles rippled as he gave his hair one last shake dry. Carrie remembered the feel of those arms around her, the incredible smoothness of his skin. She wanted to touch him again, but he stayed in the doorway all the way across the room.

"There wasn't much in the kitchen," Felipe said, "but I found some frozen vegetables and a bag of rice. The rice should be done in about five minutes. The vegetables are already hot."

He was going to play it normal, pretend that nothing between them had changed. He was going to be polite and friendly and keep his distance until the heat between them got too intense, until they ended up making love again. He wasn't going to hold her in his arms just for the sake of holding her, for the sake of closeness and comfort and warmth. And, oh, how she needed that right now.

To Carrie's horror, she felt her eyes fill with tears. Why? Why was she crying now? She never cried—well, hardly ever. And she was *damned* if she was going to cry in front of Felipe again. Fiercely blinking, she quickly turned away from him, pretending to study the view of the ocean. The blues of the water and the sky blurred together and she blinked even harder, forcing back her tears.

"Are you all right?" There was concern in his warm voice, and she heard him start to limp toward her. Heaven help her if he got too close. She'd end up crying in his arms, and that was the *last* thing she wanted. She wanted him to hold her, but not out of pity.

She took a deep breath and turned to face him, forcing her mouth into a smile. He wasn't fooled—she could see that from his eyes, but he stopped on the other side of the couch that bisected the room.

"The thought of rice and vegetables always gets me choked up," she said breezily.

He smiled at her words, but the concern didn't leave his eyes. No doubt he'd figured out that she'd fallen in love with him. No doubt it was a common occurrence. Every woman he'd ever slept with probably fell in love with him. And no doubt the concern in his eyes came from his imagining all the grief she was going to give him—the jealous phone calls, the tears, the desperate visits to him at work….

Except that he was a suspected murderer on the run. And *she* wasn't like all the other women he'd ever known. She had backbone. She had grit. She had pride.

"What happens now?" she asked, holding her chin high, letting him see that her eyes were dry as she walked past him into the kitchen. It was a big room, with cabinets and tiled counters lining the walls, a center island with a sink in the middle of the room, and a huge, round, butcher-block-style table off to the side in a breakfast nook. Windows and skylights were everywhere, letting in the sunshine, but the trees and shrubs outside provided a screen for privacy. No one could see inside.

"We'll have lunch." He followed her.

"That's not what I meant." There were two pots on the pristine white stove and the fragrant smell of basmati rice filled the air.

"We'll stay here another night," he said, crossing to the stove and turning off the burners.

Another night here at the beach house, alone in the candlelight. Heat rushed through Carrie at the thought of Felipe with her in that king-size bed…but tonight was too far away. She didn't want to wait until tonight. Man, she was shameless.

But here and now was all she had. He'd told her that himself.

"And then what?" she asked. Her voice sounded husky, so she cleared her throat again.

"Then I try to contact Diego," Felipe said. He leaned forward, bracing his arms against the back of one of the chairs that surrounded the big wooden table, taking the weight off his injured leg. The muscles in his arms and shoulders tightened and stood out. "Hopefully, he'll be able to tell me something new, something that will tip me off as to who in the police department set this frame up."

"And if he can't?"

"If he can't, we find someplace else to hide while I figure out a way to get past the security system in Richter's mansion and—"

Shocked, Carrie's mouth dropped open. "That's incredibly dangerous." As she stared across the room at him, she remembered Rafe's words. *Felipe, he's an addict, too. He's addicted to danger.* "It's *crazy.*"

"This whole thing is crazy," he countered.

"You're planning to go—no, *break into*—the house of a man who wants you dead?" She started to pace. If

Felipe went into Richter's house, did he really stand a chance of coming out alive?

"I'll go there if necessary," he said, his eyes following her as she moved back and forth across the cool tile floor. "But I'll have to do it soon. If I wait too long, Richter and Walsh will be expecting me to show up. Right now, they know I've been shot because of all the blood in that car. They'll expect me to lie low, to recuperate." He smiled tightly. "They're probably hoping I'll die from infection."

Carrie stopped pacing. "How *is* your leg?"

"Better."

"Honestly?"

"Well, it's not getting any worse."

"Are you really going to be ready to leave here tomorrow?" Carrie asked.

"I have to be," Felipe said. "We can't stay here much longer. It's only a matter of time before someone finds the van and the police connect it to us."

"I could go out and drive it farther away from this house," Carrie suggested.

"Without me? Bad idea, remember?" he said, softening his words with a gentle smile.

Bad idea. It wasn't as bad an idea as falling in love with him. Falling in love with Felipe Salazar was about the worst idea she'd had in all of her twenty-five years.

Carrie crossed her arms and looked down at the floor. "It seems all my ideas are bad ones these days," she said.

He was silent for a very, *very* long time. In fact, he didn't speak until she glanced up at him. His expressive eyes held real sadness and disappointment.

"Caroline," he said, "are you having regrets? About making love to me?"

She couldn't hold his gaze. "I don't know what I'm feeling," she admitted.

"I never meant to take advantage of you—or of our situation," he said quietly. "Although I guess I must have—"

"Oh, cut the macho attitude," Carrie said, exasperated. "How do you know I didn't take advantage of *you?* How do you know I didn't intend to seduce you?"

"Are you saying you worked out a plan to seduce me while we were down in that crawl space?" he said. "Nice try, but…" He shook his head. "I don't buy it."

He was smiling, and despite the heaviness in her heart, that smile was contagious. Carrie found herself smiling back.

"With your wounded leg, you couldn't exactly run away from me," she observed, putting her hairbrush down on a wicker telephone stand.

"I *did* run," he said with a broader smile that exposed his straight white teeth. "Last night. And it was *after* you, if I remember correctly."

His smile faded as he gazed at her. Carrie looked down at the floor, suddenly embarrassed by his scrutiny. She could feel his eyes studying her, watching, trying to read her mind. "I didn't want you to have any regrets," he said softly. "I'm sorry."

Her lips were dry. She moistened them with her tongue, feeling his eyes follow the slight movement. "I don't regret making love to you," she whispered. "How can I regret something that I'm dying to do again?"

She turned to look at him and found he'd silently closed the gap between them. He was standing only inches away, yet not touching her.

"Maybe you were right," he mused, gazing into her

eyes. "Maybe you did seduce me this morning. Because I think you are about to seduce me again, no?"

"What about lunch?" she breathed, lost in the whirl of heat in his eyes as he moved even closer but still didn't touch her.

"Lunch can wait," he said, watching her mouth.

He was waiting for her, Carrie realized. He was waiting for her to make the first move, to touch him, to kiss him. To seduce him.

But he didn't love her. He liked her, and he lusted after her, but he didn't love her. He said he wasn't going to let himself fall in love with her, either. Not now, not ever. That hurt. To think that he could control his emotions as easily as he controlled his body and—

But he'd lost control. When they made love this morning, Felipe had *lost control*. Who was to say the same wouldn't happen to the tight rein he held on his emotions?

Carrie wanted him to love her. It was crazy. For all she knew, he was going to spend the rest of his life in a maximum security penitentiary or—God help her—on death row for the crime of first-degree murder. For all she knew, he *had* pulled the trigger two times, sending bullets into the heads of those mobsters. Oh, she didn't *think* he was guilty. Naturally, she didn't want to believe him capable of such a thing. But she didn't truly *know*. There were no hard facts or any proof to placate the scientist that she was. And her faith in Felipe wouldn't help him in a court of law.

Yeah, she was probably certifiable for wanting this man to fall in love with her. But she wanted it. And she was *damned* if she was going to sit back and just give up, just settle for his here and now.

At the very least, she was going to give him something

to remember her by—and quite vividly—for the rest of his life.

The rays of light streaming in through the windows gave Felipe a golden glow. He looked otherworldly with his long, dark hair curling around his broad shoulders, his muscular chest gleaming and smooth. Carrie wondered if that same light accentuated her pale hair and lightly tanned skin. She wondered if she looked even half as exotic, half as sexy as he did. She sure *felt* sexy as he watched her, desire churning in his eyes.

But if she *was* going to seduce him, if she *was* going to try to loosen the hold he had on his emotions, she had to move fast before she chickened out.

With one swift movement, she pulled her shirt over her head.

His quick smile and quiet laugh told her he hadn't been expecting her to do that. That was good. She wanted to keep him off-balance.

He gazed at her silently but his eyes spoke volumes as they caressed her breasts and the curve of her smooth, tanned shoulders. She truly felt beautiful when he looked at her that way. Beautiful and sexy and powerful and capable of damn near anything. There wasn't a chance in hell she'd chicken out now. She'd set the wheels in motion, and now she'd see it through.

But he didn't reach for her. Instead, he jammed his hands hard into the front pockets of his shorts as if not touching her was a difficult task. She knew, suddenly, what he was doing. She knew why he wasn't touching her.

No regrets.

This time, he was making damn sure that it was clear *she* initiated their lovemaking. Of course, she could still regret it afterward, but this way, his own sense of guilt would be much lighter.

She could smell his clean, fresh, masculine scent. His nostrils flared, and she knew he could smell her, too. He could surely smell the faint, herbal scent of the shampoo she'd used to wash her hair, the tangy sweetness of the sun lotion she'd found in the bathroom and used in place of a moisturizer, and the fresh mint toothpaste she'd used to clean her teeth.

Felipe's eyes followed her fingers to the button of her shorts. She undid it slowly. *Very* slowly. Then she pulled the zipper down slowly. *Very* slowly. The look on his face was incredible. Every muscle in his body was tight with tension as he waited. Carrie knew he was keeping himself from reaching out and speeding the process along.

Watching him, she pushed the shorts off her hips and they fell to the floor with a soft rustle. He inhaled sharply, a reaction to her lack of underwear. She stepped out of the shorts totally naked. Except, of course, for the slight blush that heated her cheeks. Damn her fair skin anyway.

Still, she held her chin high, steadily meeting his gaze. The heat in his eyes was fast approaching a nuclear meltdown. Still, he kept his hands in his pockets. Still, he didn't move.

"We could have lunch first," she whispered, unable to hide her smile. "Are you sure you're not hungry?"

He wet his lips. "Not for rice," he countered. His gaze dropped to the golden brown curls between her legs, then back to her face.

His message couldn't have been more clear.

The sudden rush of heat that shot through her caught her off guard. She swayed toward him, and at that same moment, she saw his control snap.

He reached for her, *lunged* for her, taking her into his arms and carrying her over to that huge, wooden table.

His hands and his mouth were everywhere, touching, kissing, suckling, licking. The sensation of his tongue in her belly button made her cry out, her voice echoing through the quiet of the house. She tried to sit up, but he held her firmly in place, using his tongue to try to drive her as deliriously insane as she'd driven him.

She writhed in pleasure, and her arm knocked a sugar bowl onto the kitchen floor with a crash. But she didn't care. She didn't care about anything except that she was making love to this man whom she adored.

She tried to reach for the button that fastened his shorts. He obliged by moving closer. Her hand fumbled with the button, and he reached down, wrapping her fingers tightly around him.

He undid the button himself, and the zipper, and then his shorts were sliding off. From somewhere, maybe out of thin air—and she wouldn't have been surprised if he were capable of such magic—maybe from the depths of his wallet, he procured a condom.

And then he was on top of her, inside her, filling her completely with each urgent thrust. He groaned as he kissed her, and she moved with him, in a rhythm of love as old as time.

You're going to love me, Carrie told him with her eyes, her hands, her body. I'm going to make you love me.

But she couldn't talk, couldn't form words let alone sentences. She could only grip his shoulders more tightly and moan her pleasure.

Felipe pulled back to look at her. His eyes were wild and tinged with shock. He spoke to her. His words were in Spanish, but his meaning was clear. Now. *Now.*

Now, like this morning, he was unable to hold back. Now, like this morning, *she* had driven him to a place of wild abandonment, a place where he had absolutely no control.

That knowledge sent her soaring, rockets of pleasure bursting through her as her body tightened and clenched in a culmination too intense to be real. But it *was* real. Waves of hot and cold rushed through her, colors exploded in her head as she wrapped her legs around Felipe and tried to draw him closer, even closer to her.

She heard him cry out her name, and then something else in Spanish as he exploded, thrusting harder and deeper inside her.

And then it was over. Carrie closed her eyes as Felipe let his head fall forward next to hers. He rolled off her so as not to squash her, but then quickly gathered her into his arms in a tender embrace. Oh, how she loved him.

Together they lay there on the kitchen table.

Carrie started to laugh.

They were *lying* on the kitchen table. They'd just made *love* on the kitchen *table*. Heaven help them if they were ever invited back to this beach house for dinner. Carrie would never make it through the meal without breaking into hysterical laughter.

"You must be thinking what I'm thinking," Felipe said, kissing the top of her head.

"Dinner here," Carrie said. "With the Marshalls."

"That's what I'm thinking," he said with a laugh.

"I wonder if they'll know," Carrie mused. "Just from…I don't know, the aura, the cosmic waves of sex that will ripple forth from this table from now on."

"Hmm," Felipe said, cupping her breast with his hand.

"Or maybe," Carrie said, "the Marshalls do exactly what we just did on this table all the time."

Felipe laughed, tipping her face up so he could kiss her on the mouth. "Maybe not," he said.

Carrie gazed up into his eyes. "That was *great* sex," she said. "Are we in agreement?"

He didn't answer—not right away. Finally, he nodded. "Yes," he said. "We're in agreement."

CHAPTER THIRTEEN

GREAT SEX.

Caroline's words echoed in Felipe's head.

Great sex. Was that all it really was to her?

She was curled up on the other end of the long couch, her head resting on a throw pillow, her eyes tightly closed. She looked like an angel as she slept, with her lips slightly parted, her long eyelashes fanned out against her smooth cheeks, her hair a tangle of unearthly gold around her face. She was enveloped in what was probably Jim Keegan's old white terry-cloth robe. If she stood up with it on, it would trail behind her like the train of a wedding gown.

A wedding gown. Now that would be a vision to behold: Caroline, resplendent in a white gown, her long, blond hair elegantly arranged up off her shoulders, a whisper-thin veil covering but not hiding her beautiful smile.

The groom would be a lucky man, his destiny a life of laughter and love, sweet kisses and sleepy blue-green eyes smiling up at him after wonderful, endless, sinfully delicious nights of loving.

Felipe's destiny, on the other hand, promised a procession of cold and lonely nights, stakeouts and time spent under cover with another identity, another name and no real future. Of course, he'd still have Caroline's blue-green eyes smiling at him—they'd haunt his dreams for the rest of his days.

Suddenly chilled and feeling desperately alone, Felipe stretched his leg down the couch toward Carrie, wanting their connection to remain unbroken for as long as it possibly could.

He slipped his foot under her robe, touching the warmth of her leg with his toes. She smiled and opened her turquoise eyes, and a hand appeared from beneath the mound of white terry cloth. She rested it gently on his leg, stroking him slightly as she closed her eyes again.

Great sex.

It had been incredibly great sex. In fact, that was the way Felipe had always preferred to think of it in the privacy of his own mind. He spoke to his lovers of "making love," but love never really entered into it—at least not more than the rather general love he had for all beautiful women. Sure, he'd imagined himself in love a time or two back when he was a teenager. But either it hadn't lasted or he'd been spurned and his broken heart had quickly healed. So quickly, in fact, that he'd soon come to doubt the truth of what he'd felt.

But this thing he'd been feeling lately, this lump of emotion that was lodged in his chest was unlike anything he'd ever felt before.

Maybe it wasn't love, he told himself. Maybe he was mistaken.

Caroline sighed and opened her eyes again. "What time is it?" she murmured.

He didn't need to glance at the clock on the wall. He could tell by the angle of the sun on the horizon. "Nearly six."

She yawned and stretched, her legs entwining with his on the couch, her arms reaching for the high, beamed ceiling.

Caroline folded her hands behind her head, elbows in the air, and looked down the couch at him. With one foot, she played with the edge of his shorts. "What does 'tay-yamo' mean?"

Her question made him freeze. Even his heart seemed to stop beating for a few solid seconds.

"What did you say?" he said.

"Tay-yamo," she said again.

Te amo.

I love you.

He kept his shock carefully hidden from her curious gaze.

"You said it more than once," Caroline said. She lowered her arms and began fiddling with the belt of the robe, aware of his sudden complete silence and clearly uncertain how to interpret it. "You remember, back when we *weren't* having lunch. Remember, the kitchen table...?"

Her smile was half shy, half wicked and utterly charming.

"I remember the kitchen table." He would always remember the kitchen table. In fact, he would probably be thinking of it, ninety-five years old and on his deathbed. That is, if he lived that long.

"I was just wondering if..." She looked at him from underneath her long lashes. She wasn't being coy or trying to act cute. Her nervous shyness was as real as the sweet blush that often tinged her cheeks. It totally contradicted the woman who had brazenly and openly tempted him in the kitchen this noon, but that wasn't a shock. She was a nest of contradictions and surprises. He expected it by now.

She took a deep breath. "I was wondering if Tay-yamo was someone's name. Like an old girlfriend. Or maybe a not-so-old girlfriend...?"

Felipe shook his head. "It's not a name," he said.

"Then what does it mean?" she asked. She said it again, practicing the unfamiliar Spanish words. "Tay-yamo. Am I saying it right?"

Te amo.

I love you.

Felipe could only nod. Had he really told her that he loved her?

"What does it mean?" she asked again.

He cleared his throat. "It's...rather difficult to translate."

He'd told her he loved her as they made love. He closed his eyes, and he could hear the echo of his voice calling out those words. *Te amo.* Yes, he'd really said it.

Worse than the shock of realizing he'd slipped, of realizing it was only chance that he'd said those words in a language Caroline didn't understand, worse than that was the sudden glaring knowledge that those words he'd cried were true.

He loved her.

She tucked her legs back underneath her robe, moving away from his foot. The sudden loss of her warmth, of the sensation of the closeness was too much for Felipe. He reached forward and pulled her so that she was sitting toboggan-style between his legs, her back against his chest. He wrapped his arms around her, holding her tightly.

He couldn't deny it anymore. He loved her.

He was doomed.

"Tay-yamo," she said again, and his heart clenched. She didn't know what she was saying, and she probably wouldn't say it if she *did* know what it meant. "You really can't translate it, huh?"

He shook his head. No.

How ironic that the tables had turned on him so absolutely. Here he'd gone and fallen in love, and *she'd* had "great sex."

"Tay-yamo. You were…exuberant when you first shouted it," she mused, that same wicked light in her eyes. "Is it kind of like, I don't know…yabba dabba do?"

Felipe laughed, holding her closer, loving her, wishing with all his heart that she loved him, too. But if she did, man, what a mess that would be. A double heartbreak instead of a single one. Because he was going to leave her when this was over. He *had* to leave her. He wouldn't risk putting her in danger. It would be easier for her, much easier, if she simply didn't fall in love with him, if she simply continued to consider their relationship a source of friendship and "great sex."

"Yes," he told her, pulling up her chin and kissing her soft lips. "It's *exactly* like yabba dabba do."

FELIPE WOKE UP at nine-thirty with Caroline in his arms.

Morning sunlight was streaming in around the edges of the shades and curtains in the master bedroom, and had been for quite some time.

He'd never slept so late before.

But it didn't surprise him. These past few days had been full of firsts.

Take, for example, the fact that he was lying here with the woman that he loved in his arms. Loved. That was a very big first.

Caroline was still fast asleep. He smiled despite the tension in his stomach and shoulders that his thoughts had created. She slept fiercely, her eyes tightly closed and her fists clenched, as if she was fighting to stay asleep.

He'd kept her up late last night. But then she'd woken him up at dawn…. She was as insatiable as he.

They'd stumbled around in the gray half-light, searching the master bedroom for condoms. They'd used up the one he'd carried in his wallet, *and* the others his brother had slipped him before they'd left the halfway house.

Felipe had been prepared to improvise, or heaven help him, even risk it—now *there* was another first—when Carrie had dug up a nearly full box. They were Jim's, and they'd been buried—hidden—way, way back underneath the sink.

Felipe was going to take every single one with him when they left. Jim wouldn't need them for a while—his wife, Emily, was five months pregnant.

He looked down at Caroline again, studying the pattern of freckles that splashed across her nose and cheeks, imagining her pregnant with his child. The want that rose in him was so intense he had to close his eyes and breathe deeply until it faded.

The baby would look like him, dark hair, dark eyes. He would be big—all of the Salazar babies were big—maybe even too big for Caroline to deliver safely. She was so tiny that the thought of her heavy with child and in possible physical danger because of it, because of *him,* was nearly overwhelming. If he got her pregnant, he'd spend nine months terrified that she would somehow be hurt…or worse.

Another reason not to tell her that he loved her.

Another reason to walk away and never let her know the way she made his heart sing.

But—and it was time for yet another first—Felipe was starting to wonder if, when the time came, he'd actually have the strength to leave her.

Jim Keegan was married. Of course, he spent most of the time worried to hell about Emily. And Jim took precautions, too. He had a state-of-the-art security system and a dog the size of a small horse trained never to leave their yard. When he worked late at night, patrol cars would drive past his house, occasionally checking in with his wife. Felipe had stopped by himself, many times, as a favor to his old friend.

All that worry, all those precautions, and Jim only worked straightforward homicide. He rarely went under cover. His job was known to be far less dangerous than Felipe's.

Infiltrating street gangs and organized crime, which was what Felipe was so very, very good at, included a certain risk of retaliation or revenge. If he stayed with Caroline, if he let himself live the kind of life he longed for with her, he'd never be free from worry. His concentration would be off, and he'd probably get himself killed. Or *her* killed. And God help him, if anything happened to her, he'd never forgive himself.

No. When the time came, Felipe would find the strength to leave Caroline. Somehow, he'd manage to do it.

His leg started to ache, and he closed his eyes. Caroline snuggled against him, and he held her tighter, breathing in the sweet, familiar scent of paradise.

It wasn't going to be easy. God, even if *she* was the one who turned and walked away, it wouldn't be easy. Easier, but not easy.

Nothing would ever be easy again.

THE BLOODSTAINS hadn't quite washed out of Carrie's dress, but the blue-flowered pattern managed to hide them, at least at a distant inspection. Now that the dress was clean and dry, she'd put it back on. Despite the stains, it fit far better than anything else she'd found in this house of tall people.

She stripped the sheets from the beds they'd used and put them and their dirty towels in a laundry basket. She left a note on top, apologizing for not taking the time to wash the linens.

Felipe was in the kitchen, washing up the pots and dishes. He'd been oddly quiet all morning, a strange shadow darkening his eyes. Whether it was the thought of leaving the sanctuary of the beach house or something else, Carrie didn't know. But he was tense—more so than usual—and seemed lost in his thoughts.

Making love in a bed had seemed almost anticlimactic after the kitchen table. Still, it had been…lovely. He'd made love to her slowly, so exquisitely slowly. She could have sworn she'd seen love in his eyes, but she was probably mistaken. It was more likely only a reflection of the candlelight.

She sighed. Felipe glanced up at her and she forced her mouth into a smile.

"Ready to go?" he asked, wiping his hands on a dish towel, then hanging it on a hook near the sink. He walked toward her.

"No," she said.

He pushed her hair back from her face so very gently. "Neither am I," he said. "But we have to."

He was wearing the jeans, T-shirt and jacket he'd borrowed from his brother Rafe. He'd pulled his hair into a ponytail and his face looked sterner and harder without the softening effect of his long, dark curls. But his eyes were soft and his lips were even softer as he leaned forward to kiss her.

"Where are we going?" Carrie asked.

The shadow came back, flitting quickly across his gaze, and he looked away, toward the door that would lead them out of the house. "To a friend's," he said vaguely. "I have to get my hair cut. I need to look as different as I possibly can."

Carrie reached up and touched his ponytail. "Cut short?" she asked, unable to hide her disappointment.

He smiled, amusement in his dark eyes. "What? You like it long like this?"

"Yes," she said, freeing his hair from the ponytail and running her fingers through it. "It's…sexy."

"Hmmm," he said, closing his eyes, letting her know he enjoyed her touch. "I'm sorry. I won't get it cut too short." He looked at her and smiled. "The police have two kinds of pictures of me—some are with my hair long, like this. The others are with it cut short. You know, I always wore my hair really short until about two years ago." He looked down at his clothes and made a face. "And this is not my normal wardrobe. I always wore designer suits and ties."

Carrie laughed. She just couldn't picture it. Although he had worn that tuxedo with a certain ease and familiarity…. "I'll believe that when you show me the pictures."

He stepped slightly away from her, putting the rubber band back in his hair. "Time to go."

Carrie watched him open the kitchen door. She didn't want to walk through it, afraid of whatever might be waiting for them in the harsh world outside. She stalled. "What if the van's not there? What if it's been towed?"

"We're not taking the van."

"We're not?"

Clasping her hand, he led her out the door onto the back porch. He locked the door and slipped the key back under the flowerpot. "We're taking Diego's bike."

His...*bike?*

Carrie followed Felipe down the stairs and around the house to a detached garage. He pulled up the garage door, and there it was. A big, shiny, chrome-and-black Harley-Davidson motorcycle. Diego's bike. Of course.

"Do you really know how to ride that thing?" Carrie asked.

Felipe wheeled it out into the sunlight, then closed the garage door.

He glanced at her and smiled. "Yes."

"I've never ridden one before," she said.

"Think of it as riding a horse with a powerful engine and a narrower saddle," he said. "You did ride horses in Montana, right?"

"Of course."

He smiled at the faintly insulted tone in her voice. "You know how when you let your horse run, really run, you feel it inside? You move together, you even think together—"

She interrupted him. "You ride?"

"My uncle Manny works at the racetrack," he said. "I still sometimes go over there and pick up a few extra dollars exercising the horses that are boarded in their stables."

"I don't really know that much about you, do I?" she said.

The shadow came flitting back into his eyes. He shook his head. "No, you don't."

"I mean, I had no idea… Are you a good rider?"

"*I* think so. But I'm better at riding one of these," he said, turning away from her and slapping the seat of the motorcycle.

He swung one long leg over the bike, straddled the monster and slipped a key into the ignition.

"Climb on behind me," he said, handing her one of the helmets that had been hanging on the bike's handlebars. "Put your arms around my waist and hold on tight. Lean when I lean, move with me, okay? And careful where you put your legs and feet. The engine gets pretty hot."

She nodded, about to put the helmet on, when he suddenly pulled her tightly to him and kissed her on the mouth. It was a passionate kiss, filled with deep yearning and need, yet it was still sweetly, achingly tender.

Carrie's knees felt weak and her bones turned to jelly. When he released her, she nearly fell over. He put the helmet on her head, strapping it securely under her chin.

He started the motorcycle with a roar, wincing as he jarred his injured leg. The motor turned and caught. "Climb on," he shouted, strapping on his own helmet.

She wasn't too happy about getting on the motorcycle, but after a kiss like that, she'd probably follow him damn near anywhere.

Carrie took a deep breath, then swung her leg over the seat. The dress she was wearing wasn't exactly made for riding astride. She tried to secure it underneath her, then locked her arms around Felipe's waist.

As he drove slowly down the driveway, she looked back over her shoulder at the beach house, wishing they could have stayed there forever.

CHAPTER FOURTEEN

ST. SIMONE hadn't changed one bit during the two days they'd been away. The sun still shone endlessly down from a perfect blue sky, warming the cracked sidewalks and the tiny one- and two-bedroom houses that lined the street. This was the part of town that the tourists never came to visit.

It wasn't dangerous like the neighborhood Rafe's halfway house had been in. It was just quietly depressing. These were beach shacks, and on the water they might even have been charming or picturesque. But here, the ocean was more than a mile away. Here, they were just bleak, cheaply constructed boxes that were crumbling around their financially strapped owners.

Felipe pulled the motorcycle up to the curb and braced his feet on either side as they came to a stop. He cut the engine and the sudden silence was a blessing.

Carrie lifted the visor of her helmet and looked around. Whoever this friend was that Felipe was planning to visit, he didn't have much money. It wasn't Jim Keegan, that was for sure. Carrie couldn't picture the daughter of the people who owned that house on Sanibel Island living on this particular street.

Felipe took off his helmet and turned slightly to face

her. "We should go inside quickly," he said. "The fewer people who see us, the better."

She climbed stiffly off the motorcycle, and he led the way toward a tiny yellow house. A rusty wire fence surrounded the postage-stamp–size yard, and the gate squeaked as he pushed it open. But the yard was clean, the garden filled with beautiful flowers and the house was well kept, with a fresh coat of paint.

Felipe limped up the steps to a small landing and knocked on the screen door.

The inner door swung open and a small, freckled face looked out through the screen.

"Daddy!" a young voice cried, pushing the screen door wide. A little boy launched himself into Felipe's arms.

Daddy?

Carrie stared at Felipe in shock as the door banged shut. He met her eyes for only the briefest of moments over the top of a bright red head. His expression was unreadable.

"Oh my God," another voice said from the darkness behind the screen. "Get inside here, *fast!*"

Felipe's friend wasn't a he. His friend was a *she*.

She was tall, almost as tall as Felipe, with elegant, almost classical features, green eyes and long, wavy red hair. She was obviously the little boy's mother—the same little boy who'd called Felipe Daddy.

Good Lord, was this woman Felipe's *wife?* Carrie stared in shock, realizing that she'd never actually asked Felipe if he was married.

The green-eyed woman pushed open the screen door and pulled Felipe and the boy into the house, leaving Carrie out in the cold—only figuratively, of course, since the sun was beating warmly down on her head.

Still holding the child, Felipe pushed the screen back open. He took Carrie's arm and dragged her inside, shutting both doors tightly behind her.

Green-eyes looked at her with a mixture of curiosity and hostility. Carrie couldn't blame her. *She'd* be hostile, too, if *her* husband brought his lover home.

"What are you doing here?" Green-eyes asked Felipe. Her voice had the warm sugar-and-spice accent of the Deep South. "Everyone's looking for you. Jim Keegan was by just a few hours ago."

Felipe closed his eyes. "Damn. If only I'd known…"

The young woman was strikingly pretty, with long, pale, slender arms and legs. She was wearing a denim skirt and an off-white tank top with a gently scooped neckline. Her outfit wasn't necessarily feminine, but on her, it looked as delicate as lace. She looked like a dancer, tall and graceful. Next to her, Carrie felt like one of the seven dwarfs.

"I'm sorry," Felipe said. "I know this is awkward. But I didn't know where else to go."

"Phil, so help me God, if you screw up my life—"

"Billy, excuse your mother and me for a moment, please," Felipe said. The little boy slid down out of his arms. He gazed curiously at Carrie as he walked past her and sat down on the living room couch.

Felipe stepped closer to Green-eyes, touching her shoulder, speaking to her in a low, soft voice. Carrie couldn't make out the words, but his tone was soothing, almost seductive.

It was misery, watching him talk to her like that. Carrie stared at the worn floorboards of the living room floor, but she couldn't block the sound of his voice.

I don't really know that much about you, do I?

No, you don't.

Damn straight she didn't. She felt like a fool. She glanced up to find the little redhead watching her. She imagined she could see scorn and disgust in the youngster's eyes.

Carrie heard the answering murmur of Green-eyes's Southern accent, and her attention was drawn back to the other side of the room, where she and Felipe were having their own version of summit peace talks.

Was he touching her face? Had he kept that comforting hand on her shoulder, sliding it down her arm in a gentle, sensuous caress? Was she, right this very moment, lifting her face to his for a kiss?

Carrie couldn't keep from looking over at Felipe. She couldn't stop herself. But as soon as she did, she wished desperately that she hadn't. Because Felipe *was* touching the redheaded woman. He was pushing Green-eyes's wavy hair back from her face. Carrie's heart shriveled inside her as she remembered that he'd touched her that same way mere hours before.

How *could* he have? How could he make love to her the way he had, with his wife and child here in this little house, waiting for him to come home?

Felipe glanced up to find Carrie staring, and she quickly looked away, knowing all her hurt and jealousy were showing in her eyes.

"All right," Green-eyes said, walking across the living room and sitting on the couch next to Little Redhead. "So introduce me to your friend, why don't you?"

"Caroline," Felipe said, moving toward the couch, "meet Jewel and Billy." He didn't sit down but rather stood beside them. It was a charming family portrait. Carrie's head was spinning.

She searched the boy's face for any sign of Felipe's features, any similarities the child might have to his father.

She couldn't see a single one. The red hair, green eyes and freckles came directly from his mother. The nose was entirely the child's own, as was his chin and mouth.

"Daddy, I saw you on the news," Billy said. His small face suddenly looked pinched and nervous. "They say you're a bad man."

"Billy, hush," Green-eyes—Jewel—whispered. Her name suited her.

"No, that's okay," Felipe said. He knelt next to the boy. "You must be pretty upset, huh?"

Billy nodded.

"It's not true," Felipe said. "All that stuff they're saying on TV and in the papers. Someone made a mistake, and I'm being blamed for something that I didn't do."

"You didn't kill those guys?" the boy asked.

"No," Felipe said, "I didn't. And you know I'd never lie to you."

"I know," Billy said. He pressed his lips tightly together and stared down at his hands.

"I'm going to get it all worked out," Felipe said. "Don't worry, okay?"

"Okay." But it was said grudgingly.

"Feel any better?"

Billy shook his head.

Carrie's heart was in her throat. Felipe was gentle with the child, full of soft words and reassurances. It wasn't hard to imagine him talking to her in that same soothing tone. But there wasn't much he could say to make *her* feel any better, either.

"I'm sorry," Felipe murmured, pulling the little boy into his arms. "I wish I could wave a magic wand and make it all disappear, but I can't. I need time. Can you give me some time, Billy? Another week, maybe?"

Billy nodded, on the verge of tears. He wriggled free from Felipe's arms and ran out of the room.

Felipe started after him, but Jewel stood up and stopped him with a hand on his arm. "Let him go," she said. "He doesn't like to cry in front of anyone these days. He's a big boy, nearly seven. He's got enough to worry about—at least spare him the embarrassment."

Felipe looked as if he was about to cry, too. "I'm sorry," he said to Jewel.

"Whoever you're investigating," she said, "you sure got them scared, huh?"

"Yeah," Felipe laughed humorlessly. "We've got them shaking in their shoes, don't we, Caroline?"

She said nothing. What could she say? All she wanted to do was leave. Walk out the door, away from Felipe Salazar, away from his lies and deceit—except he'd never told her that he *wasn't* married. She'd stupidly never asked.

"It said on the news that you'd been shot," Jewel said, pushing her hair back behind her ear. "Are you all right?"

"I'm sore," Felipe said shortly. "I should stay off my leg for another week, but I don't have another week. I don't have enough time."

Jewel smiled wryly. "I know the feeling well. Come on into the kitchen. You can have something to eat while I cut your hair."

Now was Carrie's chance. She'd just stand up and let herself out the same door they'd come in.

Except Felipe took her arm and pulled her with him into the tiny kitchen.

"I need a bathing suit," he said to Jewel as he gently pushed Carrie down into a chair. "And one for Caroline, too." He took out his wallet and handed her a hundred-dollar bill. "Will you run down to Swim City and buy them for me? Caroline's a size five, and I'm still a medium. Get us something funky and young-looking. Something college kids would wear."

"Can I take a spin on that bike you drove up on?" Jewel asked. She filled a spray bottle with warm water from the sink, then dragged one of the kitchen chairs into the middle of the room.

"Sure." Felipe sat down in the chair, and Jewel wrapped a towel around his neck.

"Then it's no problem. I tell you, Phil, it kills me to cut this gorgeous hair off," Jewel said, wetting down his long curls.

"I don't need a bathing suit," Carrie said, finally finding her voice. Her numbness and disbelief were slowly being replaced by anger. That was good. Anger didn't hurt quite so much.

"You need to get out of that dress," Felipe said to her as Jewel combed his wet hair, parting it neatly on the side. "The police have probably issued a description of what you were wearing by now. And besides, we're going down to the beach. If you don't have a bathing suit, you'll stand out."

"*You* might be going to the beach," Carrie said. "But I'm not. I'm out of here."

"Don't be ridiculous—"

"Ridiculous?" she said. "*Ridiculous? This* is ridiculous, Detective. Sitting here like this…"

Jewel took a long, sharp-looking pair of scissors and began cutting Felipe's hair at cheekbone length. Long, dark curls fell on the beige linoleum floor. She glanced up at Carrie. "You got a problem with my kitchen? I admit it *is* kinda ugly…."

Carrie leaned forward. "I hate to break it to you, sister, but *Phil* here has been unfaithful."

Jewel just kept cutting his hair. "Why, you bad boy, you," she said to him.

"Caroline," Felipe started to say, but she ignored him.

"Don't you care?" Carrie asked Jewel.

Jewel smiled, quickly cutting the hair around Felipe's ears even shorter. "Nope."

"Well, *I* do," Carrie said coolly. "And I'm leaving."

Her chair squeaked as she pushed it back from the table and headed out of the room.

Felipe stood up. "Caroline, wait…"

Jewel put the scissors down. "It seems like this is a good time for me to get those things you wanted from the store."

Carrie spun back to face Felipe as he scrambled after her into the living room and followed her toward the front door. "And by the way," she said, "I have regrets. *Big* regrets. I regret the day I first laid eyes on you."

FELIPE HAD DONE IT. He'd gone and made Caroline ready and willing to walk away from him. Except he hadn't expected her to be quite this angry, quite this upset, quite this willing to walk right *now*.

He had had no idea that she would be so…jealous. *Jealous?* She *was*. She was jealous of Jewel. My God, maybe she cared about him more than she'd let on.

"And," she continued, "I *definitely* regret ever being so foolish as to make love to you, you two-timing *snake!*"

Felipe had been called quite a number of things in his

life, but "two-timing snake" wasn't one of them. Out on the street, he heard the roar of Diego's bike as Jewel rode away.

He laughed—he couldn't help it. It was a combination of her words and the giddy way he felt, knowing she was *jealous*.

"Oh, you think it's funny?" she said. "Fine. I'm leaving, and this time you can't stop me."

Felipe stopped laughing. She was dead serious, and the thought of her walking away now was instantly sobering.

"No," he said. "No, it's not— Caroline, I've misled you."

"Damn straight you did, you *bastard*."

"No," he said, pushing his freshly cut hair up and out of his eyes. "I've misled you by letting you believe I have any kind of relationship besides friendship with Jewel."

"No relationship?" she said. "Right. Your *friendship* created a son?"

"He's not my son," he said, talking low and fast as he followed her the last few steps to the door. "He calls me Daddy because he doesn't have anyone else to call that, and because I love him as if he were my son."

Carrie stopped with her hand on the doorknob. She wouldn't look at him, but he knew she was listening. It was a good thing she was listening because there was no way he would let her leave.

"I met Jewel when she was seventeen," Felipe said, talking quickly, quietly. "Billy was nearly three. She'd just come out of rehab, and her uncle was trying to hook her on crack again so he could resume his role as her pimp."

"Lord," Carrie breathed, finally looking up at him. Her eyes were wide and so blue.

"I helped put her uncle in jail," he told Caroline evenly. "She and I became friends. That's all it's ever been—friendship. I've never slept with her—I've never wanted to. I love her, but I'm not in love with her. Do you understand that?"

Caroline's eyes were brimming with tears, but she kept her head turned away. She never wanted him to see her cry. She was so tough, so independent, and at the same time, so damn fragile. She nodded her head. She understood.

"You must think I'm a fool," she said. "A jealous fool."

Jealous. She *was* jealous. Why did that make him so happy? It should worry him, make him wonder if maybe she cared about him too much. "I don't think you're a fool," he said gently.

"Well, that makes one of us," she said and went back into the kitchen.

Felipe briefly closed his eyes. She wasn't going to leave.

Not yet anyway.

"YOU LOVEBIRDS get things ironed out?" Jewel asked Carrie as they sat in the kitchen.

Jewel had returned from the store and finished cutting Felipe's hair. Now Felipe had gone to find Billy, to say goodbye to the little boy.

Carrie was wearing the bathing suit that Jewel had bought at Swim City. It was a bikini of extremely minute dimensions, in a neon orange-and-black zebra-stripe print. Supposedly it made her look like a college student. Over it, she wore a filmy gauze beach cover-up and a pair of overalls dug out of the back of Jewel's closet. The long pants would make riding the motorcycle easier, and help keep her warm if they were out all night.

Carrie shrugged. "It's not love," she said.

"I don't sleep with guys I don't love," Jewel said. She took a sip from the glass of iced tea that sat on the table in front of her. "Not anymore." She looked at Carrie. "And I don't think you do, either."

Carrie was silent, tracing a design on the table with the condensation from her glass.

"How could you not be in love with that man?" Jewel asked.

Carrie looked up into the brilliant green of the younger woman's eyes. "Are you?" she asked.

Jewel laughed. "No," she said. "Well…I used to have a crush on Phil back when we first met, but that was a long time ago." She looked at Carrie from out of the corner of her eye. "However, he *is* the best-looking man on earth."

Carrie had to smile. "Amen to that. But that haircut you gave him makes him look about eighteen years old. I feel like a cradle robber."

"Just push his hair out of his face," Jewel said. "It's only when it's in his eyes that he looks young."

"You're good at cutting hair," Carrie said.

"Thanks," Jewel said almost shyly. "It started out as a temporary career. I'm actually going to school over at the state university. I'm majoring in business, with a minor in Spanish. Although, I like cutting hair so much, I just might stay with it. With the business degree, maybe someday I can own my own salon."

"You speak Spanish?" Carrie asked, leaning forward.

"Nearly like a native of Puerto Rico, or so Mrs. Salazar tells me," Jewel said. Her tone was tongue-in-cheek, but there was some pride there, too.

"Do you know what 'Tay-yamo' means?" Carrie asked. Jewel nearly dropped her glass of iced tea. She put it carefully down in front of her. "Did Phil say that to you?" she asked, bemused.

Carrie nodded. "When I asked him what it meant, he told me it was too hard to translate."

Jewel laughed. "For Phil, yeah, it'd be really hard to translate. He's got a problem with that particular verb."

"Okay, we better roll," Felipe said, coming into the kitchen. "We've already been here to long."

With his hair cut so that it fell forward past his eyes almost to the tip of his nose, he *did* look much younger. With the combination of his hairstyle and the boldly patterned knee-length bathing suit, the extralarge T-shirt and the cheap beach sandals he was wearing, he looked like he might even pass for a high school student. Provided, of course, that his shirt stayed on to cover the hard, well-developed muscles in his chest and shoulders, and his hair stayed in his face, hiding the mature leanness of his cheeks.

He touched Carrie lightly on the shoulder. His hand was warm through the fabric of her cover-up.

Carrie was still embarrassed about her jealous reaction to Jewel. He'd made it more than clear that she had no claim to his heart. He'd told her that he could only give her here and now, and he may very well have meant their time at the beach house. Come to think of it, that poignant kiss he'd given her before they left, that could very well have been a kiss goodbye.

It was probably over—at least, that part of their relationship was over—yet Carrie had acted like a jealous, spurned lover. Of course, her reaction hadn't been all jealousy. She'd been outraged at the thought that Felipe could make love to her with such little regard for his wife. She'd been shocked and appalled and angry that she had misjudged him so thoroughly. The man she thought she knew wouldn't cheat on his wife. He wouldn't have gotten married in the first place, but if he had, he'd be sure to keep his marriage vows.

Of course, Jewel *wasn't* Felipe's wife. Jewel wasn't even his lover, present *or* past.

So now what?

Carrie had let him see her jealousy and hurt, and now he probably knew that she'd been stupid enough to fall in love with him. He'd probably treat her with the same kindness and gentle compassion he'd shown little Billy.

Terrific.

"We were discussing the translation of interesting Spanish phrases," Jewel said to Felipe. "*Te amo,* for instance."

His hand dropped from Carrie's shoulder. She glanced up to find his gaze fixed on Jewel, his expression suddenly shuttered.

Jewel laughed. "I've always felt that '*te amo*' is one of those things that needs to be explained by the person who says it. The meaning is defined by the situation in which it's spoken." She leaned toward Carrie. "I can't tell you what Felipe meant when he said it. Only he can tell you that."

CHAPTER FIFTEEN

"WHY EXACTLY are we going to the beach?" Carrie asked as she slipped the motorcycle helmet on her head. Felipe helped her on with a big, unwieldy backpack that held the rest of their clothes and a few beach towels.

"We're going to meet Diego," Felipe said, putting on his own helmet. "He and I used to eat an early dinner at the same sandwich stand on the beach every Wednesday night back when we were partners. I'm hoping that since it's Wednesday he'll show up. I need to talk to him."

"And you're sure that this Diego's not really some gorgeous woman?" Carrie said dryly. "Because if he is, I want to be prepared to go into another jealous snit. I *know* how much you must *love* that."

Felipe grabbed her around the waist and pulled her tightly to him. "I *do* love it when you're jealous," he murmured. If they hadn't been wearing the helmets, he would have kissed her. Instead, he just smiled into her eyes and ran his hands down her back, pulling her hips in closer to him. "But no, Diego's not a woman. You saw him on TV, on that news report, remember?"

Carrie nodded. She remembered. "I'm really sorry about before," she said softly. "Seriously, Felipe, I won't behave like that again. I know I don't own you. I know I never will. If I forget, just…remind me."

She'd been so quick to believe the worst of him. Of course, little Billy had called him Daddy, and she'd simply followed that to its obvious conclusion.

The truth was, she was ready to doubt Felipe Salazar. Was he a killer? She didn't think so. But if the least little bit of evidence showed up that worked against him, she'd probably start to doubt his innocence again.

And yet she loved him. It was a strange and powerful emotion, to be able to overlook the fact that this man *was* wanted by the police for murder.

Felipe started the motorcycle, and Carrie climbed on behind him, wrapping her arms around his waist. He drove slowly toward the beach, careful never to exceed the leisurely speed limit of the side streets.

They approached a patrol car, and Carrie tensed. But Felipe didn't slow, didn't even seem to notice. He was utterly cool, and they passed with no problem. The police officer didn't even glance in their direction.

And then they were at the beach. Felipe parked the motorcycle and they walked toward the food stand.

It was odd, being out in the open. They were in plain sight of anyone who happened to drive by. Except they were surrounded by dozens and dozens of people who looked just like them. Shaggy-haired young men in bright, funky bathing suits and dark glasses. Young women of all shapes and sizes, with all styles and colors of swimsuits, with all lengths and shades of hair. They milled around the sandwich stand. They sat on their towels on the nearby sand, or perched on top of the picnic tables that were scattered across that part of the beach.

It was the perfect place to hide. They were daringly hidden in plain view. No one would think to look for them here.

Except, hopefully, for Jim "Diego" Keegan.

Felipe found an empty picnic table in the shade, near a pay phone. Taking Carrie's hand, he pulled her toward it. He sat on top, not on the bench, and assumed the same relaxed slouch as the other kids. Carrie sat next to him.

"You look tense," he murmured. "Loosen up. And take off your overalls and shirt. You're the only one out here still dressed."

She stood up and slipped out of her pants. She rolled them up and set them next to her on the table. The gauze shirt she unbuttoned, but left on.

"Relax," Felipe said into her ear. "No one's going to look for us here."

She tried to loosen her shoulders, but it didn't seem to help. Felipe looped an arm around her neck, pulling her close. And then he kissed her.

It wasn't a little, polite, out-in-public kind of kiss. It was a huge, devouring, explore-the-tonsils, bone-melting kiss.

He released her, melted bones and all, keeping that possessive arm around her neck. She sagged against him, glad he was holding her up.

No one was watching. No one in this crowd of students had even noticed Felipe kissing her as if the world were coming to an end.

"Much better," he said with a flash of his straight white teeth. "Now you have that same hormone-glazed expression in your eyes that the other kids have."

"I do *not*," she said, insult tingeing her voice, knowing he was right. She pinched him in the side.

He squirmed away, laughing, but still watching the parking lot. "Do, too. You know, you look about sixteen in that bathing suit. It's real heart-attack material."

"Well, *you* look barely old enough to vote, so that makes us even," she said.

He took her hand, lacing his fingers with hers. "I wish I'd known you when you were sixteen," he said, stopping his keen perusal of the parking lot to look searchingly into her eyes. "You were probably one of those really smart, sexy girls. I bet you had every guy in high school following you around."

Carrie laughed. "I was a total nerd. No one followed me anywhere."

"I would have," Felipe said.

She glanced at him. "You would've scared me to death." She laughed. "You *still* scare me to death."

He looked out across the parking lot, squinting into the sunlight as he searched for Jim Keegan's car. "Really?"

Yes, really. Carrie was scared that the part of her heart that Felipe had invaded would never be the same after he left. She was scared that she'd never meet a man who could stand up to her memories of this one. She was scared that she'd love him forever, long after he was gone, long after he'd forgotten her.

And most of all, she was scared that she was wrong about him, that he *had* been involved in the Sandlot Murders.

She didn't answer him. Instead, she looked around in the late-afternoon light at the long, frothy line of water that pulsed and murmured at the edge of the sparkling white expanse of sand.

"I love the beach," she said. "You know, I was eighteen before I ever set eyes on the ocean, but I still loved it. I loved the pictures and the movies and TV shows. *Hawaii Five-O* repeats. *Miami Vice. Flipper.* Especially *Flipper.* Sandy and Bud, remember them? So I came out to

Florida to go to college and see the ocean. Mostly to see the ocean."

Felipe was listening to her carefully. He was also looking around, watching the cars that came and went in the parking lot, and gazing at the people passing by on the sidewalk. But every time he glanced at her, she knew from looking into his eyes that he was paying attention to every word she spoke. It was a nice feeling, knowing that someone was honestly listening to her.

"Everyone back home laughed at me because I wanted to be a marine biologist," Carrie told him. "Everyone told me that ranchers' daughters from Montana just didn't become marine biologists."

"Why not?" he asked.

She smiled and reached up to push his hair back from his face. "That's what I asked, too. Why not?" She shrugged. "No one had a good enough answer, so here I am. A marine biologist from Montana."

Felipe took her face between his hands and kissed her. His mouth was so sweet, his lips so gentle. Carrie's heart lodged in her throat, aching with love for him.

He still held her face after he kissed her, gazing deeply into her eyes.

Suddenly shy, and afraid that her feelings would show, Carrie pulled away. She looked down at her toes.

"Does that help with our cover?" she asked. "Does it make us seem more like college students when you kiss me?"

"That's not why I kissed you," Felipe said. "I kissed you because I wanted to. Because around you, Caroline, I have absolutely no control."

She looked up at him. He wasn't smiling or teasing. His face was dead serious as he gazed at the parking lot.

"No control," he murmured, the muscles working in his jaw.

Carrie gazed at him. No control. Over his body? Or over his emotions?

Hope formed in her stomach like a fragile butterfly. Maybe she *could* make him love her. Maybe…

FELIPE WAS AWARE he'd given too much away.

Caroline sat next to him, lost in her own thoughts. How long 'til she figured out the control he'd spoken of losing had to do with his heart rather than his hormones?

Of course, her jealousy earlier today had revealed to him that her feelings for him were more than merely casual. And sooner or later, she was going to run into someone who was going to translate *te amo* for her, and then she'd know.

He loved her.

What would happen if he told her? *I love you, but we can't be together because I'd fear for your safety.*

She'd laugh and talk him into ignoring his fears. She'd convince him he was suffering from an overactive imagination.

And then one day, someone like Tommy Walsh would follow him home. And then the next day, Caroline would be dead.

No, he couldn't tell her. He couldn't take that risk.

She shifted slightly and leaned her head against his shoulder. Felipe slipped his arm around her waist, amazed as he always was at how perfectly they fit together.

She rested her hand on his knee, and he felt the sharp stab of desire. Tonight. Tonight she'd be in his arms again.

But they had no place to stay, nowhere to go. God only

knows where they'd spend the night. Maybe they could get a room in a cheap motel by paying with cash and signing false names in the registry. But it would mean standing under the watchful eye of the desk clerk as he registered, hoping the guy hadn't seen the papers or the television news.

Of course, his haircut made him look quite a bit different—

Next to them, the public telephone began to ring.

Felipe was up on his feet in an instant. He answered it before it had completed the first ring.

"Yes?"

"Who's the blonde?"

It was Diego—Jim Keegan.

"Oh, man," Felipe said, relief rushing through him. "You don't know how good it is to hear your voice."

"Likewise," Diego said. "I drove by and saw you, but just as I was about to stop, I got this sense that I was being trailed. I don't know. Emily says when she got pregnant, I got paranoid. Maybe she's right. Still, I thought it would be smart to be cautious, you know?"

"Where are you calling from?" Felipe asked, glancing back at Caroline. She was watching him, trying to listen from her seat on the picnic table.

"I'm at a pay phone downtown," Jim Keegan said. "We got us a friendly line, Phil. No taps, no one listening in. So spill it. I know you didn't kill those guys in the sandlot. I got a truckload of questions. Let's start with the girl." He laughed, and Felipe had to smile at the familiar, husky sound. "I drive by, and I see you giving this great-looking blonde mouth-to-mouth. Who is she?"

"Her name is Caroline Brooks," Felipe said, glancing again at the great-looking blonde in question and lowering his voice so she wouldn't hear him. "Do you remember the lady I locked in the trunk of her car at Sea Circus?"

"You're kidding," Jim said. "You used to talk about her so much, Emily was convinced you'd be sending out wedding invitations within the year. How long have you been seeing her? What's going on? Is she helping you hide?"

"I never went back to introduce myself," Felipe admitted. "I haven't been seeing her at all." He told Jim what had happened at Schroedinger's restaurant, how by sheer chance, Caroline had been there that evening, how she had unwittingly blown his cover.

His friend was silent for a moment. "Then she's the same woman you left the restaurant with," he said. "That's why her name sounded familiar. We still don't have a picture of her, but the PR department is working on getting one to release to the press—along with a statement, my friend, that calls her your 'hostage.'"

Felipe swore softly.

"Apparently, the boyfriend's getting ready to tape an impassioned plea to *you,* trying to convince you to let the girl go. It'll be carried by all the local stations—"

"*Boy*friend?" Felipe said.

"Uh-oh," Jim said. "She didn't tell you she has a boyfriend?"

"No." Felipe turned his back to Caroline, afraid that the sudden jealousy that was making his stomach churn would show in his eyes. *Boyfriend?*

"Some ad exec. His name is—hang on a sec." Felipe could hear the sound of pages being turned as Jim skimmed his notes for the man's name. "Robert Penfield. The Third. Lah-di-dah. Big bucks, no brains. The guy's a real load, Phil. He's been doing the circuit of news programs and talk shows, milking the situation. Apparently, he was at the restaurant, when you quote, unquote 'kidnapped' Caroline—"

You two-timing snake… That's what Caroline had called him when she'd thought he was involved with Jewel, too. No way would she have been so vehement if she'd been doing some two-timing of her own, if she'd been hiding a boyfriend from him.

"He's not her boyfriend, this Penfield guy," Felipe said with sudden certainty. "A dinner date, maybe." He turned back to look at Caroline. "Do you know someone named Robert Penfield?" he said to her.

She stared at him blankly.

"The Third…?"

Recognition dawned in her eyes. "I was having dinner with him at Schroedinger's."

"Have you been out with him before?"

"No," she said. "I only met him that afternoon."

"I was right," Felipe said to Jim. "He was her dinner date."

"He's been implying that she's his fiancée," Jim said.

"She didn't even recognize his name at first," Felipe said.

"Maybe that's simply a testament to the overwhelming power you have over women," Jim teased. "When you're around, old what's-his-name's forgotten."

"You got anything else for me, man?" Felipe asked. "Any *good* news?"

"Only bad," Jim said. "*Really* bad."

Felipe braced himself.

"The police just released the ballistics report to the press," Jim continued. "Your police-issue handgun fired the bullets that killed Tony Mareidas and Steve Dupree out in that sandlot."

"Oh, *man*." Felipe closed his eyes. This *was* bad news.

"Was your gun ever taken from you in the past few weeks?" Jim asked. "Was it ever missing for any length of time?"

"No."

"Maybe while you were asleep? Or, um, otherwise preoccupied perhaps…?"

"No. I sleep with it under my pillow," Felipe said. "And I've been sleeping alone." Except for the past few nights, and hopefully again tonight….

"Then I'm right," Jim said. "Richter's got a man inside the St. Simone Police Force—and it's someone with enough rank and power to falsify a ballistics report."

"A captain," Felipe said.

"That's what I figured, too," Jim said.

Felipe told him about the mysterious Captain Rat, Richter's partner. "Last week I got a glimpse of Richter's personal schedule on his computer," Felipe said. "He's got a date to meet with this Captain Rat tomorrow at three-thirty."

"Where?"

Felipe laughed humorlessly. "That's the catch. I don't know where."

A fourteen- or fifteen-year-old kid hovered nearby, waiting to use the pay phone. Felipe turned and gave him a steady look, and within moments, the boy nervously walked away.

"Okay, look," Jim was saying, "I'll go and do some more checking around. The bitch about this Richter investigation is that I don't know who the hell knows about it, and who is clueless. And I don't want to ask—I don't want anyone to know that *I* know. Damn, it's complicated. And meanwhile, no one's asking me if *I* know, because they don't want *me* to know what *they* know." He swore disgustedly. "Phil, I'm honestly thinking of just bringing it all out into the light."

"Not yet, man," Felipe said. "Don't do that yet. Until I know who the man on the inside is, I can't risk coming in. And without me, you've got nothing."

"I got nothing now," Jim said. "Maybe it's time to shake the hornet's nest, see who gets mad."

"Not yet," Felipe said again. "Maybe in a few days—"

"I'm worried about you, Phil."

"I'll get by," Felipe said with a quiet confidence that wasn't feigned. At least not entirely. "Don't do something that will put you—and Emily—in danger."

Jim Keegan was silent, and Felipe quickly told him about the tape he'd made and left in Rafe's van. "Just in case," he added.

Jim was still silent. Then, finally, he spoke. "Maybe you should just lie low," he said. "Stay out of sight. Let me nose around a bit more. I've checked out all but two of the police captains, all but Captain Swick and Captain Patterson. Personally, I find it hard to believe Patterson could ever be involved with Richter. He's such a straight arrow. Swick, on the other hand…"

"He's never liked me," Felipe said. "I've overheard him using…derogatory language in reference to…my cultural background, shall we say?"

"He's a bigot," Jim stated bluntly. "But that doesn't automatically make him a criminal."

"He lives down near the water, doesn't he?" Felipe asked. Come to think of it, Donald Swick lived in a very nice house right on the Gulf—a house way too big and expensive for a man who'd been on the police force all his working life.

"Yeah, over on Casa del Sol Avenue," Jim said. "His wife's out of town. He's been putting in quite a few extra hours, working with Chief Earley, trying to track you down. The media's been eating it up. Captain Swick and Chief Earley, the modern Untouchables."

"Man, I got a feeling about Swick," Felipe said. "I'm going to check him out."

"Let me," Jim said. "You stay hidden."

"No, I've got to do *some*thing," Felipe said. "You look into Patterson. I'll check out Swick's house."

"Phil, at least find a safe place for Caroline and leave her there."

It was Felipe's turn to be silent. "Can you guarantee that wherever I put her, Tommy Walsh won't find her?" he finally said. "And can you guarantee that if I do find a safe place, she'll stay put?" He shook his head, even though Jim couldn't possibly see him over the telephone line. "No, she's staying with me, Diego. That way I'll *know* she's safe."

For once, Jim didn't argue. He just chuckled quietly. "It happened, huh, Felipe? You finally met your match."

"No—" The word wasn't even out of his mouth before Felipe recognized it was a lie. Diego was right. Caroline was the only woman he wanted, the only woman he'd ever want. After he said goodbye to her, he might as well enter a monastery.

"Oh good, and we're in denial, too." Jim's chuckle got louder. "You poor bastard, you don't stand a chance."

In his native language, Felipe soundly and quietly cursed out his best friend.

But Jim kept on laughing. "Just ask her to marry you and get it over with," he said. "You'll be surprised how much better you'll feel when you just give up the fight."

"I can't, man," Felipe said. "It's not possible. You *know* it's not possible."

"Rule number one," Jim said. "Nothing is impossible. Don't forget that. The first step is to wipe the street clean with Richter's face, bring down his whole organization, including this sonuvabitch on the force. After that, you can work things out with Caroline."

"Sure," Felipe said. Sure, he'd work things out by walking out. It was the only way.

After Jim had been transferred to homicide, Felipe had gotten used to working alone. He found that he *liked* working alone; he liked *being* alone. But the thought of being without Caroline made him feel achingly lonely. He'd never been lonely before, but now he knew he'd never be anything *but* lonely again.

"Remember, if you need transportation, the key to my car is on the right front wheel, where I always leave it. The car's in the lot at the precinct," Jim said. "I'm going to call you at this number same time tomorrow. Try to be here."

"I'll be here," Felipe said. "Or…" He didn't finish the sentence, but they both knew how it ended. He'd be there, or he'd be dead.

CHAPTER SIXTEEN

"WHOSE HOUSE IS THIS?" Carrie whispered.

"Don Swick," Felipe said. "He's a captain on the police force."

Carrie nodded. "Nice place," she said.

It was. It was very nice.

It had beachfront, in a section of town where beachfront didn't come cheap. Big and rambling, the single-level house sprawled across a well-manicured lawn with plenty of bushes and shrubbery to keep them hidden.

"You think this Captain Swick is your Captain Rat?" Carrie asked.

Felipe nodded. "Shh," he said, pressing one finger lightly to her lips.

It was hard to be quiet. Carrie was understandably nervous. This was the first time she'd ever broken into a police captain's house. It was the first time she'd broken into *any*one's house.

But Felipe seemed to know what he was doing. He used a tiny penlight he'd taken from the beach house to examine what looked like the access box to a complex security system.

With a Swiss Army knife Carrie didn't even realize he had been carrying, Felipe set to work. She watched for a moment, then he murmured, "Keep an eye on the street, *cara*. Tell me if a car is coming."

Carrie nodded.

She was scared to death. She was scared that this Captain Swick *was* Richter's partner and that they'd be in danger if they went into his house. And she was scared that he wasn't, that they'd break into his house and still be no closer to clearing Felipe's name.

"Got it," he said quietly.

Carrie turned to see the door swing open.

Gun drawn, Felipe went inside first. He flashed the same penlight around an enormous kitchen. It was nearly twice as big as the kitchen at the beach house.

Carrie shut the door behind them, then followed Felipe out of the kitchen and down a long, carpeted hallway. They passed a dining room and a living room, both vast and quiet and dark and filled with expensive furniture.

It was creepy being in someone else's house like this. True, the beach house had been someone else's, too, but they'd been there with Jim Keegan's unspoken blessing. Here, there wasn't even a hint of an invitation from the owners.

Carrie followed Felipe into an enormous master bedroom suite. His penlight flashed around the room, revealing an unmade bed, clothes draped over the back of several easy chairs, laundry overflowing a hamper. The shades in the windows were all pulled completely down, as if Swick hadn't bothered to open them in the morning.

Felipe went over to the lamp on one of the bedside tables and switched on the light.

There were Chinese food cartons on a TV tray, along with a half-eaten bag of chips and the TV remote control.

Books and papers were piled on the half of the bed that Swick hadn't slept in.

"He better clean this up before his wife gets home, huh?" Felipe murmured. "Man, what a mess."

"Where do we start?" Carrie asked.

"We're looking for a calendar or a date book or anything that might mention some kind of meeting tomorrow," Felipe said. "We're looking for any mention of Richter's name, or Walsh, or Mareidas and Dupree—"

"Who?"

"The men who were killed in the sandlot."

"Oh." Carrie nodded. "How about any mention of the company that's a front for Richter's illegal businesses?"

"L&R Co.," Felipe said. "Good thinking. You'd make a good cop."

"No thanks," Carrie said dryly. "This is not my idea of fun."

"You'd rather jump into a tank with a pair of killer whales, right?" Felipe teased.

"I'd take Biffy and Louise over Lawrence Richter and Tommy Walsh *any* day," Carrie said.

"To each his—or her—own," Felipe said with a smile. "Will you be all right in here by yourself? I'd like to go look for Swick's office. He must have a desk or something, where he keeps a calendar."

"I'll be fine," Carrie said, already flipping through the papers on the bed. She looked up. "Don't go far, though."

"I won't," he said. He moved toward her and kissed her, then disappeared into the darkness of the hall.

SWICK'S OFFICE was a disaster area. His desk was covered by a mountain of papers and files and scraps of envelopes and napkins with notes scribbled on them.

Cardboard file boxes were everywhere, even on top of a state-of-the-art stereo system, even on top of a large-screen TV.

Felipe pulled down the shades and closed the curtains and switched on the desk lamp. Well aware of the time, well aware that they couldn't risk staying here too much longer, he grimly set to work, searching for something, *any*thing that would link Swick to Richter's organization.

Swick had a file on his desk for every case he'd worked on in the past—God, it must be the past three years. They seemed to be in no particular order, neither chronological nor alphabetical.

Underneath a two-and-a-half-year-old arson case, Felipe found a desk calendar. It was mounted on a heavy marble stand, and there was a page devoted to each day of the week. It was open to the page dated January 3, which was more than two weeks ago, and probably the last date Swick had unearthed the calendar in this mess.

Quickly, Felipe flipped to January 20. Tomorrow's date. The date of Richter's meeting with his Captain Rat. There was something written on the calendar.

"Golf," it said. There was no mention of the time or location.

Was it some kind of code, or did it actually mean the game of golf? And if so, there were dozens of golf courses in St. Simone, dozens of possibilities for the game's—and the meeting's—location. Assuming, of course, that Swick was the Captain Rat he was looking for. Assuming that "golf" didn't mean simply golf.

One by one, Felipe opened the drawers of Swick's desk. They were as disorganized as the rest of the room. He quickly rummaged through them, but they appeared to be filled with files and papers even older than the ones on top of the police captain's desk.

He reached down to pull out the lower left drawer but it wouldn't open. He pulled harder, thinking it had jammed, but it still didn't budge. It was locked.

Using a letter opener he'd seen in the top center desk drawer, Felipe tried to jimmy the lock. He slipped the piece of metal in between the drawer and the frame, finally using it as a wedge and the butt of his gun as a hammer to splinter the wood and break the drawer open.

Pay dirt.

A manila envelope at the bottom of the drawer had "Salazar" scribbled across it in black marker.

Felipe took out the envelope and opened it.

An unmarked cassette tape fell into his hands. It was the only thing in the envelope, but Felipe was willing to bet it was all he needed. He quickly cleared the file boxes off the stereo, then popped the cassette into the tape player and turned the power on.

He hit the play button.

There were several moments of silence, then Lawrence Richter's voice came on, smooth and clearly recognizable.

"I've got a problem," he said. "A discipline problem."

"Tony and Steve," said Tommy Walsh's voice. "You want 'em snuffed. That's no problem."

"This is very difficult for me," Richter said. "Alfonse Mareidas has been a friend for a long time."

"Al knew his kid was as good as dead when word came through about the deal he and Dupree were making with the D.A.," Walsh said flatly. "If that had gone through, it would've taken down your entire westside operation. It wouldn't have touched you, but it would've been a mess. Al can't blame you for what you have to do."

"What *you* have to do," Richter said quietly.

"Of course," Walsh said.

"Make it quick and painless," Richter told him. "For Al's sake. But make a statement."

"With pleasure," Walsh said. "Consider Mareidas and Dupree permanently out of the picture."

"Have Julia send flowers to their families," Richter said, and the tape ended.

Yes.

Yes!

This tape was all the evidence Felipe needed to pin the Sandlot Murders on Richter and Walsh, and to clear his name. Now all he had to do was prove Donald Swick was Richter's Captain Rat. That was, unfortunately, easier said than done.

Felipe rewound the cassette tape and took it out of the tape player.

"Felipe!" He looked sharply to see Caroline standing in the doorway. "There's a car pulling into the driveway," she said, her eyes wide. "I saw lights, and—"

He stood up, stashing the tape in the back pocket of his jeans. "Let's get out of here," he said.

"I didn't find anything," she said as they ran down the hallway toward the kitchen door. "I didn't finish looking but—"

"I found a tape," Felipe told her. "A recording of Richter and Walsh planning the Sandlot Murders."

"My *God,*" Carrie breathed.

Felipe saw it a fraction of a second too late. A backup laser alarm had come on, probably since the other system had been off-line longer than fifteen or so minutes. Caroline was in front of him, and she reached to pull the door open before he could stop her.

The opening door interrupted the laser beam and all hell broke loose. The alarm shrieked, a high-pitched, keening sound that attempted to shatter their eardrums and announce an attempted break-in to the surrounding square mile.

Felipe grabbed Caroline's hand and pulled her out the door.

Car headlights flashed in his face, blinding him.

"Freeze!" bellowed a voice over the alarm. Swick. It was Swick.

Felipe didn't stop running.

"I said freeze!"

Shielding Caroline with his body, he took her with him as he dived for the bushes.

The booming sound of a gun being fired drowned out for a moment the relentless sound of the alarm.

Then, "God, Chief, you might've hit the girl!" Swick cried.

"Radio for backup," Chief Earley's voice rasped. "We got that son of a bitch cornered now."

Branches and vines slapped at Felipe's arms and legs as he and Caroline scrambled down the slight incline separating Swick's property from his neighbor's yard.

Lights were going on all over the neighborhood.

Felipe tried to stick to the darkness at the edges of the yards. He could hear Caroline breathing hard. He could almost smell her fear. Or maybe it was his own fear he could smell. *Madre de Dios,* she could've been shot. She *still* could be shot.

"Can you swim?" she asked him, straining for air as they hit a stretch of darkened lawn and ran full out.

"Yes," he huffed. He could hear police sirens in the distance, lots of sirens, drawing closer. Man, maybe they *were* cornered....

"Let's head for the water," Caroline gasped. "For the ocean. The tide should be pulling toward the south. We can swim down the coast."

Hope burst like a flare inside him.

"Te amo," he cried. "I *love* you! Caroline, that's brilliant!"

Cutting hard to the left, they ran west, toward the Gulf. Felipe's leg was throbbing, drumming with pain again, but he ignored it. It didn't matter. Nothing else mattered. He could only think of getting Caroline to safety.

Around them, the sound of sirens was growing louder and louder.

Felipe could smell the ocean, see the glimmer of the surf in the darkness. They were close. They were so close. One more road to cross, one more neatly manicured yard and then they'd hit the beach....

With a squeal of tires, a police car pulled onto the street and braked to a stop, cutting them off from the ocean and escape.

Felipe jerked Caroline down with him, hard, into the darkness of some bushes. He could feel her heart racing, hear her ragged breathing.

"I'm in position," the police officer said. "There's no sign of anyone out here. Shall I move on?"

"Stay where you are," the radio speaker crackled. "Keep your weapon loaded and ready. Suspect is armed and dangerous. Repeat, armed and dangerous."

"What now?" Caroline breathed into his ear.

Felipe shifted his weight off his injured leg. "I'm going to surrender," he whispered.

"No!"

"While this guy is busy with me," he said, ignoring her vehement protest, "I want you to sneak across the street and make it down to the water. Are you sure you're a strong enough swimmer?"

"I won't do it," she said tightly. "I won't let you turn yourself in. You said yourself you won't stay alive more than a day in protective custody—"

He kissed her. "I'll find a way," he said. "I'll beat the odds."

"Felipe—"

"Caroline, I won't have them shooting at you!"

"And I won't let you sacrifice yourself for me!"

"Your safety is my priority," he hissed. "Don't make this harder than it has to be."

"If you give yourself up, mister," Caroline said, her head at that determined angle, chin held high, "I'm going in with you. We're sticking together."

She wasn't going to give in. She wouldn't back down.

Felipe swore silently. He was going to have to find another way.

She touched him gently on the face, a whisper of a caress on his cheek. Her blue-green eyes were colorless in the darkness. She looked otherworldly, angelic.

When she spoke, her voice was little more than a whisper. "*Te amo,* too, you know."

CHAPTER SEVENTEEN

CARRIE KEPT RUNNING, holding tightly to Felipe's hand, splashing through the swampy underbrush.

They'd managed to creep away from the police car, crawling back the way they'd come. Carrie had hoped that they would make it to the water by cutting across the road farther down. But other police cars had arrived, their bright headlights slicing through the darkness, lighting both the street and the surrounding yards, herding the fugitives back, away from the ocean.

Dear Lord, let them reach the water.

Then Felipe froze, holding out an arm to stop her, listening hard in the darkness.

Sirens. She could hear sirens and shouting, and...

Dogs. Oh, God, *dogs.* Someone had brought dogs, trained to track by scent alone. They were baying and barking frantically in the distance.

Felipe was drenched with sweat and limping again. His leg had to be hurting. Hers ached from fatigue, and she didn't have a three-day-old bullet wound making things worse.

"Come on," he said, his voice hoarse, and somehow, *some*how, he started running again.

They didn't make it more than fifty yards before they came up against a twelve-foot-high chain-link fence.

The dogs were getting closer, and Carrie could also hear the throbbing of a helicopter in the distance. She swore. A helicopter with a searchlight would be able to pick them out of the water, no problem.

If they ever made it into the water.

Felipe was thinking the same thing. "When we hit the ocean, we'll have to be ready to swim underwater," he said.

When? *If* was more like it. Carrie could smell the tang of the salt air, but the ocean was somewhere on the other side of this fence that was more than twice her height.

They moved along the fence. It stretched out seemingly forever into the darkness.

Carrie was all turned around. She'd lost her sense of direction. She had no idea where they were, except that the ocean was out of their reach. For all she knew, they'd been running in circles.

"Caroline," Felipe gasped, "do you have the access code to Sea Circus's security system?"

What? "Yeah," she said. "Why?"

And then it hit her. This fence was the fence that surrounded the perimeter of Sea Circus. Lord, she had no clue they'd come this far. If they kept going, kept following the fence, they'd hit one of the park's three entrances. She could punch in the code, open the gates and they'd be inside. There must be a hundred places to hide in the marine park. And the dogs wouldn't be allowed inside— they'd frighten and endanger the wildlife.

And then, there it was, the entrance, one hundred yards farther along the fence. They'd have to cross part of a parking lot to get there, but the lights were out, and in the darkness they wouldn't be seen. At this part of the park, a huge wooden barrier was behind the chain-link security fence. Once they were inside, no one would be able to see them.

A police car passed on the street, going seventy miles an hour, heading up toward Swick's house.

Felipe ran across the lot, bent nearly double. Carrie followed close behind.

She pushed the numbers of the alarm override into the control panel. It flashed green. Thank the Lord! She entered the numbers to unlock the gate, and it swung open with a soft *whoosh*.

Quickly they went in through the open gate, and Carrie keyed in the numbers to close the gate and reactivate the alarm system. The light flashed yellow, then red, then yellow, then red.

What the hell…?

Then all over the park, bright spotlights came on, and sirens began to wail as the alarm went off.

"I did it right!" Carrie cried. "I *know* I did it right! Someone must've changed the access code!"

Felipe grabbed her hand, and again they were running, this time across the brightly lit marine park.

He was heading toward the fence that separated the park from the beach below. He was trying to reach the ocean and the escape it promised, despite the threat of helicopters and their searchlights.

But they weren't even halfway there when Carrie saw a police car skid onto the beach, tires sending showers of sand behind it. Felipe saw it, too, and swerved to the left, going deeper into the park.

All around them, outside the fence, police cars were pulling up, tires squealing. Felipe went around the side of the main aquarium tank and stopped for breath, holding Carrie tightly against him.

"You've got to hide," he said. "This is it, Caroline. They've got me. Let me at least save you—"

"We've been through this once already," Carrie said sharply. "Nothing's changed."

"Yes, it has," he said. "They know where we are. We're trapped."

"You hide with me," she said, "or I don't hide at all."

His hand was shaking as he pushed his hair back from his face. "Dammit, Caroline—"

"I know a place they'll never think to look," she said.

Taking his hand, she pulled him along with her faster and faster across the park. And then she stopped— directly in front of the killer whale tank.

THE KILLER WHALE TANK.

Caroline wanted them to hide in the killer whale tank.

Felipe would've laughed if he had had the time.

Outside the park, Felipe could hear the sound of the police, lots and *lots* of police, so many that he could hear them over the shrieking of the alarm. They were getting ready to come inside. There wasn't any time left.

"This is nuts," he said.

"No, it's not," Carrie said. "There's a place in the tank that can't be seen even from inside the downstairs underwater viewing room. It's a place that's covered by the planks of a walkway. We can stay at the surface, holding on to the edge of the tank. No one will ever find us."

"Except the killer whales," Felipe said, letting her pull him into a door marked Park Personnel Only.

"Move slowly and calmly inside the tank, and everything will be fine," Carrie said, leading him up a set of stairs and through a control room that contained sound equipment and a microphone for the marine show. A small window overlooked the tank. The counter in front of it was covered with piles of cassette tapes. "Biffy and Louise are very gentle."

"Caroline—"

"Trust me," she said, squeezing his hand. "It's your turn to trust *me*."

She pulled him out onto the boardwalk that ran along the edge of the tank. It was slick with water from the waves and foam splashing up onto it. Felipe's eyes widened at the sight of these two enormous beasts who were leaping out of the water, jaws open and big teeth bared.

Gentle? These creatures were *gentle?*

"They're just upset by the noise," Carrie said. "Come on." Sitting down, she dangled her feet in the water, then slipped over the side and into the tank.

Felipe heard the main gate burst open.

Carrie was watching him, holding out her hand to him. *Trust me.*

She'd trusted him when he pulled her down into that crawl space at the beach house. She'd trusted him with her life ever since that fateful meeting at the restaurant. If she said the killer whales were gentle, then the killer whales were gentle.

Felipe took the cassette tape from his pocket and held it up so that Caroline could see it. "I can't take this into the water," he said. "I'm going to hide it."

She smiled. "In plain view," she said.

"That's right," he said.

"Hurry."

He hurried. Back inside the control room, he put his tape toward the far end of the counter, on the bottom of one of the piles of tapes.

Caroline was still waiting for him at the edge of the pool. Behind her, the killer whales belly flopped into the water, creating a maelstrom.

"Quickly," she said.

Felipe went into the water, boots and backpack and all. The water was cold, colder than he expected. And his clothes and boots weighed him down.

At least the alarms were muffled under the water. Yet to a marine animal used to quiet stillness, they must have been terribly loud and confusing.

Carrie swam in front of him and he opened his eyes and followed her. With her long, blond hair floating around her, she looked like some sea creature, a mermaid or sea sprite, luring him down to his death.

But that wasn't true. She was luring him *away* from his death and—

Felipe came face-to-face with a killer whale and froze. It opened its mouth as if to snap him in two, yet still he couldn't move. His lungs were bursting from lack of oxygen as he stared at its beady little eye.

And then, suddenly, Caroline was there, next to him. She touched the *Orca,* gave it some kind of signal, then took Felipe's hand and pulled him toward the surface, safely underneath the boardwalk.

Felipe grabbed the side of the tank and drew in a deep, clean breath, gasping and filling his lungs again and again with precious air. Caroline was there next to him, holding him, pushing his wet hair back from his face, murmuring words of encouragement.

But no sooner had he started to catch his breath than the water in the tank started sloshing around again. Waves slapped him in the face.

"What's going on...?" he gasped.

Carrie pressed her mouth against his ear. "I told Biffy to keep on jumping into the air," she said. "It's one of the moves we've trained them to do. It's featured in the Sea Circus show. It makes them look very ferocious."

"They don't need to *try* to look ferocious," Felipe muttered, shivering as the cool night breeze hit his wet head and face. He looked up at the boardwalk. It wasn't more than eighteen inches overhead, slick and dripping with moisture. It seemed dark and cramped and confining. "This doesn't bother you?" he asked.

Caroline shook her head. "Not as long as I'm in the water," she said. "As long as I have space to move my arms and legs, as long as I don't feel restricted, I'm fine."

Across the park, the alarms were shut off. The sudden silence was odd. It felt heavy and threatening.

"You did the right thing when Biffy approached you," Caroline said almost silently, her mouth against his ear again. "You didn't move quickly or panic."

Felipe had to smile. "I didn't move quickly because I couldn't move at all," he whispered back into her ear. "I believe what I did is called 'being frozen with fear.'"

"You're that afraid," Carrie asked, "yet you'd get into a tank with them?"

"I trust you," Felipe said, pulling back his head to look into her eyes.

Her hair was plastered against her head, and beads of water were caught in her long eyelashes. She looked so beautiful, so delicate, so small and fragile. She was all of those things, yet she was also the toughest, most de-termined fighter he'd ever met. He would have quit twice already tonight. True, he would have quit purely to save Caroline's life, to give her a chance to get away. But she wouldn't give up; she wouldn't give in.

So here he was, in a killer whale tank, praying harder than he'd prayed in a long time that somehow, some way they'd pull this off.

Caroline's arms were around him, helping him keep his head above the surface. Even though he was holding on to the side of the tank, the water dragged at his jeans and boots and the backpack, pulling him under.

Felipe could feel the muscles in her arms. Man, she *was* strong. She might've been little, but she could more than pull her weight.

She leaned forward to kiss him. Her lips, her nose, her face were cold against his, but her mouth was warm, and he closed his eyes, losing himself in her sweetness.

But then she pulled back, and he heard footsteps on the boardwalk above.

Carrie motioned for him to take a deep breath and sink beneath the water. All he had to do was let go of the side, and he sank nearly to the bottom of the tank. Carrie reached for his hands, and her added buoyancy pulled him back up a bit.

With her hair a cloud of gold around her face, she *did* look like a mermaid. A mermaid in overalls. She smiled at him, and right at that moment, he loved her so much, he could have wept.

Te amo, too, she said. She loved him, too.

Somehow she'd figured out the translation from Spanish to English. Somehow he'd given himself away.

Felipe's lungs started to hurt, to burn, yet still he and Caroline stayed underneath the water. He dragged his gaze away from her face and looked up to the surface of the water. As he watched, the shadowy shapes he could barely see through the slats of the boardwalk moved away.

Carrie was watching, too, and as he looked back at her, she nodded, gesturing with her head toward the surface. She helped pull him up toward the air, and silently, they surfaced.

Felipe could hear Captain Swick's voice as well as Chief Earley's. He recognized Captain Patterson as well as a number of detectives from the Fourth Precinct.

And then a new voice joined them—Jim Keegan's.

"The dogs have picked up a fresh scent outside the fence, south of the park," he said in his familiar New York accent. "Our theory is that they worked their way around the perimeter, climbing along the chain link of the fence, clinging to it, you know, so the dogs couldn't track them along the ground."

Swick swore long and hard.

"That's why we lost their trail for so long," Jim said. "But the tracker thinks we've picked it up now. We've wasted a lot of time in here, sir. They're out there making good their escape. Shouldn't we get moving?"

"All right," Swick said. "Let's head south. Shut this place down."

The voices moved away.

Felipe turned to find Caroline watching him, her eyes wide. "Someone intentionally led those dogs off the track," she whispered.

"Jim Keegan," Felipe said. "Diego. He came through for me."

"He must really believe in you," Carrie said quietly.

Jim wasn't the only one who believed in him. Caroline believed in him, too.

Jim's loyalty wasn't a surprise—after all, he'd been Felipe's friend for years. But only a few days ago, Caroline had been ready to run away from him, ready to think the worst. Now, not only was she willing to risk her life to help him, but she trusted him enough to let herself fall in love with him.

It was exhilarating, and terrifying.

She loved him.

It was enough to make him feel as if he owned the world—if he lived in the kind of world that could be owned. But he didn't. His world, his life, owned him.

Caroline loved him, but he could give her nothing in return. Nothing but heartache and misery.

As Felipe listened, the police officers left the marine park. The gate was closed, the alarm system reactivated, and one by one, the lights were shut off, leaving only dim security lighting up and running.

Still, he clung to the edge of the killer whale tank, one arm around Caroline, listening and waiting, until they were sure they were alone.

CHAPTER EIGHTEEN

THERE WERE TOWELS in the control room.

Carrie stripped down to her bathing suit and dried herself off. It was chilly tonight. She took an extra towel to dry her hair, shivering slightly at the cold concrete under her feet and the coolness of the air.

Felipe was quietly taking off his own clothes, wringing out his jeans and laying them out to dry with the other things that had been in his backpack.

He glanced at her in the dim light. His eyes were unreadable, but really, what did she expect? They'd just done a triathlon—running, swimming and confessing their innermost feelings. None of it could have been easy for him—certainly not knowing that she'd managed to translate his "untranslatable" Spanish phrase.

Te amo.

She'd suspected its meaning. She'd guessed and she'd hoped, but it wasn't until they were running for their lives that he'd said it again and she'd known.

Te amo. I *love* you.

As Carrie watched, Felipe stripped naked, quickly drying himself off and tying a towel around his waist. But still he didn't say a single word.

"How's your leg?" she finally asked.

He lifted the edge of the towel, turning to show her the

wound. It looked angry and sore. "The salt water from the tank stung," he said. "But I'm okay. I thought maybe the stitches opened up from all that running, but they didn't." He looked over at her again. "Are you all right?"

She nodded. "You probably want to get out of here right away," she said. "We'll need something to wear. My wet suit's hanging by the dolphin tank, but there's probably one in here that'll fit you. George's or Simon's or—"

"No," he said. "No, we're in no hurry. I'd be willing to bet Tommy Walsh and his men are somewhere on the other side of that fence, on the off chance we're still in here. No, we'll stay here tonight and leave in the rush of the crowd tomorrow."

Walsh. Outside the fence, waiting for them. Carrie shivered again, wrapping the towel more tightly around her. "Won't Walsh still be watching for us in the morning?" she asked.

"Yes," Felipe said. "He probably will. And so will the police—particularly after they don't find us tonight."

Carrie was silent, letting his words digest. "So," she finally said, glancing up to find him still watching her, "really, what you're saying is we're not out of danger."

He shook his head. "I'm sorry, but no, we're not." He raked his wet hair back, out of his eyes. "I'm not going to lie to you, Caroline. There's a good chance we won't make it out of this park tomorrow," he said. "If Walsh is smart—and he is—he'll make arrangements for a sharpshooter to be near every entrance. And he'll have people watching for us—for me. It'll be a race to see who spots me first—Walsh's men or the police."

It didn't matter *who* found him first. Either way he'd be dead. He'd be killed immediately if it was Walsh who spotted him first, or he'd be killed later that day or the next if it was the police.

"Caroline." She looked up into the velvet blackness of his eyes. "I want to play that tape for you."

She shook her head. "There's no tape player," she said.

He stared around the room. "All this equipment, and there's no tape deck?"

"It's locked up in the main office," she said. She gestured around the room. "All this other stuff is underwater recording equipment and cameras. It doesn't have a lot of value in the local pawnshops. The tape decks, however, kept walking away."

He swore, then apologized. "I wanted you to hear this tape," he said. "It's a conversation between Lawrence Richter and Tommy Walsh. Richter orders Walsh to kill Mareidas and Dupree. It proves my innocence."

Carrie nodded, gazing steadily into his eyes. "I believe you," she said quietly. "I don't need to hear it."

His eyes filled with tears. He reached for her then, pulling her into his arms and holding her tightly against him.

This time tomorrow, Felipe could very well be dead. That wasn't a crazy, wild thought. It wasn't an extremely unlikely worst-case scenario. It was an honest-to-God possibility.

Carrie felt tears burning her own eyes, and she couldn't stop herself from speaking. She was well aware she might never have another chance.

"I do love you," she said.

She felt him draw in a deep breath as if her words had somehow stung.

"I'm sorry if you don't want to hear that," she whispered, fighting another rush of tears. "But I want you to know how I feel."

"I heard you when you said it the first time," he murmured. He kissed her gently on the lips, then pulled back to look down into her eyes and smile. It was shaky, but it *was* a smile. "Of course, you'd have every right to assume I'd have trouble with the translation."

Carrie stared up at him. He was making a joke. He had somehow found the strength to tease about something that he found so desperately serious and frightening as *love*.

"I'm not asking for anything in return," she told him softly.

He looked away at her words, unable to meet her eyes as she continued in a quiet voice.

"I know when you said you loved me—*te amo*—you probably only meant that you loved me at that moment," Carrie said.

He would've interrupted her, but she stopped him with a gentle finger against his lips.

"That's okay," she said. "It's more than I ever expected. Don't say things you think I want to hear, just because you think you won't be around to keep your promises."

Felipe shook his head. "I'm not going to die tomorrow," he said. "They're not going to catch me, and I'm not going to let them near you. We're going to get out of this park alive."

"Felipe, you just said—"

"That I wasn't going to lie to you. I know, but you've reminded me, *cara,* I've got a powerful reason to stay alive."

His hair had fallen forward over his face again, and

Carrie pushed it back. He pressed his cheek into her hand, then reached up and moved her fingers to his mouth, planting a gentle kiss in her palm.

He loved her. Carrie had to believe that he loved her, but he didn't—or couldn't—say the words. Still, she could see it in his eyes as he gazed down at her.

She wanted to believe that they would survive tomorrow simply because Felipe wanted them to. But the real truth was, all they could be absolutely certain of ever having was right here and right now.

"POTATO CHIPS, POPCORN OR PRETZELS?" Caroline asked.

Felipe stared pensively at the row of vending and gumball machines. "How much change do we have?" he asked.

"Enough for two bags and one can of soda," she said, "with a quarter left over."

Felipe shook his head in disgust. He had nearly three thousand dollars in his wallet—in big bills. The smallest he had was a twenty. The bill changer took nothing larger than a five. "I'm hungry."

"I'm hungry, too. We *could* break into a machine," Carrie suggested.

"And have the police out here first thing to investigate?" Felipe said. "No thanks." He smiled at her. "We're going to have to distract ourselves until the concession stand opens in the morning, no?"

Caroline glanced at him over her shoulder, a small smile playing at the corners of her mouth.

She looked incredible. She was wearing her wet suit— a navy blue, form-fitting unitard that hugged her curves like a second skin. It zipped up the front and she wore it slightly open at the neck. Her hair was nearly dry, and it hung, shiny and blond, around her shoulders, down between her shoulder blades.

She looked capable and in control and utterly, totally feminine.

"Potato chips, popcorn, or pretzels?" Caroline asked patiently.

"I'll have the swordfish steak, grilled in lemon butter, with a baked potato and a house salad," Felipe said. "And I'd like to see the wine list, please."

Carrie laughed. "We have a very nice root beer, dating from December."

"If the lady recommends it, how can I refuse? My goal is to wine and dine her with this gourmet meal in the hopes of finding out exactly what she is wearing underneath that wet suit."

"Aha," Caroline said. "A meal meant to seduce. In that case, pretzels, my favourite."

She put the money into one of the machines and pushed the buttons that made two tiny bags of pretzels fall out.

"Shall we dine alfresco?" she asked, taking the root beer from the soda machine. She handed him the can of soda and the last of their change—a solitary quarter.

Felipe knew exactly what to do with it.

In addition to the snack and soda machines, there was a row of six or eight gumball and candy machines, many of which held inexpensive toys in clear plastic bubbles. One boasted action-hero pencil erasers while another had cartoon-show tattoos. A third contained a collection of cheap plastic rings.

"For such a fine meal, it's only fitting that the lady be properly adorned with fine jewelry," he said solemnly, dropping the quarter into the slot and turning the handle.

One of the plastic bubbles dropped down. He flipped up the hatch and took out the bubble. Opening it with a flourish, he presented Caroline with a bright green plastic ring.

It was small, but it fit almost perfectly on her ring finger.

She looked up at him, her sea-green eyes wide.

And suddenly, this was no longer a game they were playing. Suddenly, this was real. She was in love with him, and God, he'd just given her a *ring*.

"I'll keep it forever," she whispered.

"It won't last forever," he warned her, so afraid he was going to break her heart. He felt his own heart already start to crack. "The plastic will break."

"Not if I take good care of it," she said. Her chin went up with that determined tilt that was becoming so familiar to him.

"It's not worth the trouble," he said. God, he wished the words he'd spoken weren't true. He wished he had a different life, a life that he could share with her. "It's worth nothing."

"I know what it's worth," she said quietly. "I know exactly what it's worth."

CARRIE WOKE BEFORE DAWN.

Felipe was still asleep, stretched out on the lumpy sofa bed in the dolphin trainer's room. He stirred and reached for her, wrapping his arms around her, holding her tightly.

Carrie felt safe in his arms, but she knew that that safety was only temporary. It wouldn't be long now before they'd have to wake up, get out of bed and get ready to face this day—and Tommy Walsh and his sharpshooters along with the entire St. Simone Police Department.

Last night, Felipe had called Jewel collect from the pay phones by the concession stand. She'd told Felipe that she had gone to see his brother.

According to what Rafe had heard, Lawrence Richter had raised the price on Felipe's head to a cool million, and Tommy Walsh had every available man out and looking for him and the angel—in other words, Carrie. The scuttlebutt was going around that things were going to get *really* intense. And word was spreading—if anyone sees Felipe Salazar, hit the dirt because bullets are gonna be right behind him. Rafe told Jewel to make sure Felipe knew what he was up against.

What *they* were up against, Carrie thought.

Jewel had talked Rafe into offering his halfway house to Felipe as a safe haven. That was good to know. That was *very* good to know.

Felipe hadn't done much more than report the contents of his conversation to Carrie, but she knew that Rafe's support—no matter how grudgingly given—was important to him.

Felipe had also told Jewel about the tape that incriminated Richter and Walsh in the Sandlot Murders, told her he'd hidden it underneath the sofa bed in the dolphin trainer's room here at Sea Circus. He'd told her to give this information to Jim Keegan, to deliver the message in person and written on a piece of paper so that no one could overhear.

And he'd told her to ask Jim to call him at Rafe's at one Thursday afternoon—*this* afternoon.

Richter's meeting with Captain Rat was to be at three-thirty—two and a half hours later.

They were running out of time.

Felipe stirred again, and she could tell by the change in his breathing that he was awake.

"Good morning," she whispered.

"Is it morning?" he asked. It was still dark outside.

"Almost," she said. "It's nearly five."

"What time does the park open?" he murmured, running one hand lightly along the curve of her hip.

"Nine," she said, closing her eyes. "But the staff starts showing up around six-thirty or seven."

"Are you hungry?" he asked.

Carrie smiled. "Starved. And it's another four hours 'til the concession stands open."

"Hmm," he said. "I don't suppose it's any use, trying to distract you…."

Carrie turned to look at him. His eyes were half-closed, the lower part of his face was covered by a day's growth of dark stubble, and his hair was rumpled. He looked deliciously sleepy. He smiled, a slow smile that promised neither of them was even going to *think* about food—at least not for a while.

CHAPTER NINETEEN

THERE WERE FOUR uniformed policemen, and God only knows how many plainclothes detectives, at each of Sea Circus's gates. They examined the faces of the people leaving the park, searching for Felipe Salazar— "Rogue Cop."

Felipe checked the clock over the main entrance. Eleven-thirty. Up to this point, there had only been dribs and drabs leaving the marine park. According to Caroline, the bigger groups wouldn't start to leave until after lunch—not much before noon at the earliest.

He scanned the parking lot outside the main entrance. This was definitely the way to leave Sea Circus. Both of the other gates had obvious places outside for a sniper to hide. This gate had only the flatness of the already-crowded parking lot, no trees or bushes or cover of any kind except for the rows of cars.

Of course, that also meant there'd be no place for Felipe and Carrie to hide, either, once they were outside the gate.

Caroline sat near him, cross-legged in the grass, off to the side of the crowded walkways. She was wearing Jewel's overalls over her bathing suit, with her pants rolled up to just under her knees. She'd put her hair up into a braid rather than the ponytail she usually wore.

He'd bought her a pair of sunglasses and a baseball cap at the gift shop—there were quite a few of her co-workers around who could identify her—and she wore them with a certain attitude that made her look like a young teenager.

Watching her, Felipe had an idea.

"Those school buses in the parking lot," he said, sitting down next to her. "Did you happen to notice if any of them carried a group of high school students?"

Caroline bit her lower lip, thinking hard. "I saw some really little kids—first-graders maybe, and some older kids—ten-year-olds." She turned to gaze out through the fence toward the parking lot. "There's an awful lot of buses today—one of them *must* be for a group of high school kids." She looked back at Felipe. "Why?"

"We're going to leave with them," he said.

"If they're not seniors, if they're younger, we'll stand out," Carrie said. He couldn't see her eyes behind her sunglasses, but he knew they were serious.

"Cross your fingers," Felipe said. He leaned forward and kissed her lightly. "So far we've been lucky."

She lay back against him, her head in his lap.

"I'm scared to death," she admitted, peering through her dark glasses to look up at him. "We're sitting out here in the open like this, and I keep thinking someone's going to see me, someone's going to recognize me. Or *you*. Lord, your face has been all over the papers and the TV."

"People see what they expect to see," Felipe said. "They don't expect to see St. Simone's most wanted sitting on the lawn near the main entrance to Sea Circus next to the dolphin trainer. They expect to see some Hispanic kid from the 'hood and his pretty girlfriend sitting around in the shade, wasting time. So that's what they see." He touched the side of her face, stroking her cheek lightly with his knuckles. Her skin was so soft, so delicate.

"Maybe we should separate," Carrie said. "Meet back at Rafe's by one o'clock."

"No." The word came out with more force than he'd intended, and he made himself smile to soften its impact. "We stay together."

She was quiet, and he intertwined her fingers with his.

"I'm still scared," she finally whispered.

Felipe nodded. He was scared, too.

Looking up into the vast blueness of the sky, he prayed. He prayed for Caroline's safety and for his own successful escape. And, failing that, he prayed for the ability to accept his death, to die at peace, knowing he had lived his life as best he possibly could.

But had he?

He couldn't help but wonder how differently his life might've turned out had he gone back to Sea Circus and introduced himself to Caroline Brooks that day after he'd locked her in the trunk of her car.

"Hello, my name is Felipe Salazar and I'm really a detective with the Fourth Precinct. Will you forgive me...and have dinner with me?"

She would have. Maybe not that night, but eventually she would have forgiven him.

And, as surely as she'd done over the past few days, she would have stolen her way into his heart.

And then...

What if...

What if Felipe had said no thank you to the assignment to bring down Richter? What if he had said it was time to take some greatly needed—and greatly earned—vacation time? What if he had spent that time, a month, maybe two, with Caroline, living a regular, *normal* life? What if he'd taken her out to see movies and go dancing? What if he'd moved his toothbrush and an extra change of clothes into her apartment? And what if…what if he had *liked* it?

What if his job had posed no threat, no danger? What if he had stayed away from undercover assignments for a while? What if he had transferred out of vice?

He could imagine this Felipe, this other Felipe, spending much more than twenty-five cents on a ring that was neither green nor plastic. He could imagine this other Felipe taking Caroline Brooks someplace unbearably romantic for dinner, and after sitting down at the small, secluded table, he would take her hand and gaze into her eyes and…

He could imagine their wedding day. Diego would stand up for him, slap him on the back and embrace him, happy that his best friend had also found what he and his wife, Emily, shared.

Felipe could imagine saving their money and buying a house close to Caroline's beloved ocean. He would plant flowers in the yard and bring her one every evening. And every night, he'd make sweet, perfect love to her and sleep with her in his arms.

He could imagine her round and heavy with his child. A familiar flame of fear flickered through him and he squelched it. Small women married tall men all the time. Perhaps the baby would need to be born by cesarean section, but perhaps not. Caroline was strong and tough. Either way, he'd see that she received the best possible medical attention and all the tender loving care she could possibly need.

Time moved faster in his mind, the years blending together, their children growing tall and strong. Sons he could be proud of, daughters with his dark hair and eyes and their mother's beautiful smile. His life became a blur of happiness and love, a blend of passion and tenderness, a mosaic of laughter and song.

Felipe stared up into the blue, blue sky, allowing himself to live that life, the life he had not chosen.

The life he never would have chosen—because he never would have turned down the assignment to put Richter away. He knew damn well that if he hadn't taken on Richter's organization, no one else would have. And he couldn't have lived with himself, knowing that such a man continued to run free, hurting innocent people.

But...

There had been something else, some part of his fantasy...

He closed his eyes, trying to rewind his daydream until at last he touched upon it.

What if he had transferred out of vice?

Felipe sat up suddenly, and Caroline, who'd been dozing, jumped.

"What?" she said. "Is something wrong?"

"No, shh," he said. "It's all right."

But his heart was pounding. What if he transferred out of vice? Not had—*did?* What if he did? Damn, if he lived through this mess, he'd *have* to transfer. There wouldn't be a crime lord or a drug dealer this side of Florida who wouldn't recognize his face. However he looked at it, he was washed up as an undercover detective for the vice squad—unless he moved to another town, another state. And he couldn't see doing that. St. Simone was his home.

He *would* transfer out of vice.

And *what if* he transferred to a less dangerous job, one that would pose less of a threat to Caroline, one where revenge and counterhits weren't part of the norm?

Jim Keegan had done it. He'd left vice and was happy with his new job. He was still making a difference by being a police detective.

Or hell, who said Felipe had to be a detective? He could transfer to youth services, follow in his mentor's, Jorge Gamos's, hard-to-fill footsteps.

The possibilities were endless.

He looked down at Caroline. She was watching him, concern on her face.

What if…? What *if?*

"What's wrong?" she asked.

He didn't know how to answer. He didn't know where to start. But when he opened his mouth, the words that came out were the words that he'd been unable to speak for so long. "I love you," he said simply.

She was quiet, just gazing up at him.

"Do you think…" he started to say. He cleared his throat and began again. "Do you think, after this is over…"

"Yes," she said, no hesitation in her voice.

Felipe had to smile. "You don't even know what I'm asking," he said. "How do you know I wasn't going to ask you to spend four solid weeks with me making mad, passionate love?"

She grinned back at him. "Well, *that's* an easy yes."

She took off her sunglasses and he marveled at the love he could see in her beautiful eyes.

"I want to spend time with you after this is over," he said quietly, seriously. "I want to find out if you'll still love me without all the intrigue, without all the danger."

There was another big if here—an if they both weren't bothering to mention: if, after this was over, Felipe and Caroline were both still alive.

But Caroline was thinking about it. He could see it in her eyes.

Death. His death. Her death.

The possibility was very real.

"Are you asking me to dinner or to move in with you?" Caroline asked. She was trying desperately to ignore the shadow of the Grim Reaper that was hanging over them.

Her words caught him off guard. Move in with him? His mother would have a heart attack. His father would turn over in his grave. But Felipe hadn't meant dinner, either. What *had* he meant?

Felipe knew what he meant—he just couldn't say the words. But the thought that after today he might not be alive to speak loosened his tongue.

"I'm asking," he said slowly, "for you to think about... considering the possibility of...marrying me. Taking my name, bearing my children."

God, he wanted that so much. He wanted that life he'd imagined, that sunlight and laughter. He wanted the warmth of Caroline's love forever.

Except...who was he kidding? The odds were that he was going to die. Tommy Walsh, or one of his men, was going to blow a hole in his head and that would be that. No marriage, no children, no laughter.

He'd have the forever—in the form of eternal rest.

And Caroline... God, Walsh would kill her, too.

Felipe closed his eyes, unable to stand the sight of the hope that was blooming on Caroline's face.

God give him the strength to die gracefully.

But Felipe knew with a powerful sense of certainty

that if in the course of the next few hours he were to leave this world, he'd go out kicking and screaming and fighting every step of the way.

AT SEVEN MINUTES after twelve, Felipe could hear them coming. At least three busloads of teens, ranging in age from fifteen to eighteen, were heading directly toward the Sea Circus main entrance. He hastily rose to his feet.

Caroline sat up, and he held out a hand to help her up. Still holding on to her, he led her down the sidewalk toward the sound of the shouting, rap music and laughter.

There were nearly a hundred kids, wearing a hundred different, brightly colored shirts and jeans and caps. They were carrying backpacks and purses and listening to boom boxes and Walkman stereos. They were talking— all at once—to each other, at each other.

Felipe stood with Carrie in the middle of the sidewalk and let the teenagers surround them. Like a herd of wild horses, the kids parted and flowed around them.

Then Felipe turned and began walking toward the entrance, in the same direction and at the same pace. It was crowded and someone jostled Carrie. He looped his arm around her, pulling her closer to him.

His mouth was dry and his eyes were drawn to the big clock that hung above the main gate.

Nine minutes after twelve.

Were these the last minutes of his life?

Around them, none of the teens seemed to notice that there were strangers in their midst. And if they noticed, no one cared.

As they approached the gate and the watching police-men, Felipe let his hair fall forward into his eyes. *Please,*

God, let this work. He didn't want to die. He didn't want Caroline to die. Without even looking at her, he could feel her fear. She gripped his arm even tighter.

"I love you," he breathed into her ear. "Whatever happens, I love you. Don't forget that."

"My answer is yes," she whispered back.

He glanced at her questioningly.

She explained. "I thought about it, and yes, I'll marry you."

Felipe laughed in disbelief. "Caroline—"

"Stay alive," she said, gazing into his eyes. "Whatever happens, stay alive."

He turned and kissed her on the lips.

Was that their last kiss? Maybe.

She was thinking the same thing; he could see it in her eyes. She clung to him, but he gently pulled away from her to pass through a revolving door made of metal bars. It was a one-way door—exit only. He turned, waiting for her to follow him.

There were police officers ten feet away, staring hard at the back of his neck.

Please, God…

Caroline came through the door and her smile was an explosion of sunshine. "Come on, give me a piggyback ride, Carlos!" she called out, loud enough for the watching police officers to hear. She pulled her cap off her head and shook her hair free from its braid.

Felipe barely had time to brace himself before she launched herself up and onto his back. Laughing, she clung to him, and he forced himself to smile and laugh, too. They were just a couple of kids having some fun.

Caroline leaned her head forward over Felipe's shoulder, and her long, shiny hair covered part of his face. With Caroline on his back, Felipe walked past the officers. They didn't give him a second glance.

And then they were in the parking lot. They were outside of Sea Circus. They were past the police. Now they only had to worry about Tommy Walsh.

Only worry about Walsh. The statement was a paradox.

Felipe felt the hair rise on the back of his neck as he imagined the sight of a long-range rifle aimed at his head. Every one of his senses was on edge.

He could only pray that if he was hit, Caroline would have the sense to get away from him, to get down, stay out of range and flee to safety.

As the river of teenagers approached the waiting school buses, Felipe pulled Caroline out of the crowd. They ducked down behind a row of cars.

Carrie's eyes were bright and she was breathing hard. "We made it," she said.

"So far," he said, searching the surrounding cars for a model that would be easy to hot-wire.

An ancient white Volkswagen Rabbit bearing the bumper sticker that read I Love Lee had been parked with its windows open. Felipe opened the door and, on a whim, searched under the floor mats. Caroline slipped into the passenger seat.

There was no key under the mats. He'd have to do this the hard way. Or the not-so-hard way, he realized, seeing a set of keys dangling from the ignition.

"Do you think they *want* the car to be stolen?" Carrie asked.

Felipe started the engine, then tried to roll up the windows. It soon became obvious that there were no windows to be rolled up. The driver's-side door didn't even shut properly. It had to be held closed with a piece of wire.

"Could be," he said.

Still, the old car ran smoothly. Felipe pulled it out of the Sea Circus lot and onto the main road.

The cars he could see in his rearview mirror looked innocuous enough. Just the same, he couldn't shake the feeling that Tommy Walsh was out there somewhere, following them.

This had been too easy. Too simple.

And when dealing with Tommy Walsh, nothing was *ever* simple.

CHAPTER TWENTY

HIGHBOY answered the door at Rafe's halfway house.

He didn't say a word, but he moved impossibly quickly for a man of his girth, throwing wide the door, pulling them both inside and slamming it shut again.

Carrie watched in silence as Highboy fastened every lock and bolt that was on that door. He would have let the alligators loose in the moat and raised the drawbridge if he could have.

When he turned to them, he finally spoke. "I will take you upstairs to Raphael's apartment," he said in an oddly high voice. "The fewer who see you here, the better."

Silently, they followed the heavy man up the stairs. He knocked lightly on the apartment door, and Rafe opened it. He was wearing only a pair of jeans. Carrie tried not to stare at the large dragon tattoo that nearly covered his upper right arm or the ragged scar that sliced across his chest.

"Well, well," Rafe said, "if it isn't the walking million-dollar lottery ticket and the blond angel." He stepped back, so they could come inside. "Come on in. They're talking about you on the news again."

The TV was on, and sure enough, there was a picture of Felipe on the screen behind the news anchor.

"…latest word from the precinct is that the ballistic

reports show it was, indeed, Salazar's police-issue handgun that killed Tony Mareidas and Steve Dupree last week in the downtown sandlot. In addition to this late-breaking news, a copy of a videotape that was delivered anonymously to the police several days ago has been released to us. On this tape, which is clearly dated the same evening as the slayings, Detective Salazar can be seen holding Mareidas and Dupree at gunpoint. Let's look at that tape."

Carrie sat down on the sofa, her eyes on the screen. Behind her, Rafe and Felipe were silent as they, too, watched the news report.

The anchor's face disappeared, to be replaced by the grainy footage from a home video camera. The tape showed three men coming out of an unmarked door in an unidentifiable city alleyway.

The television studio had enhanced the videotape, brightening the area around two of the men's faces. Even without the enhancement, it was clear they were Tony Mareidas and Steve Dupree. The videotape was frozen in place, and the station superimposed clear, labeled photos of the two men in the corners of the screen. Yes, those men were definitely Mareidas and Dupree.

Then the tape continued to roll and the third man turned. He had a gun aimed at the two other men, and he was, indeed, Felipe Salazar. The cheekbones, the hair, the set of his shoulders were instantly recognizable. The hard set of his mouth, however, was not. Still, it *was* Felipe.

"What is this videotape?" Rafe demanded, voicing the doubt that was flooding through Carrie. "Man, you said you had nothing to do with these murders."

Felipe shook his head. "This video was taken months ago, back when Mareidas and Dupree first got into trouble. They came to see Richter, but Richter wouldn't even talk to them. I escorted them out of the building. I walked them to their cars, and that was that."

"The date on it says it was made last week," Rafe said, his doubt rapidly turning to disbelief. "Have you *lied* to me, little brother?"

"No." Felipe answered his brother's question, but his eyes were on Carrie, begging her to trust him, imploring her to keep her faith in him. "I didn't kill those men. Tommy Walsh killed them. The proof is on an audiotape I found at Captain Swick's house."

"Where is this tape?" Rafe pressed. "Play it for me."

"It's hidden at Sea Circus," Felipe said.

"Did you hear it?" Rafe asked Carrie.

Wordlessly, she shook her head.

"Perfect," Rafe said sardonically. "There's a tape that clears your name, only you're the only one who's heard it, no? Sounds a little too convenient if you ask me."

"Why do you doubt me?" Felipe asked quietly.

Rafe gestured toward the television. "I see with my own eyes that you were with these men, right before they died."

"That tape was made in October," Felipe said evenly. "I did *not* kill those men."

Carrie moistened her dry lips. "Would you tell us if you had?" she asked. "Us," she'd said, not "me." She was siding with his brother.

He couldn't hide the disappointment in his eyes. "Ah, *cara,* don't *you* believe me?"

"Would you tell us?" she persisted.

He shook his head with a laugh that held not a breath of humor. "Probably not."

"Definitely not," Rafe said, crossing his arms.

A commercial ended and the news anchor reappeared on the screen along with a picture of Carrie.

"To date, there has been no word of Caroline Brooks, the young woman taken hostage by Salazar four days ago at Schroedinger's restaurant," the woman said. The picture changed to that of a familiar-looking man holding a press conference. Carrie leaned closer to the TV. "Despite an impassioned plea from Robert Penfield, Caroline's fiancé, Salazar has not let his hostage go, or even communicated in any way with the police."

"So the angel has a name," Rafe said. "*And* a fiancé?"

Robert Penfield? Her *fiancé?* Carrie nearly burst with indignation. "I met this man exactly *once,*" she said. "He's *not* my fiancé."

"Are you sure?" Felipe probed, his eyes burning holes into her with their intensity. "After all, don't you believe *every*thing you see on the TV news?"

Good Lord, he had a point. If Penfield could go on the air as her fiancé, then the rest of this so-called news story could also be pure fiction.

"Please," Bobby Penfield III said tearfully into the TV camera, "*please,* Detective Salazar, if you have any sense of decency at all, please let my dear Caroline go."

Oh, blech. And all of Florida actually believed she was going to marry this guy...?

"Despite that plea, there was no response from Felipe Salazar at all," the news anchor said solemnly. "And no word on whether Salazar's hostage is even still alive." She paused for only a split second before continuing. "We now go downtown, where Brett Finland is talking to the newly appointed chief of police, Jack Earley. Brett?"

"Thank you, Mary," the reporter said, and Carrie turned to look at Felipe.

He was standing behind the sofa, watching the screen, listening to the reporter. Surely he felt her eyes on his face, but he didn't so much as glance in her direction. His face was expressionless, but she could see the muscles jumping in his jaw.

She'd hurt and surprised him by not flatly discounting this news report. Hell, she'd surprised herself with how quickly she'd doubted him.

Salazar's hostage. That was as ridiculous a label as Penfield's fiancée.

Wasn't it?

On the television, Chief Earley's wide face looked tired and strained. He seemed distracted and the reporter had to keep repeating his questions.

"It's a hard job, tracking down Felipe Salazar, a man who once was one of St. Simone's finest," Brett Finland said, wrapping up the report. "Jack Earley has clearly lost some sleep over this, his first tough assignment as newly appointed police chief of this city. But Chief Earley, a man who started his law-enforcement career by tracking and trapping the enemy in their hideout tunnels in Vietnam, a man known as one of the marines' legendary 'tunnel rats,' should have no problem finding one rogue cop. This is Brett Finland, reporting live from downtown. Mary?"

"Madre de Dios!" Felipe exclaimed, his eyes still glued to the set. He fired off a rapid stream of Spanish to his brother.

Rafe frowned and shrugged, then answered, also in Spanish. He pointed next to the television. A pile of old newspapers lay there, and Felipe nearly leaped over the sofa to search through them. He scanned the tops, looking, it seemed, for one specific date.

"What?" Carrie said. "What's going on?"

"I need to find the paper that had that article on Chief Earley," Felipe said, still searching the pile.

"Why?" Carrie asked, but he didn't answer.

"Ah! Here it is." He sat down next to her on the sofa, and she moved closer, trying to read over his arm. He folded the paper so they both could see it better.

"Earley served in Vietnam as a *captain*," Felipe said. For some reason, that news really excited him. "Yes!" He looked up into Carrie's eyes. "Don't you get it?"

Puzzled, she shook her head.

He pointed to the text. "Look! It says it right here. Jack Earley served for ten months in Vietnam as an explosives expert. He went down into the tunnels where the Vietcong had been hiding, clearing them of booby traps. 'It was one of the most dangerous jobs in the entire Marine Corps, and not for the faint of heart or claustrophobic,'" he read aloud, glancing over at Carrie for that last bit.

"'Chief Earley and his men were known as the tunnel rats.'" He smacked the paper with his hand. "Captain Rat! *Earley* is Richter's Captain Rat."

"The police chief?" Carrie was shocked. It couldn't be.

Felipe checked the time on Rafe's VCR. It was a little after one o'clock. "Okay," he said. "Listen, Diego's going to call any minute—"

"No, he's not," Rafe interrupted. "He called about an hour ago—said he was going to be tied up, that he wouldn't get a chance to call without a lot of people listening in."

Felipe swore under his breath. "Man, I really could have used his help. But…all right. I can still do this. We still have time."

"Time for what?" Carrie asked.

"We're going to go down to police headquarters," Felipe said, "and follow Earley to his meeting with Richter." He turned to his brother. "You still want to help me?"

"Even if you killed those guys, I don't want you to die," Rafe said.

"That's not the blazing endorsement I would've liked, but it'll do," Felipe said. "Can you get your hands on some film and a camera? Maybe one of those disposable ones?"

"I got an old Instamatic," Rafe said, crossing to the closet and pulling a box down from the shelf. "It works okay. It's got half a roll of color film already in it."

He fished a small black camera out of the box and handed it to his brother.

Felipe would've turned away, but Rafe caught his arm. "If you killed those men," he said, "you better head for Mexico."

"I didn't kill them."

Rafe ignored him. "If you head for Mexico, I probably won't see you again."

Felipe shook his head. "You'll see me again."

"If I don't," Rafe said, "I just wanted you to know...how sorry I am that I...I let you down all those years, all those times."

Felipe was silent. Carrie could see the tears that had suddenly filled his eyes. She turned away, not wanting to intrude.

"I hope someday you'll forgive me," Rafe said almost inaudibly. "And maybe then, someday, I'll forgive myself, no?"

"Forgive yourself, Raphael," Felipe said, his voice husky with emotion. "I forgave you a long time ago."

"Gracias," Rafe whispered. "Go with God."

Felipe held out his hand, and Rafe took it. The two men, the two brothers, clasped hands, and each gazed into dark brown eyes so like his own.

And then Felipe turned and headed for the door.

"Good luck," Rafe added. "Keep your head down."

Carrie followed Felipe down the stairs. He checked his gun as he went, making sure it was properly loaded. Then he tucked it in the back waistband of his jeans, covering it with the hem of his T-shirt.

"Felipe," she said.

He glanced back at her, but didn't stop. "Yes."

"Please don't be mad at me."

He stopped by the front door then, his hand on the knob. "I'm not mad," he said. "Just…disappointed."

"I'm sorry," she said.

"How can you say that you'll marry me when you don't even trust me?" he asked, then shook his head before she had a chance to speak. "No, don't answer that," he added, rubbing his forehead as if he had a headache. "I honestly don't want to know."

"I keep wondering what if I'm wrong about you," Carrie admitted. "I see all this hard evidence against you and I can't stop thinking what if I've fallen in love with a man who's deceiving me."

Felipe was watching her steadily, his dark brown eyes echoing the disappointment she'd heard in his words.

"I can't help you with that one, Caroline," he said quietly. "It's something you've got to work out on your own. Let me know what you decide, though, okay?"

"Felipe—"

"Right now, we've got to move," he said, opening the door. "Stay close to me. We're getting in the car as quickly as we can."

Felipe took Caroline's arm, and together they went out into the bright afternoon sunlight and down the steps to the sidewalk.

Felipe felt the hair stand up on the back of his neck. Something was wrong. Something was seriously wrong.

Everything looked the same as it had when they'd arrived less than an hour ago. Children still played out in the street. Old men still sat, talking, on their stoops. People sauntered along the sidewalks, moving slowly in the sunshine.

The old white Volkswagen they'd "borrowed" from the Sea Circus parking lot was halfway down the block. Felipe moved quickly toward it, trying to shield Caroline with his body, praying his sixth sense that told him trouble was coming was wrong.

Caroline had thrown him for a loop back in Rafe's apartment. Her admission that she still didn't trust him had hurt even more than he'd let on. She needed time, he reminded himself. In time, she would learn he truly was everything he said he was.

Please, God, give him that time.

Out of the corner of his eye, Felipe saw a shadow move, and instantly, everything kicked into slow motion around him.

He turned his head and looked directly into the cold steel of Tommy Walsh's pale blue eyes.

Tommy had his gun out, hidden under a jacket he was carrying over his arm. It was pointed directly at Caroline.

If Tommy intended to kill them right here in the street, in front of all these people, they'd already be lying there dead. Still, Felipe knew if pushed too hard, Tommy would shoot. The time to move was now, while he was expecting Felipe to hesitate.

But Felipe wasn't going to hesitate. Not with Caroline's life hanging in the balance. No way was he going to let Tommy kill her. No way.

He pushed Caroline behind him and reached for the gun that rested against the small of his back. He drew smoothly, watching Tommy's finger tighten on the trigger at his sudden movement. But Tommy moved in slow motion and Felipe was faster. He aimed and fired.

The noise was incredible, as was the look of total shock on Tommy Walsh's face as the big man fell to the ground, a neat little bullet hole in the center of his forehead.

Stay detached, Felipe ordered himself. That wasn't a man he'd just killed, it was a monster. There'd be enough time later to suffer over the fact that Tommy Walsh might have a mother, maybe even a wife and children, who would mourn him. There'd be enough time—if Felipe could stay cool and concentrate on getting himself and Caroline out of there.

Somebody screamed—maybe it was Caroline—and suddenly the world moved again at its regular speed.

He stepped over Tommy's body and the blood that was pooling on the sidewalk. Stay cool. Don't look at the blood. Don't think. Just get Caroline away.

He wrenched open the door of the Volkswagen and pushed Caroline inside. Vaulting over the hood, he had the key in the ignition and the car in gear and halfway down the street before he even got the driver's-side door closed.

"MY GOD," CARRIE GASPED. "My *God!* You *killed* him!"

"Fasten your seat belt," Felipe said calmly, as if he hadn't just fired a bullet into another man's head.

He'd killed a man.

An *unarmed* man.

With sickening clarity, Carrie remembered her surprise when Felipe had suddenly grabbed her arm. She could still see that awful, almost inhuman look in his eyes as he drew his gun. They had been filled with a cold, unearthly, unfamiliar savagery that was echoed on his face. His lips had been pulled back from his mouth in a wolfish snarl as he'd violently taken another human's life.

Who was this man, this Felipe Salazar?

Did she really know him at all? Lord knows she had never seen this side of him before—*never.*

Carrie felt sick to her stomach. How could Felipe kill someone and then just…keep going? He'd stepped over the body as if it had been nothing more than a spilled bag of garbage, an inconvenience.

Unless killing was something he'd done before, something he took lightly….

My God, was it possible he'd killed those two men in the sandlot after all?

The police had all that hard evidence against Felipe— a ballistics report that proved his gun was the murder weapon and a videotape of Felipe holding the two victims at gunpoint. Felipe claimed the tape had been made months ago and that the ballistics report was doctored. But ballistics reports were done scientifically. It wouldn't be easy to falsify information….

All her doubts, all her uncertainty came rushing back, hitting her full force in the stomach.

Maybe it was possible that Felipe *had* killed those men. Maybe he *had* been the one who'd shot them in the back of the head execution-style. That savage man she'd had a glimpse of, that man with the deadly flat eyes, had certainly looked capable of such an awful deed.

She took a deep breath, trying to steady her shaking hands, trying to stop the flood of tears that was streaming down her face. She'd been following her heart for the past several days, refusing to allow the cold hard facts to interfere with her feelings for Felipe.

But now those cold hard facts included one very dead man, and she couldn't ignore them any longer.

"Are you all right?" he asked, still in that same quiet, almost unnaturally calm voice.

"No," she said. "I want to get out of the car."

"We will in a minute," Felipe said. He looked into the rearview mirror. "I just want to be sure that none of Tommy's men are following us. But then we *should* ditch this car. The police will be looking for it."

In the distance, Carrie could hear the sound of police sirens moving toward them, getting louder. A patrol car passed them going sixty miles an hour.

Felipe turned down a side street.

"No," Carrie said again. "You don't understand. I want to get out of the car—*now.*"

"Caroline, we can't—"

"Not 'we.' *Me.* I want you to pull over and let *me* get out."

Carrie felt him turn and look at her, *really* look at her. She stared down at her feet, unable to meet his gaze.

"I can't do that," he said quietly.

She did look up at him then. "Can't…or won't?"

The muscles in the side of his jaw were working hard again. This time it was Felipe who wouldn't meet her gaze.

"What difference does it make?" he returned.

"Am I your hostage?" she asked, trying to keep her voice from shaking. "Have I been all along?"

He made a sound that might've been a laugh. "What do *you* think?"

"I don't know." She *didn't* know. Had he been manipulating her right from the start? Were his words of love really empty promises, designed to make her trust him, keep her from running away? And what about her feelings for him? Was this really love she felt, or was it some kind of warped attachment of a hostage for a captor?

"Please," she said softly. "If you care anything for me at all, please let me go."

Felipe was silent as he took a left turn onto McCallister Street. "So," he said, just as quietly, "you've decided not to trust me, huh? That's too bad."

"Please," she said again. "Prove I'm not your hostage, Felipe. Let me go."

"As much as I'd like to prove that to you," he said, "I'd rather you remained alive. As long as there's a threat from Lawrence Richter, you're staying with me."

Carrie gazed out of the window, unable to speak.

"And now you're thinking, 'Ah, I *am* his hostage.'" Felipe's velvet voice surrounded her. "I have to tell you one more time, Caroline, that everything I've ever said to you is God's own truth."

Carrie closed her eyes. "I don't know *what* the truth is anymore." She only knew the facts. She'd seen him kill a man without a second thought. A ballistics report tied him to the murder weapon. A videotape showed that he was with the two men before they died.

As they stopped for a red light, Felipe reached over and picked up her hand, the hand with the green plastic ring he had given her.

"*This* is the truth," he said. "Open your eyes and look. *Look* at me!"

She opened her eyes and looked directly into the eyes of this man that she thought she knew so well, but perhaps didn't know at all. His face was so familiar—high cheekbones, lean, smooth cheeks, long, elegant nose, full lips, dark, mesmerizing eyes. She'd thought she'd seen him in every possible way. She'd seen him relaxed and laughing, tense and worried, cool and calm, thoughtful, angry, unhappy, joyful. But not murderous. At least, not until this afternoon.

Felipe took her hand, the same hand with the ring, and placed it on his chest, over his heart.

"*This* is the truth, Caroline," he whispered. "But if you don't want that truth any longer…"

As she watched, his eyes started to fill with tears, but he blinked them back, forced them away. He returned her hand to her lap.

"It's almost all over," Felipe said, putting the car into gear as the traffic light turned green. "A little bit longer, and then I won't stop you. You'll be free to go."

CHAPTER TWENTY-ONE

FELIPE was getting the job done.

He'd ditched the white Volkswagen near the parking lot of the Fourth Precinct. He'd found Jim Keegan's car in the lot. The key was hidden on top of the right front wheel, exactly where Jim had said it would be.

Now he sat outside police headquarters in Jim's gray Taurus, waiting for Chief Earley to leave for his meeting with crime lord, Lawrence Richter.

Yes, he was getting the job done.

He was trying very hard not to think about anything besides the pictures he was going to take of Earley and Richter's meeting. He was trying hard not to think about that small, permanent hole he'd put in Tommy Walsh's head or the nausea he felt as a result. And he was trying desperately not to think about Caroline Brooks.

That wasn't so easy to do, because she was sitting right next to him, and because, while he was busy getting the job done, he was having to take care that she didn't try to run away.

They had come full circle. Apparently, her doubts and suspicions had come out the victor in an emotional wrestling match. And, apparently, her love for him hadn't stood up to the test.

That hurt more than he would have believed possible.

So okay. He tried to harden his heart, tried to think about this practically, tried not to care. So he wouldn't leave the vice squad. He'd merely leave St. Simone. So what if it was his home? He hadn't lived here *all* his life. His parents had come here to make a new start. So now *he'd* go somewhere else to make his own new start. There were a lot of cities out there where his face wasn't known. Maybe he'd go up to Diego's New York, become a New York City cop. Now, *there* would be a job that was on the edge, that was filled with high risks and danger. He'd fit right in.

Man, he should be feeling lucky. Here was Caroline, ready to walk away from him, exactly the way he'd wanted their affair to end a few days ago. He wasn't going to have to worry about her safety. He wasn't going to have to deal with the restrictions that a permanent relationship would bring. Man, he was getting off easy. He'd had his fun. He'd had a series of intense sexual experiences with a beautiful, vibrant, passionate woman. He had the added satisfaction of knowing that he'd saved her life. He should be more than ready and willing to let Caroline Brooks simply fade into a fond memory as he continued on with his life as he knew it.

He should, but he couldn't.

Something had happened these past few days. Something had opened his eyes to the fact that his life wasn't winning any awards or prizes for Most Fulfilling. Yes, he was making a difference out on the streets. Yes, he was good at what he did. And yes, sometimes he even liked it. But he didn't like it all the time—and lately, he didn't like it at all.

The sorry truth was that the something that had opened his eyes had been Caroline Brooks. Caroline had shown him firsthand everything he'd been missing. She'd gone and made him fall in love with her and opened his eyes to a future that was impossibly joyful.

Impossibly indeed.

She stirred in her seat, and he couldn't keep himself from glancing at her.

She didn't trust him.

He was angry and hurt and even insulted by her mistrust, but the ultimate insult was that these emotions didn't make him stop loving her. He wanted to fall on his knees and beg her to believe him. But pride kept him in his seat.

He wanted to see her smile, hear her husky, sexy laughter. He wanted to know, just from looking in her eyes, that she'd be in his arms again tonight, surrounding him with her warmth and love. But there was not a chance in hell for that.

He wanted to weep for all he'd lost—for the love he'd probably never really had in the first place.

Because how could she have truly loved him without trust?

She was quiet and her face looked pale. She hadn't spoken a word to him since they'd taken Jim's car from the parking lot.

But now she looked up, actually meeting his gaze. The mistrust and trepidation he could see in her eyes burned like acid in his soul. But he didn't look away. He couldn't.

Maybe seeing her looking at him that way would make him love her less. But probably not.

"How many people have you killed?" she asked.

Her question caught him off guard. Of all the things he'd expected her to say to him or ask him, that wasn't one of them.

But he answered honestly. "Five," he said. "Tommy Walsh was the fifth."

"How do you sleep afterward?" she asked. "How do you do it? How do you live your life knowing that you took someone else's?"

Felipe was quiet for a moment, wondering how to answer. But there was really only one way to answer—with the truth.

"You don't sleep," he finally told her. He watched the entrance to the police station as he spoke. "Not at first. You lie in bed going over it and over it in your head. You try to figure out where you went wrong, where you made the mistake, what you could've done instead to make it turn out differently. And then, after about a week of not sleeping, when you feel like hell and you can't handle it anymore, you go visit the counselor—the precinct shrink. And then you start to work through it until you accept the choices that you made—the choices that led you to pull that trigger and take that life.

"You talk to people who were there, who witnessed the shooting," he continued. "You hang out with the person whose life you maybe saved by firing your gun and killing the perpetrator. Or you come face-to-face with the fact that it came down to the guy you killed or yourself. You look at yourself in a mirror and you remind yourself that *he* was the bad guy, not you. If he had been a little faster or a little smarter or a little luckier with his own gun, then it might very well have been *your* family holding that funeral service instead of his."

"And if he didn't have a gun?" Carrie whispered.

Felipe shook his head. "They all had guns. Starting with Benny Hammett. He was eighteen years old, just a kid, freaked out on crack. He had his father's handgun and was taking potshots at the children in the playground next to his house. One kid was dead—four years old— and two others were badly wounded. The medical teams couldn't get in to help them. The SWAT team was on its way when Hammett hit a fourth kid who'd been hiding behind some bushes. I was one of the cops who climbed down to his window from the roof and took him down. My bullet killed him.

"Then there was Thomas Freeman, age forty-seven. Took his hunting rifle and went back to where he'd been laid off, killed his boss's secretary and threatened to wipe out the entire office. I went in as a deliveryman, took him out before he killed the mail-room clerk.

"Hans Thorne, thirty-eight, escaped convict, tried to hold up a convenience store that Diego and I happened to be in. I stopped him from blowing Diego's head off.

"T. J. Cerrone, twenty-three years old. I believe you had the honor of meeting him at Sea Circus. When we busted him on drug charges, he and his friends decided they'd skip jail and go right to hell. Unfortunately, they took a few of my friends on the force with them. T.J. had access to an Uzi submachine gun when I ended his life with my .45."

Felipe kept his eyes on the entrance to the police station, but he could feel Caroline watching him.

"And Tommy Walsh?" she probed. "Where was his gun?"

Felipe turned to look at her. "It was aimed at you," he said. He could see the doubt in her eyes. *Madre de Dios,* was it possible she didn't know Tommy had been armed? "You didn't see his gun?"

"No."

"You think I would kill an unarmed man?" His voice rose in disbelief. What kind of monster did Caroline think he was anyway?

"That's what I saw."

Felipe's heart broke into a thousand tiny pieces. "Maybe you saw what you expected to see," he said quietly. "You've already decided I'm guilty, that I'm a killer. But you're wrong, and I'm going to prove that, even if it's the last thing I do."

Numbly, Felipe stared at the door to the police station. He'd lost Caroline. He'd totally lost her trust—if he'd ever even had it in the first place.

Everything around him, his entire life, seemed to be circling the drain.

Everything, *every*thing—his freedom, his reputation, his life—was riding on his conviction that Chief Earley was Lawrence Richter's partner. Everything now depended on his being right about that.

God help him if he was wrong.

TEN MINUTES AFTER THREE, and Earley still hadn't left for his alleged three-thirty meeting with Lawrence Richter.

Carrie risked a look at Felipe. He was getting more and more tense by the minute. He muttered something in Spanish, then glanced at Carrie, but didn't bother to translate.

"What if you're wrong?" she asked quietly. "What if Earley's not involved?"

"I drive you to Montana," he said, "then come back and start over again. If Earley's not this Captain Rat, then someone else is. Sooner or later, I'll find him."

He stared across the parking lot at the entrance to police headquarters. His mouth was set in grim determination and his face was lined with fatigue. His dark eyes were even more unreadable and mysterious than ever.

Where was his gun? she'd asked.

It was aimed at you, he'd said.

Was he lying?

He'd spoken with such conviction, such absolute certainty. There was a gun. She simply hadn't seen it. If he hadn't killed Tommy Walsh, Tommy would've killed her.

What if he was telling the truth? What if all along he'd been telling the truth?

Everything I've ever said to you is God's own truth.

If he *was* telling the truth, then, Lord, how she'd let him down by doubting him.

It was her head versus her heart. Her heart wanted to believe him. But her head couldn't reconcile the cold, hard facts.

And Carrie didn't know what to believe.

Felipe sat forward, gripping the steering wheel tightly in his hands. "My God," he said.

"Is it him?" Carrie tried to see where he was looking. She couldn't see anyone out on the sidewalk who looked like Chief Earley.

"It's Lawrence Richter," Felipe said. "He's going inside." He turned off the engine and unlocked the door. "Come on."

"We're going to *follow* him?" Carrie exclaimed. "Into the *police station?*"

"Yes." Felipe took the paper lunch bag that held Rafe's Instamatic camera, then grabbed her wrist. He pulled her across the bench seat and out the driver's-side door.

"Do you know how many police officers are in there?" Carrie asked in disbelief. "Do you *want* to get caught?"

"I'm not going to get caught," Felipe said shortly,

pulling her with him across the parking lot toward the wide stairs that led up to the main doors. "But if anything happens," he added, "get down behind me out of the way. Do you understand?"

Carrie dug her heels into the gravel of the parking lot, and he turned back toward her impatiently.

"Felipe, don't go in there," she said. "Someone's going to recognize you and—"

"How nice that you should care," he said without expression.

"I *do* care—"

He grabbed her shoulders and all the emotion he'd been hiding erupted to the surface. "Then *trust* me, dammit!" he hissed. "Trust me, Caroline, and know that I *have* to go in there if I want this to end."

"I don't want you to die," she whispered, staring into the burning depths of his eyes. "I don't know what you've done or not done, who you've killed or not. I don't know whether or not you've been using me right from the start. I don't know whether you deserve to go to jail or get a medal for bravery, but I *do* know that I don't want you to die."

He touched the side of her face, his hands suddenly gentle, his eyes soft and sad. "I truly have no control when it comes to you," he murmured. "I should despise you for losing your faith in me, but all I want is to kiss you, to touch you. I must be one hell of a fool." He shook his head. "You can help me, Caroline," he added, talking low and fast. "We can get in and out and no one will ever know. I need to do this. I need your help. Please."

Helping him would be aiding and abetting. She could go to jail for that.

"Please," he whispered again, and she nodded. Her

reward was a small smile, a mere shadow of Felipe's normal exuberance. "Put your hair under your hat," he said. "Hurry."

She obeyed, stuffing her long blond hair up underneath the baseball cap she was still wearing.

This was crazy. Felipe was crazy. *She* was crazy for going along with this.

He opened the door to the lobby and pulled her inside.

She should scream, run away, do *some*thing to call attention to herself. *Hello, I'm the hostage you've all been looking for all this time!*

Felipe was staring at the elevators.

"Richter got in one going down," he said, pulling her toward a door marked Stairs. "Come on." He pulled her into the stairwell with him, then started down. "Quickly. I don't want to lose him," he said, taking the stairs two at a time, all but swinging Carrie up into his arms to speed her along.

But he stopped running before he pushed open the door on the basement level. He opened it slowly—just in time to see Lawrence Richter walk sedately past.

They followed the silver-haired man into a cafeteria that was open to the general public. And the general public was there in all their various sizes and shapes. That was good. With these strange-looking people around, no one would give Felipe a second glance.

Near the door, there was an empty table against the wall, and Felipe sat down in one of the metal-framed chairs. He pulled Carrie onto his lap.

She didn't want to sit there. She didn't want to be so close to him, to be reminded of the way she had let him love her. She struggled to stand up, but he held her tightly.

"At least *pretend* you like me," he whispered.

Carrie stopped struggling. "Felipe—" she started to say.

"Shh. Richter's got a cup of coffee. He's going to sit down. Put your arm around me, for God's sake."

Carrie looped her arm around Felipe's neck. She wished she wasn't sitting here like this, so close to him, touching him. She wished she were back at Sea Circus or out on her boat, alone with the sea and sky, or hell, she even wished she were back in Montana. She wished she were anywhere but here.

Because she also wished that she could kiss him. Her attraction to this man was still there, powerful and strong. Her love was there, too, even stronger.

Head versus heart, it all boiled down to a matter of trust. Was he the Sandlot killer? Carrie didn't want to believe that he was. But wanting simply wasn't enough.

Felipe reached around her to put the lunch bag on the table. He poked a hole in the bag for the camera lens and aimed it at the table where Richter was sitting with his coffee.

And then, without any warning, Felipe kissed her.

It was a long, deep, achingly fierce kiss that caught her entirely by surprise. It left her weak and even more off center than she'd been before.

"Sorry." Felipe quietly apologized for the kiss almost before their lips had parted. "I'm sorry—Richter looked this way. I didn't know what else to do."

Oh. That hadn't really been a kiss. It had been a diversion, a form of cover.

"What is Richter doing?" Carrie asked when she finally found her voice. Sitting the way she was, her back was to the man.

"He's picked up a newspaper from the table," Felipe

said. He reached out and laid one hand on the paper bag holding the camera and took a picture of Richter. "Put your head against my shoulder and you'll be able to see him. But don't stare. Look past him, not at him."

Carrie turned slightly and leaned back against Felipe. Richter was reading the newspaper. As she watched, he took a sip of his coffee.

Felipe's hand moved on the paper bag. "Did you see that?" he murmured into Carrie's ear. "He just put an envelope in between the pages of the paper."

He did? Carrie hadn't noticed that at all.

"I got it on film," Felipe said. "Now we wait for Earley to show up...ah, he's right on time."

Looking harried, Police Chief Jack Earley, in a white short-sleeved shirt and a loosened tie and carrying his sport jacket over one arm, came into the cafeteria.

Felipe nuzzled Carrie's neck, hiding his face from the man who was leading the statewide intensive search for him.

Earley walked past Felipe and Carrie, past Lawrence Richter—who didn't even glance up—and over to the coffee vending machine. Casually, the police chief put some money into the machine and pressed the buttons for decaf with sugar, no cream.

As the cup was filling with steaming dark coffee, Lawrence Richter stood up, straightened his tie and calmly walked out of the room.

"He left," Carrie whispered to Felipe. "Richter left before the meeting!"

"He didn't take the newspaper," Felipe murmured. "It has that envelope inside it. Just watch. Earley is going to pick it up off the table."

Almost before he stopped speaking, the police chief

walked past the table where Richter had been sitting. For a moment, it looked as if the man was simply going to walk on by, but then he stopped, lingering to look down at the headlines of the sports pages.

He glanced at his watch as if in a rush, then took the paper with him, hurrying out of the room.

Felipe hustled Carrie off his lap and grabbed the bag that held the camera. Holding her hand, he pulled her along with him down the hall about fifty feet behind Jack Earley.

Earley stopped in front of the elevator and pushed the button. He took a sip of his coffee, made a face and tossed the cup and its contents into the garbage. The newspaper soon followed.

"Got it," Felipe murmured in her ear, and she realized he was holding the bag with the camera in front of him. "He put the envelope in his jacket pocket."

"I didn't see that," Carrie said.

"That's okay," Felipe said. "I got it on film."

"Now what?" Carrie whispered.

"Now we find a one-hour photo place," Felipe said.

"Holy hell, it *is* you," a voice said loudly. All across the basement lobby, heads turned in their direction. A bald-headed man in an ill-fitting suit fumbled for his sidearm. "Felipe Salazar, *you* are under arrest!"

"Or maybe we'll skip the photo place," Felipe said quietly, pulling Carrie close to him. "Play along."

From around the lobby came a murmur of voices and a wave of movement as civilians backed away and police officers began to draw their weapons.

But Felipe was ahead of them all. His gun was already drawn. He backed up until he hit the wall next to the closed elevator door. "Keep your hands up and guns down," he warned them. "I don't want to have to hurt the girl."

Play along. But was this fantasy or reality? It sure *seemed* like reality. The entire area was frozen like a tableau.

"Come on, Phil," the bald cop said, still trying to get his gun free. "Don't let's do this the hard way. Let me bring you in. I'll see that you get fair treatment."

"Put your hands up, Andy," Felipe said. "And back away."

"Someone get hold of Jim Keegan," the cop named Andy called out, lifting his hands with a sigh. "We got us a hostage situation here." He turned back to Felipe. "Phil, this is a royal pain in the ass."

This was all happening so fast. Carrie could barely breathe. Felipe had his gun pressed against her ribs. *Play along.* She didn't have to pretend to look frightened.

"Tommy Walsh killed Mareidas and Dupree," Felipe told Andy. "Not me. It was on Lawrence Richter's orders. I have proof of this."

"Richter?" Andy said, squinting as he tried to place the name. "Isn't he the guy who owns that chain of fish restaurants? My cousin got salmonella from eating there."

"He owns the restaurants—and runs a major crime syndicate," Felipe said. "Guess who else is involved?" He turned to look at Jack Earley. "You get the first guess, Chief."

Chief Earley's face was pale, his mouth a grim line. "Let the girl go, Salazar. You don't really want to see her killed, do you?" He turned to speak to his men. "He's clearly delusional. Get back and clear these civilians out of here."

"You're going down, Captain Rat," Felipe said to Earley. "I have the proof I need. When Jim gets here—"

Next to them, the door of the cargo elevator slid open, and a janitor blinked owlishly out at them from behind a dolly carrying large trash barrels.

Earley made his move. He lunged for Felipe, pulling both him and Caroline back into the big elevator.

"Get out!" he shouted at the janitor, who scrambled out the door. "The man's insane! *Get out!*"

Felipe hit the wall hard and fell to his knees, taking Carrie with him. He fired his gun, and the noise was deafening. She heard herself scream, felt Felipe try to cover her with his body.

Lord, this was it. They were going to die.

FELIPE HAD MISSED.

He'd had one shot at Earley, but he'd missed. The bullet tore up into the soundproof tile of the elevator ceiling as the door slid closed.

Earley was back behind the cover of the trash barrels in the other corner of the elevator. Felipe tried to shield Caroline from the chief's gun, but it was no use. His body would act as a shield for only so long at this close a range.

"Put your gun down," the chief shouted. "Put it down!"

Slowly, Felipe lowered his gun. He had no choice. Not with Earley aiming his own gun directly at him...and at Caroline.

Earley reached up to the elevator controls and pushed the stop button, halting their journey up to the first floor.

"Heroically, Chief Earley pulled Salazar and his hostage into an empty elevator, risking his own life for the sake of the crowd's safety," Earley said, straightening up and coming out from behind the barrels, his gun aimed levelly at Felipe. "The papers are gonna have a field day with this one. I couldn't've planned it better myself. Put your gun on the floor and kick it over to me."

Felipe set the gun down, but instead of kicking it to Earley, he slid it underneath the dolly that held the trash barrels. Caroline's eyes were wide as she looked from Felipe to Earley and then back.

"It really is a shame when a good cop turns bad," Earley mused, shaking his head.

"You should know," Felipe said. He could see his future in Earley's eyes, and it wasn't going to be a long one. Earley was going to shoot him, and then shoot Caroline with Felipe's gun. And there was nothing Felipe could do about it.

Or was there?

Jim Keegan's Rule Number One: Nothing is impossible.

Felipe's Rule Number One: If you're going to die, die fighting.

The big cargo elevator was about eight feet long by seven feet wide. The dolly holding the barrels cut off one corner of that space.

"Let go of your hostage," Earley said as Felipe slowly rose to his feet, pulling Caroline up with him.

"Te amo," Felipe said to Caroline, brushing the side of her face with his lips. "Get down behind the barrels," he breathed into her ear.

"Very touching," Earley said impatiently. "Now, let her go."

Felipe pushed Caroline hard, away from Earley and toward the trash barrels, as he leaped at Earley. "Get down! Get back!" he shouted again at Caroline.

The gun went off with a roar as he hit Earley in the face. He felt a slap, heard Caroline scream, saw a spray of blood hit the elevator wall.

Felipe had been hit. Where, he couldn't begin to say. All he knew was that the bullet hadn't killed him—he was still alive. And until his heart stopped beating, he was going to fight like the devil himself to save Caroline's life.

He hit Earley again, and the chief's gun flew out of his hand and into the corner.

Earley fought back, trying to get to his gun. He used his hands like a club, striking Felipe hard on the shoulder.

God, he knew now where that bullet had struck him. Earley hit his wounded shoulder again and again and Felipe reeled back in mind-numbing pain. Somehow he managed to kick out at the older man, and his foot connected with Earley's knee. The chief went down with a grunt but scrambled quickly to his feet, assuming a street-fighter's stance.

"Freeze!" Caroline shouted from behind the barrels. "I said *freeze*, dammit!"

She was holding Felipe's gun, and she had Earley's gun behind her on the floor.

Earley straightened up, lifting both his hands as she pointed the gun from him to Felipe and back again.

"Good job, miss," Earley said, starting toward Felipe. "We've got him now."

"Don't you move!" Caroline warned him. He froze.

"You're kidding, right?" Earley said. He gestured toward Felipe. "This man's the known felon. He's the kidnapper, the *murderer*. He's the one who's been holding you hostage all this time."

Caroline's eyes flicked from Earley to Felipe.

Felipe didn't say a word. What could he say? He just looked at her. *Trust me.*

She looked into his eyes, searching for answers, searching for the truth. He hoped she could see it—the truth was clearly there, written permanently in his heart.

Te amo. I love you.

Earley started forward. "Give me the gun, miss."

She turned sharply, pointing the weapon at St. Simone's chief of police.

"Don't come closer, mister, or I'll put a hole in you," she said.

Relief flooded through Felipe. Caroline had followed her heart and trusted him.

He staggered slightly—his knees felt odd, weak. He realized that his shoulder was still bleeding quite heavily. Blood ran down his arm and dripped onto the floor from his fingers.

"You're hurt," Caroline said to Felipe, her eyes still locked on Earley. Her voice shook slightly, but her hands were steady. "Is it bad?"

Felipe shook his head. "I'll live," he said. He moved across the elevator and reached over to take back his gun.

She glanced up at him then. "So will I," she said. "Because of you, I think."

"Hands on your head," Felipe ordered Earley. "Sit down. There, in the corner."

"You're not going to get away with this," Earley said.

"You wanna bet?" Felipe said.

Overhead, an intercom speaker clicked on.

"This is Detective Jim Keegan from the Fourth Precinct," came a familiar voice. "Felipe, are you there? Pick up the telephone in the control panel."

The metal panel swung open with a squawk, and Felipe picked up the red receiver.

"Diego?"

"Phil! *Yes!* I heard a shot and I was afraid—is everyone all right?"

"I've been hit," Felipe said, "but I've cornered my Captain Rat."

"Jack Earley?" Jim said.

"That's right."

"The chief of police."

"Uh-huh."

Jim Keegan laughed. "You got proof?"

"Uh-huh. Photos of him accepting a payoff from Lawrence Richter."

"Well, isn't that dandy," Jim said. "That and the tape you left for me at Sea Circus should just about change your tag from Rogue Cop to Local Hero. I'll have the boys bring in Richter and his pals."

"That's cool, but meanwhile, I've got Andy and the entire police force ready to blow me away when these elevator doors open," Felipe said.

"Go on up to the first floor," Jim's voice said. "Captain Swick will be waiting for you there. Believe it or not, he's one of the good guys. That's why he had that tape of Walsh and Richter planning the Sandlot Murders. He was holding it to clear your name when the time came. He was working *with* you on this case, and he'd suspected Earley for some time now."

Felipe pulled out the stop button and the elevator started with a jerk.

"Keep your hands on your head," Caroline warned Earley.

"This isn't over," Earley hissed.

"Yes," Felipe told him, "it is."

And the elevator doors slid open.

FELIPE WAS SITTING on the lobby floor, leaning against the wall by the elevators, waiting for the paramedics to arrive.

A man Carrie recognized as Andy, and several other police officers, were around Felipe, trying to stem the flow of blood from his shoulder.

Earley had been taken away and reporters were gathering outside for an enormous press conference. In a matter of hours, word would hit the newsstands and TVs that Felipe Salazar was *not* a menace to society. His name would be cleared.

As Carrie watched, Felipe glanced around the lobby, looking for something or someone. Looking for *her*. His eyes landed on her, and he visibly relaxed.

He held her gaze. She could see pain in his dark brown eyes and at the edges of his mouth. His shoulder hurt more than he was letting on. Hell, for all *she* knew, his wounded leg still hurt him, too.

The ambulance was on its way. The paramedics would arrive and take Felipe to the hospital.

What then? Was she simply free to go? Should she just walk out of the police station, hail a taxi and go home to her apartment?

Andy approached her. "Uh, excuse me. You're Caroline, right?"

She nodded.

"Uh, Phil was wondering if you'd mind coming over for a sec before you go," Andy said.

Before you go. Felipe expected her just to walk away, to leave. It was over. All of it. Including any future they might've had together. She'd destroyed that with her doubts and mistrust.

Still, as she walked toward Felipe, she tried to smile.

The other police officers moved tactfully away.

"You trusted me," Felipe said, looking up at her from his seat on the floor. He patted the tile and she sat cross-legged next to him.

"I didn't for a while there," she said. She looked at her hands clasped tightly in her lap, unable to meet his eyes.

"When it came down to the bottom line—" Felipe's soft accent seemed to caress her "—you were there for me."

"No," Carrie said, closing her eyes. "You were there for *me*. All along, you protected me. You risked your life for mine."

"I was glad to," he said simply.

"I let you down," she said. Her voice shook and she couldn't hide it.

"It was hard for you to trust me," he said gently. "The way we started…" He shook his head. "I don't blame you, Caroline."

Carrie nodded. She still couldn't meet his eyes. "I'm so sorry."

"I am, too."

"It could've been really good, couldn't it have?" She risked a glance up at him. His dark eyes were serious and as mysterious as the midnight sky.

He nodded slowly. "Yes," he said. "It could have been remarkably good."

He was just sitting there, watching her. She wanted desperately for him to reach out, to touch her, to pull her into his arms—or at least the one that wasn't hurting. But that wasn't going to happen. Their love affair was over. She'd killed it, smothered it with her mistrust.

"Now what?" she asked quietly.

He held out his hand—his good hand—to her. "Hello. My name is Felipe Salazar," he said, "and I'm a police detective with the Fourth Precinct. I'm with the vice squad right now, but I won't be for much longer. I'm thinking about putting in for an assignment as an urban youth officer." He brought her fingers to his lips and kissed them one at a time. "You've got to be the most intriguing woman I've ever met. Will you have dinner with me tonight?"

Tears flooded Carrie's eyes and hope flooded her heart. "You want to start over?" she whispered.

"I would love to start over," he said. "Will you have dinner with me?"

"Oh, Felipe, can you really forgive me?"

"If we're starting over," he said, with a small smile, "there's nothing to forgive." His eyes were liquid brown and so very warm as he gazed at her. "Even though we've just met, would it be forward of me to ask for a kiss?"

With a trembling smile, Carrie shook her head.

Felipe leaned toward her, careful not to jar his shoulder. Carrie met him halfway in a kiss so sweet, so pure and tender, it brought a fresh rush of tears to her eyes.

"This may be the shortest courtship in the history of the Western Hemisphere," Felipe breathed, desire sparking in his eyes.

"I hope so," Carrie said.

He touched the side of her face as he looked searchingly at her. "Caroline, there *is* a catch to this. I'm about to go into protective custody. As the chief witness against Richter and Earley, I'll have to be kept safe until after the trial. For your own safety, you should come with me.

Richter may figure out he can get to me through you. But it's your choice. You don't have to come. If you choose not to, I won't be able to see you until it's over and done. It could be nine or ten months. Longer."

Carrie was silent for a moment. Not see him for nearly a *year?* "I'd have to quit my job," she finally said.

"A leave of absence," Felipe said. Hope lighted his eyes and he leaned forward to kiss her again. "Your position would surely be waiting for you when you returned."

"Returned from where?"

He smiled. "I don't know. Where do you want to go?"

Carrie smiled back at him, her heart exploding with love for Felipe Salazar, who was man enough to give her a second chance. "Someplace where we can go out on a boat," she said. "Someplace near the ocean."

"I know of this great beach house on Sanibel Island," Felipe said. "The owners are friends of mine. Although we may need to go farther away from St. Simone, this beach house might be a good place to start."

Carrie kissed him, closing her eyes and drinking in the softness of his lips, the sweetness of his mouth.

"It would be the perfect place to start."

* * * * *

Desperate young widow Abigail McMurray steals a pickup to flee an abusive relationship, never realizing the truck's owner, K-9 deputy Cade Latimer, is in the back.

Read on for a sneak peek of

LATIMER'S LAW

by Mel Sterling, coming May 2014 from Harlequin® Romantic Suspense.

"Let me see, Abigail. I won't hurt you, but I need to know bruises are the worst of it."

"That…that *crummy* button!" The words came out in the most embarrassed, horrified tone Cade had ever heard a woman use.

He couldn't tell whether the trembling that shook her entire body was laughter, tears, fear, pain or all of the above. She swayed on her feet like an exhausted toddler, and he realized she might fall if she remained standing. He sank back onto the picnic table bench and drew her down with him. She drooped like a flower with a crushed stem, and it was the most natural thing in the world to put an arm around her. In all his thug-tracking days he'd never comforted a criminal like this. How many of them had wept and gazed at him with pitiful, wet eyes? How easily had he withstood those bids for sympathy and lenience? How many of them ended up in the back of the patrol car on the way to jail, where they belonged?

But how quickly, in just moments, had Abigail McMurray and her gigantic problem become the thing he most needed to fix in the world. He felt her stiffness melting away like snow in the Florida sun, and shortly she was leaning against his chest, her hands creeping up to hang on to his shoulders as if he were the only solid thing left on the planet.

Now I have the truth.

He had what he thought he wanted, yes. But knowing what had pushed Abigail to take his truck wasn't enough. Now he wanted the man who had done the damage, wanted him fiercely, with a dark, chill fury that was more vendetta than justice. He shouldn't feel this way—his law enforcement training should have kept him from the brink. He hardly knew Abigail, and the fact she'd stolen his truck didn't make her domestic abuse issues his problem.

But somehow they were.

He felt her tears soaking his shirt, her sobs shaking her body, and stared over her head toward the tea-dark river, where something had taken the lure on his fishing line and was merrily dragging his pole down the sandy bank into the water.

Aw, hell. You know it's bad when I choose a sobbing woman over the best reel I own. Goodbye, pole. Hello, trouble.

**Don't miss
LATIMER'S LAW
by Mel Sterling, coming May 2014 from
Harlequin® Romantic Suspense.**

ROMANTIC suspense

EXECUTIVE PROTECTION
by Jennifer Morey
He's trained to be prepared for anything...but this

When his politician mother is shot, jaded cop Thad Winston gets more than he bargained for during the investigation with the spirited Lucy Sinclair, his mother's nurse. And when a stalker sets his sights on Lucy—possibly the same man who tried to kill his mother—Thad realizes just how much he has to lose.

Look for EXECUTIVE PROTECTION by Jennifer Morey in May 2014. Book 2 in *The Adair Legacy* miniseries. Available wherever books and ebooks are sold.

Also from *The Adair Legacy* miniseries:

HER SECRET, HIS DUTY by Carla Cassidy

Available wherever ebooks are sold.

Heart-racing romance, high-stakes suspense!

HARLEQUIN®

ROMANTIC suspense

TRAITOROUS ATTRACTION
by C.J. Miller

**From steamy jungles to opulent palaces...
it's nonstop action, danger...and passion!**

To find a "dead" agent, intelligence analyst Kate Squire
needs the man's brother—retired Sphere operative Connor
West. His skills as a trained assassin are essential for her
mission...but not so much her slamming, raw attraction for
the man himself....

For a loner like Connor, trekking into the jungle with a
secretive killer blonde at his side is not textbook. Caught
between armed insurgents and hungry predators, he fears
Kate may be his deadliest threat...until their very agency
turns on them. Stranded, outmanned and outgunned,
Connor has nowhere else to turn. Trusting Kate may be the
only way to get them out alive....

Look for the TRAITOROUS ATTRACTION
by C.J. Miller in May 2014.

Available wherever ebooks are sold.

Heart-racing romance, high-stakes suspense!

www.Harlequin.com

HRS27872

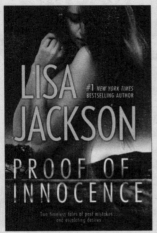